To Shannon Bone
Thanks!

RESURRECTION DAWN 2014

M. Sue Alexander

M. Sue Alexander

SUZANDER PUBLISHING, LLC
RESURRECTION DAWN 2014
FIRST EDITION 2003, USA

ISBN: 0-9740140-0-1

Cover design by Lisa Akins, ALLEGRA PRINT & IMAGING OF DICKSON, TENNESSEE and Ron Watson of Clarksville, Tennessee
Author photo by Karen Haddad of Orlando, Florida.

To order books, send money order of price listed to:
SUZANDER PULISHING, LLC
PO BOX 135
VANLEER, TN 37181
Visit our Web site today at
www.suzanderresurrectiondawn.net

READER OPINIONS

"I HAVE NOW READ OVER 25,000 MANUSCRIPTS. *Resurrection Dawn* rates at the top for intrigue and spellbinding Christian fiction and will keep you glued to its pages from start to finish. Writing is superb."

—Joseph S. Johnson, Jr.Retired Editor
of Inspirational/Trade Books for
Broadman & Holman Press
Nashville, Tennessee

"THIS NOVEL CAPTURES MY CUROUS NATURE. Surprise twists in plot kept me guessing. I can't wait to read the next book in the sequel."

—Karen Haddad
Marketing Agent
Orlando, Florida

'SHOCKING. DISTURBING. INSPIRATIONAL." Author writes with amazing insight into the future, the very near future. A must read!"

—Shirley Mitchell
Retired Teacher
Atlanta, Georgia

"ONE OF THE BETTER CHRISTIAN BOOKS I HAVE READ!"

—Mary Ann Haller
Great grandmother
Miami, Florida

"AN INTRIGUING ROMANTIC CRIME MYSTERY." Couldn't put it down.

—Joyce Wallace
Architecture & house designer
Dickson, Tennessee

"THIS BOOK IS A FAST-MOVING BEST SELLER IN MY OPINION. Couldn't wait to see what happened next!"

—Nell Meriwether
Editor & Retired teacher
Baton Rouge, Louisiana

"THIS IS AN ACTION-PACKED MYSTERY! Great to see a main character portraying Christian values. I cheer Victoria Tempest on each time she acts on her beliefs."

—Nicole Anna Alexander
Pastor's wife & Women's Ministries
Jacksonville, Florida

"AWESOME! WHEN I READ THIS ANOINTED BOOK IT STIRRED BY SOUL. Anyone who reads this book will be blessed."

—Linda Williams
Assisted Living Caretaker
Bon Aqua, Tennessee

"COULDN'T PUT THIS STORY DOWN! Would highly recommend it to any reader—good as any Christian book I've ever read."

—Sharon Haller
Insurance Claims
Miami, Florida

"BETTER THAN MOST NOVELS I'VE READ. Impressed with author's writing, wouldn't be at all surprised if *Resurrection Dawn* hit the best seller list."

—Linda Ragland
Bible teacher & homemaker
Dickson, Tennessee

"ENTERTAINING SUSPENSEFUL ROMANCE THAT PULLS YOU INTO THE STORY. When I started reading I couldn't stop until I finished. Wow!"

—Christine Daughrity
Local Board for CARENET
Dickson, Tennessee

Author's Dedication

To God for loving me, my family who encourages me, especially my mother who has taught me invaluable lessons about how to live my life. A special thanks to Editors Joe Johnson and Nell Meriwether for their faithful friendship and editing suggestions, and the many other friends who have read this work and offered opinions.

Author's Note

Resurrection Dawn is a futuristic crime novel set into the arena of pre-Rapture, Biblical "end times." The author has chosen a specific time frame that best depicts this story, but no one can be certain when the Antichrist will achieve power and rule the world. The town of Fernwood, Tennessee does not exist, and the characters and events portrayed in this story are a creation of the author's imagination.

"Truth is nowhere to be found, and whoever shuns evil becomes a prey." Isaiah 59:15

MONDAY, APRIL 14

1

Dawning draped its gauzy mist over Victoria Tempest's waking neighborhood. On the horizon, the sun winked before lathering a melon glow over the countryside. The florescent street lighting above blinked, then went out. What seemed like any ordinary morning wasn't. Something important had happened. *What?*

Victoria spun around in confusion, a troubled expression clawing at her pretty face as she inhaled the sweet honeysuckle odor permeating the crisp April air. It was morning. Dawn. Calm with no wind to speak of. Skies were clear and bluing.

Where am I? And what's happened to Hillside Estates?

Impossible as it seemed, an entire 1950s subdivision had been instantaneously displaced by concrete condos. Victoria heard her name called and glanced up.

A woman in a pink robe frantically waved from a second-story balcony. "Mother! Get the morning paper and come inside before you catch a death."

Mother? Victoria hadn't a clue how she'd ended up in the middle of the street.

"Come inside, please. It's too chilly for a morning stroll."

The voice was familiar but the woman wasn't. Victoria attempted to shake the cobwebs from her confused mind. *The girl thinks she's my daughter.* Victoria leaned over to pick up the *Fernwood Gazette* and was struck by a sharp pain in the temple.

"Ouch! What was that?"

"Mother? Want me to come down and help?"

Victoria glared at the morning headlines. *Monday, April 14, 2014, another impossibility!* She slapped the paper as an uncomfortable lump lodged in her throat. *Yesterday was Thursday, April 13, 1989, wasn't it?*

Someone had to be playing a cruel joke on her. But who? "It

has to be Jeffrey!" A light bulb switched on in Victoria's mind. After fourteen years of marriage, her feisty husband was still up to his cute little tricks. *Well, well . . .*

"Hey, you down there! The paper."

"What?" Victoria focused suspicious coffee-brown eyes on the pushy lady, who was about to torch her last nerve.

Have it your way. She cradled the newspaper under one arm and indignantly marched across the lawn, determined to resolve the kinship matter.

What was that? Sharp pains jabbed at Victoria's temples. She mounted the steps, managing to maintain her balance though her heart unmercifully rocked.

"Need some help, Mother?" the young woman asked, impatiently waiting at the top of the steps.

"You just hold your horses, young lady!" Victoria pointed an accusing finger, reaching the landing in record time. "I . . ." she looked into the girl's face and was shocked to see how very much she resembled her own daughter, Karen.

"What's going on, Mother? This better be good!" Hazel eyes were aimed at Victoria like daggers. "I am really starting to worry about you. Are you sick?"

"No, I'm not sick." The morning paper unconsciously slipped from Victoria's grasp and thumped on the concrete floor. She'd had about enough of this, this . . .

"So, what's the deal?" the stranger asked.

"I don't know your game, lady, but you're not my Karen? Who put you up to this?" Victoria was on the verge of striking the woman, ready to turn and run . . . where?

Her beautiful home had disappeared, she assumed, with all her friendly neighbors and their dogs. And this imposter claiming to be her daughter was in her face. She just needed to wake up. "If this is one of Jeffrey's tricks, he'll pay plenty later!"

"What are you babbling about, Mother? You're not making a shred of sense." The imposter opened the sliders. "You're pale as a ghost."

"I'm not a ghost!" Victoria huffed. "And I'm not your mother!" Black spots clouded the periphery of her vision. "Where's my daughter?"

"Enough is enough, Mother!" The woman grasped Victoria's arm and pulled her inside the condo. "You need your morning cup of coffee to clear your head."

Duh. Victoria stepped into the vaulted den bathed in subdued lighting, her pupils dilating as she surveyed the unfamiliar surroundings. *Where am I?*

"Okay, sit down, Mother. I'm not in the best of moods, but I'll dote on you a bit. Don't you move a hair, you hear?" She hurried from the room.

Forget about the woman! There were more important issues to resolve—like where she had come from earlier. *So I get out of bed. I go outside to get the morning paper. And . . .*

"Oh, I give up!" Victoria tossed her hands in the air, shutting her eyes and praying that the ridiculous scenario would end so her life could return to normal. But it didn't.

"What?" Victoria's eyes popped open. The actress Jeffrey had hired was in the kitchen, banging pans around, bent on serving her coffee as if it were the fix of all fixes. *Get real.*

Had she been sleepwalking? Or experienced a mild stroke? That would certainly account for the headache and confusion. But this bordered on the twilight zone.

"Here's your coffee." The woman returned to the den. "Relax and enjoy it like a good girl." Her lazy gaze swam on Victoria. "Now, please tell me what's really bothering you!"

Bothering me? Victoria had no clue. Goldfish swam around in her queasy stomach as she contemplated on which planet she had landed. The coffee smelled wonderful, but out of pure stubbornness, she resisted the urge to grab the mug.

I don't live here. Victoria closed her eyes and envisioned her two-story Victorian home in Hillside Estates, the most family-oriented neighborhood in Fernwood. Streets lined with pretty trees. Spacious manicured lawns and sidewalks with curbs. *I live there.*

She'd never forget the day when her smart attorney husband had reported his fantastic real estate find. "Sweetheart, are you sitting down?" Jeffrey had said. "I found us a beautiful home, close enough to my office so I can come home for lunch. I can't wait for you to see it!"

Luckily, he had been the first to preview the property and put in a bid. "There's no question you'll love it," he had said. And she had with all her heart.

On the back porch of Victoria's mind, she heard the imposter's voice. *Forget about the woman!*

Yes . . . it seemed like only yesterday when she and Jeffrey had stood on the big front porch watching the wind gently push the swing. The kids were playing on the gym set out back, left by the former owner. It was their first home and special.

Their first remodeling project was to rip out the old-gold carpet and refurbish the floors with blond hardwoods. Of course, her favorite room in the house was the gourmet kitchen, equipped with all the bells and whistles. It was so true: the way to a man's heart is through his stomach.

Jeffrey and the kids loved the den and its real wood-burning fireplace. With bountiful window light to brighten every room, the quaint forties home was large enough to accommodate a growing family, yet cozy enough for cheerful love.

Home is where I should be. Victoria enjoyed the illusion, shutting out the world until the woman opened her mouth again.

"Mother! Pay attention, I have limited patience."

"What?" Victoria's eyes flew open in protest.

Forget about the woman.

Victoria closed her eyes and listened to the familiar sounds of life. Outdoors, birds happily twittered as cars swished by. Children played. Overhead, a jet roared past.

Inside the condo, the air-conditioning unit grunted as it kicked on. A ceiling fan swished overhead. A drippy faucet pinged against a metal spoon in the kitchen sink.

Normal, everyday sounds. Victoria sighed, growing mellow from reminiscing. The aroma of freshly brewed coffee pleasantly sifted into her nostrils. Eyes popping open, she wanted her morning coffee. No, *needed* it!

But not now, she closed her eyes again. A vanilla-scented candle had recently been burned in the room. She inhaled the blended odors of cinnamon disinfectant spray, charred wood remnants and burnt toast. Ordinary odors, pleasant and offensive, found in any house on any day of the week.

Feeling safe with her illusions, Victoria opened her eyes. It was foolish to ignore the woman any longer. In some strange way, she was part of the nasty little nightmare. "I—" Victoria was uncertain how to begin her inquiry into the bizarre.

"Here, Mother." The pretentious woman shoved a coffee mug in Victoria's face. "Don't make me stand here holding your coffee! You hate cold coffee!"

True, Sister. I'm learning to hate a lot of things!

Neither of them made a move. In some silly way, it reminded Victoria of a standoff: *Pull your gun first and I'll pull mine.* She foolishly grinned, shaking her head.

"At least, you're smiling," said the imposter, Victoria's coffee mug lingering between them like a peace offering.

What if this illusion persists? Victoria had a sickening thought. *The former things have passed away*, lightly trickled across her brain synapses.

"Mother?" The woman leaned into Victoria's face

"Yes?" She lent the actress limp brown eyes.

"Here. Take this and drink it all! You never were much good without your morning coffee. I won't stand for no." A solemn gaze solidified her determination.

"Oh, all right! Did you add cream?" Victoria grabbed the mug, grateful that she still remembered liking cream.

In some weird way, had Karen been in her mid-thirties, she might have resembled the actress since they shared the same warm hazel eyes and spacious smile . . . when the troublemaker wasn't frowning.

And the imposter's frosted hair was brown. Brown, like Karen's. You couldn't hide roots. Like family, roots prevailed. *Ah, where is this getting me?* Victoria jumped when a cold hand touched her forehead. "What?"

"No temp. We can be thankful for that," the imposter made light of the situation.

"Of course, I don't have a fever!" Victoria snapped.

"But something's amiss."

Hooray! The woman finally got the picture.

"No, I feel fine." Victoria felt terrible. "Just tell me who you are and we can part as friends."

"Friends?" The woman's troubled face reflected genuine concern. "Look at me, Mother." She leaned into Victoria's face. "It's me. Karen! What gives?"

She's good, really good! Victoria hoped that Jeffrey had paid the actress well because he really had her going this time.

"Okay, time out. No way you're my daughter!" A guttural laugh spilled from Victoria's trembling lips. "I don't mean to be unkind, dear, but you must tell me who you really are. Did my husband, Jeffrey, put you up to this?" A civil approach was best.

"Cut it out, Mother, you're starting to scare me!"

"Join the crowd!" Victoria leaped from the sofa. "You drag me inside this place and call me *Mother*, then expect me to believe your baloney?"

"What?"

"Well, I'm not buying."

"You're teasing me. Right?"

"No speak'a *Inglés*?" Victoria spouted.

"Stop it, Mother!" The imposter's face washed out white.

"Stop calling me *Mother*! Enough is enough!" Victoria grabbed the girl by the shoulders and shook her. "I won't stand for this another second!"

"Stop it, Mother! Have you lost your mind?"

Victoria stared. *Had she?*

"I can't believe this! You really don't recognize me, do you?"

Fear soared from the imposter's vibrating pupils. "Oh my!"

"I said I didn't, didn't I? Where's Jeffrey? Where's my husband? I want to talk to him. I want to go home! I'm tired, I don't feel well."

"Sit down, Mother. I'm going to call Mark right now!"

Mark James? Victoria knew Dr. Curtis Mark James, her lifelong friend and family physician. *Oh, to get their stories straight*, she bet.

"While you're on the phone, why don't you call Jeffrey?" Victoria suggested. "And tell him to bring Paul and Karen with him when they come to pick me up."

The phone hit the floor. "Mother. Paul is dead!"

"No, it's a lie!" Victoria's heart pounded in her chest. Bitter acid rose from her stomach, scalding the back of her throat. "Where's Jeffrey? Give me back my family!"

2

Prompted by Victoria's hysteria, Karen picked the receiver off the floor and hurriedly dialed Mark's number. "Come on, come on," she chanted until the phone line connected. "Thank God you're home! Something terrible has happened."

"What is it, Karen?" Mark's mind raced in uncertain directions.

"Mother's gone hysterical on me, doesn't know who I am," Karen spewed. "Doesn't know Paul died two years ago. And she asked for Dad. Mark? What am I supposed to do?"

Victoria was amused as she listened to the curious conversation between her would-be daughter and Mark James. Maybe it was Jeffrey at the other end of the line. It would be just like him to pull a trick on their fourteenth wedding anniversary.

But that she was the subject under grueling discussion was totally obvious. *Who are these people and what are their motives?*

Mark heard Karen's complaints about her mother, suppressing his irritation at her ranting. It was only a power play to get his attention, too early in the morning to take her seriously.

Even cockroaches had trouble stirring at this hour, much less civilized people. Having barely crawled from the sheets, he repressed a rude yawn, attempting to process Karen's rapidly fired words, thinking she was blowing the incident out of proportion.

"Mark, I'm coming unglued. I don't know what to think."

"I understand your concern, dear." He traced surgical hands through his mane of disheveled salt-and-pepper hair, thinking how he'd felt nearly serene before Karen had phoned. "Maybe Vicki's confusion will pass."

"But what if it doesn't?" Karen fired back. "Mother's on the sofa, staring at me like I'm the enemy," she rambled on with more details. "Tell me what to do!"

Do? This was not a diversion he needed this morning. The new day had already dumped far too much on his work plate with two morning surgeries. "Try to calm down, Karen. Your hysteria isn't helping your mother."

"Calm down?" Karen reacted. "Mark! You're not getting this picture!" She gathered steam. "So let me spell it out for you in plain English! I can't handle this again!"

"By this, I assume you mean Vicki's memory thing." Mark's skin felt infested with crawling spiders. "I understand your concern, dear. Really." Karen had a valid concern.

"It's just that you've caught me off guard," Mark continued, "and it's still early at my place. I'm having difficulty getting my juices going. So how 'bout starting over from the beginning and telling me exactly what's happened to upset you so?"

While listening to the detailed replay of the morning's occurrences, Mark's pulse quickened at Karen's description of Vicki's newest dilemma. Fear jammed in his face. Always the strong one, he should remain calm.

"Sweetheart, I don't want to alarm you, but from the way you're describing your mother's condition, she may have experienced a mild stroke. Or . . ."

"Or what, Mark?" Karen's thoughts splintered. "Now you're really freaking me out!"

"Don't overreact, dear. Just listen."

"Don't tell me not to overreact! I've got a real situation going on over here! If you have any brilliant ideas, doctor, feel free!" Her pulsating voice popped the phone line.

"Karen, sweetheart . . ." Mark cautiously softened his voice, "if Vicki has experienced a mild stroke and is still conscious, her condition isn't life threatening."

"Go on, Mark." Karen processed her mentor's words, wary eyes tracing her mother's distraught face for visible signs of a stroke, silently willing her beating heart not to take flight.

"Another thought. Maybe there's a simpler explanation for all this," he considered the worst possible scenario. "Your mother might be regaining her memories."

"What?" Karen shrieked. "After twenty-five years! How is that possible?"

"The mind's a funny thing." Mark's professionalism kicked in. "In the case of amnesia, confusion often floods the memory before full comprehension returns. Your mother—"

"Ohmygod! It must be Mother's memory. She's acting disoriented and doesn't know me. She's talking out of her head, accusing me of playing tricks on her, asking to see Dad and Paul!" Karen struggled with oscillating emotions. "What does it mean, Mark?"

"Karen, pay attention. You must calm down," Mark warned. "Your hysteria will only make matters worse for Victoria." His pulse was jumping. "Do you have Benadryl?"

"I think so," Karen fought back fear. "Benadryl. Yes."

"Give Victoria a couple of tablets." Mark's heart thumped irregularly. "That should relax Vicki until I have a chance to make my rounds at the hospital. I'll be over as soon as I can."

"Okay, okay," Karen chanted with chattering teeth.

"And Karen," Mark added, "take a Benadryl yourself."

"Wait! Can you come over now?" Karen panicked. "We really need you." *I need you.*

The breath was sucked from Mark's lungs as he mopped his sweaty brow with a damp washcloth. "Maybe I'd better. Soon as I can get dressed." He'd need to postpone a surgery first.

Cradling the phone to her breast, Karen focused moist eyes on her mother. "Mark's coming over to check on you. We'll be just fine." He was amazing. "He'll know what to do."

"So I hear," Victoria wasn't at all convinced. *I am fine*, she told herself. *But was she?*

Karen realized that she could no longer helplessly stand by and do nothing. Her confused mother needed help. Somehow she had to pull herself together and respond rationally, do as Mark said. *Find the Benadryl.* Karen hurried down the hall.

What is going on? Victoria watched the imposter scurry from the room like a bat out of hell. Obviously deranged, the girl really believed her own lies. *So Mark is coming over.*

Karen hurriedly retrieved the antihistamine from the bathroom medicine cabinet and popped a capsule in her mouth. When she returned to the den, she found her mother sitting on the sofa, eyes downcast at the carpet. "Mother?" She carefully chose her words.

Victoria gazed at the fireplace, refusing to look the imposter in the face, hoping the surreal nightmare would dissipate any second.

"Mark wants you to take this medication." Karen opened the palm of her hand, revealing two small pink-and-white capsules. "Don't be afraid, they won't hurt you."

"Afraid?" Victoria's eyes targeted her worthy opponent. "I'm not afraid of those little pills. Or you, for that matter!" *Humph.* "And for your information I played in the mud with the mysterious Dr. Mark James before you were born. So get a grip!"

"Huh?" Karen's sudden motion sent Victoria's coffee mug sailing off the coffee table, spewing dark liquid all over the beige Berber carpeting. "You remember . . . *before*?"

"Of course, I remember. What's wrong with you? I'm leaving now." Victoria got up and started for the door, uncertain where she would go since she had no idea where she lived.

Karen's mind raced in a thousand directions. "Wait!"

"What?" Victoria kept her hand on the slider, about to leave the way she'd come.

"You can't go." Karen closed the gap between them. "You live here, Mother."

"What?" Victoria suddenly remembered something important.

Yesterday she had been in her Mazda on her way into town to meet Jeffrey for a private fourteenth-wedding-anniversary celebration. The night was threatening as black skies viciously swirled overhead and lightning licked its way across the heavens.

But she had struck out in the storm anyhow. Soon, strong winds snapped trees like they were matchsticks, haphazardly slinging limbs across the highway. Any second, a tornado would manifest itself and swoop down. *Fear.* It never let up.

What else had happened that night? *Thursday, April 13, 1989, wasn't it?* Victoria struggled to get her days straight. *How can today be Monday?*

Remembers? No, it's not possible! Too much time had passed since her mother's terrible accident out on Highway 64 and her father's death. Karen fought back hysteria.

But, if by chance, Victoria Martin Tempest was recovering from amnesia, did recall those terrible events, how would she react? Everything else was relative.

Karen popped a second Benadryl in her mouth.

3

When the phone line clicked, Mark hung up. Karen Tempest had a right to be concerned about her mother. They had both been to hell and back over Vicki's amnesia.

Hadn't he always been there when their lives went askew?

Mark grasped the marble sink, leaning forward to study his tawdry image in the bathroom mirror. He'd always thought of himself as a settling catalyst for the Tempest family, a guardian angel, although he hadn't totally been able to shield them from harm's way. Aside from Jeffrey, Mark believed he understood Vicki better than anyone else ever had.

My word! The Martins, James's and Tempests were old bloodlines with deep intertwining roots that went as far back as the Civil War. Their forefathers founded Fernwood. He and Jeffrey had played together as children, gone to the same schools, known the same people, and done the same stupid teenage things!

They were the Warring Wildcats' star football quarterbacks.

And Vicki, three years younger, had clung to their coattails and done everything they did until she grew up.

Gracious, she looked cute in that short, sassy cheerleader outfit!

Oh, he'd even been a little jealous when Jeffrey beat him to the punch and asked Vicki out on a date. *His mistake.* But back then, Mark James hadn't known his heart.

Still, despite friendly competition, the three of them had remained the best of friends through the years. But a *friend* was all he'd ever been to Vicki until a year ago.

Sure, high school was a blast but the crazy times were short-lived. Following graduation, his 1971 classmates had disbursed like confetti in the wind. Some married or took off for college. Others moved away to work or joined a branch of the armed forces. But given time, the faithful few had returned.

Vicki was among the first of her classmates to come home. After three years at Memphis State University, love had wooed her back to Fernwood to marry Jeffrey, who had by that time set up his own law practice in the tradition of his father and grandfather.

Mark was interning at Vanderbilt when the news clip of their announcement came by mail. Not long afterwards, Jeffrey had phoned and asked him to be his best man. Although jealous, he'd said yes. What else could a friend do?

As expected, the wedding ceremony was beautiful. They should've put Vicki's picture on the front cover of a bridal magazine. Jeffrey, too. Handsome as a Brad Pitt in his black tuxedo and bow tie.

Eventually, Mark's chief-of-staff father had pulled strings to get him on staff at the Hardeman County General Hospital. And it suited him just fine. Dr. Curtis Mark James, specializing in cosmetic surgery, opted to return home like every other generation James.

Where else was there to go?

Besides, he had missed a hometown setting like Fernwood with its uncomplicated schedules, comfortable friends that he could always count on, and a supportive family.

And landmarks. Wood and concrete weren't going anywhere. Let others see the world, slay the dragons! Give him friendly faces, old hangouts and drinking buddies.

Not long after moving back to Fernwood, the newlyweds had him over for a meal at their apartment. Playing Cupid, Victoria had invited Beverly Yates, a sorority sister from Memphis State University. The evening had been fun.

Bev was a good looker and a heart staker, a little on the wild side, but that was okay with him. After a zany romance, they eloped. And for a while, the marriage was comfortable. They liked each other and had fun. *Didn't that outweigh love?*

With true loyalty, the Tempests and James's had stuck like glue through thick and thin. Mark couldn't count the number of social occasions they'd shared. Bev and Vicki, always the best of friends, did all those social things that women do. And at every opportunity, he and Jeffrey had slipped away from work to play a few holes of golf.

Everyone had been so happy back then. *So happy . . .*

Now, the hurt never went away. Mark choked up, his mirrored image fogged by his steamy bad breath. Swallowing a mouthful of Listerine, he reined in the mounting guilt. Life was never the same after that awful night. *Never the same . . .*

Shrugging off sad memories, Mark cranked his head to one side, noting that he needed a trim around the ears. Too many wrinkles crouched under his weary blue eyes. *Fat cheeks*, he blew them out. His partner, Allen, should grab hold of him and cut away a little of the blubber. *Nearly sixty . . . time was a zoomer.*

Back when he was a young doctor, life seemed less complicated. Choices had been wide open, limited only by the imagination. Decades passed and he hadn't always gotten life on his own terms. He helped Karen move past a disastrous marriage, but he was divorced and lonely. Casual affairs proved unsatisfying and risky to his career.

Just when Dr. Mark James had determined that life sucked from baggage piled on top of baggage, he turned a brand new corner. Finally, like finding gold, he and Vicki earned a chance at a late-life romance. And life shined again.

Mark scrubbed his hairy chest like Tarzan, rearing back his slouchy shoulders. If he'd listened to his heart decades ago, it would have told him that Vicki was the only girl for him.

No sir, making a personal house call to help out his woman was his pleasure. And Dr. Mark James always took pleasure seriously. But now he had to quit thinking and get moving.

After a quick shave and shower, Mark towel-dried his body and patted his sagging chin with *Calvin Kline* cologne. Stepping into a pair of khaki slacks, he pulled on his new *Tommy Hilfiger* shirt and stepped into a shiny pair of *Bally* oxfords.

Feeling like a male hulk fresh off the front page of *Bachelor*, he grabbed his lightweight jacket from the hall closet, pausing to assess if he'd forgotten anything. On his way out the door, Mark switched off the lights and keyed in the security code. Call him paranoid, but people couldn't be trusted. He double-checked the door locks.

His shiny sunflower-yellow remodeled Z-3 BMW was easy to spot in the Parisian parking garage. It functioned like a good woman when it came to handling. Fast and rewarding.

With the canvas top rolled back, he whipped out of the florescent-lit garage into the gathering daylight.

The chilly morning was lightly scented with jasmine, stimulating Mark's senses, making him feel more alive. An invigorating breeze kicked at the tentacles of green foliage lining the parkway as the sun-flamed horizon dazzled the dew-laden blades of grass. Spring had finally arrived in Tennessee.

Suppressing negative thoughts over Karen's description of Vicki's morning malady, Mark counted his many blessings. By human standards, he had nearly everything a man could want: a tremendous medical career, a good woman at his side, and more money than he'd ever spend.

Certainly, Parisian Condominium Estate Living was adequate, although at first he'd wondered if he'd been crazy to trade a huge two-story on the Hatchie River for a single parking space in a garage.

But who needed all that space? Wasn't his bachelor pad the perfect hangout? No hassle, no yard upkeep and just minutes from his office.

Parisian even had its own gym and pool with tennis and golfing facilities. And when he had time, the opportunity for recreation was unlimited.

Mark wasn't in a hurry. It was only a fifteen-minute drive over to Karen's condo. Only minutes after sunrise, the roadragers had not yet emerged. His classic sports car zipped over the maze of streets with no problem.

So what would life with Vicki be like if her memories had returned? Mark posed the dreaded question. Only recently had she come to terms with Paul's untimely death. And even though she didn't recall Jeffrey's demise, it had still taken years for her to adjust to lost years.

Hugging the steering wheel, Mark suffered unprecedented remorse. He was sorry for leaving Jeffrey's murder unsolved, repulsed by Paul's brutal death, and bitter at Fate for stealing so much of Vicki's life. But most of all: for his irresponsible contribution to their suffering. Unfortunately, he knew of no easy solution to vindicate the multitude of wrongs done by many.

Knowledge was a powerful bedfellow and the tragic memories never left him. Besides, there were certain facts surrounding Jeffrey's death that should never come to light—privileged information that the good citizens of Fernwood should never learn for everyone's sake, especially Vicki's. And in that, Mark found solace.

Life happens, like it or not.

Karen's condominium complex suddenly loomed ahead. Weighty thoughts had launched him on a lofty mental plane, but now it was time to touch down and face the real world. He whipped the BMW over to the curb and killed the engine.

Straightening his collar, Mark cleared his throat, stepped up to the challenge, and rang the doorbell. It was time to rule. Seconds later, the door flew open.

"Thank God, you're here!" Karen grabbed Mark's arm and pulled him inside the swanky condo, her teary eyes wagging with worry. "I'm at my wit's end."

"Where's Vicki?" His mind shot back to the night Jeffrey was assaulted. No one had expected the storm to drive the attorney back to his law office to retrieve his umbrella. Jeffrey must have been holding the phone in his hand when it rang and alerted the thieves to his presence. *Wrong place. Wrong time.*

Caught off guard, Jeffrey had no opportunity to defend himself against the experienced thugs. Shot twice through the chest, one deadly bullet had penetrated a lung, the other his heart. So began the bizarre night that changed so many lives.

The police later traced the call to Vicki's car phone. She was on her way to town to meet Jeffrey. Driving conditions had been deplorable. Whatever happened—fear of the storm, the slick pavement, panic at hearing gunshots when Jeffrey answered the phone—she'd ended up in a twisted car at the bottom of a ravine.

Simultaneously, husband and wife had been rushed to Hardeman County General Hospital for treatment. Jeffrey was pronounced dead on arrival, Vicki with irreparable head injuries. She never had the chance to tell Jeffrey why she called him or to say goodbye. *The rest was sad history.*

When the swelling in Vicki's brain subsided, she'd been left in a coma. The prognosis was grim. No one had expected her to recover so quickly. The doctors were ecstatic when she suddenly woke up ninety days later. The news media gobbled up the story and spat it out over the major networks. Fernwood attracted national attention as folks applauded God's generosity.

However, Vicki's recovery wasn't as bright as proclaimed. It soon became apparent that she was experiencing amnesia. With no clue of what had happened before the accident, she was a new person in an unfamiliar world. She even treated her own children like strangers.

The name *Jeffrey* meant absolutely nothing. Mark shrugged his shoulders. When he looked into her eyes, she was unresponsive to his caring. No one knew how to help.

On top of everything else, he'd been the one to break the sad news to Vicki—that Jeffrey was dead. But even that meant nothing to her.

No memories, no grief or remorse.

Back then, he had questioned her ability to cope with Jeffrey's brutal death had she remembered. And today, twenty-five years later, he was still haunted by the idea that those tragic memories just might be coming home to roost. *Yet another Victoria tragedy!*

"Mother's resting quietly in her bedroom. I'll go get her," Karen was saying. "Why don't you wait in the den?" She was already making her way down the hall.

Mark's mind catapulted to the present. Complacently nodding, he ventured into the den and collapsed like a jellyfish on the sofa, suffering from mental wounds he believed had healed.

Cornered by memories, he thought of young Paul and Karen, devastated over losing both parents at once. Over time, Jeffrey's son had proven the weaker of the two siblings, never having coped with suddenly losing both parents.

But Karen, a blossoming vivacious teen, had demonstrated amazing strength, sacrificing her own social needs to help nurse her mother back to health.

Quite oppositely, Paul had only become more detached and despondent as time passed. At sixteen, he'd been nearly suicidal, foolishly seeking relief in alcohol and experimental drugs.

Karen had tried to help her stubborn brother, but Paul had refused advice. As Jon Branson's brash sidekick, the kid had hellishly blazed a destructive trail. Discounting the costs to himself, family members, and friends, he had acted selfishly out of confusion and despair.

Oh, yes, there had been periods in Paul Tempest's life when he'd played the good citizen and held down a job. "I'm rehabilitated," he had promised.

And Santa Claus is real.

Never lacking for money, Vicki's son had refused wise counsel, burning the candle at both ends as he and Jon recklessly played with their lives like balls chancing a win on a roulette table. As a result, Paul was never able to sustain a loving, permanent relationship. Mark wished his life had turned out differently.

But life was what it was.

Two short years before, Paul was found dead in the back room of a gay bar. A drug overdose, the police had said. Only thirty-eight years old, the lad's demise was yet another tragic event in the already stormy history of the Tempest family. *Sad but true.*

4

"Mother, are you asleep?" Karen switched on the leaded-glass lamp beside Victoria's bed. "Mark's here to see you. Do you feel like talking to him?"

Selfishly, she dreaded dealing with her mother's memory problem again. Once in a lifetime had been quite enough. Observing her slow recovery from the debilitating accident had nearly destroyed her life, too. "Do you need some help?"

Karen made no effort to assist, aware that her indifference was an act of defiance. As a teen, she hadn't understood *karma* very well. But today, a wiser woman, she realized that fate and karma were duo-kickers.

"The Tempest tragedy," aptly coined by the local residents, had placed her and Paul at the center of town pity. "*Those poor Tempest children . . .*" she'd overheard their well-meaning whispers as she'd unsuccessfully dealt with an uncontrollable older brother who'd refused sound advice. When he wasn't talking on the phone to crazy Jon Branson, he was behind the house smoking pot or guzzling cheap alcohol.

Karen shook her head. *If her mother only knew* . . . her precious Paul did more damage in his short life than she ever cared to know about. *But at least Paul had ended his misery.*

"Mark is here?" Victoria's eyelids fluttered.

"Take all the time you need, Mother."

Karen retraced her steps to the den and spied Mark on his haunches beside the glowing fireplace, hands extended to absorb the flowing warmth. "She's on her way. Do you want something to drink?"

"No, thank you. I had a cup of coffee before I left home."

Having Mark near was a comfort. Karen knew she never would have emotionally survived without his continual help over the years. Always her firm anchor, she depended on his creative judgment. But how would he handle yet another change in his *beloved*?

"What is it, dear?" Mark noted Karen's melancholic expression.

"Come over here, my little kitten." He crooked his finger, morning sluggishly tugging at his heels.

Did he know how tremendously grateful she was to have him in her life? Karen lent him a teary gaze. *He didn't, because he had eyes only for her mother.*

"You're cold, dear," he said to her. "You need to let me handle things from here." Karen nodded, walking into his embrace as if she belonged there, enjoying the faint odor of Mark's cologne, the touch of his strong hands.

After her mother's accident, he'd taken charge of everything, paid the family bills when the insurance money played out, even hired a private nurse to take care of them.

"You're mighty quiet, dear." The physician's lips slightly curled. "Did Vicki say anything that might tell us what's going on with her?" Mark hid his worry.

"She'll be out in a moment." Karen gazed into his flame-blue eyes glistening with concern. "Thank you for coming over."

"Of course I would come. I'm family." Mark enjoyed his pseudo-filial responsibility. Together, they would hurdle another crisis.

Victoria sat up in bed. Attempting to internalize the events of the past hour, she added two plus two and came up with an uneven five. With no leap of insight, she swung her legs off the side of the bed, slipped her cold toes into a silky pair of pink house shoes, and shuffled down the hall toward the den.

Nothing made any sense this morning—not where she was or what she was doing before she'd lost time. *Lost time. That was it!* Victoria groggily stood in the hall shadows, pressing fingertips to her temples as pictures flashed through her mind.

As a secret door to the vault of her memory opened, she recalled having placed her Bible on the car seat before leaving to meet Jeffrey in town. *Yesterday, wasn't it?*

Jeffrey had invited her to meet him for dinner, in honor of their fourteenth wedding anniversary. Where they were dining that evening was his best-kept secret. Excited over a romantic evening out on the town, she had purchased a classy new dress for the occasion. But something happened to keep her from going into town.

What was it? Her mind thrummed with speculation.

She had left Paul in charge of babysitting Karen—not that either of her children needed looking after. In her book they were near perfect, reared with church values and dependable. Paul balked at the idea. *Why?*

Like a lid popping off, Victoria's mind opened up a vat of memories. Staggering down the hall, holding her head like it was about to fall off her neck, she recalled leaving the house and driving down Highway 64 toward Fernwood in a terrible storm. When a DJ on the radio reported that a funnel cloud had been sighted, she'd refused to turn the car around and miss her date.

But something stopped her from going.

Victoria sauntered into the den, swaying with confusion. *Dear Jesus, what was it?* She peered at the two strangers cozily cuddled.

More scheming?

"Mother," the imposter said. "Do you need some help? You look pale." Hazel eyes darted between Victoria and the man.

"I don't think so." *Give it up, honey!*

"Mark has been waiting to speak to you."

Where is he? Victoria stumbled toward the sofa, attempting to dislodge the confusion nesting in her brain. Probably from the medication she had taken earlier.

Who are these people and what is their game?

"Don't be afraid, Mother."

"Afraid?" Victoria collapsed on the sofa. "I thought you said Mark James was here." She stared at the gentleman. "You ought to be ashamed of yourself. Was this your idea?"

"Don't you know me, Vicki?" He came closer.

"Mark?" She peered into his intelligent blue eyes. Decades older, the actor actually resembled her friend. But her Mark worked out at the gym.

"Can you describe how you feel?" He made the mistake of touching Victoria. Repulsed, she shrank away.

"You're not my Mark! Get your hands off me!"

"You *do* know me . . ." Mark cast a wary glance at Karen. "We know what's happening to you, Vicki." His worst fear materialized. "Try to relax, honey."

"Get away from me now! I don't know who you are, but you're not Mark James!" She would not cooperate with these people.

"You're remembering, that's all." Mark motioned for Karen to hand him his medical bag. "Don't be alarmed, dear. Just hold real still." He pulled out a syringe.

"No!" Victoria's eyes widened in horror. "What are you doing?" She pushed away the threatening needle. "Stop! I don't need a shot! Help! Somebody, help me!"

"Hush, Mother! We're only trying to help you!" Karen harnessed Victoria's hands while Mark gripped her arm.

"Be still, Vicki. I'm giving you a sedative. It will barely sting and you will soon feel much calmer." He hadn't seen her so distraught since the day Paul was buried.

"No," Victoria resisted. "Somebody help me! Why are you trying to hurt me? I don't want a shot! You're not my Mark. He's younger than you are—where's Jeffrey?"

For now, Mark had done what he could for Victoria. She would soon respond to the medication and sleep. However, Karen seemed in even worse shape. Rigorously shaking, the girl's teary eyes were ablaze with horror. She needed his help, too.

"Sweetheart . . ." Mark turned to his fragile kitten. "Help me get your mother on the sofa." He hoped his command would jar her sensibility. "We mustn't let your mother fall." He kept his voice low-key, worried that Karen might faint on him.

Mark guided Victoria to the sofa and peered at his helper. "Why don't you sit down a minute?" he said to Karen. "You're pale as a sheet."

The morning wasn't going well at all. Mark was late for work, and now he had two helpless women looking to him for support. He only hoped that Karen would not see how truly upset he was.

How disastrous it would be for everyone if Victoria's memories had returned! She would have questions about the past that would stir up a hornet's nest and turn everybody's life upside down.

No, it was better to lie to her.

"I feel dizzy." Victoria swooned. "Somebody help me, please!"

"We're both here, Mother." Karen squeezed her mother's hand tightly. "You're going to be just fine. Don't fight the sedative."

Mark gazed at Victoria helplessly lying on the sofa. She looked so fragile, but he knew that she was amazingly strong. When she had more of the equation, how would she react?

The cold winds of truth blew through Mark's troubled heart. His *Little Vicki* would never be able to handle reality. Her resurrected memories would be the dragon to slay her. As passionately as she loved, she would hate.

Worse, the crushing reality of truth might send her crashing into a black vat of nothingness all over again. And it would partially be his fault. Regardless how this new scenario played out, she must never learn what took place on that stormy night when Jeffrey died! The truth would not set her free. It would crush them all.

Mark settled on his knees beside the sofa as the building guilt walloped him. The medication had forced Victoria's eyelids to close. She would sleep now. But who would salve the doctor's conscience?

Moving beyond caring who these people were, Victoria longed for sweet rest. A lazy wash of wooziness soon invaded her mindscape. *Sleepy, very sleepy . . .*

Karen covered her mother's cool body with an afghan, breathing more easily. "She's out, Mark. The medication did its job. Let her sleep it off on the sofa."

Mark crept to his feet and stared down at Victoria's limp body. "Seeing her sleep so peacefully, you wouldn't think she'd been through so much," he shook his head. "Poor baby."

"Do you think Mother will be all right?" Karen whispered.

"I hope so, dear."

Mark's fears coupled with compassion had drained him. He'd hate to fill Vicki's shoes. She had much to face if she were truly remembering. But all he could do now was wait and see.

Before Mark realized it, Karen's arms were tightly bound about his neck, her light, but passionate kiss, capturing his lips. "Thanks for coming, Mark. Mother's so lucky."

Mark blinked, rubbing his mouth with the back of his knuckles. Distressed over Karen's sudden display of affection, he was uncertain how to respond.

"Does it bother you so much that I care for you, Mark?" Karen despised her brash display of affection. *Had she no pride?* "It's not the first time you've been kissed."

"No, dear. Of course not," a kinder, fatherly Mark responded. "I just think we should concentrate on your mother's getting well. Let's table this topic, shall we?"

Glaring at the doctor, Karen didn't want to table the topic. Resentment surfaced. She wanted to shake her fist at God!

Why couldn't Mark love me?

5

Victoria's pillow was soft as a silk cloud. *Heavenly*. Unaware of anyone else in the room, she drifted into a historic dreamscape. It was Thursday, April 13, 1989.

She was in the kitchen tidying up while Karen lounged on the sofa in the den, glued to one of her favorite TV soaps that portrayed worldly people with few Christian values. Pushing imagination to the limits, the actors appeared fickle whether they were married, involved in love triangles, or so-called friends.

Certainly not my cup of tea, Victoria hummed as she worked.

Home early from school, Paul skidded across the freshly polished kitchen floor. "I got a football game Saturday afternoon!" he announced while rummaging through the refrigerator. Grabbing a half-filled carton of chocolate milk, he guzzled it down in record time. "Do you think Dad will come see me play?" Spirited brown eyes lazily shifted toward his mother.

"I'm sure your father will want to come." Victoria used potholders to retrieve a cherry pie from the oven, carefully placing it on a metal rack. "If it rains, he won't be playing golf."

"Duh, Mom!" Paul scowled. "If it rains the game will be called off anyhow!"

Victoria locked a disapproving gaze on her impertinent son, then almost felt sorry for him as she watched the lad's countenance take a tumble. "Your dad does what he can, son."

"He won't come. He's always too busy." Paul's shoulders slumped in defeat.

"Actually . . ." Victoria placed a fond hand on her son's shoulder. "It's quite possible your dad and I will be gone overnight on Saturday." They had in mind a romantic weekend.

"For what?" Paul stole a cookie from the jar. "Why can't Ka and I go?" His big brown eyes were silver dollars.

"Because," Victoria sheepishly grinned, "your father and I are celebrating fourteen years of marriage with dinner out tonight and a honeymoon trip planned over the weekend." A milestone many of their friends hadn't reached. God had always been faithful.

"Cool!" Paul bared his even white teeth. "Hope I don't stay married to one person that long!" He snapped a hand towel. "Yuk! Imagine lookin' at the same ol' boring face!"

"Paul!" Victoria reacted. "It's your mother you're talkin' to!" She was appalled at his casual attitude toward relationships. Kids didn't have a clue about the importance of family.

"My friend . . ." Paul dug his hands into his slouchy Polo jeans, "he said his dad got divorced just before they moved here. Holy Toledo, Mom! You should see Jon's new step-mom! Curves in the right places and real cool, a whole bunch younger than his dad."

"That's enough, Paul!" Victoria's patience was taxed. "You know the Bible tells us that God doesn't approve of divorce. Your father and I didn't bring you up to think like that!"

"God doesn't live in today's world, Ma. It's way different now. You have no clue." Paul glared at his mother. "It's not like it was two thousand years ago. No way."

"I totally disagree!" Victoria informed Paul, shedding her apron and tossing it on a kitchen barstool. "God's principles never change. His Word is eternal and still applies today."

"Yeah, I guess," Paul mewed. "Gotta go now and knock out some algebra before me and Jon play pool later tonight." He tossed out the idea, halfway out the kitchen door.

"Wait, Paul!" Victoria's summons halted Paul. "Sorry, but you can't go out tonight. Remember? I have plans. Anyhow, I don't like you hanging out at the pool hall."

Paul spun around, scowling at his mother. "Jeeze, Mom! Give me a break!"

"That's enough, Paul. I don't want to hear another word of profanity coming out of your mouth! And don't you dare look at me like that!" Victoria warned. "I only want what's best for you and I don't know this boy, Jon what's his name? Who are his parents?"

"Jon's family moved to Fernwood last fall," Paul mumbled,

shuffling his feet in a hurry to leave. "Shoot, you never let me have no fun!" He hoped she'd change her mind.

"Fun can be dangerous," Victoria wisely counseled. "That's why you have parents."

"I'll be home early, I promise." Paul refused to give up. "You don't even have to drive me 'cause Jon's got his own set of wheels. Please, Ma? I won't stay out late, I promise."

"Oh?" *Jon has his own set of wheels?* "So exactly how old is your friend?" She worried about Paul hanging around an older, more-experienced boy. Influence molded character.

"C'mon, Ma!" Paul wasn't through pitching. "Jon's a good kid. He's fifteen. His dad manages that meat factory. You know, out on that ol' dump site where the tannery used to be."

"You still can't go out," Victoria held firm to her decision.

"What time's supper?" Paul asked, not a happy camper. The boy knew when he'd pushed the limits.

"You get to order pizza in. Go out another evening, after I've met your friend. Besides, it's stormy tonight. You and Karen are grounded!"

"But—"

"No *buts*, Paul. You know how afraid I am of storms."

"But I ain't scared of no storm!" Paul scowled. "Can I help it if Granny lived in Oklahoma and was in three tornadoes? *Jeeze*, Mom! Give me a break!"

"That's enough, Paul. Jesus Christ, our Savior, is not an exclamation!" The younger generation lacked proper respect.

"Sorry." Paul visibly softened. "Can I go to my room now?"

"Pizza and Coke, finished off with homemade cherry pie topped with ice-cream," Victoria embellished her supper proposal. "Don't be mad. I really need you home, son."

"I said okay, didn't I?" Paul's haughtiness was imbedded.

"Tonight is special for your father and me, Paul. Don't go and ruin it."

"I won't. Promise." He sassily winked.

"You!" Victoria preferred the lighter mood of her son's dark personality. Give him time to grow up. Time seasoned people.

"No problem-o. Sis and I can mind the store while you two play lovers." Paul pushed his teasing further, hoping to get a rise out of his mother. "Like Romeo and Juliet."

Victoria's cheeks flushed as she realized her son must know about sex, although he hadn't yet brought up the subject. Jeffrey should talk to Paul, the sooner the better.

"If I can't go out, can my friend come over?" Paul asked.

"No!" Victoria exclaimed. "Go. Study. I need to get ready if I'm gonna meet your father in town by seven." She was looking forward to their private anniversary celebration.

"Yeah." Paul shrugged. "Sure thing." He jumped, touching the ceiling fan with his fingertips. "Oh, and Paul," Victoria hurriedly added. "Will you phone in the pizza order when you and Karen are ready? I'll leave enough cash on the kitchen table for a nice tip."

"Whatever!" Paul hollered as he scampered from the kitchen and bounded up the stairs toward his second-story bedroom.

Seconds later, Victoria heard his door slam followed by a loud blast of riotous music from one of those satanic rock albums that so mesmerized teenagers!

With no leap of insight in wise parenting, Victoria glanced around at her clean kitchen before retreating to her bedroom. Leaning against the closed door, she cherished the prospect of spending an entire evening alone with Jeffrey with no distraction from TV, ringing phones, or kids. No question that she loved her children, but romance had its rightful place, too.

During the past weeks, Jeffrey's work had escalated and swamped him. She couldn't recall when they'd last had a heart-to-heart. He came home late at night so exhausted he had literally fallen into bed fully dressed. Seconds later he was sleeping.

Long ago Victoria had decided that law was beyond her understanding and definitely wouldn't cure loneliness! What she most needed was a quality dose of TLC from her husband.

Sighing, Victoria pulled her new black-lace dress from its hang-er and spread it neatly across the bed, enticed by the idea of a bubbly soak in the garden tub.

Thirty minutes later, she crawled from the soapy water. Wrapping a towel about her, she blew her long brown hair dry and dressed. Not too bad after fourteen years of marriage, she viewed her polished image in the mirror.

Feeling grateful for a Christian home and a caring husband, she removed her Bible from the nightstand and opened the pages to one of her favorite Scriptures: "I can do all things through Christ who strengthens me."

Nobody said it any better than the Apostle Paul.

Like her own Paul, the New Testament teacher had struggled with making right choices as faith took root. Victoria smiled back at her image in the mirror. If her young son had any of Jeffrey's genes he would turn out all right. The Tempests were survivors.

"Nothing was new under the sun," her mother had once remarked. "Temptation is a given in any generation." Except the Biblical Paul never compromised or caved in to society's pressures. He always tried to do things God's way.

Pressing on toward a higher calling . . .

Victoria only prayed that her Paul would cling to Christian values defined by love, integrity, and regard for others. "Love the Lord God with all your heart, mind, and soul. And love your neighbor as yourself." Jesus couldn't have said it better.

"Listen to your heart, my son."

Although uncertain how either of her children might react to adversity, Victoria trusted that *nothing* could separate them from the love of God. If there were one true virtue in life, it was the substance of faith. And on faith in Jesus Christ hope was built.

***

When Victoria awakened around noon, a brilliant shaft of sunlight leaked through the parted window curtains of the den. The house was ominously silent. She was alone.

Sleepily creeping into the kitchen, she found a note on the bar written to her by the pretentious woman stating that she'd gone out to show a house.

So the imposter is a real estate agent, Victoria haphazardly tossed the note aside while considering the sincerity of the man calling himself Mark James. *Was he part of the charade?*

If so, the doctor played a pretty good game. Victoria puzzled over Mark's premature graying and aggressive aging. But if she chose to accept him for face value, then the woman calling herself Karen must also be the real deal.

Except overnight aging was impossible, wasn't it?

Surely there was a plausible explanation for the lapse in time. Victoria nosed around in the den for evidence of the fact when she noticed Karen's business card lying on her desk.

Curiously, she picked it up and read the inscription. Printed in bold ink were the names of the three realty owners: Jones, Cohen & Hussein Associates, Inc. with the business address, phone numbers, e-mail and fax, all of which seemed foreign to Victoria.

Strange, Victoria mused. So what was the likelihood of a Christian, a Jew, and an Arab forming an amiable partnership? Three people of such different cultural and religious backgrounds, how did they find enough commonality to establish a business?

She dropped the card on the desk, distracted by the rich aroma of fresh-ground Colombian coffee seeping from the kitchen, deciding that caffeine was exactly the punch she needed to clear her thinking. Perhaps a *normal* cup of coffee would sharpen her senses, give her greater perspective on her situation.

Dear God, it had been an awful day.

And the actual date was still up for grabs. There was a questionable gap between April 13, 1989, and April 14, 2014. Victoria mulled over the missing time as she inserted a gourmet filter pad into the sophisticated coffee maker and hit the *On* button.

Feeling hungry, unable to recall when she'd last eaten, Victoria located some packaged ham in the refrigerator along with fresh tomatoes, onion and lettuce. Grabbing a loaf of bread from the pantry closet, she started stacking. Being hungry was quite normal.

When Victoria had put everything on her sandwich thinkable, she bit into her triple-decker sandwich and sighed with relief. Everything would turn out just fine. She just needed more faith and nourishment. Life had a way of working out the wrinkles as time progressed.

After pouring herself a stiff cup of coffee steeped with real cream, Victoria satisfied her ferocious appetite, stewing over her unusual predicament. Had she somehow stepped through a time warp? Her illusive surroundings felt quite real, although existing in the Twilight Zone.

Perhaps, Victoria considered her options, *it's time to take the offensive regarding my weird state of mental affairs and quit second-guessing the imposters.*

Her smart attorney-husband would insist she explore the facts before leaping to any conclusions. *After all* . . . Victoria giggled. *I didn't just fall off a turnip truck!*

Foremost, Jeffrey believed in cause and effect—a consequence for every action. He would encourage her to investigate the reasons why she felt disoriented earlier that morning, why she hadn't recognized her subdivision, home or daughter.

Or Mark, her best friend.

Following the serious little chat with herself, Victoria felt so much better. With a coffee mug in hand, she ventured outdoors and peered over the balcony railing. A few hours ago, she had stood in the deserted street below while life as she knew it vanished. It was unrealistic to believe her quaint neighborhood had been instantaneously displaced by rows of condominiums since time was required to tear down the old and reconstruct the new.

So what had really happened? Victoria cautiously examined the physical evidence, preferring to forget about the imposters and disregard her apparent loss of time. But Jeffrey would require that she face the truth. And remembering was crucial, even if painful.

Victoria was unsure how long she'd contemplated her precarious plight before the floodgates holding back chained memories suddenly lifted and unleashed a stream of terrifying and confusing details about her chilling past. A scream knotted in her stomach.

"*NO!*" Hysterical gasps rose in Victoria's throat as a night of horrors impacted. Gale force winds had forced her Mazda to hydroplane on Highway 64, tossing it like a tin can into a deep ravine. The sounds of metal crunching had filled her ears as the car landed with a thud and gut-wrenching pain ripped through her body, terrorizing her mind.

Dear Lord, I nearly died that night! Victoria grasped the balcony. Now the date on the morning newspaper made sense, why she had been so confused earlier that day, and why yesterday felt like April 13, 1989. As bizarre as it seemed, in the blink of an eye, she had traded one set of memories for another. It was the only reasonable explanation for Karen's and Mark's seemingly rapid aging and why she'd been unable to recall where she was or what she was doing seconds before.

Something else important happened that fated Thursday. Victoria struggled to leave no memory chip unturned, ready to swallow the bitter pill of truth. *What was it?*

"Yes!" Victoria gasped as more recall surfaced. She'd been driving down Highway 64 toward Fernwood. Before her accident she had called Jeffrey to tell him she was running late.

But their anniversary evening never happened.

She could still hear the ringing phone like it was yesterday. And when Jeffrey answered his office phone, she heard a series of loud pops. *Crack! Crack! Crack!*

She'd been terrified. *Gun shots?* "Jeffrey! Jeffrey!" She'd screamed at hearing his phone drop to the floor. Seconds later she'd lost control of her Mazda. The rest was history.

"There are so many unanswered questions," she mumbled.

Closing her eyes to review the details of her revelation, she now understood why life as she knew it was unfamiliar. "Flip-flopped" memories had confused her. She presently lived with her real-estate daughter, for reasons she had yet to discover. And apparently, Mark James was still her doctor. But what had happened to Jeffrey? Had he died that night like Karen said?

"And where is my son, Paul?" Victoria voiced her concern.

And there were other issues that needed to be resolved—like what had happened to the Bible she carried with her in the car that stormy evening. And who hurt Jeffrey?

Ready for answers, Victoria vowed to learn why her family had suffered so tragically. Resolving the past was necessary in order to recreate a new one for the third time.

In a moment of hope, Victoria considered she was wrong, that perhaps Jeffrey hadn't died from gun wounds. Maybe he'd only grown tired of dealing with her amnesia and divorced her years before. He could still be alive and living somewhere else, maybe even remarried. She could forgive him anything.

Come back to me, darling.

And Paul had probably moved to Texas. He'd always been a cowboy at heart like Bruce Willis. She might even have grandchildren. Maybe her son did skilled work with his hands. Victoria smiled. He used to make crosses with Popsicle sticks.

But rationally, Victoria knew that the fantasy wasn't true. Jeffrey was dead. And so was Paul. No one had reason to lie about them. She hated not being able to recall the years when Paul and Karen were growing up. Despised that Jeffrey's comforting arms would never wrap about her again. Detested that they had not grown older together. It just wasn't fair.

Dear Jesus! I want my wonderful life back.

6

As the afternoon shadows deepened, Victoria comfortably reclined in a patio chaise lounge with no particular agenda in mind. She had spent most of the day thinking about the early morning events and how she had jumped to all the wrong conclusions. One simple phone call had confirmed her suspicion that the year was 2014. Ma Bell could usually be trusted.

Victoria heard the glass sliders open and turned around. Unable to constrain joyous love, she rushed over and tenderly hugged Karen, recognition miraculously emanating from her Hershey-brown eyes. "I'm so glad you're home, dear. We need to talk."

"Mother? You know it's me." Karen's cascading tears soaked her pink cheeks. "I'm so sorry about everything." She embraced Victoria with vitality. "It must be terrible for you."

"Come here, sweetheart." Victoria grasped Karen's hand. "Sit down beside your mother, out here in God's pure cleansing sunlight. I want you to tell me what happened after my accident, and all about your father."

"You remember your accident?" Karen's hazel eyes glistened, confusion flooding her expression. "But how?" The wreck had left her mother in a coma that resulted in amnesia.

"Only God knows," Victoria softly replied, amazed. "I must have been injured badly," she grimaced, now wide open to hearing the grueling truth. "The event is a blank."

"You nearly died, Mother!" Karen gasped. "You were in a coma for three months."

"Where is your father now? Did he divorce me?"

"No, Mother. Dad wouldn't do that!" Karen raked a frosted curl off her forehead. "No couple was more perfectly matched." She choked on gathering emotions. "You were the love of his life."

"Jeffrey died, didn't he?" Victoria had known the answer before she asked.

"Dead on arrival. From gun wounds in the lung and heart."

Karen sucked in a breath. "It was a burglary at his office. Dad caught them—he didn't have time to suffer, Mother."

"Good, I'm glad." Victoria remained composed, resigned to hearing Karen out. "Did they ever find out who killed Jeffrey?"

She wanted to know if justice had been done.

Karen's diffused gaze latched onto Victoria. "Mother? You don't recall the police investigation?" She nervously wrung her hands. "Please tell me you remember."

"I'm afraid I don't," Victoria admitted. "Why don't you tell me."

"Now I'm confused," Karen said. "How is that possible?"

"Possible? I'm not sure." Victoria turned sympathetic eyes on her daughter. "It appears that my amnesia has flip-flopped."

"What?" Horror struck Karen's face.

"It's true. Now that I remember *before*, I don't recall afterwards." A faint smile trembled on Victoria's lips.

"I don't know what to say, Mother." Karen was stunned.

"Just tell me the truth! Don't be afraid, I can handle it." Doubt crouched. "Did they prosecute your father's killers?"

"No." Karen's illusive gaze shifted off Victoria. "The police determined it was kids looking," her voice cracked, "for money."

"But you don't think it was?" Victoria lifted Karen's chin, redirecting her gaze. "Look me in the eye, honey. This is important. Don't hold any information back."

"It's all in the past now." Karen wanted to keep it that way.

"Nothing's in the past!" Victoria passionately declared.

"What?" Karen looked at her mother, horrified.

"I'm back." Victoria glared back. "And I want Jeffrey's killers brought to justice."

"No, Mother! You can't!" Karen rasped. "You don't understand. They gave us money to pay for Dad's funeral and your medical bills! For my college tuition and your nursing care! We never would have survived without financial help."

Victoria moved beyond speechless, weak in the knees.

"Mother, we can't go there again!" Karen's eyes were hauntingly fearful. "Don't push this issue any further."

Victoria's mind raced in widening circles as she processed Karen's response, taking every possible scenario into consideration. Bottom line: she was blown away.

"You took money from the *scum* who killed your father?"

"No!" Karen's face was horrified. "I wouldn't do that!"

Victoria grabbed her daughter by the shoulders and was shaking her before she realized it. "Karen! How could you do such a thing? That's accepting *blood money*!"

"We thought," Karen choked, "we believed you would never come out of the coma." She was on the verge of bawling. "Paul and I were kids. Dad was gone, and you might as well have been. We were left penniless when the insurance money played out. We didn't know what else to do!" She backed away. "We did the best we could."

Victoria fought back raging anger, trying to understand an eleven-year-old's response to a crisis, needing to believe that Karen wanted to do what was right, yet detesting her unwise choices.

"Mark James helped us," Karen said in her defense.

"Mark?" Victoria's pupils widened. "What's he got to do with this?"

"Everything. He was wonderful!" Karen's voice brightened. "Mark received an anonymous note from someone saying they were sorry, that Dad's death had been an accident."

"The killers wrote to Mark?" Karen's bizarre story shot up to the level of creative genius. "You knew their names and didn't tell the police?" *What was I doing all this time?*

"No, Mother! They didn't give their names. And I didn't care who they were at the time. Mark thought we should take the money. He said we couldn't bring Dad back and we might never track down his killers, so Paul and I agreed."

"Mark said that? Jeffrey's good friend?" *Unbelievable.*

"Mark is the trustee to our family Gift Trust Fund. He took over everything, settled your hospital debt and hired a nurse to take care of you so Paul and I could concentrate on growing up. When you surfaced from your coma, he helped you start a new life."

"Wow!" was all Victoria could think to say.

"Mother! A few months ago you agreed to marry Mark!"

"What?" Victoria's mind thrashed about to grasp the possibility. Forcing her eyes upon the third finger of her left hand, she spied the glittering diamond.

"I need to sit down." Victoria's knees were shaky, heart cumbersome with latent guilt for letting others control her life.

"Mother, Mark is a good man," Karen said. "You love him."

No, I don't. Victoria's lungs contracted so tightly she couldn't speak. Truth's weight was an anchor around her neck.

"Say something, Mother," Karen's voice pulsed.

"I need to be alone to deal with this news."

"No, Mother. You shouldn't be alone. Not at this time like this."

"I'm a stronger woman than you might believe, Karen," Victoria declared with resolve. "I'll be just fine." She stood tall with dignity. "God is with me. He'll see me through this."

Karen didn't budge a muscle.

"Look, dear, why don't you go back to work?" Victoria said. "Show a house or do something useful. I need time alone. Please!" Revelation left emotional residues. Mark, Karen and Paul—they had all made decisions for her because she couldn't.

"You're sure? I hate leaving you alone like this."

"Positive." Victoria lifted her chin with resolve.

"Then I'll take a long walk," Karen decided. "Be back in an hour."

"You do that." Victoria grasped the patio railing to steady herself. "I just realized I haven't seen myself in the mirror yet." A smile tugged at her full lips. "I still have to face some issues alone. You can't help with this. Honestly." She was older, too. Ugh!

"I'm so sorry," Karen apologized, "for all you've been through."

"It's not your fault, dear. What happened to our family wrecked all our lives." Victoria grasped Karen's hand. "Just one more question?" She peered into her daughter's lovely face.

"What?" Karen's dark eyelashes nervously fluttered.

"After my accident? Did I recognize you and Paul?"

"No, Mother," Karen sighed, a deep sadness emanating from her eyes. "You required round-the-clock nursing care for the next eighteen months. Although you were told that we were your children, you treated us like strangers."

"You must have suffered terribly!" Victoria's remorse capitulated, longing to recall why she'd been so callous. "It's all my fault!"

"No, Mother!" Karen reacted. "How can you possibly believe that? Accidents happen. You mustn't think that Dad's death was your fault! It was all a twist of Fate."

"No, not Fate, Karen!" Victoria bit into her lower lip. "Fate is a fabrication of humankind. *Faith* is a better choice!"

"Faith?" Karen reacted. "After all that's happened, you have faith?"

"Nothing happens in this world without God's knowledge or permission." Victoria guarded her heart. "I believe our Almighty Father has a purpose for everything He does. Even for my accident," she swallowed hard. "And for your father's death."

"Then you're a bigger person than I am, Mother!" Karen's caustic words were searing. "Very noble, but still completely foolish." She'd long ago concluded that the only one she could trust was herself.

"Karen, what happened to your *faith*?"

"Oh, Mother! If I were you I wouldn't go around preaching Christianity. Religious thought has drastically changed."

"Changed?" Victoria huffed. "What about God ever changes?"

Karen offered no comment. Above Victoria a flicker of sunlight escaped a dark cloud, warming her face and reminding her of an important Biblical principle: *I can do all things through Jesus Christ, in His strength.* The principle still applied.

"People view God differently now," Karen's voice was reduced to a bare whisper. "That's the way it is, Mother."

"I guess I've got quite a lot to learn, haven't I?"

"Yes, Mother, you do."

7

After a thought-provoking walk, Karen drove over to her real estate office to check on a pending sale. Besides, her mother needed more time to cope with the impact of change.

It dawned on Karen that Mark should be apprised of the recent developments with her mother's memory. He wouldn't be pleased that his *Little Vicki* was scheming to track down her daddy's killers. Using her cell phone, she dialed Mark's office and was put into rotation.

Mark had helped her through more than one crisis, so why not help him? If her mother didn't have the good judgment to stand by her man, she would. The smart doctor had no clue how very attractive she found him, despite their age difference.

Answer the phone, Mark! I know you're there.

Karen pictured Mark's cobalt-blue eyes ablaze with intelligence, the strong maturity lines that riveted his distinguished face. In her book, the rock-solid man was ageless.

Come on, somebody answer the blasted phone!

Nervously, Karen tapped her pencil to the rhythm of the programmed music, sensitive to her physical need to be near Mark, to shamelessly declare her love regardless of what others thought. Not only was Mark a respected surgeon, he was a remarkable human being. Should he ask her, she would marry him tomorrow.

Regardless of changing circumstances, Mark had proven to be a true friend over the years. He'd acted unselfishly on so many occasions and had guided her through a horrendous period following her husband's death, a time in her life more terrifying than when her mother first came home from the hospital.

"Please stay on the line," said a robotic voice.

Answer the phone, Mark! You need to hear this!

If only the talented doctor hadn't treated her like a daughter over the years, she might have recognized the direction their relationship needed to take. By now, she should happily be Mrs. Mark James. Hanging up, she pushed the redial button.

Seconds later Mark's secretary answered. "It's about time," she fussed. "This is Karen Tempest. Put me through to Dr. James."

How could Mark have overlooked her obvious love? While waiting for him to make the first move, she had realized that he was courting her mother with serious intent, canceling any moves she was about to make on him.

She had herself to blame for bad timing. Sadly, it had taken half a lifetime for her to recognize it was how a guy treats a girl that matters and not their age difference.

But now that her mother's mental condition had fluctuated, dare she hope for a more intimate relationship with Mark? After all, the impossible trio was playing life on a different board game guided by a new set of rules and circumstances.

And who could say what might happen now that life had spun out of control again?

"Mark James, here."

"Thank heavens. Finally!"

"Hello, Karen. Something else happen with Vicki?"

"Can you talk?" Her nerves felt on the verge of snapping.

"I can spare a couple minutes." Mark considered how his escalating practice cut more and more into his social schedule.

Twenty-first century Americans were vain, demanding that he deliver physical perfection. Kids thirteen, fourteen, convinced parents that they needed their fat globules surgically removed. Breast enhancement and tummy tucks were the rage.

"I hate to bother you a second time today." Karen felt a little rush speaking to Mark. "But this is important."

"No, I'm glad you called. So how is Vicki doing?"

"We really need to talk." Karen leaned elbows on her office desk. "Privately."

"What is there to say that Vicki can't hear?" Mark had difficulty concentrating, worried over what Jeffrey might have told Victoria before he was shot. Specifically, had he recognized any of his assailants?

"I'm at my wit's end." Karen leaned on Mark. "Can we meet?"

"Now?" He was in the middle of work. "Can't you just tell me over the phone what's bothering you?"

"I'd rather not." Karen heaved a sigh. "I hope you're sitting down because you aren't going to like what I'm about to say."

"Why did you call? I'm working."

"Mother intends to reopen Dad's murder investigation." She paused to let her words sink in. "I tried to discourage her, but you know how noble Mother is. She wants *justice*."

"What?" *Reopen that catastrophic can of worms?* "That would be a huge mistake." His esophagus burned with acid reflux.

"I absolutely agree. And don't think I didn't reassure my mother that the police had done everything possible to locate Dad's killers before they filed his case away as unresolved."

"What do you think we should do?" Mark wrestled with panic.

"I don't think anything we say will make any difference." Karen moaned. "Mother's out there on a limb, sermonizing on the topic of the truth, counting on her faith to resolve twenty-five years of mistakes."

"I'm afraid you lost me, Karen." Mark used his white handkerchief to mop his leaky forehead. "Has Vicki recalled any specific details about your father's death?"

Life as he knew it could end.

"Not to my knowledge." Karen winced. "I keep asking myself how Mother can still believe that God is in control." She was struck by her morality. "She actually thinks our family tragedy has some lofty purpose."

"Wow! Guess we'll have to find a way to calm down all that zeal." He was grateful for little favors, though Victoria's dilemma was becoming everybody's problem. Especially his.

"Mother's a strong-willed woman," Karen's verbal pace escalated. "I know that one condition of the Gift Trust Fund involved signing away our family's future rights to reopen my father's murder investigation, but Mother didn't sign that document!"

A suffocating fear gripped Mark's chest. Having difficulty handling this bit of new information, he reached for a nitroglycerin tablet tucked in his desk drawer.

"Mark, are you all right?" Karen heard his heavy breathing.

"Yes, just a little stressed." He struggled with how he'd falsely believed Victoria would never get her memories back, how he'd foolishly committed to a relationship with this beautiful, complicated chameleon-of-a woman.

"Mark? What should we do?"

"Do?" His thoughts vacillated. "Can I get back to you on this?"

"Mark, if you think Mother will sell out her principles for any reason, especially money, you don't know her as well as you think you do."

"No, it's not that. I love Vicki because of her principles. She's changed me in so many ways, you have no idea." He feared a confession of his past sins would only muddy the waters. "I just need a little time to adjust to these new rules."

"All right by me. But we must talk this out, and soon." Karen emphasized soon. "We need an infallible plan of action. Things are happening extremely fast with Mother."

"Karen? Does Victoria know about *us*?"

"Mother knows that she is wearing *your* engagement ring. But what she thinks about it is still up for grabs."

"What do you mean?"

"Her mind is not on you, Dr. James. About now, Victoria Martin Tempest is probably discovering herself."

"How so?" Mark's plentiful gray eyebrows lifted.

"Last I heard Mother was going to view herself in the mirror."

"I'm not following you, dear." The panorama grew wider.

"I'm afraid Mother's condition is more complicated than we first believed. In recouping her old memories, apparently she's lost half a lifetime." Let him chew on that one.

"What?" Mark's mind circled and boomeranged with enlightenment. "Are you saying that Vicki doesn't remember growing old?" The idea was mind-boggling.

"That's exactly what I'm saying."

"That explains why Vicki didn't recognize us earlier this morning. Your mother always manages to astound me." Mark grinned. "Can you imagine her shock at seeing how she's changed over the years?" She was still a beguiling woman.

"It's so weird," Karen mused. "Mother woke up this morning thinking her accident happened yesterday. In her mind, there was no sense of passing time, nothing in between."

"That's incredible." Mark's imagination rolled into a tailspin.

"There's no way to predict how she's going to handle all this sudden change!" She'd given Mark plenty to think about. "Hey, my other line's ringing!" Karen fired, "Catch you later."

"Go get 'em, girl!" He managed to sound positive.

An hour later, after digesting Karen's comments regarding Victoria's zeal for reopening Jeffrey's case, Mark phoned Dick Branson. "We've got a problem."

8

Victoria couldn't stop staring at the engagement ring glittering on her left hand. It wasn't how she wanted to spend her time. For the life of her, she couldn't comprehend what possessed her to accept it. On the verge of tossing the ring down a drain, she was forced to admit that it was the most gorgeous, most expensive piece of jewelry she recalled owning.

Jeffrey would never have purchased so luxurious a gift although she knew that he had loved her as dearly as his own life. No man gave an extravagant gift without a motive.

So Mark? What's yours? Love, or something else?

"It takes two to tango," Victoria lamented.

Hadn't she agreed to marry Mark? At the time she accepted his ring, she must have loved him. Revelation grew more complicated by the minute.

But what in the world happened to Mark's first wife? Had he divorced Bev? Or was her name already attached to a tombstone?

Victoria wanted to speak to Beverly Yates James about Mark's character and ask if she thought he could be trusted. Jeffrey's former friend seemed awfully nervous about something.

Oh, it was a given that much had changed over a twenty-five year period. Assessing her present situation without all the facts was impossible. Ignorance altered the perspective of truth.

It had only recently occurred to Victoria to view herself in a mirror, which she hadn't done. For some silly reason the familiar phrase "mirror, mirror on the wall" came to mind.

Choosing a full-length mirror to deliver the initial shock, she eased inside Karen's bedroom and approached the closet door.

End the fear, Victoria!

Eyes shut tight, hands at her side, fingers crossed, feet together, she positioned herself in front of the image-maker. It was time to put the moment behind so she could face more serious issues. "Victoria Martin Tempest, open your eyes! This is your life!"

***

It was around five Thursday afternoon when Victoria began the initial preparations for supper. She'd always had a knack with pasta, recalling a wonderful New Orleans Cajun recipe. Karen inhaled the spicy aroma the second she opened the kitchen door.

"Is that Shrimp Delicious I smell cooking?" Her eyes widened.

"Yep." Victoria's hands were busy at the task.

"You haven't made that dish in years."

"Your mother may have forgotten a few scenic details along the way, sweetness, but she still can cook!" Victoria happily exclaimed. "Would you mind tossing the salad, dear?"

"Sure. Let me change clothes first." Karen jaunted down the hall to her bedroom. Discovering her clothes strewn about, she retraced her steps to the kitchen.

"Why are my clothes scattered about my room?"

"Oh, that. I'll explain later," Victoria replied with a sheepish grin. "Get changed and we'll sit down to a normal meal tonight." She considered how being fifty-six wasn't so bad.

Five minutes later, Karen peered into the hull of the refrigerator and spied the bag of fresh-cut veggies. "You still like onion?" She teasingly looked over at her mother.

"Of course!" Victoria winked. "I didn't lose my taste buds."

Karen laughed. "Or your sense of humor."

Victoria had borrowed Karen's curling iron to style her shoulder-length brown hair the way she'd worn it back in the eighties. Cloud nine didn't describe how she'd felt when she squeezed into a pair of her daughter's size ten jeans.

"I haven't seen you in jeans in ten years!" Karen exclaimed. "In fact, those are mine you're wearing. And that's my new workout tee! You've been trying on my clothes!"

"Bingo!" Victoria waved her soupspoon in the air, stealing a slender uncut carrot from Karen's bowl. "Hmm, delicious."

"What's going on?" Her mother's enthusiasm was contagious.

"Oh, Ka . . ." Victoria had a ton of unanswered questions.

"Tell me how I stayed so youthful after all these years. And I don't mean my hair color—I know that's fake."

"Mother," Karen giggled, "you had a facelift."

"Just as I suspected." Victoria plopped down on a barstool.

"It's no big deal, Mother." Karen noted her mother's distress. "Cosmetic surgery is common today. Besides, it's Mark's forté."

"Seems he's good at a lot of things." Victoria wrestled with catastrophic emotions. "So how's the real estate business?"

"Work is going great." Karen was always ready to talk about her career. "I don't suppose you recall my success in the past year?"

"No, dear, I'm afraid I don't." Victoria hopped off the barstool and tossed a package of pasta into a stainless steel container of boiling water. "So tell me." She peered at her daughter.

"Well . . . I was licensed to sell commercial properties a year ago. The courses were hard, but I passed. And now I'm making excellent money." Karen traipsed over to the sink with the fresh vegetables. "But it's not the money that really matters."

"What do you mean, the money doesn't matter?"

"We don't need money, we have plenty!" Karen used the cutting board to slice the carrots and radishes. "After Dad's death and your accident, you collected quite a bundle from the insurance companies. Besides, the Gift Trust Fund adequately provides for us."

"I still don't understand how an ordinary family like ours received a Gift Trust Fund." Victoria moved to the stove to stir her pasta soup.

You don't have to, just enjoy it, Mother."

"Mark James is—was—your father's best friend. I can't imagine him recommending that you accept a payoff to get your father's murderer off your back!"

"That's not how it happened." Karen stopped chopping vegetables and peered at Victoria. "Dad's death was an accident. He wasn't supposed to be there when the perpetrators broke into his office."

"Now that alone sounds pretty suspicious!" Victoria reacted, eyebrows raised as she peeked into the pot of boiling pasta. "Who broke into Jeffrey's office? Give me names!"

Hesitating, Karen said, "I can't." Mark had made it crystal clear that any further investigation into her father's death was potentially dangerous. Above all, she wanted to keep her family safe—what was left of it.

"Karen, talk to me," Victoria insisted. "Tell me about the Gift Trust Fund, how you used it. Help me to understand why Jeffrey's best friend was so involved in our decisions."

"Mother! Mark cares about us. Isn't it obvious that we had to pay our bills? Talk to him. He'll do a better job of explaining than I can," Karen declared. "Let's eat, I'm starved."

TUESDAY, APRIL 15

9

Tuesday morning, after Karen had left for work, Victoria located Beverly Yates James' name in the phonebook. While dialing Bev's number, she concluded that peeling away the layers of deception to unveil the truth would involve some rather skillful maneuvering.

"Hello," a lilting voice pealed forth.

"Bev, this is Victoria Tempest. Please don't hang up!" She wasn't sure why she had added that last tidbit. "I hope I haven't called at a bad time." Her heart was pumping adrenalin.

"Victoria Tempest!" Beverly's tone was unduly haughty. "We haven't spoken in some time. Heard you finally snagged my ex. I do hope he treats you better than he did me."

Bev's derogatory attitude left Victoria momentarily speechless.

"I know this sounds strange, but do you suppose we could meet somewhere?" Face to face was always better when pursuing truth.

"You mean, like in the same room?" Bev's words were icy.

Victoria sucked in oxygen. "I've gotten my memory back!"

"What? Oh. My. God."

"It is God, Bev," Victoria professed. "He's so good. And He's restored my memories. Well, most of them," she admitted. "I really do need your input." She prayed that Bev would help unravel some of the mystery.

"I bet you do!" Bev exclaimed, coming off her high horse. "Hopefully you forgot all the ugly moments," her voice had less edge. "So why did you decide to ask for my help?"

"You're my oldest and dearest friend," Victoria pointed out. "And I have a huge problem." She gathered steam. "Although I recall my life before my accident, well, ur, everything since is a big blank. Simply said, I've misplaced twenty-five years of my life!"

"Oh, my! I guess you do want to talk to me—with your engagement to Mark and all." Bev was pumped up to help.

"Yeah, that sums it up. How soon can we meet?"

"You say, and I'll make the time."

"Today, if you can swing it." *There's no time like the present.*

"Honey, for a chance to fill you in on my ex, I'll give you all the time you want!" Bev seemed anxious to air her dirty laundry. "I'd hate for you to make the same mistake I did."

"Thank you, Bev." *Score one for me.*

"My place? Oh, say, high noon?"

"Sounds great!" Victoria was elated.

"We can enjoy a bite of lunch while having a nice, long informative chat."

"What's the address? Never mind. Is the one in the phone directory correct?"

"Yep. I'll be on pins and needles." Beverly hung up the phone.

***

Dick Branson's office was impressive. Over two and a half decades ago, the ol' barracuda had converted it into a plush bachelor pad with everything in it but Marilyn Monroe. *Some desires were unattainable.* Mark James pushed open the front door.

"Oh hi, Mark." Dick's ravishing young secretary glanced up from her computer. "What can we do for you today?" Jeannie jerked a paper from the printer and laid it in a tray.

"Tell Dick I need to see him." Mark parked his hands in his pants pockets, the pearly-beige carpet swallowing the soles of his shoes like quicksand.

Dick's office cried one word: prosperity. And the smart businessman had scads of it. In fact, he probably owned one of the finest collections of antique furniture in the world. No doubt, his trophy portraits were meant to remind visitors of his hunting success, in the field and off.

"Mr. Branson will see you now," Jeannie flashed a smile, her oversized Audrey Hepburn eyes widening. Standing, she wiggled to straighten and lengthen her tight-fitted leather skirt.

"Thanks." Mark winked at Jeannie, cute as a pinup. He could easily get tangled in her riotous mane of long curly-red hair and never climb out.

Almost as hot as Marilyn. Mark curbed his roaming eyes and ventured into Dick's luxurious office. Yes sir, the old geezer could sure pick the lookers.

"Mark!" The tycoon's belly spilled over his belt like Jello.

Too much good beef on the table every day, Mark supposed.

"Come in." Dick's pudgy hand pointed to a cushy chair. "Whut's up, my man?" He didn't have time for chatter.

Mark slammed the office door behind him.

"Uh oh. That testy attitude spells trouble." Dick's toady-brown eyes focused on Mark. "So what takes you away from your important work to see me? Don't be bashful, now."

"Can Jeannie hear us?" Mark asked, swearing that the glint in Dick's eye had been surgically implanted. He fully expected Dick to overreact at the news he was bringing.

"This room is as secure as Fort Knox," Dick bellowed, collapsing in his padded swivel rocker. "I swear, boy! You look like you gotta a load on your shoulders you need to dump!"

Mark glared at his confidant. Dick had a way with words. He'd give him credit for that.

"Go ahead, unload!" Dick spewed, lit up a Havana cigar, and offered one to Mark.

"No, thanks." Mark backed into a chair and collapsed. It had already been a trying morning. Silence and smoke filled the room for the next sixty seconds. "Well . . ."

"A deep subject. I can see this isn't going to be a casual chat." Dick wheezed heavily, a ring of pungent smoke circling his bald eagle crown. "Well, I'm a busy man, so get on with it!"

There was no easy way to deliver the news. Mark uneasily shifted in his chair. He'd just say it: "Victoria has her memories back, Dick. Just thought you should know."

Rising like a demon in the midst of smoke, Dick coughed and

sputtered like a train in trouble. "Remembers?" His face was pinched, flushed with anger. "You'd better explain."

Mark suppressed a grin, giving Dick a few minutes to digest the unsavory news.

"Does Victoria *know*?" Dick's serpentine eyes narrowed. "You know . . ." he nodded.

"About Jeffrey's death?" Mark liked seeing the old devil squirm. "Yeah, she knows her husband was murdered."

"No, stupid!" Dick wanted to climb over his desk and choke the information out of Mark, his stout knuckles having trouble supporting his pompous frame. "Does Victoria know *who* killed Jeffrey?" Mark's answer determined how he would handle the situation.

"Now, that's the jackpot question!" The muscles in Mark's shoulders knotted as he stretched out his arms and rocked his head from side to side, neck bones cracking like ice.

"Well, you'd best ask her!" Dick raced around his desk and got up in Mark's face. "What do you think this is? Some party Victoria has invited you to? It could be your funeral."

Mark defensively raised his hands. "Don't blow this out of proportion, you hear? Nothing devastating has happened that changes anything between us."

"So now I'm calm." Dick puttered behind his desk and sat down.

"I don't know if Vicki trusts me anymore," Mark dropped the news bomb and smoothed the lapels of his sports jacket with his hands. Life should be so simple. "Just thought you'd want to know." The tragedy had layers like an onion.

"Humph." Dick jiggled his tight belt with his right thumb, loosening his necktie with his left hand. The room was too warm. He walked over and turned down the AC.

"So what's your take on this?" Dick turned and faced Mark.

"If I'm right, Vicki's feelings toward me have probably changed." Mark didn't move a muscle, comfortable where he sat.

"We both knew the day might come when she'd get back her memories. It just took longer than we expected."

"Oh, man," Dick swore. "I knew I was under a bad sign today. My zodiac chart was all off." Sweat beaded his bulky, red-wrinkled neck as he collapsed in his chair. "I need to call my psychic in Dallas." He thumbed through an old-fashioned Rolodex.

Mark didn't rely on zodiac signs any more than he trusted faith. Carefully choosing his words, he wanted to make sure that Dick understood his sphere of influence regarding Victoria.

"Oh." Mark pointed a finger at Dick. "Did I tell you Vicki forgot she was engaged to me?" He toyed with his confidant. "Apparently all I am to her now is a very good *friend*."

"How can that be?" Dick scratched his chin, chewing on the nub of his charred cigar as he rocked back and forth to comfort his psyche. "Your little Vicki is a real puzzle."

"Fact is, Dick. It appears she has forgotten everything since her automobile accident."

"But she remembers before?" Dick came to his feet, marble-hard eyes narrowing. "Now that might prove to be a problem."

"Not if we keep our mouths shut." Mark cleared his throat, a tinge of pain crouching in his chest. The precarious situation was putting added stress on his health.

"Mark! This is serious! It took years to get Victoria thinking our way." The woman was far too independent for her own good.

"What we did is called *manipulation*, Dick." Mark was guilty. "And now she's in the driver's seat again because she's thinking differently. Could I have a drink of water?"

Dick paged Jeannie to bring a pitcher of ice water.

"Thank you," Mark said when Jeannie handed him a glass.

Dick guzzled his water and plopped the empty glass on the desk. "So what's your take on this, Mark?" He locked his bulky fingers across his watermelon belly and rocked back in his chair. "If you don't want me to take action, you better talk."

"This is my concern over Vicki's restored memories: Will she recall Jeffrey saying anything over the phone that would incriminate us?"

"Hell's bells!" Dick's vision was clouded with scenarios.

"Maybe Vicki won't ever remember," Mark pointed out.

"And maybe she will." Dick's mind whirred.

Mark studied her powerful contender. "And if she does?"

"Your *Little Vicki's* a loose cannon, Mark." Dick placed his feet solidly on the floor, grasped the desk with both hands and came to his feet. "She made an awfully cute cheerleader back in high school, but she's cheering for the wrong team now."

Unable to refute Dick's reasoning Mark stood to leave.

"One more thing. Find out how much your betrothed recalls." Dick pointed a pudgy finger. "And make it your priority to learn what Victoria's got up her pretty sleeves. If you succeed, I just might have another mil to feed into your already fat bank account."

"This isn't about money, Dick!" Mark exclaimed. "It's not that simple." He tugged at his necktie. "Victoria has principles and she can't be bought!"

"Principles, my eye!" Dick roared with laughter.

Mark was not in the least amused.

"Ain't nobody got those kind of principles!" Dick tottered around his desk to face Mark. "Everybody's got a price, friend! The proof's in the pudding, haven't you heard?"

Although Dick called him a *friend*, Mark knew his disreputable business associate had his limits to loyalty. Wealth purchased a slew of faithful followers, the police not excluded. With political friends in high places, Dick would not be easily crossed.

"Now don't go gettin' all down in the mouth." Dick patted Mark on the back, changing tactics. "I've got confidence you can handle our little problem." He was gooey nice. "You just make sure that Vicki's principles don't get out of hand and we'll all be just fine."

"And if she decides to reopen Jeffrey's investigation?"

She'd better not!" Dick's voice was charged with a hiss.

"Yeah." Mark swore. "I can let myself out."

"I don't want any more unexplained accidents, you hear?"

Mark peered at Dick a second, having read his subtle threat.

"Well, don't be long coming back," Dick said as Mark exited the room. "And remember whose side you are on."

10

Victoria knocked on Beverly James' front door and it opened. The wiry Beverly Yates James was still a beautiful woman, though the melodrama of fifty-five years of hard living showed in her tired face, unlike her gray roots disguised by a full head of short highlighted blond hair.

"Well, just don't stand there. Come inside." Bev grabbed Victoria by the arm, her big baby blues suspiciously scanning the front yard. "You weren't followed, were you?"

"Goodness no!" Victoria replied. "Why would you think that?"

"Shush!" Bev put a finger to her lips, quickly closing the door and locking it. "I recently added an extra bolt."

"You don't have to whisper," Victoria remarked. "I came alone because I want to talk to you about Mark." *Why beat around the bush?* "Nobody followed me, why would they?"

"We'll discuss Mark later." Bev led Victoria deeper into the den. "Take a load off your feet." She pointed to a floral sofa, a smile blossoming on her salon-tan face.

Victoria glanced around and saw nothing remotely familiar.

"Take a gander at you!" Bev circled Victoria like she was a mannequin on display. "I gotta admit that facelift Mark gave you took off fifteen years," she jealously remarked.

"Huh? Oh that!" Victoria flushed with embarrassment, feeling at a loss to discuss a surgery she didn't recall.

"Wish I had the do-re-me to remake my mug," Bev croaked. "Do you know what a facelift costs today?" She waltzed over to the window and drew the curtains.

Victoria offered no solution.

"You hungry?" Bev asked. "I made us a grilled chicken salad."

"Sounds enticing." Victoria produced an honest smile, genuinely liking Bev. They went way back to college days.

"What's wrong?" Beverly noted apprehension in Victoria's pensive gaze. "Did Mark do something to hurt you?"

"What, girlfriend? Cat got your tongue?"

Victoria bit into her lower lip. "I was just going to say, uh, if I've ever done anything to hurt you in the past, I'm truly sorry."

Appearing as if a straw could knock her over, tears swelled in Bev's eyes. Victoria was unprepared for how profoundly her apology would impact her friend.

"Why, Vicki!" Bev caught her breath. "I think that's the sweetest thing anybody's said to me in years." She mopped her bleary eyes with a tissue and gave Victoria a tight hug.

"Then I'm forgiven?" Victoria felt the weight of remorse lift.

"Clean slate." Bev widely smiled, even white teeth showing. "So how can I help?" She sauntered into the kitchen. "Want a cup of fresh-brewed Starbucks?"

"Love some." Victoria ventured into the kitchen and sat down at the oversized breakfast bar. "Actually, I wanted to talk to you about Mark. I need to know how he fits into my life."

"Wow! Talk about being direct. No games, this time."

Games? Victoria wondered who she had been a week ago.

"No, I'm not. I'm looking for missing puzzle parts to complete my picture of what happened the evening Jeffrey died."

Victoria was prepared to linger as long as necessary.

"Some things are best left unsaid," Bev casually remarked as she slid a chilled bowl of chicken avocado salad across the breakfast bar. "You still use cream?" she asked.

"Sure." Victoria measured out two tablespoons of the non-fat dairy creamer and added it to her coffee mug, recalling how Karen had basically embraced the same philosophy. *What was everyone afraid to talk about? Didn't they want to know the truth?*

Or did they know and hoped she wouldn't find out?

"So Victoria . . ." Beverly glared with interest. "What exactly do you remember?" She wiped the counter clean and sat down.

"Nothing after my accident." Victoria forked her salad. "This is delicious!"

"Nothing?" Bev ignored the compliment, going straight to being stunned. "You don't recall coming out of your coma or getting that fantastic trust fund worth millions?"

What? "No, I don't." Victoria blinked. "How did you find out about the trust?" The money was a sore subject with her.

"I read the newspapers, girlfriend." Bev chomped on a raw carrot stick. "But you do recall Karen getting married and having an abortion?" Her pencil-thin eyebrows arched.

"What?" A knife sliced through Victoria's skittering heart.

"Oops!" Bev realized her mistake when she saw alarm resting in Victoria's blushing-red expression.

"My Karen had an abortion! I don't believe it!" Victoria shoved back her plate, no longer hungry, trembling at the idea of something so heinous happening in her family.

"Like I said, some things are best left unsaid." Bev played with her paper napkin. "Maybe I ought to let you ask the questions and I'll answer the best I can without volunteering anything extra." She squirmed in her seat.

Cover-up was written all over the conversation. Victoria hated the idea of being spoon-fed information. Still too much knowledge all at once could prove emotionally overwhelming. "Whatever," she agreed to Bev's terms.

"So ask." The hostess began eating again.

"First of all, when did I get engaged to Mark?"

"Just before Christmas." Bev crunched a cucumber between her teeth. "It was the feature story on Fernwood's society page. Made me mad as hell!" She cursed like a sailor.

"Bev!" Victoria despised profanity, although liberally used by most Fernwood residents as if words didn't matter anymore.

Wasn't there anything society considered sacred?

"Sorry," Bev apologized. "You'd been dating Mark a year. Folks kind of expected you'd eventually get married, though knowing didn't make it any easier on me."

"Was I—?" Victoria choked on her question.

"Sleeping with Mark? Oh, yes," Bev confirmed Victoria's suspicion. "It's common knowledge you two lovebirds kept an apartment in Jackson where you could nest. "From your odd expression, this must be a discovery that would stun even a Sherlock Holmes."

Victoria shuddered at the news. Attempting to decipher the motives of others was indeed a challenge, but not nearly as mind-boggling as getting to know herself.

What happened that caused me to betray my Christian principles?

***

By the time Victoria had returned home, a headache clawed at her temples from what she had and hadn't learned from Mark's spirited ex. She was fast learning that in today's vernacular, the term *friend* was tentative. *Or had she somehow misread Bev?*

Victoria thought not. Bev's guarded words had suggested that she was frightened of something, or someone. While her college sorority sister had freely elaborated on Mark's career climb as a plastic surgeon and his unorthodox friendship with Dick Branson, she had not delivered the unedited truth, or revealed the underlying motives of the personalities involved.

And why was that? Victoria grimaced as she trudged into the bathroom to retrieve a box of antacid tablets from her medicine cabinet. Bev's edited information was proving difficult to digest alongside her spicy chicken salad. The conversation had not put her mind at ease. On the contrary, she felt put on notice. Warned!

Victoria pondered how to use the siphoned tidbits fed her, realizing a correct diagnosis of her situation might exceed her expertise. Maybe it was time to hire a real professional. She gulped down a fizzing glass of Alka-Seltzer.

The mirror did her no favors. Victoria peered at her pathetic image, dark shadows crouching beneath her bewildered eyes.

"My life has been derailed," she lamented. "Why did God put me in this predicament? A wild woman wallowing around in all this detective mess?"

Why didn't Jesus send me to Heaven the night of my accident?

Fatigued to the core, Victoria limped across the bedroom like a wounded animal, hoping to put her troubling thoughts to bed.

Who could she trust? Dr. Mark James, the man who was in cahoots with Dick Branson? Her daughter, Karen, Mark's ally? Or her former best friend—the illusive Beverly James?

Please, God, tell me who?

Victoria recalled her mother once saying that God didn't respond to demands. He had a reason for allowing trouble to interrupt the lives of human beings. Prayer was answered in God's own time and at the right moment. She should count on that.

How could she do nothing? Surely God expected more from her than regrets. And a courageous detective would certainly confront Mark regarding the details of her family's Gift Trust Fund, ask him what tied him to Dick Branson.

Victoria wondered if the reason she hadn't approached Mark about Jeffrey's death had something to do with fear, a problem that had stayed with her over the years.

However, she wasn't the only one afraid. Just look at Bev. She'd changed from a gutsy lady who had once leaped out of airplanes to a weaseling wimp. The girl she knew from college would never back down from a fight if she truly believed in the cause.

So did Bev really believe her condo was bugged?

"Get real, Victoria!" Goose pimples raised the hair on her arms. Fear would certainly explain Bev's cloak-and-danger behavior, Victoria decided. And if someone had been watching Bev's place . . . she leaped to a shadowy conclusion.

She should think twice before publicly advertising her judicial agenda. Alerting those responsible for the break-in at Jeffrey's office might provoke a counterattack. Why give anyone the chance to obscure the facts?

Victoria was beginning to realize the world had become far more complicated than a quarter-century before. These were times in which devious people purposely masked their true feelings while moving around in relationships with selfish motives.

Trust was nearly extinct.

Perhaps Bev had guarded her revelations in order to escape

harm's way. Did she believe telling the truth would bring the bad wolves to her door? *Or worse, get her killed.*

Victoria shivered at her unavoidable involvement. Jeffrey had been her world and she could never put his memory to rest until his killers were found and convicted. Practicing the law had been his life's work, and he had expected the U.S. justice system to work.

Didn't she owe loyalty to her family? Victoria thought she deserved to know the truth. And with God's divine guidance, she would apply justice.

But at all times, she should act cautiously and reevaluate her progress. Sherlock Holmes would never reveal his plan until he had assessed whom he could trust. And that was?

"Where is my Bible?" Victoria climbed out of bed, realizing she'd let an entire day slip by without reading God's Word. Foremost, she needed the Heavenly Father's gracious insight.

"Jesus is a lamp unto my feet, a light onto my pathway," came to mind as Victoria searched the condo for her missing Bible. Stumbling upon a copy of *The United Baptist News Bulletin*, she curiously reviewed the list of weekly church activities:

Tuesday 9 a.m.: Women's Meditation Techniques
Tuesday Noon: Men's Self-awareness Luncheon
Tuesday 7 p.m.: Ladies Self-awareness Seminar
Wednesday 4 p.m.: Children's Combined Choir
Wednesday 6 p.m.: United Power Prayer Hour
Wednesday, 7 p.m: Choir practice
Sunday 10 a.m.: Church Services

Something felt terribly wrong with this schedule. Self-centered in concept, had Christianity boiled down to utilizing techniques of self-awareness? What in the world was her church thinking? Had she awakened on another planet?

Victoria knelt beside her bed to pray. "Dear Lord, I'm truly confused. Spiritually, I know I've been reborn . . ." The cleansing tears began to flow. "Yet I'm terrified about what's happened to me over the years. How can I survive this mental confusion? Lord, I need for You to speak to me. I need my Bible. Show me what to do next about Jeffrey's murder. As always, protect me from my enemies."

Victoria stood and thought about when she had last seen her Bible. Yes! It was yesterday, in her car! No, that wasn't right!

It had been in her Mazda twenty-five years before, the night she struck out in the storm to meet Jeffrey for their anniversary celebration. Which meant . . . it probably hadn't survived the crash.

Stumbling into the den, Victoria perused Karen's collection of religious books and removed from the shelf a little pocket book entitled *SELECTED PASSAGES FROM THE BOOK OF PSALMS*.

Tears trickled down her cheeks as she slumped into the soft folds of the beige sofa and randomly opened the pages. Beautiful, comforting words written by David the Psalmist over four hundred years before Jesus was born leaped from its historic pages:

To the faithful you show yourself faithful,
to the blameless you show yourself blameless,
to the pure you show yourself pure,
but to the crooked you show yourself shrewd.

You save the humble
but bring low those whose eyes are haughty.
You, O Lord, keep my lamp burning;
my God turns my darkness into light.

With your help I can advance against a troop;
with my God I can scale a wall.

This was God's timely message for her, written a thousand years before Christ was born, King David's Psalm 18:25-29 was a voice of encouragement in a dark hour.

With her human spirit soaring to the very throne of God,

Victoria knelt beside her bed and began to worship. Before long she was singing "Amazing Grace" and weeping grateful tears.

God is still with me and very much in control.

Victoria was unsure of how much time passed before she heard the ringing phone. Encouraged by God's Holy Spirit and Word, she now felt emotionally equipped to effectively stand tall in a world with a history of trampling God's truth.

"It's time to act!" Victoria grabbed the phone. "Hello."

"Vicki? This is Mark."

"Mark?" He was the last person she expected to call.

"Your voice sounds so cold. It's me, honey."

Honey? Victoria had no idea how to respond since she had no attachment to Mark other than being his friend. And even that was questionable. "What do you want me to say?"

"Say you'll have dinner with me tomorrow night."

Thinking of saying no, Victoria decided that spending time with Mark would afford her an opportunity to learn more about herself. Particularly, why she had fallen in love with her husband's best friend and what it was about him that bred distrust.

"What time shall I meet you?" she asked.

"I'll pick you up." He sounded elated. "I don't want you to drive yet. Those headaches you've been experiencing—well, I'm not sure what they might mean."

Victoria hadn't yet considered what triggered her erratic headaches. Did she have a brain tumor, or a lesion that had developed as a result of the accident? Evidently, some change had occurred to induce her memories after so long a time. *What*?

"Vicki?" Mark had begun to think she had hung up on him.

"Yes?" She gathered courage. "Do you suspect a brain tumor?"

"Well, I certainly hope not!" Mark reacted as if the idea were foreign. "However, it is important to get you checked into the hospital to run a battery of tests."

Just to be on the safe side. "Whatever you think."

"Meanwhile, the good doctor recommends healthy food and

tender-loving care," his erotic voice softened to a whisper. "And I can provide both, Vicki."

I bet you could! She thought about their little love escapades in Jackson. Unsure of what her former lover expected from her, the conclusion to their evening would not turn out as he anticipated.

"What time shall I be ready?"

"Seven. And wear that sexy black dress I gave you for the New Year's Eve party," he said. "Sure," she replied, having no idea which dress Mark meant.

"Until then, sweetheart."

WEDNESDAY, APRIL 16

11

Victoria lounged around the condo in her pajamas Wednesday morning, skipping lunch to fast and pray. Late afternoon, she chose to pamper herself in a steamy tub of water before opening Pandora's closet.

Thumbing through a huge wall of *Shelly Henson* originals, Victoria was appalled at her opulence. A pair of shoes for every outfit, plus matching purses and hats?

My goodness, the old Victoria was quite extravagant and obviously vain. So what had changed her over the years? Bent her? Was it the fact she had no memory of her religious upbringing? No realization of the person she was in Christ Jesus?

Slipping into the black dress Mark wanted her to wear, Victoria viewed herself in Karen's full-length mirror and decided it was indecently short and cut way too low in the bodice. The obscene cutouts at the back didn't help.

No, this was definitely not something she would wear. Victoria tossed Mark's scanty choice on the floor. So what would she wear? Didn't she want to look good for a date that she couldn't afford to miss?

God willing, she intended to open Mark up like a can and make him spill all the beans. *Victoria, the bombshell*! He wouldn't have a clue what had hit him.

Smiling, she became more realistic and selected a tea-length, antique-white lace dress featuring puffy chiffon sleeves that teased the shoulders. A row of tiny seed pearls bordered the round neckline of the fitted bodice, and the A-line cut nicely accentuated her waistline.

Yes! This is so much better. Victoria stood barefoot before Karen's mirrored closet door, deciding that she looked almost angelic.

I can live with that. She only hoped Mark could.

Moments later, it dawned on Victoria where to begin her investigation into Jeffrey's murder. She certainly had no intention of involving the local police who had done a shoddy job in the first place. She would check out the Fernwood Public Library and read about her accident. Maybe there were eyewitnesses.

Nothing like being educated.

"Wow! You look fantastic!" Karen's mouth fell open when she arrived home around 6:30 p. m.. "Hot date, huh?" The weary real estate agent tossed her leather briefcase on the desk.

"Hi, dear," Victoria said, blushing at Karen's compliment. "Hope you don't mind that I didn't make supper for us?" She spun around, modeling her dress. "So what do you think?"

"You're going out with Mark?" Karen's gaze widened with discovery. "I didn't think you remembered Mark."

"If you mean do I remember us as a couple, the answer is no." Victoria drew in a slow breath. "We're going out as friends."

"Does Mark know that?" Karen raised an eyebrow. "Goodness, Mother! I never thought of you as a tease."

"A tease?" Victoria mulled over Karen's opinion. "How so?"

"Look and don't touch, something like that," Karen replied.

"You think I'm baiting Mark?"

"I know you are," Karen declared with certainty. "I just don't know why. Want to tell me, Mother?" She plopped down on a barstool. "Hey! I've got nothing better to do than listen."

"The situation is much too complicated to explain on the spur of the moment." Victoria put Karen off. "Maybe I'll share what I've got up my sleeve with you one day soon."

"And those are very sexy sleeves!" Karen teased, her arched eyebrows seesawing. "It appears that Victoria Martin Tempest has an agenda. What is it, I wonder?"

"Oh, you!" Victoria patted her hot cheeks. "I forgot how much fun you could be." She watched Karen walk over to the refrigerator, open the door, and explore its sparse contents.

"Know what?" Karen bent over the shrink-wrapped salad mix in the crisper drawer. "I'm sick to death of eating healthy. I want something sinful tonight like fattening pizza!"

"You always did like pizza." Victoria recalled that stormy evening she had left Karen home with Paul to venture into town for a quiet anniversary dinner with Jeffrey.

"Oh!" Karen erected herself, stiffening. "I didn't mean to bring all that up, Mother." Her strained face reflected regret. "Sorry." She wanted to forget that awful night.

"You love pizza. It's as simple as that." Victoria smiled, though tears peppered her luminous brown eyes. "What kind of pizza did Paul decide to order that night?"

"Pepperoni on a thick crust. Extra cheese with sausage, onion and black olives," Karen spouted. "Gee, Mom! That's was twenty-five years ago!" She held a Diet Coke in her hand.

"But you still remember, don't you?" Memories were gold nuggets in the stream of life.

"Only because I order the same pizza every time." Karen popped the lid on the soda pop and took a swig.

"I wonder where Mark is taking me tonight?" Victoria peered through an oval window arching the kitchen sink. Exotic shades of strawberry and amber were splayed across the graying skies. Darkness slowly unveiled one lone glittering star.

Venus, the goddess of love . . . Victoria thought of Jeffrey.

"We've got several swanky restaurants in town," Karen said with a yawn, leaning sharp elbows on the breakfast bar for support. "Thanks to Dick Branson for putting Fernwood on the map."

"Isn't Branson that new company located on the old tannery site?" Victoria recalled young Paul mentioning that his friend's father worked for the packing company.

"Yes. Only it isn't new anymore." Karen clipped a pizza coupon from an advertisement flier. "When Hearty Meats opened, hundreds of employees moved into town, boosting our local economy and turning Fernwood into a thriving metropolis."

"Sounds like Superman arrived," Victoria huffed.

"I don't suppose you recall Mark's friendship with Dick."

Karen gazed at her mother. "They became close around the time Dick bought the company and attached his name."

"And why is that?" Victoria carried her hot tea into the den.

"Why is what?" Karen collapsed on the carpet by her mother.

"Why do you suppose a doctor like Mark and a meatpacker like Dick hit it off so well? Doesn't seem they'd have all that much in common." Victoria glanced out the sliders. Another day was passing without answers.

"Guess I've never thought of their friendship quite like that," Karen admitted. "But you're right. If you knew Dick, you'd soon realize he's not anything like Mark."

"Sorry." Victoria sighed. "Wish I could comment on their similarities and differences, but I can't since not one blooming fact about Dick Branson is logged in my memory bank."

"That is so weird, Mother." Karen shook her head. "I don't see how it's possible to recall events before your accident and not afterwards. Do you think it's psychological?"

"Goodness, I hadn't thought of that!" Victoria reacted. "You think I don't want to remember, that the trendy lifestyle of the post-Victoria so contradicts the values of the pre-Victoria that the newest version has somehow suppressed selective memories?"

"That's quite a mouthful, Mother. But I must admit that you've summarized your predicament fairly well for someone not in the profession. I know one thing for certain: given time, you're smart enough to figure it all out for yourself."

"I certainly hope so." Victoria planned on using what was left of her reasoning power to solve Jeffrey's murder rather than self-analysis. She wondered if she should share her recent conversation with Beverly James with Karen.

"What? I see that brain working." Karen's eyelashes fluttered with curiosity. "What's bothering you, Mother?"

"Nothing of importance," Victoria replied.

Can I trust Karen when it comes to Mark?

"But something." Karen refused to let up. "Tell me, Mother!"

"Do you know about Mark's gambling habit?" Victoria bit her quick tongue. Like Bev said, some things were best left unsaid.

"What?" Karen appeared shocked. "No, Mother! Where in the world did you ever get that ridiculous idea? Mark James, your friend, has always been very responsible with money."

"Are you sure, dear? You said he was handling our gift estate. Do you know exactly how much money we have left?" Victoria purposely planted doubt in Karen's mind.

Unfortunately, her lovely daughter seemed dangerously enamored with a man nearly twice her age. Karen should reexamine Mark's motives, a mature single male who'd likely been a popular womanizer over the years. Certainly, Bev could provide a list of fornicators. Or had Dr. James already worked his magic on Karen?

"Me thinks you ponder too deeply," Karen noted her mother's paranoia. "Why don't you just spell out what's on your mind? Consider it a therapeutic beginning."

Victoria felt cornered, suspecting that she was about to be bombarded with questions she didn't want to answer. Luckily, the doorbell saved her. "Hold that thought." She raced to the door.

"Mother!" Karen barked. "We haven't finished talking."

"Come in, Mark." Victoria produced a radiant smile.

Karen didn't fail to notice how Mark's mouth dropped open as his gaze swallowed her mother's pristine image. She had the distinct feeling that no matter what delicacies he lavished on his date, it was certain to get him nowhere.

"Hi, Mark." Karen coyly stepped in his pathway, toying with the strands of her frosted hair. "Your lust is showing," she leaned over and whispered in his ear.

"Hi, chickadee!" Mark brushed past Karen. Feeling discarded, she grabbed his arm. "You haven't called me that in years!"

"Huh?" Mark sidestepped Karen and grasped Victoria's hands. "Cold hands, warm heart." He planted a wet kiss on her cheek. "You look amazing."

Did her mother just blush? Karen was hot with jealousy.

"Have I told you lately how much I love you, Vicki?"

Karen rolled her eyes, disgusted. Mark only had eyes for his Little Vicki. Her heart had actually leaped at his adoring words.

"Will I need a jacket?" Victoria ignored Mark's amorous remark. Wearing the slightest hint of lime, his stimulating cologne melted into her senses and put a lump in her throat.

"Wear a shawl, darlin', you might need it." Mark had trouble keeping his hands to himself. "I'm letting down the top to my BMW tonight." He whistled *I'm in the Mood for Love.* "Who knows? We might just find us a lover's lane somewhere."

At hearing his proclamation, Victoria exited the den in record time.

"Well, that was certainly debonair," Karen remarked

"What?" Mark spun around to face Karen. "You don't think your mother's ready for Lover's Lane?" He crooked his head to one side.

"I know she's not. And if you try anything, you'll be sorry."

Victoria hurried down the hall to her bedroom and closed the door. Was the tiger's bite as ferocious as his roar? If so, she was in trouble. She jerked a white cashmere sweater from the clothes rack and headed to the den.

"So, kiddo, did anything unusual happen today?" Mark asked Karen.

No doubt, he's referring to my mother.

"What? You peeved at me?"

"Have you ever gambled, Mark?"

"What?" he sputtered. "Where did that come from?"

"Mother said—"

"Mother said what?" Victoria made her presence known.

"Uh—" Mark was caught off guard. "Karen was just saying how the two of you were having such a great time getting reacquainted."

"Yes, we are." Victoria fondly captured Karen's eye. "My daughter is a remarkable woman." Didn't they share family genes?

"That she is!" Mark walked over to Victoria and squared her shoulders with his hands. "And so are you, Vicki. Pretty as a bride!"

Stunned at his opinion, it was the last image Victoria had intended to portray. *Angelic . . . maybe. A bride, never!* Keeping Mark at bay all evening would indeed prove challenging.

"Let's go! We've got a seven forty-five seating." Mark grasped Victoria's elbow and nudged her out the front door. "Oh, and Karen," he peeked around the door and winked, "I'm feelin' lucky tonight so don't wait up for us!" He scooted down the steps.

Don't wait up for us! Karen cursed and kicked the door shut. *He did that to purposely antagonize me.* Her mother hadn't won yet!

12

Victoria was comfortably seated in Mark's immaculately clean BMW before asking, "Where are we dining tonight?" His mint cologne pleasantly teased her nostrils.

"The Branson-Fernwood Country Club." Mark's powerful engine exploded beneath his skilled hands, shooting away from the curb like a cannon fired into the ongoing traffic.

"Woe, boy!" The forward thrust socked Victoria in the gut. "Aren't you taking it a little fast?" She tossed him a scourging glance, wondering if the old Victoria had been more daring.

"I'm real fast," Mark winked. "Hold on, Vicki! I'm giving you the ride of the century!"

Victoria suspected Mark wasn't just talking about the drive. He had busy hands, used to having their way. And she hadn't always declined his sexual overtures.

She soon relaxed and began to enjoy the scenery, realizing the ride was going to be bumpy. As was her date. A glorious milky-melon moon had emerged on the horizon, promising a spectacular spring evening. As the skies lightened, God's myriad of starry candles began to blink out. Heaven appeared in perfect order.

It was people who didn't line up with His Word.

With temperatures dipping into the low sixties, Victoria gratefully snuggled inside her warm sweater. Relishing the sights and odors of the silent night, she said nothing for miles, until finally, her thoughts evolved into words.

"Mark," she made eye contact. "You said we were dining at the Branson-Fernwood Country Club. Does Dick own everything in town?"

"Why does it matter?" Mark reacted by swerving the car sharply, slamming his foot on the brakes before accelerating again. "Do you recall Dick?" His gaze was harsh.

"Does my question annoy you?" She raised her voice to compensate for the haughty wind and noisy engine. "Karen said Dick was a powerful contender in Fernwood. I can't help but wonder how the two of you became friends."

Mark eased his foot off the accelerator before whipping off the interstate and letting the classic convertible trickle to a stop.

"So why did we stop at this roadside park?"

"To talk," Mark grumbled. "Why the second degree?"

Victoria glared at him in disbelief. "I wasn't grilling you!"

"Yes, you were. I want to know why?"

"I don't know what you mean." Victoria struggled to maintain her composure, for the first time hearing the chirruping sounds of crickets in the woods. Mark's disturbed face was cloaked in dancing tree shadows. "It was a simple question, not an interrogation."

"Oh, is that what it was?" Mark was irritated to the core.

Talk about starting a date on the left foot, Victoria lamented. "I'm sorry if I offended you, Mark." She estimated her leverage.

He didn't say anything.

"I was only trying to understand you better. I can't do that without asking questions." That was as plain as she was going to get.

"That's viable," Mark used a medical term to describe his feelings. "I suppose you have a right to know about others who have influenced your life." He gazed into starlit space.

"Thank you for your patience." Victoria breathed a sigh of relief.

"Let me see," Mark gathered his scattered thoughts, "I met Dick through Paul. While you were recuperating in the hospital, he became good friends with Jon, Dick's son."

Jon Branson, the friend Paul mentioned the day of her accident?

"Quite a lot happened the summer you slept." Mark grasped Victoria's hand. "With Jon hanging around the hospital talking to Paul, Dick naturally came by now and then to ask how you were doing. At that point, we were merely acquaintances."

"So how did you become close?"

"Some months later, in October I believe, Dick's third wife ventured into my office and asked me to give her a tummy tuck." He casually draped an arm about Victoria's shoulders.

"Marjorie's surgery was a huge success," he recalled. "When Dick invited me over to see the new country club he'd financed, naturally I accepted." Mark nuzzled his nose into Victoria's cold cheek. "You smell so good, honey."

"So that's how you and Dick became an item," Victoria remarked, paralyzed as Mark's forefinger began to trace her moist lips, warmly stimulated by his maleness.

"I don't want to talk about Dick, Vicki." Mark's hand moved to where it shouldn't.

"No!" Victoria gasped, anticipating his next move. "I can't."

A spurned lover's look coursed his stern face as he jerked away his hand.

Great! Victoria scooted against the car door. "Sorry." She lent him her eyes. "Guess I'm not ready for *all that* yet."

It took him a couple of minutes for Mark to regain his composure, for the fire to die from his eyes. "Forgiven," he accepted her apology. "Guess we should proceed to the country club."

"Mark?" He was pitifully slumped over the steering wheel.

"What, dear?" He was tender despite having suffered rejection.

"What Karen said about Dick being so rich and powerful . . . I guess I don't understand how the meatpacking business can turn a whole town into a thriving metropolis."

"Oh, Dick isn't one enterprise," he replied.

"What do you mean?"

"Heavens! Nobody knows how many businesses the old tycoon has sponsored over the years. Why, Branson ships fresh meats all over the world. Dick even makes donations to impoverished nations. For his generosity, he gets a big tax write-off."

"I should have known there were still taxes."

"As I recall," Mark thought back, "the Fernwood operation was struggling until Dick purchased the business in 1991, attached his signature, and made some positive changes."

Obviously, a sign of vanity, Victoria determined.

"Dick's enterprise is a huge conglomerate now. There's absolutely nothing small about his financial investments!" Mark exuded enthusiasm. "The self-made man is to be admired."

Victoria listened, her dislike for Dick unwavering.

"Fact is, Branson went public on the Stock Market Exchange a few years back," Mark declared. "I even received free options," he bragged. "Dick's been a good friend to me."

"Really?" Mark's raving over Dick's success irked her.

"Vicki . . ." he plucked at the loose strands of brown hair teasing her forehead. "Do you think there's any way we can get back to what we had?" He was a man in love.

Engulfed by Mark's majestic blue gaze, Victoria was unsure how to answer him. The ring on her finger was a reminder they had been linked.

"Tell me, Vicki. Tell us. I'll do anything to get us back!"

"I feel close to you, Mark. I really do." Victoria felt she had to say something positive. "After all, we've been friends for a long time, although I'm missing a few years."

"Uh oh! I feel a Dear John coming on." He uncomfortably shifted in his seat.

"No, Mark! I'm only being honest!" Victoria felt on the verge of tears. "One thing I do know . . . it's impossible to recapture twenty-five years of lost feelings in one evening."

Mark's gaze softened like butter melting. "You're absolutely right, Vicki." He grasped the steering wheel. "I don't like it, but I won't pressure you. It took awhile for us to get close, and decades for you to get over Jeffrey's death and realize you love me."

Victoria moaned. "How close were we, Mark?"

"Close, intimate. Lovers." Mark didn't mince words.

"I was afraid of that!" Beverly had said as much. She couldn't look him in the eye. "My memories of Jeffrey are as fresh as yesterday. You have a right to know that."

"Victoria, you love *me*. What we have together. I never forced you!" He reached over and grabbed her shoulders. "Please promise you'll try to get us back."

"It's complicated." Victoria gently pushed his hands away, shifting sad eyes toward the woods. "I'm terribly sorry our love story turned out this way." *This was not how I planned it.*

"Sorry! For what?" Mark became indignant. "For being intimate with me? Or not remembering how much you love me?" he rasped. "Either way stinks!" His face was contorted.

"Both!" Victoria refused to be manipulated by his emotional outburst. "Premarital sex violates the principles of my faith," she exclaimed. "Mark . . . I still love my husband!"

"My word, Victoria!" He angrily bolted from the BMW to let off some steam. "Jeffrey's been dead for decades! In the new millennium, people write their own rules!"

"How insensitive of you to say that to me!" Victoria opened the car door and got out to face him. "I'm sorry if learning the truth upsets you, but I care about my actions. And God cares, too."

Mark was confused, torn between kissing Victoria and slapping her. Bewildered over whether to accept this new, more prudish Victoria into his life, or to abandon such an insane, impossible, incompatible relationship based on a one-sided love.

***

For Victoria, the evening had begun on a wrong foot and ended the same way. Clashing with Mark at every turn of the conversation, she had early on decided that she should cut short their failed attempt at togetherness. Had she been the stubborn one? Or had Mark purposely tormented her because she had spurned his attempt at romance earlier that evening?

Regardless of who was at fault, she had been emotionally unequipped to handle Mark's male arrogance. Excusing herself to use the restroom, she had called a cab to take her home. Saying goodbye was out of the question under the circumstances.

She had sneaked into the condo around eleven, careful not to wake Karen lest she become bombarded with a lot of unsettling questions that would only disturb her sleep.

"Home again, such as it is." Victoria shut her bedroom door.

Any way she looked at it, the evening had been disastrous. Having extracted little information from Mark, she'd constantly fought his roving hands. Worse, he tried to drink the bar dry.

Victoria thought she understood how a lost puppy felt as she slowly peeled away her fancy dress, hung it on a padded rack, and placed it in her overstuffed closet. Kicking off her shoes, she puttered into the bathroom to brush her teeth and prepare for bed.

By now, Mark would realize that she had walked out on him without an explanation. He would be hurt. No, angry! Caught up in her trauma, he had become a victim, too. In that, she empathized.

But to try and force her into a relationship was selfish. But wasn't everyone guilty when it came to needing?

Victoria stared at her face in the mirror while removing her makeup with Wonder Cream. There should be such a thing for life! She angrily switched on her electric toothbrush. Her life had come unplugged and there was no battery replacement.

She marched into the bedroom, retrieved a ratty pair of pajamas from her chest of drawers and put them on. Caving into bed, she half expected the ceiling to collapse. *The sky is falling . . . the sky is falling . . .* so said Chicken Little.

Sleep was impossible. Victoria turned and tossed and tangled in the sheets, attempting to come to terms with her crazy world! What choice was left but to deal with it?

Although life had dealt her a horrendous set of circumstances, Victoria still believed the Creator would somehow enable her to cope if she persevered. The key to Kingdom living was in not giving up, not giving in, and not forgetting God's divine love.

Nor His divine power to intervene in human lives and solve problems.

Victoria bolted from bed and said aloud, "Why not keep a diary?" It was a God-sent idea. She could record her daily impressions of conversations with people. Later on, when she felt defeated or confused or depressed, she could review what she'd written and make wiser choices about her future.

Somehow if she clawed through enough confusion, swam through enough muddy waters of deceit, and leaped blindly off enough lying cliffs, she would succeed in understanding fully why her husband had tragically died.

And in the process nail Jeffrey's killers and find her Bible.

Victoria leaped from the bed and scrambled through drawers, finally locating a notebook that would serve her purpose. With renewed faith in God's ability to use her, she wrote:

Wednesday, April 16, 2014

Dear Diary,

Today I met with Beverly Yates—a former Memphis State sorority sister. Bev was married to Mark James at the time of my auto accident, but since divorced him in 1991 after discovering that his gambling habit had nearly bankrupted them.

Apparently, all those times Mark claimed he was fishing on the Mississippi Gulf Coast, he'd been gambling in the casinos. Bev found records of old debts dating back to 1985 that Mark finally paid off in 1991. (Personal comment: Isn't it convenient that the Gift Trust Fund became available around the same time?)

Anyhow, the dishonesty and distrust between Bev and Mark was enough to shatter their shaky marriage. Bev said Mark had been an unfaithful husband and involved with people she neither liked nor trusted. Wisely, she'd asked for a quiet divorce.

Bev is of the opinion that some things are best left unsaid. I believe she told me as much as she dared. I also think she was hiding something important about her ex-husband's activities in order to protect the both of us. Although Bev realizes that my motives are pure in wanting Jeffrey's killers brought to justice, she truly believes it is in everyone's best interest to leave well enough alone.

I had dinner with Mark tonight, but knowing what I do about him makes it difficult to sustain any kind of sane relationship. I abhor his drinking and he wants more affection from me fast. I don't know how much longer I can put him off before he asks me to return his engagement ring. I pray that I can maintain a peaceful relationship with Mark until I learn his true reasons for befriending rude Dick Branson. Friend or foe, I need Mark's input to solve Jeffrey's crime.

My take on Mark: His ability to pay off his gambling debts, Dick Branson's arrival in Fernwood, and Jeffrey's death are all somehow connected.

What deadly secret is everyone afraid to tell?

THURSDAY, APRIL 17

13

Victoria woke up late Thursday morning and found the note Karen had left stating she was tying down a big commercial deal at the office and couldn't say what time she'd be home.

Good, thought Victoria. *I can keep my visit to the library under wraps. At least, until I have qualified evidence to reopen Jeffrey's murder case.*

The library wasn't located where it had once been. In its place, a six-story FEDERATION CHILDCARE CENTER had been erected. Progress marches on.

Clutching the steering wheel, slouched in her parked car, Victoria observed how people paraded their young children in and out of the front door of the gigantic center. Somehow the facility's federal name troubled her. Whenever government funds were appropriated, it usually meant a list of requirements was attached.

Had that limited the opportunity for Christian Bible reading and prayer?

Victoria strapped on her courage and located Fernwood's new library on the next corner where an old Sears Merchant Store had once stood. Peering at the dazzling, gray reflector-glass complex, it was obvious that no expense had been spared to enlighten the mind. No doubt, library technology had greatly changed since the late eighties.

Entering through the library's revolving glass doors felt more like stepping into Buck Rogers' territory. After reviewing the layout of the library in the lighted diagram, she glanced through the double-arched doorway and spied a series of cascading escalators busily delivering library-goers to the second and third levels.

Well, well, she was definitely impressed.

Venturing deeper into Fernwood's intellectual temple, she stepped on a sea of scud-proof, skid-resistant flooring where supporting columns rose out of the floor like giant muscular arms and grasped the arched Greco-Roman ceiling above. World-famous paintings from the dawn of culture were rampant on the stucco-swirled beige walls.

I can do this. Victoria sucked in a breath and walked toward the INFORMATION CENTER where library-goers swarmed the circular maze of computer terminals like bees drawn to honey, busily donning earphones while gazing into laser screens.

Uncertain of protocol, Victoria trailed a woman to a terminal and soon realized that the she was conversing with a voice-activated screen that answered her questions and directed her to the desired information. *Pretty tricky!*

Victoria stepped up to a terminal. After following the easy teleprompt, she quickly learned where the historical newspaper articles were housed. With information electronically recorded on computer chips, it was a good guess that bound books had become obsolete, except for historians who maintained private libraries.

Taking the escalator to the Third Level, Victoria claimed a cubicle and looked at the equipment. Befuddled, she glanced around for assistance and spied a woman behind the Help Desk frantically waving. Having no clue how to react, she casually waved back.

Victoria had better decide quickly since the stranger was headed over to speak to her. Luckily, Kathryn Billingsly was wearing a name badge.

"Good morning, Kathryn." She invented a smile.

"My, my! You're out and about early," the librarian noted.

Offering no response didn't deter the loquacious Kathryn. Trapped in a one-sided conversation, Victoria seized the opportunity to learn more about herself from someone who apparently knew her well. An occasional nod kept the dialog moving along.

"We missed you at bridge last week." Kathryn crouched beside Victoria's cubicle. "Have you been ill, dear?" She infringed on Victoria's comfort zone.

"Well, I haven't quite been myself." Victoria was amused at her choice of words, unable to recall if she'd ever known how to play bridge. *Scrabble, maybe.*

"Tabitha Barnes is hosting next week," Kathryn chattered on as if Victoria cared. "Did you know her daughter was divorcing?" She elaborated on the gory details.

"No!" Victoria tried to sound truly alarmed. "I do hope things will work out."

"Hubby Charles has a new girl friend," Kathryn embellished on Tabitha's sordid tale. "Can't be too careful whom you trust these days. Wolves in sheep's clothing, you know." She patted her inflated hairdo. "So how's Karen?" She flipped to a new page.

"Fine." Victoria nervously fumbled with the keypad. "We've both been busy." She was polite, but evasive, not about to share her heart with the town gossip.

"With your wedding, I suppose," Miss Congeniality opened a disturbing subject. In response, Victoria grunted, hoping the subject of Mark James would die on the vine.

"So what are you researching today, dear? Biorhythms?"

Biorhythms? Victoria swung her head toward Kathryn.

"Or sexual fetishes," Kathryn whispered. "I hear you and Mark are tying the knot permanently in June. But I suppose the textbooks have nothing new to offer you."

"No!" Victoria gasped. "I'm doing research for an article on," her mind whirred, "on coma victims!"

"I bet you are interested in that subject!" Kathryn's clear gray eyes widened behind her thick round spectacles. "You were a coma victim once. Three months, wasn't it?"

"Yes." Victoria nervously played with the mouse. "I was fortunate to have awakened from my coma. Except for God's mercy, I might have died."

"Oh!" Horrified, Kathryn clasped together the bony knuckles of her hand. "The thought of going through something like that gives me the willies! But Victoria . . . you are a survivor."

"Yes, I am." She graciously received the compliment.

"Well, good luck with your research," Kathryn said, about to walk away.

"Oh, Kathryn?" Victoria grappled for a way to enlist help.

"What else can I do for you, dear?" She sweetly smiled.

"I've got a sore finger." Victoria shook her right hand. "I don't believe I can operate the keyboard." She had absolutely no idea how the machinery worked. "Do you mind?"

"Boot you up?" Kathryn's professionalism kicked in. "Of course." She scooted Victoria out of the way. "It'll only take a minute. How far back shall we go?"

"Let's start with articles printed in 1989." Kathryn's limber finger maneuvers were to be applauded. "I want to read about my automobile accident."

"Oh, now, that's nervy." Kathryn lifted hands from the computer keyboard, her sharp nose wrinkling as her eyes widened with curiosity. "You're a braver soul than I. Why you'd want to revisit that tragedy mystifies me. You're positive you want to do this?"

"I'm sure." Victoria thought any recollection of pain would have been brief from so severe an accident. But wasn't getting in touch with her feelings the primary purpose of her research? No, reading the article was necessary. "I'd appreciate your help."

"Well," said Kathryn as the screen magically lit up with information. Nimble fingers ran the gambit of the keyboard, clicking like lightning as the skilled librarian zeroed in on the needed information. Finally, a list of some two hundred articles appeared.

"Looks as if you have your work cut out." Kathryn narrowed the list of articles down to those residing in the state of Tennessee, then Hardeman County. "Here, dear, you have fifteen articles from which to select. Will that be enough?"

"Perfect." Victoria was ecstatic. "Thank you so much."

"Anytime," Kathryn replied. "By the way, what magazine are you writing for?"

"What?" Victoria glanced up. "Oh, the article. Just free-lancing."

"I'll be at the counter across the way. Call if you need me." Kathryn observed Victoria as she highlighted an article. "Your finger seems to be working just fine now."

Victoria blushed, realizing her error. "I guess the Tylenol has had time to take effect," she lied, her eyes glued to the topic on the screen because she couldn't look at Kathryn.

COMA VICTIM FIGHTS FOR LIFE

Victoria Martin Tempest, coma victim of a recent automobile accident, is reported doing poorly at Hardeman County General Hospital. Attorney Jeffrey Tempest, the victim's husband, was simultaneously shot to death in a break-in at his office. It is believed that Mrs. Tempest alerted the shooters of her husband's presence in his office when she telephoned him on her car phone. Traveling alone, hearing the gunshots, the inclement weather conditions apparently contributed to Mrs. Tempest losing control of her Mazda and flipping over a steep embankment on Highway 64 near Fernwood, Tennessee. An anonymous caller dialed 911 and reported the accident from a nearby pay phone.

An anonymous caller reported her accident? Who else was there besides the police officers who filed her accident report and the Emergency Medical Service?

But even if they had names, in twenty-five years, people moved, quit their jobs, divorced, retired and *died.*

While Victoria grimaced over unfavorable circumstances, she felt the weight of Kathryn's watchful eye. To appear diligent in her research, she read a couple of other coma articles and made notes before offering her computer to a kid looking for a cubicle.

Getting out of the stuffy library was liberating. The radiant spring morning waiting outdoors was the exact stimulant she needed to persevere in the shadow of momentary setbacks. With eyes of faith, she scanned the royal-blue heavens void of any blemishes, determined to see beyond any physical limitations.

A step back, two steps forward.

Locating her parked blue Mercedes Benz, Victoria popped the locks and climbed inside. In no mood to go home, she drove around Fernwood's canonized square, belaboring the fact that she recognized few names attached to the retail stores.

Out with the old, in with the new.

While she'd been locked away in a time capsule, Fernwood had marched on. But at least the *Olde Soda Shoppe* was still in business.

So be it!

It was time to investigate her high school hangout, enjoy an old-fashioned chocolate soda, and try like crazy to discredit the maxi calories. Victoria prayed she'd be fortunate enough to bump into someone from her past.

14

Walking into the old drugstore proved a definite leap into Fernwood's historic past. Victoria inhaled the familiar medley of odors unique to an old drug store, delighted to see that the old soda-fountain bar was still intact and exactly where it had stood for over a century, its shiny black-and-white marble surface a true testimony of its immortality.

Behind the twenty-foot dessert bar on mirrored glass shelves was the same antique collection of green-and-bronzed medicinal bottles she remembered from high school. And on her left, the molded-plastic red booths still welcomed thirsty customers.

Is that a frown or a grin? Victoria wondered as Gloria Gordon stepped from the back room. "Vicki Martin!" Her high school classmate spurted. "I'm surprised to see you in here after so many years! I thought you'd come up too far in this world for this ol' soda dive."

"I haven't changed all that much," Victoria professed. "I still like chocolate sodas!" She walked over and hugged Gloria, laughing with enthusiasm. "Of course, the calories won't do me any favors!"

"It's so great to see you!" Gloria's black eyes gleamed. "We got some great memories, huh?" She wrinkled her nose. "A whole lot of water under the bridge."

"Can you still make a soda like in the good old days?"

"Some things don't change!" Gloria sauntered behind the counter and grabbed a chilled steel container. Scooping up two heaping spoonfuls of twenty-five percent, fat-filled vanilla ice cream from the cooler, she began constructing a mountain of calories before adding a rich lather of chocolate syrup over the top.

Victoria's gaze widened as her taste buds ignited.

"So why did you suddenly want a chocolate soda?" Gloria admired her sweet creation at arm's length as her peppered gaze came to rest on Victoria. "Today of all days?"

"I'm not quite certain." Victoria mounted the barstool like

she'd done a thousand times in high school. If she turned around, she might even see a younger Jeffrey and Mark hunkered down in a booth, wolfing down hamburgers, acting like stupid fools.

Nostalgia took its toll as Victoria's eyes glazed over. Jeffrey's memory had cut a fresh wound in her heart, opening up a locked closet of forgotten feelings.

"Sometimes you just gotta get out of routine and smell the roses." Victoria sucked in oxygen and reined in skyrocketing emotions.

"I hear that, girlfriend." Gloria's grin was strangely crooked. "So you and the Doc still got plans to hook up permanently?" Her eyebrows lifted. "Never figured that to happen in a million years."

"Why would you think that?" Gloria added a packet of vanilla flavoring and gave the soda a whip in the blender.

"You know . . ." Gloria whispered over the counter, warily glancing around. "Because of all that money."

"No, I don't. Mark was Jeffrey's best friend."

"Humph!" Gloria huffed, then stiffened. "Maybe."

"And why do you say *maybe*?"

When Gloria gazed into space, Victoria feared she had somehow offended a well-meaning friend. The last thing she intended to do was alienate a possible wellspring of information vital to Jeffrey's investigation. What should she do now?

"Anyhow . . ." Victoria attempted to get past the uncomfortable moment. "I wonder why Mark James and I are such big items?"

Gloria's lacquered eyelashes fluttered and lifted. "Gosh, Victoria. You're high society!" She topped the soda with an extra scoop of chocolate ice cream and squished on a mountain of high-calorie real whipping cream.

"Oh?" Victoria's lusty eye was on the dessert.

"And folks talk, you know." Gloria's eyelashes shuttered, her gaze centered on the task at hand. "And *they* wonder about *all* that money you collected?"

"They?" Victoria reacted. "Who are they?" She despised the

fact her affluence had turned her into an untouchable and made her the subject of continuing gossip.

"Never mind. Forget what I just said." Gloria shrugged her shoulders. "None of my business anyhow." Her gaze drifted to a booth across the room. "I got other customers—"

"Wait!" Victoria restrained Gloria with a firm hand. "That's a strange comment, not one I'm likely to overlook. Are you certain there isn't something more you'd like to tell me?"

"Look Victoria, I like you and all . . . but I don't think Dr. Mark would approve of me talking to you like this!" Gloria jerked away, attempting to wiggle out of answering.

Mark again! Did she exist beyond his shadow?

"It's done!" Gloria announced.

"What?" Victoria's disgruntled gaze targeted Gloria.

"Your soda, sweetie." The awkward moment passed.

Victoria wanted to grab Gloria's creation and slurp it down. Instead, she watched her friend garnish it with two cherries and teasingly scoot it across the bar.

"Two straws, please."

"What?"

"I need two straws for my soda," Victoria replied.

Gloria waved her hand and reached under the counter, coming up with a handful of colored straws. "Your choice. Pick one."

"Thanks." Victoria selected the blue and poked it in her soda. About to imbibe, Gloria's next statement stopped her.

"Mercy me, Victoria Martin Tempest and Dr. Mark James gettin' hitched! Never thought I'd live long enough to see that!" Gloria patted her puffy blond sixties' do.

"And why is that?" Victoria inhaled the soda's flavor.

"It just isn't something you would do, Vicki Martin!"

"Tell me, Gloria." Victoria shoved her soda aside. "Am I so different now than I was in high school?" She wanted to know how others viewed her.

"We're all different, honey." Gloria leaned into Victoria's face, eyeball to eyeball. "But you gotta know Mark James was in the middle of that thing with your husband."

"What do you mean that *thing*?" Victoria gasped. "Jeffrey's murder?" It was inconceivable that Mark would plot to hurt him.

Hearing the tinkling door chimes, Gloria glanced at the front door and trotted off like the starting bell had rung for the next horse race. "Wait!" Victoria called out as she disappeared behind Door 2, the back room where supplies were kept.

Spinning around on the barstool, Victoria spied a motorcyclist dressed in a black leather jacket and wearing boots to his knees. Looming in the doorway like Darth Vader, he cradled a Harley-Davidson helmet in his right hand. Seeing his kind lime eyes and pleasant expression, she wondered what about the young man intimidated Gloria to the point she ran away with no explanation.

Ten minutes later, when Gloria hadn't return, Victoria finished her chocolate soda, paid the cashier, and left the drugstore.

The day had taken on a fresh linen odor as the warm, humid air absorbing the blended potpourri odors seeping from the giant clay pots lining the sidewalk.

Across the street, washed sunlight cast a silvery glow over the stately three-story eighteenth-century courthouse. Filled with a renewed sense of hometown pride, Victoria hurried toward her parked car, mulling over Gloria's questionable opinion of Mark.

Was her former lover capable of betrayal?

Although Mark had professed to be Jeffrey's best friend for decades, his level of sincerity seemed questionable.

Was he the type to stab a friend in the back?

Victoria hopped into her car, making a quick decision to visit Fernwood's shaker-mover at his place of business. It was time she got to know the real Richard Branson, the Third.

***

Kathryn Billingsly took her break soon after Victoria left the library. Locating an unoccupied pay phone in the foyer, she telephoned Dick Branson at his office.

"Dick, this is Kathryn. You asked me to phone if Victoria Tempest came by the library. Well, she just did." The librarian suffered some remorse tattling on Victoria.

"Oh? Thank you so much for calling me, Kathryn." Dick lightly cradled the receiver to one ear. "And what did our Victoria want?

"She said she was writing an article on coma victims."

A stream of dirty words flushed out of Dick's mouth before he checked himself and apologized to Kathryn. As usual, the prudish librarian ignored his brutal personality because she was a good friend of his third wife, Marjorie. *Ah, the benefits of friendship.*

"Victoria said she wanted to read articles about her car accident," Kathryn blabbered. "My goodness, that's old news, Dick. Do you have any idea what's going on?"

"None." Dick heard his second line buzz. "I need to put you on hold, Kathryn. It'll only take a minute."

"Sure." The librarian listened to elevator music while she waited, buffing her manicured nails with an emery board.

"What is it, Jeannie?" Dick learned he had a visitor. Punching a button on his phone, he reconnected Kathryn. "Thank you for calling me, dear. Can I catch you later?" His words were butter-smooth.

"Sure, I'm busy too!" Kathryn was blunt. "Have a nice day. And give Marjorie my best," she said, remaining courageously courteous.

"I will. And, you take care now, you hear?" Dick hurriedly hung up the receiver, then buzzed the front desk.

"Who is it, Jeannie?"

"Victoria Tempest is here to see you."

So the fly came to the spider, Dick grinned.

15

Dick was bewildered. Victoria was here? The woman was all over the place like a bad dream that wouldn't go away.

"Send my visitor on in." He straightened his silk tie, tugging at his baggy pants failing to grip his bulging belly.

Bring on the tigress.

Victoria stepped into Dick's office, uncertain how to begin her interrogation.

"Vicki! How nice of you to pay me a visit!" Dick's whimsical grin revealed a mouthful of white-capped front teeth as he rushed over to greet his guest.

Victoria glared at the pompous sixty-five-year-old toad squeezed into an expensive tailored suit half a size too small, unable to recall ever having met him, though he was certainly working hard at being friendly.

So why the big front? She wasn't his friend.

"Thank you for seeing me." Victoria managed to smile.

"Here now, Victoria." Dick catered to her. "You just sit down in this nice, comfortable chair, and I'll have Jeannie bring us some fresh hot coffee. Or would you prefer a soda?"

Dick's lush-politeness was sickening.

"No, thank you. I'm coffeed out." Victoria sank uneasily into his Queen Anne. "I have a matter to discuss that shouldn't take long." She glanced around at the opulent office.

"Oh? About your honeymoon?" Dick attempted to take control of the conversation. "Oh, yes indeed, I told Mark I wanted to foot the bill as a wedding gift. Hell's bells! The sky's the limit! Take a month and go around the world if you like." He waited to see if she'd bite.

Dick's profane generosity left Victoria speechless. Did he think paying her off would get rid of her so easily? And he should do something about his vulgar language.

"This isn't about my marriage to Mark," Victoria said, attempting to hide her distaste for the manipulative meatpacker. "Or our honeymoon. I've come to talk about *me*."

"Well, now isn't that a delightful subject?" Dick chuckled. "I'm listening, little lady. Just tell me how I can help." He dug a lighter out of his desk drawer and ignited a half-smoked Havana cigar. "You don't mind if I smoke, do you?" He was already puffing.

"No," Victoria replied. After all, she was on his turf.

Sighing, he sheepishly grinned. "Obviously, you've come for a reason, so what is it?"

Victoria briefly considered the level of Dick's pretense.

"Have you spoken with Mark recently?" *Let's skip the verbal fore-play, shall we?* "Do you know about my . . . condition?" *Would Dick say if he did?*

"What? No!" Dick's gyrations were theatrical as he threw his cigar aside and played dumb. "I do hope you don't have some dreaded disease, Victoria!" Surprise was on his face.

She couldn't help but smile. Dick Branson was good. *Really good.* He must have invented social games. The expression on his face hadn't varied one iota.

"No, nothing like that." Victoria glared at the gifted man of illusions. She didn't believe for one second that Dick hadn't heard about her "awakening." Beverly James had made it crystal clear that the vulgar meatpacker and doctor were tight as ticks on a mangy hound.

"Then what?" Dick's lips were pursed as he rocked gently in his high-tech office chair. "Speak up, woman! How can I be of help otherwise?"

Is he for real? "Maybe you could help."

In speculation, Dick tilted his head to one side. "How so?"

"I'm working on an article about coma victims. I was hoping you might offer some insight into my past." She wasn't about to tell him about her flip-flopped memories.

"Like what?" Dick coughed and spewed, waving his hand to clear the cigar smog from his view. Bulging eyes, muddy as a swamp, squatted in his contorted face.

Dick Branson was too much! *Really*!

"Come now, don't be bashful," he toyed with her. "Tell me, although I have to wonder why in the world you want to drag up all that sad history."

Victoria was not intimidated by Dick's oratory. "A few months before my automobile accident, your company moved to Fernwood and . . ." she coughed as acrid smoke infiltrated her lungs.

Seeing her discomfort, Dick snuffed out his cigar. "Go on, I'm all ears." He laced his bulky fingers over his belly.

"That day . . ." Dick would know which day she meant, "Paul mentioned he'd met a kid at school whose father worked at the meatpacking factory. By chance, was that boy your son?"

"Jon?" Dick tugged at his sagging pants. "Oh yes, indeed, it very well may have been my boy. You know my son Jon and your Paul were best of friends for years and years."

Were? Victoria wasn't yet prepared to discuss her son's death.

"I'd like to speak with Jon as soon as possible!" Dick shouldn't mind if he had nothing to hide. But if he proved difficult . . .

"Why?" Dick suspiciously glared, chewing on the nub of his charred cigar.

"I have my reasons," she replied. "Shortly before I left the house on the eve of my unfortunate accident, Paul asked me if he could go into town and play pool with a friend. Of course, I said he couldn't, not while Jeffrey and I were out."

Dick attentively listened, not commenting.

"I wondered if—"

"No, Jon wasn't at your house *that* night!" Dick emphatically responded, kicking his desk as he swiveled around to face her, an arrogant smirk tucked away in his gaze.

Fists clinched, Victoria guarded her spiraling temper. "You're sure?"

Supported by pulpy fists, Dick rose with undaunted passion, perilously leaning across his cluttered desk. "I know for a fact my

Jon wasn't at your house that night." He fell back into his swivel rocker, dragged down by his obesity.

"You're positive?" Disappointment sabotaged Victoria's hope.

"Oh, yes indeed. It was a terrible night." Dick descriptively embellished the scene replaying in his brain. "Awful weather, tornado warnings out everywhere."

"And you're absolutely certain that Jon was home all evening?"

"No, I didn't say that!" Dick blinked. "Crazy kid took a motorcycle ride in the storm. Came home around nine o'clock soaking wet. Caught a chill and was sick for four days."

"I'd still like Jon's phone number," Victoria insisted. "I'd prefer asking him myself." Maybe the lad had more integrity than his father.

"Jon's out of town. On vacation." Dick stalled for time so he could contact his son first. The kid didn't always think about what he was gonna say before he let it all hang out.

Victoria knew that she'd hit a brick wall. One way or another, she would speak with Jon. Dick could take that to the bank. "Just tell your son to phone me when he returns."

"Sure. Why not?" Dick played with his shiny Bic lighter. "The kid should be home in a couple of weeks." Dick's quaking smile made his mustache quiver.

Although clever, Dick didn't lie very well.

"Vicki?" Dick waddled around his desk and grasped her hand. "Do you mind telling me why you want to drag up this terrible tragedy after all this time?" Sincerity oozed like honey from a comb.

"I think you already know the answer to that!" She shook loose of Dick's clammy hold, pleased that her words had torched a spark of worry in his disgruntled face.

"As you wish." Dick bowed ever so slightly, conceding momentary defeat. The smoke, the lies, the pretense clouded his aura.

"I can let myself out," Victoria concluded her visit.

"Now you be sure and tell that good lookin' fella of yours hello for me." He made a last-ditch effort to mimic Emily Post. "And do come back when you have more time."

Suppressing an ugly remark, Victoria quickly exited the building. Shakily standing outside Dick's office, she realized that Dick Branson was a man she instinctively distrusted. A poor excuse for a human being, he was crass and manipulative, certainly powerful enough to deploy friends in high places and enemies in rat holes. Those calling him a *friend* should not be trusted.

Mark James not excluded.

About to drive away, Victoria decided to have a quick look around the premises. But spying the NO TRESPASSING posted signs, she turned the car around and headed toward the front entrance, recalling she'd read somewhere how the leather-tanning process left soil pollutants.

When chemical wastes weren't properly removed, didn't they leak into the community's water table and make people sick?

It seemed socially irresponsible that no one had complained when Hearty Meats swept into Fernwood overnight and plopped down on the old tannery site. Come to think of it, she could not recall one press article addressing the potential health problem. As far as she knew, there had never been a formal environmental complaint filed against the tannery or the meat packing company.

Stranger things happened.

But she would be the first to admit that on the surface the Branson premises appeared immaculate, suggesting that a professional landscaper had designed the lovely manicured entrances and floral walkways. And considering how prosperous Fernwood's economy had been since the company arrived in town, who would want to contest so lucrative a business?

Obviously no one! Victoria whizzed past the exit gate.

Still, to her way of thinking, it all seemed pretty fishy. Wouldn't the Environmental Protection Agency have required a soil report before giving the company clearance to do business? And who kept those reports on file for citizens to review?

Victoria felt on the verge of an important revelation, a critical clue that would contribute to solving Jeffrey's murder. Prior to her accident, he had mentioned working on a case of extreme importance that would potentially impact everyone who lived in Fernwood. He had told her not to worry, that he was sure to win.

But now, she wondered why he had said that. Had Jeffrey been worried? *If so, why?*

Most of her husband's legal work had dealt with marital separation, divorce decrees, or an occasional lawsuit that he filed over an accident claim, but nothing of monumental importance.

Yet, Jeffrey had indicated that this case was one of "extreme importance."

In retrospect, Victoria could kick herself. She should have shown more interest in her husband's work and asked him what kept him out late at night. If she'd only taken decisive action back then, her life and his might have turned out differently.

The milk was spilt! Victoria thought her mother's old adage aptly applied in this situation. Here she was twenty-five years after the fact, trying to solve the crime that took Jeffrey's life without one shred of physical evidence to support her murder theory.

What am I thinking? Detective work was beyond her expertise.

But you couldn't commit a crime without leaving evidence, could you? And whoever broke into Jeffrey's office was bound to have had motive.

Maybe the motive was tucked away in Jeffrey's office records. *Did those files still exist?* If so, they possibly harbored damaging secrets that would address why Jeffrey's office had been ransacked that stormy night. Possibly, name his killers.

Tormented, Victoria rationalized that Jeffrey's case may have been so confidential that he wouldn't have discussed it with her anyhow. But at least, she could have asked.

Deliberating over her next move, she vowed to stand by her man. Jeffrey had been her husband and lover, the father of their two wonderful children. A man of staunch faith, he would have given his life to shut down any business that contaminated his community. *And he had.*

Perhaps the connection between Dick Branson and Jeffrey had been the "case of extreme importance."

Maybe they had been mortal enemies.

As Victoria drove away from the Branson complex, she had the uncanny feeling that Dick's son held a key that would unlock the mystery of what happened the night she crashed.

It wasn't over until it was over.

16

As soon as Victoria had gone, Dick Branson phoned Mark James at his office. "I thought you said you'd take care of her." He was direct, barking like a chained dog.

"What's Vicki done now?" Mark cringed, the ill effects of last night's foolish drinking binge at the country club still plaguing him. Now he had to deal with this!

Dick exploded in a heated tirade over Victoria's recent office visit, his lengthy complaints requiring more patience than Mark could muster. He was keenly aware of his fiancée's intolerance.

Hadn't she left him high, and not so dry, last night without one word? Never had Dr. Mark James swallowed so much pride as when he had tried to explain Vicki's sudden departure to his tipsy friends.

Second mistake, he'd hung around the bar one drink too many. Hours after everyone had gone, a looker half his age offered him a lift home. What happened after that was a blank.

"Mark! You hearing me?" Dick's voice escalated two decibels.

"Yeah," Mark grimaced, unable to recall if he'd given the girl the hundred-dollar bill missing from his wallet when he awakened this morning, which may have meant something.

"Well, boy! How do you intend to handle this!" Dick croaked. "I'm putting this mess in your lap." He heard his partner-in-crime grunt at the other end of the line. "You don't sound well at all," he wheezed. "You been digesting what I've been sayin' about Victoria?"

"Uh, er." Mark stammered as his head exploded in little episodes. He was in no shape to defend Victoria against the big bad wolf.

"As I said before," Dick plowed new territory, "your Little Vicki burst into my office askin' a lot of questions about Jon. Now why do you suppose she wants to talk to my son?"

"Jon? I have no idea!" Discounting the fact he hadn't smoked in five years, Mark rummaged through the nightstand in search of a loose cigarette. From the way the day was going, he would need one. Nerves shot, hands trembling, not a good MO for a surgeon.

"Well, guess what, Mark?" Dick ranted. "I know the answer to my own question!" Venom spewed in his words. "Victoria wants to know all about the night of her accident!"

"That doesn't surprise me," Mark said, grinning at finding a stale Camel.

"What worries me is that Jon might tell Victoria the *truth*."

"Huh? What more could Jon possibly know about Vicki's accident than we already know?" Mark introduced a rush of nicotine into his virgin lungs, his head drumming with pain.

"I never told you," Dick swore, "but my boy was the anonymous caller who reported Victoria's accident." He leaned back in his comfortable chair waiting for the news to impact.

"What?" Mark dropped his flaming cigarette on the floor, flushing a menu of dirty words as it burned a hole in his new office carpet. "Ouch." He retrieved the burning butt.

"Yes, indeedy!" Dick enjoyed his little drama. "It was yours truly who advised Jon not to get involved with the police that evening. Fact is, I never told a soul until now."

"Well, Dick, I don't know why," perspiration broke out on Mark's forehead, "but that doesn't make me feel a whole lot better. The least you could have done was warn me!"

Acid recoiled in Mark's rolling stomach. The situation with Victoria was not improving.

"Telling you didn't seem necessary at the time." Dick mused. "It was all in *our* past. At least, until now." He waited for Mark's ingenious input.

"So what do you expect me to do? Tie Vicki up and gag her?"

"No, but your fiancée needs to calm down a bit, be a little more cautious. Who knows what tomorrow will hold?" Dick cleared the phlegm from his throat. "Think before she acts."

That's an understatement, Mark thought to himself.

"Upset like Victoria is, she might have another mishap. Accidents happen, you know," Dick added for absolute clarity.

Mark's pulse leaped at his confidant's less-than-subtle threat.

Dropping the phone, he rushed to the john and emptied the contents of his alcoholic stomach. A few minutes later, he picked the receiver off the floor. The ranting tycoon had hung up on him.

Like it or not, Mark realized he was still tied to some nasty business that he'd believed was behind him. It was way too late for plea-bargaining. *The dye was cast.*

Mark stood at his office window, speculating if he were willing to risk everything for one woman? Lay his comfortable life aside all for the sake of love?

He would have to think about it.

***

After a lengthy conversation with his father, Jon Branson cradled the phone, surprised to learn that Paul Tempest's mother had gotten her memories back after so long a time. He'd been fifteen when Victoria's accident had occurred.

Everyone was so . . . different now.

As always, his daddy spoke his mind. Once again, a father who tolerated no mistakes had raked his son over the hot coals about how to handle past mistakes. And quite clearly, the influential man meant for him to lie again about his involvement with Victoria's accident. Except obeying his father *now* posed a huge problem.

Twenty-five years ago, the *old* Jon would have agreed to lie in a heartbeat. Loyal to *Number One*, a snotty-nosed rebellious, pot-smoking teen who rode a mean motorcycle, had no qualms about perverting the truth.

But today, he felt differently. The new Jon had a heart-adjustment of the God-kind. The change had occurred after Paul Tempest OD'd on cocaine.

Up until the summer of 2012, he and Paul had been nearly inseparable, buddies working alongside each other packing his daddy's meats. Goofing off on the job had come easy for them. *Party* had been their middle name with every two-week's paycheck going to support their gambling and womanizing habits. With no regrets, they'd ridden life like it was a wild bronco.

Then, a couple of weeks before Paul had died, he mentioned overhearing an unusual phone conversation that had taken place between Dr. Mark James and Jon's father. They were discussing his mother's automobile accident and Paul wondered why.

At that time, he honestly had no clue.

"Jon?" Paul was hunkered over a foaming beer he'd just purchased at Cavalier's Pub, a gathering waterhole for singles.

"What?" It was Friday afternoon around kick-butt time, Happy Hour two-for-ones. Feeling tipsy from smoking a marijuana cigarette, he had a hungry eye on a juicy sixteen-ounce steak the man next to him had ordered. No worries to mention, the old Jon was one of the bombed-out, over-indulgent X-generation. "Is there a problem?"

"Doc was telling your father something over the telephone that started me to thinking." He caught Jon's eye.

"Yeah, what?" The old Jon ignited an expensive Havana cigar lifted from his father's desk.

"Doc told your old man he wished he could forget about his part in Jeffrey's death. Seemed weird to me."

Stunned that Paul had brought up the subject after twenty-three years, he'd clamed up like an oyster. *No one must know*, his daddy had said.

"Jon? You'd tell me the truth, wouldn't you?" Paul's determined expression said he expected a straight answer from his best friend. "So what'd you think Doc meant by that statement?"

Paul's question effectively brought back memories of the chilling events that had taken place the night that changed so many lives. After arguing with his father, he had rushed headstrong out of the house, unconcerned for his safety, bent on tasting danger as he rode his motorcycle like wildfire in the violent storm.

The eerie night had taken on a doomsday appearance. Lightning crackled in the unstable atmosphere; thunder quaked the landscape. Raging winds pressed against his sweaty face as he furiously rode his motorcycle toward Paul's house in a futile attempt to outrun the hellish storm.

The incident had happened so long ago . . . why drag it out of the closet? Seated next to Paul on a barstool at Cavalier's, choked up on all *those* memories, the old Jon had lacked the courage to tell his best friend what he'd done that fateful night.

"Do you think it means that Doc had something to do with my father's death?" Paul had the telltale cat by the tail slinging it.

"You probably misunderstood, man," he had barely whispered.

"Probably nothing, huh?" Paul's gaze was centered on his frothy beer.

"Yeah, probably nothing."

Later, when the party had wound down at Cavalier's Pub and Paul had gone home, he had rushed over to his father's house to point-blank ask him about his phone conversation with Mark James, to learn if he had anything to do with the break-in at Jeffrey Tempest's office.

At first, his less-than-diplomatic father had been outraged and claimed that Paul had misinterpreted his conversation with Mark James, insisting that it was ludicrous to believe that either of them would intentionally harm Jeffrey or Victoria Tempest.

So, a dutiful son, the *old* Jon had let the matter drop. Even forgotten about it until Paul turned up overdosed in the back room of a gay bar. *A gay bar!* That was when he had realized that something was terribly wrong. Despising homosexuality, Paul never frequented gay bars.

No, the timing was too uncanny, like maybe Paul had asked one too many questions and there was far more to the young attorney's death than appeared on the muddy surface.

Following Paul's funeral, Jon had decided to dig up what he had secretly buried decades before: Victoria's Bible. It was true he'd witnessed the accident; true, he'd called 911. But Paul hadn't known it. Nobody knew the full truth of his mischievous involvement with Victoria Tempest's accident—that something more had happened that night.

"Curiosity killed the cat" would aptly describe young Jon's rash actions when he'd returned to the crash site and steered his Harley down the steep embankment toward the smoking Mazda, thinking whoever was inside that wreck must be "deader 'n a doornail."

Peeking through the broken window glass, he'd spied a woman inside the mangled car scrunched against the steering wheel's screaming horn, blood oozing down her forehead.

Most likely dead, he'd determined, *so why try to pull the woman out?* She could have a broken neck and moving her was dangerous. Somebody would soon come and help.

Jon had been a kid back then, hadn't known he was supposed to help. But he certainly would have tried had he known it was Paul's mother lying inside the demolished car.

Unfortunately, his curiosity didn't let up. Poking his head through the broken glass window on the passenger's side, he'd spotted a book. *A Holy Bible!* Just lying on the car seat like it hadn't felt the bumpy ride down the ravine.

"Wasn't that some kind of miracle?"

Curiosity was a kicker. Reaching through the broken glass car window, he had grabbed the book and shoved it inside his leather jacket so it wouldn't get rain-soaked. Lightning slithered across the blistering skies and thunder rolled as erratic winds whistled about him.

Cloaked in the night's eerie shadows, he had revved the motorcycle engine and climbed up the slick embankment in search of safe shelter. It was a night he'd never forget.

Later on, when he'd gone home and confessed to reporting the accident, his daddy had been disturbed over the news, making it crystal clear that no one else was to know. *Ever!*

So after midnight, he'd decided to ditch the evidence that would connect him with the accident. *My word*, Jon recalled, *I'd forgotten all about the Good Book until Paul died.*

Once reminded of that night, Victoria's buried treasure haunted him. The Bible must have been special or why else would it have been spared? The idea wouldn't let him rest.

Not that he had believed in God at the time, but those had been his thoughts. What he'd seen and done that stormy evening was still fresh in his memory like it had happened yesterday.

But the new Jon didn't have time to think about that now. He had to prepare a counter-attack to any evil plans that his daddy had up his sleeves for the beautiful, resurrected lady.

Did Victoria have any idea of the danger she was in?

17

After leaving Dick Branson's office Thursday morning, Victoria aimlessly drove around Fernwood attempting to corral her anxious thoughts before returning home.

So what did Karen think about Dick's business practices? She plugged her Mercedes into her usual parking space in the garage.

"Karen?" Victoria called out as she unlocked the kitchen door.

The ominously silent condo signaled that nobody was home. Disappointed that she couldn't quiz her daughter regarding Dick's trustworthiness, she changed into a pair of Karen's shorts and a white tee. Unfriendly thoughts tortured Victoria's mind as she considered the possibility that the material evidence pointing to Jeffrey's killers might no longer exist.

Then what would she do? With leads quickly vaporizing, did she honestly believe she could solve a twenty-five-year-old crime when the police couldn't?

Victoria browsed through Karen's library, keeping a sharp eye on the clock. Maybe she'd watch some TV. *Where was it?* She glanced around the den. Surely television hadn't become obsolete! Change was too new and too fast. She grunted with exasperation.

She found the operating manual on the fireplace mantel and flipped a switch on the remote. *Well, well, science is pretty tricky.* She watched a big screen roll down the wall. Settling into a rocker, she prepared to be entertained.

But watching the five o'clock news had been a huge mistake since it painfully reminded her of how drastically society had changed. *Why me, Lord?* Victoria crouched in the deepening shadows of the dying day, depression settling like a black fog.

When Karen hadn't returned by six thirty, she made herself a bologna sandwich and read some Scripture from one of the International Religious Ethics Committee's approved literature selections. An hour of so passed and Victoria grew nervous.

Where is Karen? She agonized, anxious to quiz her daughter regarding the weird bond between Dick Branson and Mark James.

Worse, dare she ask Karen if she had an abortion? It was inconceivable that she had resided in the same town with her daughter and allowed such a thing to happen. There were alternative choices to abortion like adoption. How could she have stood by and let anyone kill her own grandchild?

As the hour grew late, Victoria switched on the radio to pass the time. Tuning the dial to her favorite Christian gospel station, she immediately noticed a style change in the music. A few of the slower songs sounded weirdly off key. New Age, they called it.

Others songs had chaotic melodies, their lyrics too repetitive, producing an uneasiness in her spirit. The writers had sadly missed conveying salvation's critical message: *Jesus is the way, the truth, and the life!* She continued to listen, to be fair in her evaluation.

It wasn't long before the station management issued a statement regarding the edited comments and musical selections, claiming an IREC committee had edited the program.

"What a cop-out!" Victoria lamented.

Who did these buzzards think they were?

"Censorship! That's what it meant." No longer could the gospel truth be aired. So who proclaimed Jesus Christ's death, burial, and resurrection to the unsaved world?

Victoria switched off the radio and sat in silent darkness. Fighting discouragement, she did not want to believe that her own daughter had aborted a baby or that Christian radio had bowed down to secularism. This was a different world than she remembered.

Tears stung the retinas of Victoria's eyes like angry bees. Restored memories had only heightened her suffering. The inability to think would be far better.

Self-pity bears the stamp of pride, Victoria reminded herself. Satan functions well alongside the sulking, self-absorbed Christian, promoting creative ways to indulge the psyche.

"What happened to my enthusiastic belief, 'I can do all things through Jesus Christ?'" Her weighty thoughts became audible complaints. Tromping into her bedroom, she removed her diary from its secret hiding place and began penning her morose thoughts:

Thursday, April 17, 2014

I've had my old memories back now for four days. What I've learned about my society and how people think and choose to live disgusts me. Because I had a sexual relationship with a man outside of marriage, I distrust even myself.

I apologize for irresponsible choices made outside my faith-based beliefs. Dear God, please forgive my unholy life style. It was foolish of me to have substituted "blood money" for the truth, the Trust Fund for trust in You. I should have questioned my husband's untimely death and sought justice.

O Lord, please forgive my deceitful friends who have used me for selfish motives. I have been spiritually weak and morally gullible, fully deserving punishment. I accepted the world's standards, forsaking my first love in Christ Jesus.

Time did a number on me, Lord, and erased my spiritual history, making it far easier to accept false beliefs. I apologize for not standing up for my convictions, for surrendering my principles, and letting society's New-Age thinking rape me.

I was stripped of my dignity without even realizing it. Truth was trampled in the streets and I walked all over it. Dear God, if it weren't for Your redeeming grace, I would be condemned and judged unclean this very moment . . .

Victoria could no longer bear to record her troubling thoughts in the diary as tears dripped from her eyelids, smudging the black ink on the paper. Falling on her knees, she humbled herself before God and prayed that He would forgive her for miserably failing.

Reminded of Elijah, the Bible prophet who had prayed for rain to quench a thirsty land, Victoria petitioned God to rain down hope in her soul. Not until she had felt the Holy Spirit's powerful touch and experienced God's cleansing forgiveness did she arise and prepare for bed. Sleep would be blissfully sweet now.

A smile curled Victoria's lips. The depression had lifted. God had granted her the supernatural courage to face all her tomorrows and make wiser choices. Lifting hands in adoration, Victoria now felt equipped to bear a Christian witness to a misinformed society.

SUNDAY, APRIL 20

18

Victoria remained cloistered in her bedroom all day Friday and Saturday like an oyster in its shell. Karen had agreed that she needed time to rest and think before acting on her emotions and she used the time alone to meditate.

By Sunday morning, she had pretty much sorted through her strangled feelings and awakened feeling refreshed and slightly optimistic. While Karen slept soundly in her bedroom, she crept through the den and peered out the sliding-glass doors.

The patio flowers in red clay pots were wet with dew. Sweetly yawning, they lifted their frosted-pink heads sunward as if to say "good morning." Birds happily flitted from post to pillar, musically tweeting in their secretive languages, announcing another glorious sunrise.

Nature was rejoicing and Victoria thought she should, too.

Stepping outdoors, she inhaled the fresh spring air fragrant with herbs and newborn grasses. "Good morning," she heard Karen say.

Startled, Victoria spun around. "I thought you were asleep, dear." Her daughter looked a little weary around the eyes. "Late night?" Rest was required to maintain good health.

"Saturday is *Girls Night Out*, haven't you heard?" Karen joined Victoria on the patio. "Guess I'll go down for the morning paper," she yawned. "As the world turns, you know."

"I can do that," Victoria volunteered. "You sit and rest."

"No, I don't think so." Karen tossed a sideward glance. "Last time you did that you came back a changed woman! Think I'll perform this little task all by myself." She skipped down the steps.

A husband and a couple of kids would tone down my daughter's cynical attitude a bit! Victoria huffed to herself.

At least, Karen should have an adoring guy in her life, someone who would occasionally surprise her with fresh flowers or take her out to dinner.

Girls Night Out, my eye! Karen's marriage had done a real number on her. Victoria watched her child racing across the yard, carefree as a seven-year old on a Popsicle mission.

"Brrr, it's chilly out this morning!" Karen remarked as she returned with the paper. "Didn't somebody tell the weatherman it was spring? Here, you read the news while I make the coffee." Karen handed her mother *The Fernwood Gazette* and rushed indoors.

"Wait! I'm coming, too." Victoria trailed Karen into the den, tightly closing the sliders behind her, eyes glued to the startling headline: WORLD LEADER REIGNS WITH GRACE.

"Now, that's rather scary!" Victoria envisioned the Antichrist figure in the Bible as she read the entire article, ignoring the lump rising in her throat. *This is unbelievable!*

"So what's new?" Karen sauntered into the den and lit a fire in the hearth. "Me." Victoria handed her the paper. "The news is beyond me."

"Mother! That's a weird stance to take regarding current events!" Karen reacted rather harshly. "You can't ignore progress!" She wasn't smiling. "You need to get real."

Victoria stiffened, retrieving a book from the library shelf entitled *Selections from the Bible: The Minor Prophets.* "Real? Would you mind telling me why there isn't a complete version of the Bible in your vast book collection? That's real." *Progress stinks.*

Karen sharply eyed her mother. "Sure. Because there isn't one."

"What?" Victoria's heart quickened.

"Mother, a great deal has happened that you don't recall."

"Obviously," Victoria mumbled before trudging into the kitchen. "Can I get your coffee, dear?" The Lord's Day wasn't getting off to as great a start as she'd envisioned.

"Sure. Cream and one sweetener, please," Karen replied.

Heart-stung over the news article, Victoria fixed their coffees and returned to the den. Handing Karen a steamy mug, she cradled her own cup as she crouched beside the fire.

"What you said about the news . . . well, you were right."

"Right about what?" Karen curiously peered at her mother.

"About me. There's a gap in my memory as large as the Grand Canyon. I'm not exactly up on current issues, you know . . . so why don't you tell me what I've missed?"

"I'll have to give it to you, Mother, you're a brave soul." Karen's mind recycled as she recalled headlines of old. "Well, for starters, Russia collapsed in 1990."

"Russia did what?" Victoria nearly dumped her coffee mug.

"It just crumbled inwardly, Mother. Tired of Communism, the citizens of Russia were emotionally, spiritually and economically broken. The revolt favored free enterprise."

"I don't believe it!" Victoria's mind did a tailspin. "After four decades of cold war and the arms race?" Her temples pulsated with anticipation. "What else happened?"

"The Berlin wall came down and a unified Germany existed for the first time in half a century." Karen set her mug on the coffee table, grabbed a fire iron, and poked the sizzling logs until flames leaped. "The nineties were troubled years." Karen collapsed on the carpet, feet doubled under her. "Terrorism increased."

"Terrorism?" Victoria sighed, having difficulty comprehending all she was hearing. *Why can't I recall those events?*

"Oh, and the Oklahoma City Federal Building got nuked."

Appall riveted Victoria's face. "People were killed?"

"Hundreds of them. Children, too," Karen sadly replied. "They caught the guilty guy and executed him. Turned out he was a disgruntled American soldier with a grievance to air."

"I'm listening." Victoria prepared her heart for the worst.

"The World Trade Center in New York was bombed in '92," Karen continued. "Scores of people were injured." She paused, noting the shock on her mother's face.

"In 2001, in the name of Allah, the Arabs came back to finish the job. They drove two airplanes into the twin towers and took them down. Thousands of people were working that morning when the commercial airliners hit."

Horror reflected on Victoria's shadow-washed face. "Innocent people on planes died?" There was no way to process the devastation and grief that must have followed.

"Are you all right, Mother?" Karen realized she'd covered a great deal of information. "We don't have to do this today."

"Yes, continue please," Victoria consented to more revelation.

"Computers became indispensable in the late nineties as more people began to transact business over the Internet, and—"

"Karen," Victoria interrupted. "I don't understand how the Internet works." Kathryn Billingsly had tried to explain and failed.

"It's a media system that operates off satellite. You dial up a service on your telephone and connect to any other computer at any location in the world. You can type a message at your personal terminal and launch it in seconds. They call it e-mail."

Victoria swallowed hard. "What about the Bible?"

"I'm getting to that." Karen's thoughts raced ahead. "Electronics were being developed at warp speed in the nineties. Technology exploded, particularly in the field of genetics. Cloning became possible with sheep. Oh, yeah, in 1999, our president was caught with his pants down and nearly got impeached!" She giggled, though it was far from funny then.

"What?" Victoria gasped. "I'm afraid you've lost me."

"Infidelity, Mom. Our Democratic President became involved with a woman half his age," Karen explained. "The House voted to impeach him, but the Senate acquitted him."

"Was he actually guilty?" Hot coffee stung Victoria's tongue.

"Yep, but nobody wanted to kick him out. He was, after all, our President." Karen preferred to dismiss the past and look to the future.

"What about the Bible?" Victoria remained focused.

"Patience, Mother, I'm getting to that," Karen replied. "Terrorism worsened toward the close of the century. School bombings and mass murders occurred. In some cases, kids did it."

"What?" The coffee sloshed in Victoria's mug.

"U.S. embassies around the world became the targets of Arab terrorists. NATO waged a war in Kosovo against the Serbs to protect its Albanian population from religious annihilation."

Victoria gritted her teeth at Karen's devastating details.

"Mother! Religious sects were at each other's throats. The Arabs and Jews argued over Palestinian territory, practicing terrorism while they went through the motions of negotiating a peace settlement. While Irish Protestants and Catholics failed to resolve their differences, the Curia was falling apart because of homosexual acts committed by priests."

"Karen! This is unbelievable."

"I'm not finished," Karen continued. "Minority races were victimized. Nazism was on the rise in Germany, and the Ku-Klux-Klan revitalized its efforts in America. Right-winged Christians harassed Prochoicers for supporting women's abortion rights while pleading with Congress to change the law that supported it!"

"Need I go on?" Karen grabbed a breath.

"Karen, why was abortion such a problem?" Victoria found an inroad to question her daughter regarding Beverly James' recent accusations, to clear up the misunderstanding once and for all.

"Isn't it obvious that women around the world want the right to make choices about their own bodies?" Karen's words wore barbs.

So she had touched a festering spot . . .

"No one should dictate when a woman can have a baby!" Karen flared. "Sometimes it's best if you don't give birth!"

Karen's eyes were ablaze with churning emotions. "You're talking about yourself now, aren't you, dear?" It was time to say something.

"How did you know, Mother? Did Mark tell you?"

"No, I just heard." She didn't want to involve Bev in hearsay.

"You don't, uh, know the whole story, Mother!" Karen stuttered, growing more upset. "No way would I have had that monster's baby." She was emotionally unraveling.

Monster? Victoria was shocked at Karen's description of her deceased husband. "Isn't that a little harsh, dear? Certainly, I'd like to hear your version of the incident when you're prepared to tell me. As your mother, I'll try to keep an open mind."

"Thank you." Karen's stern gaze crumbled. "That's the sweetest thing you've said to me since, since . . ." she didn't complete her sentence, exasperated from her tirade.

Since her memories had returned. Victoria felt ashamed for handling relationships so poorly. Haughty and overly pious, not unlike the Pharisees had acted toward Jesus Christ, she had made unjust demands on Karen and Mark, misjudging friends like Kathryn Billingsley and Gloria Gordon who only wanted to help.

"What about the Bible?" Victoria asked again.

"I can see that the Bible is important to you." Karen's misty eyes, swirling in browns and greens, rolled on her mother. "To say that religious conflict became a problem is a vast understatement."

"Tell me," said Victoria. "All of it."

"1999 was a scary year. People feared the confusion the new millennium would bring. Panicking over the unknown, propelled by the news media, thousands of people rushed out to purchase home-survival kits and electric generators. Since computers were not programmed to handle dates past year 2000, businesses spent millions updating their electronic equipment.

"Wow!" Fear did weird things to people.

"Most computer glitches were repaired by the time the dome fell at Times Square," Karen continued. "But at one point, the U.S. lost control of one of its surveillance satellites."

"That must have been frightening!" Victoria imagined the resulting chaos.

"Naw," Karen said. "Nobody knew about it until after the fact. Anyhow, that's the short version of Y2K." She hugged herself, shivering slightly from the chill in the room.

"2YK?" Victoria was puzzled.

"Y. 2. K. Year 2000, the millennium," Karen explained.

"Oh," Victoria mumbled, feeling stupid for asking.

"With the passage of the twentieth century, the volatility of the stock market increased. Shocked investors hastily scrambled to dump their stocks and reinvest their money elsewhere, only to reenter the market when the economy looked favorable. With day-traders playing investment-roulette, financial analysts had difficulty accurately predicting market changes."

"Wait, who's a daytrader?" Victoria inquired.

"People who buy and sell stocks over the Internet from their home office," Karen explained. "Before 2002 Internet stocks sky-rocketed, inflating the prices of both NASDAQ and BLUE CHIP stocks. Investors remained optimistic that prosperity would last."

"And it didn't, I assume," said Victoria.

"No, Enron came along, and the War on Terrorism didn't help."

"Enron? What war? I'm confused?"

"It's a lot to take in, isn't it?" Karen peered at her mother."

"Oh, brother, am I behind on the times."

"By 2005, human relationships worsened as people attempted to impose their brand of faith or politics on others. Any person in their right mind recognized it wasn't working."

"What wasn't working?" Victoria lost focus in taking it all in.

"The world, Mother!" Karen revealed. "Fortunately, a smart businessman recognized the need for a truce to end the bitterness and fighting between religious factions."

Uneasiness crept into Victoria's spirit as she listened.

"Most people were pleased when Alexander Luceres Ramnes and his committee devised a workable plan to end religious conflict." Karen's eyes sparkled with intrigue.

"The man mentioned in this morning's paper, the one who reigns with grace?"

"Exactly. NATO approved IREC's document requiring that the most basic precepts of all holy doctrines be incorporated into one Holy Creed to which all peoples could relate."

A cold wind blew through Victoria's heart.

"Fourteen months ago, representatives from all faiths signed a peace pact agreeing to create a new document that would reflect a consensus of religious thought."

"Even the Jews?" Victoria's eyes widened.

"Well, the Jews are still a problem," Karen admitted.

"So what happened to the *real* Christian Bible?"

Karen sucked in her breath. "The IREC appealed to religious persons around the world to give up their religious documents and—"

Victoria gasped. "And they burned Bibles."

"No, nothing as dramatic as that!" Karen shook her head. "Affiliates of all religions voluntarily turned in their Bibles in lieu of an updated IREC approved version."

"What document can improve on the Bible?"

Karen digested her mother's narrow view. "Primarily, the one-world document dealing with human relationships. It's called the *International Book of Religious Ethics*."

"So what happened to the *real* Bibles?" Victoria was relentless.

"Book presses extracted those portions of the Bible that didn't comply with IREC regulations and rebound them," Karen explained. "You've seen the various editions in my book case."

"Ah so . . . the creation of books like *SELECTED PASSAGES FROM THE BOOK OF PSALMS* and *NEW TESTAMENT HIGH-LIGHTS*." Victoria had become a misfit in her world.

"Exactly." Pride rested in Karen's face. "Wasn't that a neat idea?"

19

Later Sunday, Victoria accompanied Karen to the United Baptist Church of Fernwood. Standing on the front steps of the historic brick structure, she peered up at the church steeple and heard the ringing bells. Within these hallowed walls, she had accepted Jesus Christ as her personal Savior.

Taking a moment to regain her composure, Victoria climbed the concrete steps and followed Karen inside. Having been warned that people dressed less formally for services, she was wearing a dark tweed pantsuit, a white blouse, and comfortable pumps.

Friendly parishioners cordially greeted one another and found their seats in the sanctuary. From all the rows of empty cushioned pews, Karen selected a seat near the back.

Typical Baptist, thought Victoria, troubled that the church's treasured eighteenth-century cross no longer stood behind the baptistery. In its place was a dove, the symbol for peace.

"Good morning, Vicki." Mark smiled from across the aisle.

Did she imagine it, or was there really a smirk on his clean-shaven face? "Oh, hello, Mark," she said, shocked that he had even bothered coming to church after his drunken behavior at the country club. But then, church was for sinners.

With no encouragement, Mark scooted from his seat, moved into the aisle, and stood at the end of Victoria's pew. "Vicki? Mind if I sit by you?"

Heads turned at Mark's loud overture. The engagement ring on Victoria's left hand burned a hole through her third finger as she reluctantly scooted over to make room for him.

"Thank you, sweetheart." He acted as if the country club scene had never happened. Squeaky clean and wearing his usual brand of mint cologne, he was polished to perfection.

Daring to look Mark in the eye, Victoria considered how his outrageous fire-engine-red tie seemed to assassinate his dark suit like blood splattered against a black wall. But Mark wasn't a victim like Jeffrey.

Behind his fond words, did he have an insidious agenda?

Seated indecently close, Mark leaned over and loudly whispered, "So Vicki, what do you think of the sanctuary's alterations?"

Sharply elbowing his side, she wanted to crawl under the church pew as scourging parishioners' eyes came to rest on them. Refusing to answer him, she focused on the talented musician playing a loud pipe-organ prelude.

Mark soon got the message and shut up.

When Victoria was a youngster, the old sanctuary had accommodated a couple hundred people. Now, with the enlargement of the foyer and choir loft, many more graciously smiling faces could fit into its plush padded pews had they chosen to come.

"They took down the big wooden cross," Victoria softly lamented. "Yes, they did." Mark patted her hand. "People don't like to be reminded of suffering."

"That's a strange remark for a Christian," she retorted, noting that Dr. Mark James was a continuation of negative surprises. "Shuu!" She scolded him when he attempted to explain.

The choir loft soon filled with trained voices offering a beautiful rendition of an unfamiliar choral arrangement. A youthful pastor wearing a regal-black robe and a winsome smile approached the pulpit and perused his congregation.

"Good morning," Dr. Daye said.

"Good morning" came the unanimous response.

"Please turn to page 114 in your *Universal Prayer Book*."

Victoria located the little green book in the back slot of the pew and turned to the reading taken from Psalms 6:1.

"Read with me," Dr. Daye said.

O Lord, do not rebuke me in your anger
or discipline me in your wrath.
Be merciful to me, Lord, for I am faint;
O Lord, heal me, for my bones are in agony.

My soul is in anguish.
How long, O Lord, how long?
Turn O Lord, and deliver me;
save me because of your unfailing love.
No one remembers you when he is dead.
Who praises you from the grave?

Following Dr. Daye's scripted prayer, the choir director signaled for the congregation to be seated. Sixty voices accompanied by a talented orchestra sang a beautiful arrangement of "Have Faith in God," its words and harmonies lifting spirits.

Distracted by Mark's overt behavior, Victoria had trouble concentrating on the service. At every opportunity, he made physical contact, whether in sharing a song book or fondling her shoulder as he nonchalantly placed his arm on the back of the pew.

At hearing the pastor's sermon on the stimulating topic of life's outpouring cup of suffering and pain, Victoria nudged Mark to remind him of his previous comment on hardships. In response, he playfully smiled.

Dr. Daye proved an eloquent speaker, using graphic illustrations of life's unfairness as he discussed the plight of disabled children and starving nations. Certainly, it was a timely subject to which Victoria could readily identify.

Hadn't her family unjustly suffered?

"Limited only by humanity's lack of faith," Dr. Daye said, "God desires to heal human frailties. But without a spiritually harmonized church, whose members accept human imperfections, the Creator's agape love cannot function at its highest level."

Pricked with guilt for having constantly criticized Mark's behavior, Victoria was forced to agree with what Dr. Daye said. She badly needed to work on her level of tolerance.

In conclusion, Pastor Daye implored his congregation to meditate on the Scriptures, rid their minds of disruptive thoughts counterproductive to faith, and firmly commit their daily lives to caring for others. Then church was suddenly over.

What? Pastor Daye had at no time mentioned the word sin or offered an altar call to the unsaved. Where was the old-fashioned invitation for salvation, the pastor's plea for sinners to be washed clean in Christ's holy blood?

Stunned, Victoria slipped from the sanctuary. So religion had come to this! Simply an invention of man's self-worthiness!

Couldn't people see they were missing the mark?

"How about lunch, Vicki?" Mark draped an arm about her shoulder. "Or we could take a drive into Jackson?"

Resenting his suggestion, Victoria quickly said, "Karen and I, uh, we already have lunch plans." Her eyes chased after Karen.

"I don't have plans," Karen said to Mark.

"Then why don't we go somewhere nice and have a wonderful Sunday brunch?" His gaze shifted to Victoria. "Of course, you're welcome to tag along if you like."

"We'd love to!" Karen caught Mark's arm, glancing Victoria's way. "Unless you want to make us all lunch, Mother."

Outvoted. What more could she say?

The day was bright with low humidity. A southerly wind disbursed a delicate floral fragrance in the air as the temperature comfortably approached the high sixties.

Mark walked over to his BMW to make sure it was locked. "We'll ride with you, Karen." Three people wouldn't fit in his convertible.

"Fine." Karen retrieved her keys from her purse and popped the locks to her Cadillac. "You drive and I'll sit in the back." She tossed Mark the keys and climbed inside.

Mark walked around the front of the car and politely opened the door for Victoria. "Where are we going?" She prayed the destination wasn't Jackson.

"Since my first idea seems distasteful . . ." Mark had the audacity to wink at Karen. "Why don't we take a drive over to Whiteville. I hear a lovely new restaurant has recently opened."

Karen agreed it was a fine idea and Victoria consented.

The paved highway cut a white swath through the rolling green countryside. Wherever Victoria looked, new developments were springing up, condominium copycats like all the others she had seen. Being *different* had become a problem for Americans.

A few miles down the road, Victoria noticed the antiquated buildings on the premises of the mental institution. "What's happened to Western State Hospital?" It looked deserted.

"Pretty much shut down," Mark replied. "A couple buildings are still occupied, housing mostly indigents who can't afford private psychiatric care." He noted Victoria's distress.

"Why is that?" she inquired.

"Well, the majority of the mentally disturbed live in private hospitals or group homes nowadays." Mark hoped his explanation would satisfy Victoria's curiosity.

"What a shame! You'd think our government would take better care of the sick, elderly and deranged!" she passionately declared.

"There are few sick and elderly," Karen interjected.

"What?" Victoria glanced back at her daughter.

"What Karen means . . ." Mark took over, worry tainting the corners of his blue eyes, "is that few people reach that existence before choosing voluntary cessation."

"What?" Victoria cranked her body to the side and eyed Karen. "What about Mother and Dad? Are they still living?"

How could she have forgotten about her parents?

The dark centers of Karen's hazel eyes raced between Mark and her mother's poignant gaze. "Grammy is still alive. She is in an assisted-living facility near Nashville."

"What about Dad?" Alarm circled Victoria's brain.

"He chose voluntary cessation six months ago," Mark said.

"You mean my father killed himself," Victoria said it plain and simple. "I don't believe it!" The idea gutted her. "Please tell me it isn't true."

"It's true, Vicki!" Mark slowed the Cadillac to a crawl, pulling off on the shoulder of the road before killing the engine. "I'm sorry you heard the news like this," he empathized.

Please, God, no! Victoria internalized the hurt.

"Vicki, look at me," Mark said. "It's not a bad thing. Your father was the best!" Could she understand he wanted it that way?

Devastated, Victoria's dilated pupils twitched as her liquid-brown eyes latched onto Mark's sympathetic blue gaze, a hurricane of nausea threatening to topple her.

"I'm sorry." Any explanation was grossly inadequate. "David Martin was one of the bravest souls I've ever known." He grasped Victoria's shoulders to steady her. "You should know that you shared quality time with him before his decision was finalized."

Quality time she didn't recall. "He chose to die?"

"Yes," came Mark and Karen's unified answer.

"Dear Lord, no!" Victoria doubled over and bitterly wept.

Mark and Karen waited a moment before tapping Victoria on the shoulder. "You should know that Big Daddy was ill with Alzheimer's." Her eyes flickered to Mark. "An attorney prepared the papers, so when he was deemed incompetent . . ."

"A doctor could end his life," Victoria finished Karen's sentence. Although her mind rapidly processed Karen's words, the grief of losing her father was nonetheless overwhelming.

Mercy killing had finally been approved in America. The courageous sick and elderly were expected to voluntarily remove themselves when they became a burden to society. The good of the whole outweighed individual rights.

Thomas Jefferson, turn over in your grave!

"Are you all right, Vicki?" Mark lent Karen his eyes.

Was there some kind of conspiracy going on here?

"Not really!" Victoria's temples throbbed with pain. In the shakiest of places, she envisioned a doctor standing over her father's bed administering a lethal dose of death. *God, help us all!*

"Can't you see she's not all right?" Karen barked at Mark. "How can we help, Mother?"

Transferring her sorrowful gaze on Karen, Victoria expressed the one desire of her heart. "When can I see my mother?" She was the prodigal daughter needing to go home.

"We'll go to Nashville next week," Karen promised. "I'll take a day off work. We'll visit Grammy on Wednesday. She loves for us to come. You'll see, it'll be all right."

"Oh, I don't know, Karen," Mark interrupted, putting a damper on the idea. "Vicki should schedule a visit to the hospital first. She needs a thorough exam to determine—"

"No, I won't go!" Victoria blurted out. "Scratch that idea for now! I don't intend to see the inside of a hospital until I have some answers about my life that makes some real sense!"

MONDAY, APRIL 21

20

Victoria decided to revisit Beverly James on Monday morning, purposely vague when Karen asked where she was going. Around nine, she slipped out of the condo.

After ringing Beverly's doorbell several times, Victoria was disappointed when no one answered. *Where are you, Bev?* About to turn and leave, someone called out to her.

"Excuse me." She noticed that a nosy neighbor stood a few feet away on his front porch steps. "Lady's moved away. Packed up her things on Friday and left out on Saturday."

"What?" Shock ricocheted through Victoria. "Do you have any idea where my friend has gone?" It seemed rather odd Bev hadn't mentioned moving.

"Heard she got assigned a new territory. For her cosmetics business, you know," the older gent recollected. "Seems to me the wife said it was somewhere out in Colorado."

"Oh." Victoria felt her chance at gathering evidence dissolving. Without an eyewitness testimony, who would believe a word she said, a crazy woman with amnesia on a mission impossible?

"Did Bev leave a forwarding address or phone number?"

"Nope. None of my business anyhow, Miss, uh . . ." the neighborly fellow crooked his head to one side.

"It's *Mrs.* Victoria Tempest," she introduced herself to the lone cowboy wearing scuffed boots, overall jeans, and a multi-colored western shirt. "And you would be?"

"Pretty name, Victoria," he replied with a toothless grin. No spring chicken, Bev's elderly neighbor was sturdily built and appeared in good health. "Once had a cousin named Victoria, but she died. Folks call me Frank." He ventured into the yard.

"I'm sorry about your cousin, Frank." Victoria took a step toward him, sensitive to his loss. "I'd really appreciate your help." Desperation overshadowed caution.

"Folks don't ask a lot of questions around here." Frank dug his roughened hands into his overall pockets. "A wrong answer just might get a feller into a heap of trouble."

Victoria was disappointed but not surprised. She'd heard that sermon before. *Some things are best left unsaid.* It might be a newer world, but it certainly wasn't a better one.

"If my friend comes back, will you tell her I'm looking for her?" Victoria pleaded more with her eyes. Frank's genuineness was the mark of a trustworthy fellow. "It's important."

"Sure." Frank chewed on a blade of grass, in no hurry to end the conversation.

"Thanks for coming out to talk to me." Victoria walked over and offered Frank her right hand, guessing she'd reached a stalemate. "You've been a big help."

"Anytime." Frank grasped Victoria's hand. "Cold hands, warm heart. Not a bad combination."

His comment seemed a little fresh, but warm-hearted nevertheless. Victoria gently pulled her hand from Frank's roughened grasp, thinking *not always.*

"Well . . . guess I'll be going now." She clutched her purse.

"See ya," he called out. "Don't be a stranger, ya hear?"

Glancing back, Victoria spied Frank's sly grin and half-wave, conscious of his watchful eyes on her back as she hurried to her Mercedes and slid behind the wheel. After he had gone inside, she sat in her parked car for a while contemplating the next move. She had one idea that just might pay off big.

Victoria cranked the engine and drove downtown. Luckily, she found a vacant parking space in front of the *Olde Soda Shoppe.* After locking up the car, she fed a couple coins into the timed parking meter and went inside. Maybe Gloria Gordon knew why Beverly James had left town so suddenly. She glanced around the drugstore. *Doggit!* The daffy blond was nowhere in sight.

The investigation into Jeffrey's murder wasn't going well. Victoria plopped down in a booth, struggling with depression.

"Can I get you anything, Miss?" A lad hustled over to the table and asked.

"Yeah. A banana split with all the trimmings." *A teen-impulse flashback thing*, Victoria supposed as she assessed her progress in solving Jeffrey's murder and became more depressed.

The dessert was as great as it had been back in high school. Halfway through it, she snagged the coattail of a waitress and inquired if Gloria had taken the day off.

"No," Sissy replied. "Miss Gordon quit her job on Saturday."

Quit? Victoria shoved the ice cream aside as it turned to lumps of soap on her palate. Her head began to throb as a knot formed in the pit of her stomach. What was going on? Was she being watched? Victoria reminded herself she was being paranoid.

In the event Gloria Gordon had taken a new job in town she would find her. But if her high school buddy had flown the coop like Bev had . . . her disappearance could mean more.

Victoria massaged her aching temples with her fingertips. *Who was keeping tabs on her?* She hunkered down in the booth. Was it Mark or Dick Branson? *Dear God! Please don't let it be my Karen!*

***

According to Kathryn Billingsly, Pearlynne Blackstone was the registered nurse who had provided home care for Victoria while she recuperated from her automobile accident. Perhaps Pearlynne could shed some light on her shadowy past.

Grabbing her purse from the table, Victoria ran out of the drugstore, leaped in her car, and drove straight over to the public library. Deciding to let her fingers do the walking, she located the public phone booth in the foyer and frantically perused the Yellow Pages.

"What are *you* doing?" A voice from behind startled Victoria.

"What?" She spun around too quickly and dropped her heavy alligator purse on her left big toe.

"Ouch! You frightened me, Kathryn!" Victoria grabbed her

aching foot with a hand, hopping around like a bunny on the other foot. "Shame on you for sneaking up on me like that!"

"I wasn't sneaking." The nosy librarian shifted her gaze to Victoria's injured foot. "What are you doing?" She picked Victoria's purse off the floor.

"I heard you the first time!" Victoria nastily snatched her purse from Kathryn's hand. "What does it look like I'm doing?"

"You can use my desk phone if you need to make a call."

"Thank you," Victoria said, uncertain if she'd broken a toe.

"Who were you phoning, anyhow?" Kathryn glared.

Was she genuinely interested or just prying? Victoria wondered. Dare she involve the town gossip? Hadn't everyone she questioned thus far turned up missing?

"Actually . . ." Victoria said, "I was about to call my daughter's office to let her know where I was." A lump of conviction clogged her throat as the little white lie slipped out.

"Oh?" Kathryn's penciled eyebrows lifted. "Is this in connection with the coma article you are writing?"

Why didn't the fuddy-duddy go back to work? Victoria considered coming clean, telling Kathryn the article had been a ruse and she was looking for her old nurse.

"Victoria? You're green around the gills."

"I'm fine." She was shaking from the lies.

"I was about to take a break, dear. Do you have luncheon plans?" Kathryn's feathers didn't appear the least bit ruffled. "Perhaps you would like to join me?"

"Sure, why not?" Victoria had nothing better to do. Besides, she was hungry and it would give her the opportunity to question Kathryn regarding the whereabouts of her old nurse.

"Why don't you leave your car in the library parking lot and we'll take my Honda?" Kathryn suggested. "I have my own reserved parking place in the high-rise garage."

Whoop-de-do. Victoria trailed the librarian outside. Inhaling the pollen seed odors from a variety of budding plants, she unexpectedly sneezed three times.

"Oh, excuse me." Victoria scrubbed her leaky nose.

"Bless you!" Kathryn crossed the street. "You need an antihistamine."

"Right." Victoria sneezed again. "Guess I've got hay fever." She pulled a tissue from her purse and vigorously blew. It wasn't like her to be allergic. At least, not that she recalled.

"Oh, dear, I hope you're not catching a cold." Kathryn was the overprotective type. "Maybe you should see a doctor."

"I'm usually pretty healthy." Victoria hoped it was true.

"So when can we expect you back at bridge?" They entered the parking garage and took an elevator to the fourth floor.

Bridge was not a subject Victoria cared to discuss so she answered offhand, "Oh, I'm taking a little break." Kathryn rather insistently discussed the complexity of party bridge as they hopped into her Honda and zipped out of the garage.

Already regretting having accepted the luncheon invitation, Victoria thought she could better identify with a lonely twig snipped from its life source than the rules of party bridge.

"Oh, my." Kathryn noted her guest's pensive mood. "I've never seen you so quiet. Are you worried about the many details of pulling off a wedding?" The Honda turned a corner.

"Where are we going to lunch?" Victoria skirted the "wedding" subject, needing more time to organize her comments regarding her projected life. Certainly, she was unprepared to publicly announce that she had no intention of ever marrying Mark James.

Besides, there were far more important issues at hand than analyzing her uncertain relationship with the popular physician. At the top of her list was locating the misplaced Beverly James! And she'd give blood to know why Gloria Gordon quit her job.

"I know Mark is ecstatic about your wedding," Kathryn filled in the uncomfortable silence. "My guess is Allen will be his best man." She peeked over half-rimmed spectacles.

"Allen?" Victoria drew a blank. *Who the devil was Allen?*

"Allen Taylor, Mark's business partner," said Kathryn, as if to read Victoria's thoughts.

Caught! Victoria's face flushed a bright pink.

"Are you certain you're all right, dear?"

"Actually, I'm developing a terrible migraine." Victoria clasped her forehead. Stress was a murderous ally.

"Oh, I'm so sorry," the librarian whipped her Honda into a parking space outside an impressive two-story restaurant. "If you don't feel like eating . . ."

"I do. I'm hungry." Victoria managed a smile. "Really."

"Good, because I checked and the blackberry cobbler is on the dessert menu today." Skinny Kathryn never counted calories.

"I didn't think the fruit was in season yet. July, isn't it?"

"Bud gets his blackberries from all over. His chef is world-renowned. We may be small town, but folks here think big."

"Yeah," said Victoria, thinking of Dick Branson's big ego.

"Shall we go inside?" Kathryn asked. "I want to get a table before the restaurant gets crowded." She opened her car door and got out. "Coming, dear?"

21

Victoria peered up at the tremendous white columns supporting the massive front porch of the prestigious eighteenth-century home turned restaurant. Elegant French doors steadily opened and closed as customers passed from the present into the home's enchanting historic foyer. Mounting the steps, Victoria only hoped that the food would be as enticing.

"They've recently changed the luncheon buffet," Kathryn said. "Everyone is raving over the food. By the way, didn't Bud Lindsey graduate with you?"

"High school?" Victoria recalled a skinny red-haired lad a couple years younger who had played a mean clarinet in the band. "Oh, yes. Bud!" She fumbled through her purse for Tylenol.

Kathryn placed their names on the restaurant's waiting list while Victoria located an empty seat by the door. Still early for the working luncheon crowd, the wait was short.

Victoria trailed Kathryn into the restaurant proper and was greeted by several people who apparently knew her well.

Or believed they did.

They were seated at a round, glass-topped table with a nice window view of the herb gardens out back. After their server had brought them cloth napkins, silverware, menus and water glasses, Victoria gulped down two painkillers. Maybe Mark was right to suggest that she see someone about her headaches. One little upset and the pain was hopping.

"Baby, I didn't know you were planning to lunch here," a husky voice pierced the cacophony of restaurant sounds.

"Mark!" Victoria's thrashing hands nearly dumped her glass of water. Did he just call her *baby*? "What are you doing here?"

"I'm glad to see you, too." Mark planted his hands on the table and fondly leaned over, blowing his breath in her ear.

Obviously embarrassed, Kathryn lowered her head.

"Hello, Kathryn." Mark erected his body, hooking his arms over his chest in preparation to linger. "How's George doin'?"

George was Kathryn's husband—that much Victoria knew.

"Want to join us for lunch?" Kathryn asked Mark.

Victoria choked on her water. *Get a grip.*

"Thanks, but no thanks," Mark declined, seeing the idea troubled Victoria. "Allen and I have business to discuss."

"Allen's here?" Victoria's quick eye-frisk of the restaurant landed on a tall, baldheaded, jockey-type in his fifties on his way over to their table. A giraffe in motion, the surgeon's violet eyes sparkled with such vigor they upstaged any other shortcomings he might have had. Her breath was taken away as Allen's dynamic personality and booming voice stormed the table.

"Mark, there you are!" Allen's gaze landed on Victoria. "You ravishing creature, where have you been keeping yourself?" His resonant laugh was deep. "I'd be jealous if you didn't belong to my partner here! Hope you don't mind if I borrow your man for lunch."

"No problem." Relief swept over Victoria. "Actually, I'm Kathryn's guest and we have a few things we need to discuss, too."

"Good." Allen chuckled. "Then I won't feel guilty for stealing Mark away from you this once." He crossed workout arms over his pumped-up chest. "Did you already get us a table?" He asked Mark.

"Vicki, can I see you tonight?" Mark whispered in Victoria's ear.

"Call me at home later," she mumbled, embarrassed over Mark's drooling. Kathryn was soaking in the scene like a sponge, her opinion likely to spill all over Fernwood at some point.

"Ain't love grand? Nothin' like the real thing!" Allen remarked.

"Yeah!" Mark snapped to attention. "Call you later, Vicki." He tossed a sassy wink and strutted off, leaving Victoria to wonder why his presence had disturbed her so deeply.

In all fairness to Mark, she must have once loved him. Wasn't she still wearing his engagement ring?

Alone at the table with Kathryn again, Victoria considered how to broach the subject of Nurse Pearlynne Blackstone. About to pop the question, the perky waiter showed up.

"What shall it be, ladies?" Joe inquired. "Be sure and leave room for our great desserts. The blackberry cobbler is superb." His electronic pen was poised to take their orders.

"What will you have, dear?" Kathryn looked at Victoria.

"The luncheon buffet is fine by me." She shut her menu.

"Make that two buffets and put it on my bill," Kathryn generously announced.

"You don't have to do that, Kathryn. Dutch is fine by me."

"No, I want to," she replied. "You've been through so—"

"Much!" Victoria jumped in. "Kathryn, I don't want your pity."

"No. Lunch is my pleasure. Honestly."

"Then thank you," said Victoria, thinking that in some weird way Kathryn would have made a better weasel than a human being. Reminded of Dr. Daye's Sunday sermon on tolerance, she shoved aside judgmental thoughts. "Kathryn?"

"What, dear?" The librarian's open gaze reflected interest.

Victoria mustered the courage to pop her question. "I was just thinking I'd like to invite my old nurse to my wedding."

"Pearlynne Blackstone?" It was Kathryn's turn to strangle on her water. "Whatever for? I haven't heard that woman's name mentioned in eons! She'd be old as sin by now."

Victoria ignored Kathryn's smugness. "I just think it would be nice to include as many of my, our old friends at the wedding as possible." She quickly corrected her pronoun.

"Isn't this a drastic change of plans, Victoria? I was under the distinct impression that the wedding was a private affair." Kathryn punctuated private. "At least, according to Mark."

According to Mark, Victoria reddened. That wasn't a Bible quote. Kathryn was probably upset because she hadn't yet been invited to Fernwood's most talked-about wedding.

"Of course, you and George are to be included," Victoria hurriedly spouted, quickly rectifying her social error. Kathryn had been most helpful and didn't deserve to be overlooked.

"I wasn't fishing for an invitation, Victoria!" Kathryn seemed truly embarrassed as she shifted her colorless gray eyes to the window. "The flower garden is lovely, isn't it?"

Victoria placed her hand over Kathryn's. "Look, inviting you to the wedding was my idea. How could you have possibly known that we were expanding out guest list?"

"You're sure that George and I won't be intruding?" Delight rested on Kathryn's rather plain face. "Shouldn't you consult Mark first?"

"It's not necessary." *If there is a wedding.* "Inviting Pearlynne to our wedding is entirely my idea, as a wedding surprise for Mark."

"Oh, the doctor will be surprised! Really surprised." Kathryn patted her dainty lips with her napkin. "Believe me, Victoria, I'd pay plenty for a front row seat to that event!"

When were the lily-white lies going to stop?

Flabbergasted over the depth of deceit she proliferated, Victoria said, "I have a confession to make, Kathryn. When you saw me at the library earlier, I was actually looking for Pearlynne's phone number."

"Goodness, Victoria, why didn't you say so in the first place?" The old helpful Kathryn bounced back. "You certainly won't find her name in the Fernwood Phone Directory!"

"What?" Victoria's head did a forty-five.

"Pearlynne moved to Memphis some years back to work for the Methodist General Hospital. The downtown branch, I believe. I'm surprised you didn't know that."

"Oh, I'd forgotten," Victoria shot back, the truth this time. Why not drive over to Memphis and look for Pearlynne. While there, she could contact a reputable detective agency.

"I'm sure if you contacted the hospital, they would know how to find Pearlynne." Kathryn leaned her arms on the table.

"You think?" Victoria was encouraged.

"My goodness, your old nurse would be pushing ninety by now. She never married and has no living relatives to my knowledge. It's my guess she still volunteers every time they let her."

They both had a good chuckle.

"Thank you, Kathryn. I appreciate your valuable input. And do you mind keeping my guest list secret? I really do want to surprise Mark."

"Sure," Kathryn agreed. "Why not?"

"I'm starved, let's eat!" Victoria tossed her napkin aside.

22

After lunch at Lindsey's Restaurant, Kathryn quietly drove Victoria back to the library. "Oh, dear me, would you look at the time?" The punctual librarian rolled the green Honda into her designated slot in the parking garage and shut down the motor.

"Thanks for a lovely lunch." Victoria eyed Kathryn as she hopped out of the car. "Don't worry about me, I'll take the elevator down. I know my way around, you go on to work."

While driving away in her Mercedes, Victoria found herself planning a dinner menu that would please Mark James. No, scheming was a better word for what she was doing.

So what's up my slippery sleeve now?

Although Victoria's agenda was not totally formulated, the benefits of inviting Mark over for supper outweighed the risks. And what she needed to do next zeroed in loud and clear.

Locked away in Mark's calculating mind were clues she needed to proceed with her murder investigation. Once a little of his gray matter had been pried loose, some truth was bound to fall. To insure privacy, she would ask Karen to dine out.

Bearing down on the accelerator, tires screeched at every corner turned. *Time is of the essence.* Victoria squeezed the steering wheel. In the path of present dangers, there was no alternative game but to play Mark out. Hopefully, her plan would work.

A chill gripped Victoria's heart as she realized that solving a murder was a dangerous game she was unqualified to play. Whatever the outcome, she had to bait Mark. *Just do it!*

Biting the bullet, she located Mark's office building and ventured inside the impressive six-story concrete structure built around the turn of the twenty-first century.

The elevator ascended to the fourth floor and let Victoria out in the waiting room. From the number of people jamming his office, she guessed that the popular surgeon had absolute customer satisfaction.

The receptionist immediately recognized Victoria and told her that Mark was with a patient. Thanking Lillian, she took a seat and waited alongside the others. It wasn't long before Mark stuck his head around his office door and motioned for her to step inside his office. His wide grin expressed extreme pleasure.

"Vicki!" He kicked the door shut and corralled her in a bear hug. Uncertain how to respond, she prayed for courage.

"This is such a great surprise!" His shocking-blue eyes were alight with astonishment.

"What can I say? That I was in the neighborhood?" She tossed her purse on a chair and moved forward with her plan—which hadn't included Mark applying a moist wet kiss to her lips. Responding despite her resolve, she failed to squelch the unexpected thrill coursing her senses. Her suitor certainly had the ammunition to entice any woman.

"I see that mind working, Vicki." He released her and straightened his navy blue necktie. "What's up?"

"Mark, I—" nervousness stole Victoria's thunder as she realized how vulnerable she was to his charm. Standing so close, inhaling his cologne, pretending to care was so easy. She was considering chunking her plan.

"Why, honey," Mark sheepishly grinned, "you're blushing."

"No!" she adamantly denied it. "Yes." She giggled. "Actually, I am a little embarrassed over the kiss."

"Because it felt good?" He was delighted.

"The reason I'm here is to invite you to supper. At my place, can you come over around seven?" she blurted out.

"Sweetheart!" Mark embraced Victoria and wickedly nipped at her right ear. "You know I'm all yours."

"It's supper, Mark." She gently pushed him away, embarrassed over responding to him in the slightest way, realizing she had dug a muddy trench and would have to wallow in it, come what may.

"Maybe we could just skip supper and take a drive over to our place in Jackson. It's been way too long, Vicki." He kissed the soft tissue of her upturned palm. Then, noting her dour expression, he released her hand and chuckled. "Oh, well. Guess I'll have to wait until you're ready, Lady. Fasting always did pique my appetite."

Fasting? That's what he called it. Victoria bit back a negative response and said, "Then I'll see you later at my place. Don't be early, I still need to grocery shop."

"Surprise me!" Mark winked. "*Really* surprise me."

Victoria was certain that what she had in mind would surprise Mark. And she had several hours in which to devise her verbal menu. *Come on, Tiger, I'll be ready this time.*

"Oh, something else, Vicki." Mark fondly rubbed her shoulders. "I want you to check into the hospital and have an MRI. We'll schedule it for one day next week if that's suitable. Of course, after you've had a chance to visit your mother in Nashville," he sweetly added.

Touched over Mark's sensitivity, Victoria felt somewhat guilty for her scheming. But not enough to cancel her dinner plans. Still, the issue over her health was a valid concern.

"Sure, why not? I suppose I should find out what's causing my recurring headaches, though it's likely stress." Victoria sighed. "I'm not looking forward to being a patient again."

"Wise choice, Vicki!" Mark rocked on his toes, love written in his poignant gaze. "You're making a whole lot more sense than you did last week." He politely opened the door.

"Thank you again, Mark," Victoria smiled, squeezing his hand.

"For what?" He held tightly to her hand.

"Being concerned. For me and my worries over Mother."

"It's my pleasure," he grinned. "And I always take my pleasure seriously." He walked her to the elevator.

Mark's admiring gaze swallowed Victoria until the elevator doors closed between them. Queasy from the rapid descent, she had an unsettling thought. While attempting to manipulate him had she fallen victim to his charm?

A wise woman would proceed with caution! The talented Doctor Mark James was used to being in the driver's seat. *And he drives fast.*

She spied Jenson's Gourmet Market a few blocks away and

wheeled into the parking lot. Using a payphone, she called Karen's office to tell her about her supper plans.

"It's me," Victoria said when Karen answered, going on to explain why she had called. Gratefully, without being asked, her sweet daughter volunteered to make herself scarce.

Feeling she had the cat by the tail, Victoria hung up the phone and went inside the grocery store. Bob Jenson's mom-and-pop grocery had been in business for fifty years and still specialized in selling fresh meats, fruits and vegetables.

Bob saw her come in and waved.

After perusing the attractive array of crisp products splayed over ice chips, Victoria selected two pounds of large gulf shrimp and a variety of Chinese vegetables, preferring to make her own oriental sauce. Topping off her hand-carried basket with a variety of fresh herbs, she headed down the aisle toward the front of the store, passing the cooler. Should she serve wine with dinner?

Quickly deciding no, Victoria was aware of how poorly Mark usually handled any form of alcohol. And didn't she want to set a Christian example?

After checking out and paying her tab, Victoria drove a few streets over and pulled into a bakery. As a grand finale to her scrumptious meal, she was serving raspberry cheesecake.

Walking out of the bakery with two loaves of French bread under one arm, Victoria was pleased that she hadn't forgotten how to plan a meal, cook and graciously serve it.

Thanks to her wonderful mother.

Victoria was pleased to see that the cleaning service had paid a visit to the condo while she was away. All she needed to do now was prepare the meal, light a few scented candles, and get knock down gorgeous. As the minutes flew by, excitement mounted.

High on optimism, she felt close to a breakthrough in solving Jeffrey's murder. *Just stay focused.*

Around five thirty, Karen breezed in and out, pausing only to make a quick change of clothes, commenting that she was uncertain what time she'd be returning home.

Fine, Victoria had said, reminding Karen to phone if she had any problems. *A motherly thing*, she guessed.

After tossing aside several outfits, Victoria selected a pair of teal-blue polyester slacks to wear with a fluffy white angora sweater. Taking extra care in styling her hair, she applied a thin layer of makeup to her face and the slightest hint of mauve blush to her cheeks. Last to go on were jewelry, flats, and a hint of *Oscar de la Renta* perfume. *Perfect, let the games begin.*

After taking a final walk through the condo, Victoria lowered the thermostat, lit a host of scented candles, and set a glowing fire in the hearth. Stumbling on some old fifties music, she arranged the CDs in the desired sequence and set the sound system's timer.

Done.

Victoria spun around like a found Cinderella, surveying the den for aesthetic affects. Hearing soft romantic music in the flickering candlelight and inhaling the sumptuous odor of simmering Oriental sauce while warming by glowing embers was bound to weaken Mark's defensives.

She had set the perfect stage for revelation. Before the evening ended Dr. Mark James would tell her everything she wanted to know. *How could he resist?*

23

Although Victoria had planned for hours, she nearly jumped out of her skin when the doorbell rang. *Calm down, you don't have to do anything you don't want to do.* She sucked in a breath and hurried to open the door. As expected, it was Mark.

"Hi." A wide Cheshire grin spread across his pleased-as-punch face as he stepped inside the condo and closed the door behind him. "Wow! You look great."

"Hi, Mark." Victoria felt a lump rising in her throat. Having recently shaved and changed into casual clothes, Mark was wearing that same brand of mint cologne that spooked her every time. In his right hand was clasped a lovely bouquet of petit roses.

Am I making a mistake? She considered canceling their date.

"You don't know how happy you have made me, Vicki." Mark's eyes were huge windows of delight. "Here." He handed over the bouquet.

"Thank you, Mark. They're lovely." Victoria shakily walked over to the kitchen sink and placed the flowers in a crystal vase. Adding water, she set them on the dining table.

"The table you've set for us looks beautiful." Mark glanced around the den. "And just look at all the trouble you've gone to. Candlelight and everything." He inhaled the wonderful aroma of simmering Oriental sauce. "What's that I smell cooking?"

"We're having Chinese cuisine tonight," said Victoria, suddenly ashamed of her ruse. Perhaps she'd misjudged Mark's motives. Only a very foolish woman would sabotage a second chance at happiness. So what was she doing here?

"What is it?" Mark stepped closer.

"Nothing." She turned away when he grasped her hand.

"No so fast." He slowly rotated her around until they faced. "Don't look so troubled, honey. Let's just let tonight happen, all right? We have much to celebrate."

Celebrate? Victoria thought not. But then, how could Mark possibly understand? He'd never lost half a lifetime of memories, had a mate murdered, or suffered a traumatic accident.

"I'm taking it slow, remember?"

"You have to know how I feel about you, Vicki." Mark swept her into an embrace, a raging passion burning through his gaze. "Doesn't this feel right? Like we fit?"

Victoria longed to recall her former lover, his touch and her trust. But due to twisted circumstances Mark was only a friend, a very risky friend.

"We had so much together . . ." he choked up, "then suddenly, it was all snatched away. You weren't there for me anymore, Vicki. And I can't stand the loss."

"Loss?" She grasped Mark's hurt. "I changed, didn't I?"

"Change again, Vicki." Mark sweetly kissed her on the lips. "Give me back that wonderful woman who turned my life upside down and satisfied my every desire."

"I invited you to dinner, no—" the words slipped from Victoria's brain as Mark's arms closed around her and he whispered, "I love you so much, baby." Hearing his endearing words, it took all the willpower she could muster to resist falling under love's spell.

"No, Mark!" Victoria set her boundaries. "I've told you that I need more time to discover who I am before I know who we are."

Disappointment slapped him in the face.

Did Mark really believe that a kiss would change her mind? Is sex all their relationship was about?

"Patience is not my strong suit!" Mark's upper lip trembled as he let her go. "My arms are used to holding you."

"I know, and I'm sorry," she said, "but I need a little more time." She had to keep him pacified.

"How can I refuse when you ask like that?"

"Thank you." Victoria took Mark by the hand and led him like a little child into the den. "Sit here, on the sofa, and enjoy the fire while I bring in our meal." A CD kicked in on queue.

"Don't be long," Mark said. "Elvis Presley?"

"Yes," Victoria answered from the kitchen. "I found a few of Karen's old fifties CD's earlier today. Guess I'm not a modern girl anymore." She hurriedly prepared their plates.

"You never were," Mark called back.

"That's good, isn't it?" She suspected the former Victoria had been more daring. Now that her *Garden of Eden* was staged, what would she do next? Give Mark an apple and watch him eat? He was only human. And was she above temptation?

"Regardless, I'm back." *Didn't an actor coin that phrase?*

"Yes, you are," said Mark, chuckling.

Victoria placed their prepared plates on the coffee table, slumping down on a puffy pillow across from Mark. Grateful to God for His goodness, she bowed her head.

Mark stared a second, then followed suit.

"Dear Lord," Victoria began, "thank You for this food we are about to partake. Grant us the wisdom and patience to do Your will. Amen." She opened her eyes and looked at Mark. "Dig in, tiger."

"The blessing was nice, Vicki. You truly have a good heart."

"Why thank you, Mark." She fumbled with the Chinese chopsticks.

"Did I ever know how to use these?" He played the sticks on the coffee table like a drummer. "It was a joke, Vicki." He smiled.

During dinner Mark talked little, ate heartily, and tore into the generous portion of the cheesecake. Once again, Mark seemed like the good friend Victoria had so often counted on in high school.

Jeffrey had once written a sweet note on a napkin and sent it to her by Mark, his go-for. The girls on her cheerleader team had giggled when he traipsed out on the football field and delivered Jeffrey's message. The note said, "I miss you, Vicki."

Back then, when life's opportunities seemed unlimited, she had truly believed that there was nothing she and Jeffrey couldn't accomplish together. He was her anchor.

"Would you like seconds?" Victoria found her manners.

"No thanks." Mark came to his feet and smiled. "I can't recall ever being served a more tantalizing meal. I feel like a king in his palace!" He carried their used plates to the sink while she filled two mugs with hazelnut-flavored coffee.

"I thought you deserved a nice gesture," Victoria exclaimed, watching the surgeon wipe germs from the kitchen countertop with paper towels.

Removing her apron, Victoria headed into the den with their mugs. "Coming? Forget about the dishes. Let's sit and talk." She motioned with her head.

"I needed this," he sighed. "I thought I'd lost you." Mark sank to the floor, propping an elbow on a pillow with his back soaking in the fire's warmth. Cradling the mug with his right hand, he adoringly watched Victoria.

"I'm sorry, Mark. I've treated you poorly since—"

"Don't apologize, baby." He came to his feet and walked over to the sofa. "I can't imagine filling your shoes. You've been an amazingly strong woman."

"Have I?" Amusement clouded Victoria's vision.

"I only hope tonight means that you feel more at ease with me," Mark said. "Dinner was perfect. As you can see, I'm perfectly content to sit beside you, and . . ." he paused.

"And what?" Victoria curiously asked.

"I was going to say 'not touch you.' " He grinned. "So do I get an A for patience?" At least, he was trying. "Heavens, Victoria! I've trusted you with my heart!"

"Yes, you have." She nervously bit her lower lip. "Mark?"

"What?" He reached over and began to gently massage Victoria's neck with one hand. "Feel good, honey?" He set his mug aside and used both hands. "You are so tense."

"What about the 'no touch' policy?" The massage felt great.

"Oh," he said, removing his hands. "I forgot."

If she was ever going to get the truth out of Mark, it was now. "There's probably not ever going to be a right time . . ."

"Oh dear, I feel a serious question coming on."

"You promise you won't be mad," Victoria plowed infertile

ground. "I need to know if—" the words became glue on the roof of her mouth.

"Know what, sweetheart?" Mark had a quizzical expression.

"If *you* know why Jeffrey's killers were never prosecuted?"

Mark blinked with understanding, sat up, distaste flickering in his chilly gaze. His not saying anything was worse than a tongue-lashing.

"Is it so difficult for you to tell me the truth?"

Mark threaded his fingers through his hair, leaned forward and cupped his hands over his knees in preparation to stand. "So Vicki, is this why you asked me to dinner?"

"It's not a sixty-four-thousand-dollar question," Victoria exclaimed. "Either you know something about Jeffrey's death or you don't."

Disappointment crouched in Mark's blue gaze. "When you came by my office earlier today, I got the distinct impression you wanted to concentrate on us! Don't mind me, though, I'm a *sucker* for a good meal." There was no fool like an old fool.

"I've offended you, I'm sorry." Victoria didn't feel like apologizing, but she did. "I worked hard to prepare a meal that would please you. We had a wonderful time, didn't we? But you must realize there is no us until I solve Jeffrey's crime!"

Mark's head drooped; his lips, hard set. Pitiful half-shaded puppy eyes glared at Victoria in disbelief. "I had hoped tonight was about us! Above all, I believed you cared for me. We're not children anymore."

Victoria blinked with understanding. Mark was hurt.

"Is it so terrible to want to concentrate on *our* future?" He grasped Victoria's arm with force. "Look me in the eye, Vicki. Tell me that you don't care about me."

"I can't, because I do." It was the truth, though undefined.

"We've shared out souls and bodies, Vicki. You can't forget something like that. Don't torture yourself over Jeffrey's death. Let his soul rest."

"Don't you care what happened to Jeffrey the night he died?" She couldn't dismiss Mark's callous attitude toward her deceased husband. "You were his best friend."

"Of course, I care. But this is between you and me."

"Don't you think Jeffrey's angry that his killers were never brought to justice?" Victoria came to her feet and faced Mark. "Wouldn't you be?"

"Vicki, will you listen to yourself!" Mark squeezed her shoulders between his strong hands. "Jeffrey *is* dead!" His expression was raw. "You have to find the strength to carry on with your life. Isn't my love enough to satisfy you?" He was out of patience.

Hot tears dripped on Victoria's cheeks. "I wish I could respond to your love, Mark. I do. But I just can't! Not until I can put Jeffrey's memory to rest, once and for all."

Mark walked over to the fireplace and grasped the mantel with both hands. "You have to drop this matter! Jeffrey's investigation is over and closed. There is no recourse."

"There's recourse if I say there is!"

Mark turned around, his razor-sharp gaze slicing through Victoria's heart.

"Another matter is bothering me," she said.

"Should I ask? You're going to tell me anyhow," Mark's voice softened to a raspy whisper. "Get it out."

"What happened between you and *your* wife?"

"Beverly?" Mark reacted. "What's she got to do with this?"

"Maybe nothing." She would give him a chance to come clean.

"Exactly what is it you want to know about my past?" Mark felt like he was on trial. "Quizzing me like this is crazy, Vicki."

"Not if you're on my page," she declared. "Why did you divorce Bev?"

"Why are you bringing up old hurts, Vicki?"

"What secrets are you hiding, Mark?"

"This conversation is over." He picked up his jacket and walked over to the door. "I see nothing positive coming from this conversation. Dinner was nice and I'll see you tomorrow. Goodnight."

"Wait!" Victoria chased after Mark, making a U-turn in her strategy. He lingered a moment with his hand on the door handle.

"Unless you're going to apologize, I see no reason to stay," he said with his face to the door. "Seeing the way you feel, why would you want me to?"

"Granted I may have come on a little strong with my questions." Victoria made a last-ditch effort. "I apologize if I hurt your feelings. Please don't go yet." Mark was in her life, like it or not.

"Oh, honey . . ." Mark turned around and engulfed her in his arms. Like the ending to a perfect movie, he was so ready to forgive and let bygones be bygones. "We have so much to lose if we look back."

"That's not what I'm doing." Victoria's emotions intensified. "But I do have valid concerns about the past." She had Mark's undivided attention. "I need to hear from you why your marriage failed. From *you*, Mark!"

"And that will be the last of the questions?"

"Yes, if you'll tell me where you were the night Jeffrey died."

"I am not a suspect in Jeffrey's murder, if that's what you're asking. Vicki, I'm all you have." He could protect her.

Was he? "I'm having difficulty resolving your past into my future." Had the same money source that paid Mark's gambling debt also established her family's Gift Trust Fund?

"About my divorce," Mark decided to attack her first question. "Bev and I realized that we weren't in love. In fact, we questioned whether we'd ever been."

How shallow, Victoria thought. "Go on."

"It was Bev's decision to leave me."

"I know that," Victoria said too quickly.

"What? How could you know?"

"Because I recently spoke to her. And she had *quite* a lot to say about you." Would Mark lie to save face?

"You saw Bev?" Fear flooded his face. "What did she say? Tell me!" He cursed and grabbed Victoria's shoulders in a fit of rage, shaking her until her teeth chattered.

"Stop it, Mark!" She pounded his chest. "You're hurting me!"

Letting her go suddenly, Mark backed up as if he'd touched a hot poker, his palms upturned in a defense mode. "I didn't mean to hurt you, Vicki. Honestly."

"When have you been honest with me?" She was furious at his manhandling outburst. "You can't force me to do anything!"

"I don't mean to frighten you—" Mark's face was so close Victoria could feel his hot breath against her cheeks. "But you must tell me exactly what Beverly said. And don't *dare* leave anything out. You'll have to trust me on this one."

Trust? Victoria stepped away. *Tender, yet so violent.*

"I went to see Bev one day last week to tell her I had my memories back. She told me that you had acquired some debt back in the eighties."

Shock registered on Mark's face. Unlike her suitor, she was not afraid to tell the truth. "Your wife didn't trust you," Victoria cut to the chase. "Maybe I shouldn't either."

Mark's mouth fell open, clearly traumatized. "It's true I used to gamble, but I paid all my debts and quit," he admitted. "Do you believe me?"

"Maybe." She wasn't yet finished.

"Vicki, I love you. You changed me. Can't you see that?"

Had she? Mark could have fooled her.

"Please say you believe me. I've paid for my sins." Mark's gaze was icy blue. "I came by the money honestly. I have proof."

"All right, I believe you unless I find out otherwise."

"Thank you, Vicki." Mark's next move nearly sent her over the edge. She hadn't seen the guarded lust crouching in his eyes. Seconds later he was all over her, hands everywhere, smothering her in kisses and caresses.

"No, Mark! I can't! Stop!" She shoved him off her.

"Don't push me away!" His dark gaze was frightening.

Great! Now she faced a spurned lover.

"I want you to leave, Mark. Now!"

"No!" He pinned Victoria against the door. "You want this as much as I do." He made intimate advances.

"Stop it!" She kicked at Mark's shins as his hot hand covered her mouth. "Back off, Mark!" She broke his vise and clawed at his shirt. "If this is how you show love, I don't want any part of it." She ran into the kitchen and took a knife from the drawer.

"Get out!" She guarded her territory.

"This is so stupid." Mark regained his composure. "If I didn't love you so much, I wouldn't care so much. Go on, find your killers and see what happens to you."

"I'm not afraid of you, or Dick Branson."

"Listen to yourself, Victoria! You're inventing a crime scenario to satisfy your need for revenge. If you're smart, you'll marry me and try to be happy."

"Don't threaten me, Mark James. I won't be the recipient of your anger. Take your lust somewhere else and spend it on someone who cares!"

"Well, well," said Mark. "You've gotten to be quite the little psychologist, haven't you?" He saw her in a new light.

"Go ahead and make fun of me. But you can take this to heart! With or without your help, I'll see Jeffrey's killers brought to justice and behind bars if it's the last breath I take."

"Let it go, Vicki! You'll never live to learn the truth!"

"Threats again?" Victoria refused to be intimidated.

"You must know I'd never intentionally hurt you or Jeffrey." Mark's back was against the proverbial wall. How could he tell her the truth without incriminating himself?

"But you did agree to be the administrator of my family's trust fund!" Victoria lashed out. "And you did have my children sign a document stating they'd never reopen Jeffrey's murder investigation! Did you also have a part in Jeffrey's death?"

"Stop it, Vicki! His death was an accident."

"No!" Victoria shouted. "I'll never accept that!"

Mark's face was wrenched. "You need me, Vicki."

"No, I don't need you."

"Drop this matter now or . . ."

"Or what, Mark?" The knife was shaking in her hand.

"Or you'll be bitterly sorry if you don't!"

"I can't!" Sobbing, Victoria's knees buckled beneath.

"I'm so sorry, Vicki!" The knife hit the tile floor as Mark grabbed her. "I was too hard on you, baby." He rubbed her hair and kissed her cheeks. "Are you okay?"

"Am I really in danger if I pursue the truth?" Victoria pitifully lifted her troubled eyes, wanting to entrust her safety to Mark.

Mark stood up, fists knotted at his side.

"Answer me, Mark! For God's sake!" Victoria crawled to her feet. "Yes or no?" Was there an enemy lurking about?

Stern with restraint, Mark said nothing.

"And you say you love me! You hypocrite!"

"Yes! You're in danger!" Mark rasped.

TUESDAY, APRIL 22

24

Closed for Monday, Branson Meatpacking Company had long grown silent. Alone in his office after midnight, as was his preference, Dick planned to catch up on his real work. Outside, half a dozen night watchmen rambled about guarding Dick's prosperous enterprise. And in the old cold-storage warehouse, a trusted skeleton crew packed crates to ship overseas.

Although it was past time to go home Dick wasn't yet ready. In fact, he seldom wanted to go home at the end of any day. Not that he didn't love Marjorie dearly, he did.

Oh, she had her quirks and sometimes irritated him with her constant chattering, but what wife was perfect?

And he knew she would do her best to wait up for him, have something nice warming in the oven, just in case he did arrive home at a decent hour. Fact was Marjorie was probably way too good for him. Hadn't she stuck by him through two failed marriages?

Goodness, Dick kicked back in his chair. Marjorie had been his mistress decades before they decided to tie the permanent knot of respectability. She probably understood him better than his own mother. Despite his shortcomings, he truly believed she loved him.

Now that was the bones of a good marriage.

Over the years Dick had shared a lot of his chicken-soup soul with his third wife. However, Marjorie had no clue how he really earned his millions, and he preferred keeping it that way. He fondled a box of shrink-wrapped Havana cigars. After all, if she didn't know his daily agenda, how could she snitch on him?

Oh, Dick realized that if he delayed going home long enough, Marjorie would fall asleep on the sofa with the TV blaring and he'd have to wake her up and point her to the bed.

But he never apologized for coming home late. Why should he? A man had a right to his privacy.

All things considered, he didn't feel guilty about missing supper or getting home late. Besides, Marjorie always knew he'd do his best to make it up to her the next morning with a little extra tender loving. They had an understanding, a reasonable bond.

Dick heard the electronic humming of the wall clock, aware that it was after midnight. In Europe it was already Tuesday morning. He turned to his computer and keyed in the telephone number of his newest potential contractor, a man named Peter Coates.

"Peter! It's Dick Branson, here in the States. Hope I didn't catch you at a bad time." Dick was energized when working.

"No, Sir! What can I do for you?" The Tennessee businessman's picture flashed on Peter's computer screen, fading in and out due to a solar storm.

"Oh, just a friendly call." Dick wheezed as he drew in a breath. "Thought you'd be happy to know the shipment from Miami will be arriving at my place in a day or two. We'll be repackin' a sample and shippin' it your way by the end of the week."

"Great!" Peter exclaimed. "Our suppliers are antsy to get their hands on the, uh, merchandise." He almost said drugs, a no-no.

"I like to hear my product is in demand." Dick chuckled. "Puts a sense of pride in a man." He loosened his tight collar.

"Always pleased to do business with a man of stability and vision." Peter was aware that Dick had run a prosperous drug-trafficking enterprise since the early nineties.

"New business is my pride and joy," Dick said. "A man's gotta have goals, you know." He thought of his derelict son, Jon.

"So how's the family?" Peter cordially asked, having heard that Dick's third wife was a keeper. Few women were.

"Oh, Marjorie is fine. Little woman's a handful, though." Dick was a chatterbox. "Just us at home now. Jon's got an apartment, works part-time with me when he's not off chasing women."

Peter had heard that Dick's boy didn't take kindly to drug dealing, but wasn't the sort to make waves as long as Daddy fattened his bank account. Jon was born right after Dick married his high school sweetheart, but she hadn't stayed deluded too long.

Rumor had it that Dick met his fate over the toss of a dice. Jon would've been in his teens when his papa took a Miami cruise and happened on a drug lord. The young entrepreneur had envisioned his financial future when he had decided that shipping packaged meats was the perfect cover for supplying the world with its daily drug-fix. When Dick's Mafia buddy said, "Name the time, place, and amount," he hadn't hesitated to cut a pact with the devil.

"What did you say?" Peter zoomed in on Dick's words.

"I said, 'exactly who's headin' up this proposed expansion'?"

"The name of our corporation is Taurus."

"Taurus, yes." Dick tugged at his tight belt. "A bullish crew."

"Exactly!" Peter laughed. "Outside of me, our investors prefer to remain anonymous for obvious reasons. It's the Middle East we want to target." He didn't want to say too much over the airways.

"Intriguing." Dick skimmed the clear plastic wrapper from a box of cigars. Russia had tried distributing drugs to the Arabs and failed. The Muslims were more morally strict than Christians.

"I hear you've got plenty on your plate without taking on that motley bunch," Peter ventured to say. His cup was not yet full.

"Who am I to stop a man from trying?" Dick rudely belched. Hungry again, he never felt quite full after a meal. It was his nature to want more of everything.

"If you're ready to do business, it's time we meet over a friendly drink." Peter laid the groundwork for a contract.

"Somethin' too important to say over cyberspace! Humph, now you've grabbed my interest." Dick gnawed on a cigar. "A meeting might just be arranged. Oh, say in June?"

"June?" Peter was overjoyed.

"I'm expectin' to receive an important invitation from Rome. An invite to attend the grand NATO festivities the big Whigs got planned for their future chairman of the ECMC."

"The what?" Peter wasn't up to snuff on world politics.

"The Economic Common Market Committee." Dick's mental wheels whirred. "The Alliance liked the work their boy-genius did on the International Religious Ethics Committee so well they're going to give him another top-dog job. Don't you listen to CNN?"

"Exactly what will their boy be doing?" Peter inquired.

"Miracles!" Dick chuckled. "Alexander Luceres Ramnes is a name to remember. The ECMC is slated to devise a financial plan targeted at stabilizing the world's economy."

"That would take a miracle," Peter replied, considering the feat virtually impossible. "So you'll be coming to Rome in June. Alone?" He was anxious to nail down a time.

"Oh, no, Marjorie loves parties. She's comin' with me."

"Italy's weather should be super by then." Peter's mind raced forward. "Maybe we can arrange a seaside rendezvous."

"The Mediterranean? Marjorie would love that! We're boating enthusiasts, you know." She wouldn't miss an opportunity to hob-nob with the world's most influential women.

"I'm divorced again," Peter admitted. It was his fourth marriage, but women were fickle. "But I'll arrange to bring along a date. To make it look like a real vacation."

"Good boy!" Dick warmed to the idea. "Make sure your sweet thing likes to play cards. It'll keep the women occupied while we discuss more important issues."

Eve still had her place in the world.

"Got to go now," Dick tired of talking. "I'll get things moving here on my end. You just get that bullish crew of yours organized and ready to go by the time I get to Rome."

"Count on it!" Peter's voice pulsed. "Call me on an exact date."

"Oh, I will." Dick shut the phone down, not a bit sleepy. He didn't need rest. Propelled by the idea of making more money was manna enough. An occasional steak didn't hurt either, along with a tasty glass of wine and a good woman by his side.

Kicking back in his swivel rocker, Dick was on top of Mount Everest as he switched on his desktop Bose. Using his little electronic gizmo, he tuned to a New Orleans jazz station.

Yesirree! As long as the drugs kept coming out of South America, he'd be sittin' pretty on planet Earth. *Great balls of fire!*

He could saturate the world with his good-feelin' product now that he was franchising like McDonald's!

Dick wondered if he'd qualify for additional federal funds.

Probably not! He sighed and poured himself a glass of liquor.

Relaxing a bit, Dick lit up a Havana cigar. He had a whole kit of cigar accessories from Club Havana—humidors, cutters, and lighters.

Bearing no remorse for supplying folks with a little pleasure, Dick recalled having read somewhere that man couldn't live by meat alone. *People had free wills, didn't they?*

Why should he feel guilty? Everybody used drugs of some variation for all kinds of reasons. Anything from controlled substances like Prozac or Viagra to whatever would satisfy their greedy needs. He was in the *"whatever"* business.

Nope, Dick was convinced what he did wasn't wrong, even if it was illegal. Peter Coates was right in thinking that the Middle East Arab leaders were primed to control their masses with mind-altering drugs. An operation in Baghdad would be profitable.

But first he would need an official international charter to expand his business interests into the Arab markets. With the world operating under the control of a chosen few, it was time to cultivate internationally influential friends.

In exchange for the Big Boys' permission to market his product, Branson Meatpacking Company would be prepared to pay a healthy surcharge on its profit. *Nosiree*, he wasn't selfish.

Let them set up an account at the World Central Bank to receive direct deposits. No one need know where the money originated.

I'll scratch their backs and they can scratch mine.

Why, the Big Boys could earmark his generous contribution to underwrite the world's shaky currency. Dick's thoughts shifted to the battlefront at home. "And Victoria, my pretty rose with excessive thorns . . ." the pesky woman turned Dick's stomach.

"You and I need to have another little talk real soon. Who knows, I might even decide to share a box of my expensive cigars with you as sort of a farewell gift."

25

Tuesday morning slid in like an oil tanker for Victoria. Feeling drained, she was totally unprepared for Karen's distasteful menu of questions regarding dinner with Mark.

"We had a nice time," she chattered about incidentals to avoid specifics. "Mark is still pushing me to check into the hospital and get these headaches checked out." Kimberly Ann came to mind. "Are we still going to see Mother in Nashville tomorrow?"

"Relax, I've already arranged for someone to cover for me at the office." Karen recognized her mother's avoidance tactics.

"Thank you, dear. I'm worried over your grandmother's welfare."

It was futile to tell her mother not to worry, so Karen said, "Think I'll stir up an omelet." She pulled an egg carton from the refrigerator and set it on the counter. "Shall I make extra?"

"Sure." Victoria had no appetite, still distraught over her combative evening with Mark whose rash actions had ranged from love to loathing. Afraid that Karen might side with him, she dared not touch the subject.

"Grammy will be pleased as punch to see us." Karen whisked the eggs, onions and cheeses in a stainless steel bowl. "I think she misses family."

"Then why don't we invite Mother to live with us for a while?"

Karen frowned at the brilliant idea. "I'm afraid that's impossible! Do you want extra cheese?" she asked, eyeballing Victoria.

"What? Oh, the omelet." Victoria was still processing her daughter's odd response. "Wait a minute, Karen. Why is it *impossible* for Mother to move in with us?"

"Well . . ." Karen took a moment to collect her thoughts. "Obviously, there's a great deal more you don't recall than I first realized." She dumped the egg mixture into a saucepan.

"Like what?" Victoria's interest piqued.

"I really don't have the time to get into this discussion today."

"KISS." Victoria smiled. "Why can't Mother live here?"

Keep it simple, stupid. Karen added pepper to the omelet and said, "It isn't easy to check out of a federal care facility once you have agreed to the terms and signed a lease. Most people reside there until—"

"Until they die?" Victoria solved the equation.

"Oh, Mother! Don't be so melodramatic!" Karen flipped the omelet. "It's how our restored society works. In the long run, it's the best solution." Her wary eyes cut over on her mother.

"Says who?" Victoria was on target to argue.

"When we began this conversation, I thought the subject was Mark!" Karen slid half the omelet on a plate and plopped it on the counter in front of Victoria. "Breakfast is done and so am I!"

"Wait a minute!" Victoria had no intention of abandoning the cliffhanger. Karen moved to the bar and sat down and asked: "Couldn't we table this conversation?"

"No, we can't," Victoria replied. "You were the one who first brought up the subject of Mark! It seems to me that you're interest in him is—hmmm, Karen! This is a great omelet."

"My interest in Mark is what?" Karen's fork dangled midair.

Victoria considered whether to express her opinion.

"Spit it out!" Karen cried. "Mother to daughter, no secrets."

"I was just going to say that your interest in Mark seems a bit unbalanced." Victoria decided to elaborate a little. "Considering there's quite a difference in your ages."

Karen opened her mouth and shut it again, looking away with tears in her eyes. Should she tell her mother that she loved Mark and wanted to marry him?

"May I have a glass of orange juice?"

"OJ? Sure." Karen obediently puttered over to the refrigerator. "Large or small?"

"Large, like your teary-eyed response."

"What?" Karen lifted her half-filled glass. "Here's to unbalanced." Sarcasm dripped like acid from her pursed lips.

"Don't make light of it, dear. Forgive me if I'm wrong, but it concerns me that your life seemingly revolves around Mark, a man twice your age," Victoria declared.

"Drop it, Mother!" Karen raked her half-eaten omelet into the sink. "I don't need your permission to do whatever with any of my friends, especially when it comes to Mark. I'm a grown woman."

Drop it? Victoria recalled how Mark had said the same thing when she presented the idea of reopening Jeffrey's murder investigation. In the past Mark had functioned as a father figure and financial advisor to her children. Had he also been Karen's lover?

"Mother?" Karen cleaned the counter with a wet sponge. "I'm not innocent as you might think." She flipped the switch to the garbage disposal.

Do I really want to hear this? Victoria wondered.

"I know about men." Karen glanced over at her mother. "It's time you learned about Teddy, my eccentric, deceased spouse." She dried her hands on a dishtowel and tossed it.

Victoria was uncertain if she wanted to hear what happened to Karen's marriage, having come to the same shallow conclusion as Beverly James: Some things are best left unsaid!

Too bad she had the spine of a melting marshmallow!

"Take a seat, Mother. You need to hear this." Karen carried her coffee into the den. "Theodore Lawrence Carter . . ." she plopped down on the sofa showing plenty of leg and attitude, "was quite the womanizer."

Victoria collapsed on the sofa beside her distraught daughter.

"Good ol' Teddy to all his friends. Best lookin' in his high school annual. Star pitcher for the Selmer baseball team, Mr. All-around with a four-year scholarship to Ole Miss. Minor league a year before he moved to Fernwood. Mr. Catch-me Wonderful!"

"Doesn't sound like such a bad guy!" Victoria huffed. "You could have done worse." She had when she agreed to marry Mark.

"Ah, but Mother, appearances can be misleading! Of all people, you should know that." Pretending to care for Mark was hypocrisy.

"That's the most profound statement I've heard you make. So tell me what happened to your marriage, dear?"

"To say Teddy wined and dined me is an understatement," Karen stiffened with resolve. "I was swept off my feet from the moment I laid eyes on him at the country club."

"Well?" Victoria wanted the rest of the story.

"In Teddy's book I must have seemed filthy rich. I'm sure he'd heard rumors of my family's trust fund. Since he wasn't all that savvy in business, I suppose he liked the idea of marrying money." Karen glared beyond the sliders as unpleasant memories surfaced.

"You don't think Teddy loved you?" Victoria found Karen's opinion questionable.

"Oh, I don't know, maybe at first. I suppose I'll never really know." She had become cynical over the years. "First thing Teddy did after we got married was run up a ton of bills. Business, he said. I was naïve at first. Later, I learned he had a girl in every port."

"Your husband cheated on you!" Victoria was appalled. "That's a terrible way to live!"

"It got worse," Karen continued, growing more agitated by the moment. "After we'd been married a while, Teddy's lovemaking got kinky." *Why not share the sordid details?*

"Kinky?" Victoria reacted. "How do you mean, dear?"

"Teddy was weird, Mother." Karen cursed. "He beat me while we made love. Locked me in my room for hours and threatened to kill me if I told anyone. He was the king of jerks!"

"You were abused." Victoria was floored. "Did you ever tell anyone? Karen, why didn't I help you?" She struggled with knowing she had somehow failed her daughter.

"Mother!" Karen scowled. "You were so involved with your frivolous rich friends and keeping up with your social schedule, you hardly knew I was in town. Shall I say more?"

"What?" Victoria's pulse quickened at her daughter's disparaging opinion. "Karen! I can't believe you thought I was like that!" Her self-image took a dive.

"I didn't just think it, Mother. You were like that!" Karen's words bordered on cruelty. "That's why I'm having a real hard time accepting the values of the latest Victoria Tempest."

Dear God, was I that self-indulgent?

Karen sighed deeply. "Is it any wonder I keep waiting for the axe to fall." When she evaluated her life, the results stunk.

"That's a terrible thing to say!" Victoria was heart-stung when Karen didn't apologize. "But, of course, you had to leave Teddy," she rationalized, unable to imagine a marriage relationship so horrible. "Had you stayed, Teddy might have killed you."

"He almost did." Tears squatted in the corners of Karen's huge hazel eyes. "I did something terrible Mother," she said in a grave voice. "Something I deeply regret."

Victoria couldn't imagine anything worse than suffering physical and mental abuse.

"I put sleeping pills in Teddy's drink one night . . ." Karen bit into her lower lip. "He didn't wake up the next morning." The weight of guilt was stronger than grief.

"He died?" Victoria reacted. *Murder?* She couldn't bring herself to speak the word.

"But Teddy drank heavily, didn't he?" The parent in her searched for a plausible excuse. "Isn't it possible he overdosed on alcohol?" It was the only defense she could think to offer.

"Doesn't matter!" Karen gritted her teeth. "I gave Teddy sleeping pills and he didn't wake up. That's all that counts. No one can erase the past. Except you, Mother."

Victoria didn't care what her daughter thought of her, whether she believed that her amnesia was real or imagined. "Did you tell anyone?" She was worried over Karen being prosecuted.

"Mark knows. He took care of the autopsy."

Isn't eradicating evidence a criminal act? "Why?"

"To protect me. Mark's been wonderful to both of us."

The pain forming in Victoria's skull threatened to topple her.

"There's more," Karen went on. "A week after Teddy was buried I found out I was pregnant. I had an abortion."

She noted the distress in her mother's face.

"Don't you see that I had to do it?" Karen's defense heightened. "There was no way on earth I was going to have that creep's offspring! His family would have hounded me for the rest of my days."

Karen's confession buried Victoria under an avalanche of confusion. How could she express her deep sense of loss at losing a grandchild? Or excuse Karen's irresponsible actions?

"So, Mother, what do you think of your sweet little girl now?" Bitterness quickened on Karen's tongue. "A mistress to murder?" She had heard the townspeople's scorn: *guilty*.

"I suppose I can understand your reasons for wanting to escape an abusive relationship, possibly even killing Teddy in self-defense. But Karen, murdering your own baby?"

"That's why I love Mark so much. He stood by me when others didn't. And he never, never judged me."

Love? Victoria glared into Karen's wounded eyes: soft brown on the rims, hard green toward the core. Karen was guilty of much.

Considering the sinless nature of God's only Son, when Jesus had the opportunity to judge a sinful woman and stone her, He chose to forgive. *He who is without sin, let him cast the first stone!*

Neither should she. "Thank you for telling me the truth, Karen." Victoria let go of the hurt as she forgave. "Now if you don't mind, I'd like another cup of coffee."

"What?" Karen was blown away. "Coffee? Right." She trotted off to the kitchen to accomplish a task far easier than making the right choices in life.

Victoria realized that her vulnerable daughter wasn't yet ready to hear about God's unconditional mercy or forgiveness. For now, she needed only to know that she was *loved.*

Later that morning, as mother and daughter sat on the veranda quietly listening to the twitter of birds, Victoria said: "You know, dear, birds have a love language of their own."

Overhead, a passing jet left its white mark on the blue sky. Life had left its impression on Karen, too. A dark and dismal one that shadowed her dreams and clouded her optimism.

"Mother. You know I would change my past if I could."

"I know that, Karen. And I do love you, sweetheart." Victoria hugged Karen. "I'll always love you no matter what happens."

It was important to be the parent Karen needed.

"I love you so much, Mother." Karen snuggled close, drinking in the comfort. Just as the birds would have it, true love remained unconditional.

26

Although Victoria was eager to question Pearlynne Blackstone about her past, the Memphis trip would have to wait until she'd visited her mother at the Nashville care facility. Besides, she had an idea that required Kathryn Billingsley's help again.

Actually, Karen had supplied the inspiration when she mentioned that the Internet was the telephone tool connecting the world. Just maybe Beverly James could be located on the World Wide Web. Victoria located her car keys and headed out the door.

Kathryn was astounded that Victoria didn't know how to use the Internet. "I can't imagine you not getting on line at least to shop!" The testy librarian booted up the system.

"Guess I've had my head in the sand." Victoria squeaked a smile. "Just hope you can teach an old dog new tricks!" She was not ready to discuss her unusual amnesia with Kathryn.

"It's not all that difficult." The librarian's teaching skills kicked in. "If I hadn't had the proper instruction in the beginning, the world's new technology might have stumped even me."

Lightning reflexes in Kathryn's fingers made all the right connections. "I'm getting you into Yahoo." Her squinted gray eyes targeted the screen. "From there you can do just about anything you want."

"Yahoo?" Victoria's mind raced to the TV sitcom, *The Beverly Hillbillies*, and chuckled despite her restraint.

"Don't laugh!" Kathryn said. "Yahoo's an Internet service that breezes through volumes of information in seconds. Are you still working on your coma article?"

"No, I'm finished with that," Victoria replied. "You might recall that I mentioned expanding *our* wedding list," she reminded Kathryn. "I'm trying to locate a particular friend who has recently moved so I can invite her to the wedding."

"Anyone I know?"

"Probably not."

"And you think Mark will be pleased if she comes?" Kathryn asked, getting a little too inquisitive to suit Victoria.

"Sure, I wouldn't do it otherwise." She lied like a pro.

"Then I'd go into a chatroom if I were you." Kathryn clicked a few more routes to achieve the designated location. "Let's try the Senior Citizens Link-up."

Amazed at the leap in technology, Victoria wondered if she had known how to operate the Internet and forgotten when her memories flip-flopped. Back in the eighties, she recalled Paul asking for a home computer when Jeffrey purchased one for his office.

A self-indulged housewife, she'd had little interest in technology outside of microwaves and beepers.

"Do you know where your friend last lived?" Kathryn inquired. "A state would be helpful." Her fingers skillfully glided over the keyboard. "The computer responds to facts."

"I think Be—my friend," she coughed to cover her goof, "lives in the Colorado area." Victoria recalled what Beverly's nosy neighbor, Frank, had said. "Try Denver."

"I could plug in a name, but it's not usually done that way." Kathryn's eyes were aimed at the screen. "People don't usually give out their real names over the Web."

"Why not?" Victoria wondered, paying close attention to Kathryn's keyboard skills.

"Much too dangerous for private intrusion." The librarian's milk-toast gaze shifted on Victoria. "Most people use symbols to represent themselves when communicating with others," Kathryn explained. "It's called a *handle*. For example, you might choose a cartoon character."

"Like Bugs Bunny? How can I find someone like that? It seems like such a game."

"Exactly!" Kathryn exclaimed. "Internet chatrooms are very social avenues. In fact, people have been known to find their life's mate via the system. Love is universal, you know."

"Really?" Victoria tried to visualize agreeing to marry a cartoon character.

"Well, why don't you decide on a handle, dear. Then we'll place you in a chatroom where you can start greeting people." Kathryn looked to Victoria for a decision.

"It all sounds pretty risky. Could some kook track me down?"

"Not likely if you don't give your real name and address. Keep your questions simple and wait for answers. Remember that thousands of people will be roaming around on the Web with you. Some of them may even be listening in on your conversations with others."

"I gather you've done this before," Victoria said.

Kathryn blushed. "Occasionally."

Assuming that she had intruded into a private area of Kathryn's life where she wasn't welcome, Victoria quickly moved forward. "What else should I know?"

"The icon you select should be easily identifiable by your friend—a symbolic something the both of you will recognize. Like some visual trigger from a previous conversation."

"Oh, I get the idea! A clue." *Why didn't Kathryn just say so?*

"Exactly!" The prim librarian beamed with pride.

"Try the Sherlock Homes icon," Victoria decided.

"That's an—uh, ordinary choice," Kathryn mumbled as she clicked on a pool of characters and found the Holmes icon. "You're sure that's the best idea you can muster?"

"Absolutely!" Victoria flashed a winning smile.

"Well," Kathryn frowned, "here's how it works. Use the mouse to move around in the chatroom until someone hits on you."

"Wait! Hits on me?" Victoria was puzzled.

"Not literally!" Kathryn rolled her eyes. "A hit is when somebody responds to you. Once you begin surfing, you'll get the idea. Go ahead, you try it."

"Surfing?" Victoria batted her eyelids. "It sounds more like I'm going for a swim." The terminology was blowing her away.

"Trust me, dear." Kathryn sighed. "Operating the Internet is no big deal. Everybody does it. In response to a hit, just click right here." She pointed to the screen and got out of the way.

"It appears simple enough." Victoria took Kathryn's seat.

"You'll do just fine." Kathryn's nervous gaze flickered over to her desk. "Oh, dear, I'm afraid I must get back to work." People were in line waiting for her. "Can you handle this?"

"Yes. Sorry to have put you to so much trouble."

"No problem, dear. Glad to be of service," Kathryn bubbled. "It's my job, you know. Just wave if you get stumped."

"I'll handle it from here." Victoria grabbed the mouse as Kathryn rushed off to take care of business.

It didn't take long for a *hit*, as Kathryn had put it. The computerized voice asked the Sherlock Holmes icon if she were male or female?

"I'm female," Victoria responded. "I'm searching for a friend in the Denver area who sells a new line of cosmetics via the Internet."

"Do you sell cosmetics, too?" an eerie voice came back. "I'd like to buy something from you. When can we meet?"

She, or *he*, seemed overanxious for a personal encounter. Nervous that she might be having a conversation with a serial killer, Victoria said, "I don't think so. My friend left town without giving a forwarding address. I owe her something."

"Money?" the weird voice perked up. "I've got lots of money. I have a great job and I travel a lot. I probably come to your town occasionally. Where did you say you live?"

"No, it isn't money. It's a *personal* matter." Victoria was uncomfortable with the weird conversation. "I should go now."

"No, don't! I like *personal*," an innuendo came forth.

"Perhaps you've heard of a new cosmetic line that just started up in the state of Colorado, sold exclusively via Internet?"

"Can't say that I have, but my wife might know."

What a jerk! "Could I speak with your wife, then?"

The line immediately fell dead.

Not surprised, Victoria proceeded to try again. Another hit occurred but it turned out to be unproductive. Then a third try, but she was unsuccessful in locating Beverly James. *Jesus, I need your help.*

As Victoria was about to exit the program, someone typed a message on the screen: "Meet me in the Private Study."

Grabbing the mouse, she trailed the little strawberry-blond character through a mirrored wall into *The Private Study* and asked, "Do you sell cosmetics?"

"Yes," a robotic voice came back. "What do we have in common?"

Is this Bev on the line?

"College." Victoria's breath was shallow. "MSU."

"Affirmative."

"Did you live in the same town as your ex until last Friday?"

"Affirmative."

"Information needed to solve a murder."

"Will correspond by e-mail."

E-mail. "What's e-mail?"

"Get an address. Same place, same time on Friday."

The strawberry blond icon disappeared from the screen like a bubble popping. *That was it?* Victoria's pulse took a leap. *Thirty seconds and Bev was gone?*

Victoria had no way of knowing for sure she had communicated with Beverly James, but it sure felt like it. Ready to log off, a kid around nine took over the computer. By the time she was walking away, he was already on line and calling up a list of games.

If that doesn't make me feel plum stupid . . .

As Victoria exited the library she made a snap decision to revisit the *Olde Soda Shoppe.* Knowing every shortcut to avoid the traffic, she rolled into a vacant parking space in front of the courthouse ten minutes later. A woman on a mission, she grabbed her purse, locked up the car with the clicker gizmo, and half ran across the street, praying that somebody at the drugstore could tell her why Gloria Gordon had quit her job on Saturday.

More importantly, where was Gloria?

Taking a moment to regain her composure, Victoria pushed open the front door and was greeted by tinkling bells and the rich aroma of fresh-brewed espresso. Over in a corner booth sat a red-haired boy wolfing down a large chocolate shake.

A dead ringer for Bud Lindsey. Victoria thought the boy had to be one of Bud's grandsons. "Hi." She approached the booth.

Four boys around ten looked up at her.

"Excuse me," she singled out the red-haired lad, "but you look exactly like someone I know. By chance, are you kin to Bud Lindsey?"

"Yep." The kid sharply eyed Victoria. "Whut about it?"

"Don't talk to strangers," said the Lindsey kid's buddy.

"Mrs. Victoria ain't no stranger!" He elbowed his friend.

The kid knew her? Victoria was surprised, then realized that most people who had lived in Fernwood for very long would have recognized her. A pillar of the community, her picture had probably appeared on the society page of the local newspaper on more than one occasion. Her engagement to Mark might have made the six o'clock news. Unfortunately, fame had its pitfalls.

"It's Cory." The Lindsey kid found his manners. "Cory Lindsey." He wiped chocolate syrup from his freckled face.

"That's a nice name, Cory." Like Bud's, his russet eyes matched the color of his hair. "I didn't mean to interrupt your treat, but I'm looking for Gloria Gordon. Do you know her?"

"I know Miss Gordon," the kid beside Cory answered for him. "She left town on a vacation. Got a big check from some relative, I heard my mom tell somebody over the phone."

"Oh?" Victoria's eyebrows lifted. "And who are you?"

"He's Matthew Page," Cory took over the three-way conversation, mouthing at the other three boys to leave him alone.

Victoria peered into Matthew's eyes, soft as the petals of a violet. She'd seen those eyes before. *Where?* Obviously the boys were best of friends since they answered for one another.

"You're Dr. Allen Page's son?" Victoria made the connection.

"Yep," Cory chimed in. "The famous plastic surgeon who works with Dr. Mark." He grinned at Matthew. "You must know him, Mrs. Victoria. Dr. Page sure knows you."

Trapped, Victoria realized her fragile position. If Allen Page discovered that she had been grilling the boys over Gloria's disappearance, he was bound to inform Mark. Sighing, she opened her billfold and handed the boys two crisp bills.

"Whut's this five dollars for?" Cory eyeballed Matthew.

"Favor money," Victoria said with a sheepish grin. "For not telling anyone I'm looking for Miss Gloria. I've got a big surprise for her," she said to appease their curiosity.

"All right!" The two boys slapped a high five, going into rap gyrations. When Cory's two other friends scowled at the transaction, Victoria decided to cover her bases by rewarding them, too.

After Victoria had paid out another ten dollars and joked around awhile, the gang of four seemed willing to play along. She could only hope they would keep their lips sealed as promised.

Skipping dessert, she thanked the boys for the information and hurried outdoors, hoping that her thirty-minute parking meter hadn't run out. The instant Victoria popped her door locks, a policeman ticketed her windshield.

"Just one minute!" She raised an eyebrow.

"Yes, Ma'am?" The young rookie was polite despite his rude challenger. "Obviously, I owe a fine for letting my meter expire!" She huffed, unable to recall if she had put in adequate coinage. "I'll be more than glad to write a check to pay my parking fine."

"Oh, that's not necessary, Ma'am." The muscle-bound policeman continued writing. "Here. You can mail in this form with your check or money order." He handed over a self-addressed, stamped envelope. "Have a nice day, lady." He turned to walk away.

Have a nice day, Victoria grumbled.

"No, wait. Really!" She chased after the traffic cop. "I want to pay this ticket now if it's permissible. I'll follow you down to the station in my car." The last thing she wanted was a police record.

"Suit yourself." The cop hopped on his motorcycle like Roy Rogers, revved his engine, and eased into the flow of traffic.

"I do!" Victoria called out as she leaped behind the wheel of her car and followed, grateful that the rookie cop hadn't turned on his bleating red lights. *Oh, boy!*

The Fernwood Police Precinct was housed in a renovated municipal building on the other side of the square. When Officer Roy parked his black boot against the curb and pointed to the front door, Victoria realized he wasn't going inside.

Waving goodbye, she pulled into a parking space marked "visitor" and entered the complex, thinking she was there by God's design. Hadn't she intended on visiting the precinct anyhow? To ask about her accident report filed in 1989?

This was a break. She'd simply maintain a low profile, pay her fine, and look for the right opportunity to ask questions. *Here goes.*

Victoria walked straight up to the female officer in charge and said, "Excuse me. I just got a parking ticket and I'd like to pay it now. If you'd be so kind," she tempered her request.

"Over there." The lady cop pointed.

Spinning around, at first Victoria saw no one.

"Sarah!" Lady-lungs screamed. "Git this woman's ticket money and record it."

Behind a glassed-in booth, a curly mop of black hair bobbed up and down like a fishing cork. Victoria walked over to the counter and patiently waited for the officer to resurface before speaking.

"Sarah, I'm Victoria Tempest. I owe a fine for letting my parking meter expire. Here." She handed over more than enough cash.

"Can you verify where this cash came from?" Sarah dragged out her syllables like a true born-and-bred southerner. "'Cause if you can't, it's our policy not to take it."

Oh dear?" The money wasn't stolen, but Victoria couldn't verify a bank account since she couldn't recall ever having opened one. "Guess I'll have to send in my fine by mail, after all."

Sarah grunted, then disappeared again.

"Wait! I have one other question," Victoria hollered.

"Whut is it?" The officer erected herself. "Josh! Get that cotton-pickin' phone line!"

"I'm doing some research for an article I'm writing on a particular automobile accident." Victoria lowered her voice and glanced around. "May I ask you a few questions?"

"You a reporter or sum 'in?" Sarah wrinkled her shiny black nose.

"No, freelance," Victoria fabricated. "How would I get hold of an old police report dating back to, oh say, 1989?"

"Heaven forbid, honey child! That's a long time ago!" Sarah waved a hand. "Those old reports are probably packed away somewhere in the police archives."

"Where is that located?" Victoria raised her voice above the noisy entourage arriving as four husky policemen escorted a motley crew of tipsy teens into the interrogation room.

"Josh! I said get the blasted phone!" Sarah screamed at her associate again. "This place is too busy to talk archives." The officer grabbed her notebook off the counter.

"This is important, Sarah," Victoria made a plea.

"Look, lady. I gotta late lunch break comin' up. Maybe I could ask around and find out where they keep those ol' reports."

"Oh, Sarah! Would you mind checking? I'd be sure to make mention of your name in my article." Victoria bargained for Sarah's time.

"Meet me out front at two o'clock and we'll talk."

"Thank you!" Victoria was rudely shoved aside to make room for more incoming traffic.

"If you wanna live, you better git out now!" Sarah pointed to a side door.

27

Earlier, Victoria had noticed a deli around the corner from the precinct. Loading an hour's coinage in the parking meter, she took off walking. By the time she'd finished a bowl of soup and walked back, Sarah would be on break.

Lunch was good and Victoria was prompt in returning. Unfortunately, Sarah was running late. *Or worse, had forgotten.*

Victoria lurked outside the station, casually thumbing through a free-shopper flier.

It was 2:20 when her newfound friend stepped out the side door. Victoria immediately pounced on her.

"Sarah! It's me!"

"Oh, hi." The officer appeared tentative. "Look, I—"

"Thank you for agreeing to talk to me. I only have a few questions to ask you," Victoria hurriedly said, sensing the helpful officer was close to reneging on her promise. She whipped out a pen and an official-looking notepad and presented her best smile. "Please, Sarah."

"Walk with me." She nodded, taking long strides forward.

Falling into step beside Sarah, Victoria asked, "You headed to the deli for lunch?"

"Yep, wanna eat?" Sarah's almond-brown eyes were bright with intelligence.

"I was just there," Victoria replied, "but I could sure use a cup of coffee." She quickened her pace to keep up with the fit officer. "Thank you for taking the time to help me."

"Exactly what are you lookin' for?" Sarah's demeanor was direct, no fooling around.

"Actually," Victoria began, "I was in an automobile accident in 1989. After recovering from a coma, I was left with amnesia."

"Wow!" Sarah tossed a sideward glance. "So how can I help?"

"I promised to keep it short, so I will. I'm interested in finding the person who pulled me from my wrecked car and saved my life." Victoria was becoming short-winded. "I will be glad to pay for the information." She paused to catch her breath.

"Seriously?" Sarah halted. "You gonna give a ree-ward?" The officer's gaze burned with interest. "'Cause if you are, I can't accept it." She started walking again. "Against police policy."

Victoria caught up with Sarah. "I certainly respect your reasons for not accepting my money." She bolstered Sarah's esteem. "However, if I could locate the person who dialed 911 to report my accident, I'd be plenty grateful."

"Wull, I can tell you . . ." Sarah turned the corner, "you gotta have an affidavit to open up one of them archive cases."

"I was afraid of that." Victoria grimaced to herself. "Sarah, I need to get past all the protocol. There'll be a nice, uh, *gift* for someone willing to help."

Sarah reconsidered the idea. "Give me a few days?"

"You got it." She grasped Sarah's hand. "And would you keep *this* between us?" The secrets were piling up, a lot of them hers.

"Sure." They reached the deli's entrance. "If you already ate, Victoria, you don't have to waste time hanging out with me."

"Thank you, Sarah. Think I'll pass on the coffee. Are you clear on what I need?" The officer was a light in the darkness.

"Got the facts up here." Sarah fingered her right temple. "I already got an idea myself and my mama tol' me to keep my word."

"Wait! My phone number." Victoria scribbled her name on the back of Karen's business card. "If my daughter answers the phone, hang up and call back later."

"Just between us." Sarah grabbed the card and shoved it into her shirt pocket. "Trust me, I'll call."

"Thanks, Sarah. Thanks a bunch."

"Sherlock Holmes, you ain't doing so bad," Victoria mumbled as she walked toward her parked vehicle. While buckling up, she recalled Karen's painful confession regarding her disastrous marriage. *Poor baby, she must be carrying a load of guilt.*

What concerned Victoria more than Karen's ranting was her

silence. It wasn't a good sign for rebuilding a mother-daughter relationship. *So how did Teddy dupe her smart daughter?*

Cruel and controlling, although dead, he'd still win the Classic Jerk Award if she were judging. But that was God's job.

Worse, Karen's unfortunate experience with Teddy was bound to distort her opinion of marriage. *Or had she already settled for casual relationships?* Victoria had no idea how Karen felt about the subject of love or spent her free time, but it was time she found out.

Victoria let herself inside the condo with a key. Switching on some lights, she set her purse on the kitchen bar and thumbed through the mail on Karen's desk. A wedding invitation had arrived. Toni Kippinger's return address was engraved on the envelope. *Hadn't Toni been in Karen's ninth grade class?*

Judging by modern standards, Victoria guessed Toni would have lost in love at least once by now and been about to take a second or third plunge. Back in the eighties, half of the marriages in America were predicted to fail. Probably the rate of survival was even less today.

Then, maybe not, Victoria picked a fight with herself. People didn't seem to rely on marriage to maintain a stable relationship anymore. In that case, the divorce rates could have improved.

Why am I going down this mental road? She rummaged through the refrigerator. *I'll cook*. She busied herself with marinating two chicken breasts she had thawed in the microwave. Aware of how cautious Karen guarded her figure, she tossed a fresh spinach salad and shoved the glass bowl into the refrigerator.

After steaming a few caffeine-free tea bags, she was tempted to invent a pie but checked her chocolate urge. Dessert was a definite calorie bomb neither she nor Karen needed. Low-fat yogurt would substitute nicely. Topped with fresh blueberries.

Victoria already felt much calmer. At home in the kitchen she could forget about what year it was. When she had finished, she took a shower and changed clothes.

Mark phoned around four, acting as if nothing had happened.

"So Vicki, how are you doing?"

"Fine." She was in no mood to forgive him.

"I didn't like the way we ended things Monday," he said.

"Me either." Victoria swallowed her pride. "I hate fighting." She inwardly struggled with the way Mark had forced his affections on her after she'd served him a delicious meal.

However, she realized the sour ending to a tasteful meal had partially been her fault. After luring Mark into her clever den, had she really expected the tiger wouldn't try to bite?

Deciding to practice what she preached, Victoria embarked on honesty, a commodity difficult to identify in modern society. Little white lies came entirely too easy to save face.

"Mark? I think we need to discuss what happened between us the other night." Victoria wanted more perspective on how things got so out of hand. "Let me tell you how I *really* feel."

"Do I want to hear this?" Mark chuckled. "Up to more games?"

"Touché." Victoria had that coming. "I felt threatened by your actions. Don't overreact and bear with me. Assuming Jeffrey's murder was an accident, give me one good reason why you refuse to answer my questions. All I'm asking for is your opinion."

"You're absolutely right, Vicki." Mark switched the phone to his other ear. "Assuming that I have nothing to hide, you should feel free to ask me anything and expect an answer."

"Not just an answer, Mark. The *truth*!"

"Ah, but dear, truth is tricky. One person's reality is another person's misconception. It's all relative to the situation," Mark toyed with Victoria, starting to enjoy the verbal banter.

"That's hogwash New-Age bull based on situation ethics! It's like saying that if you hate someone, it's okay as long as it makes you feel good!" Her voice popped the phone line.

"I see you've done your homework." Mark was astounded at his fiancée's new posture. "When did you become the expert on New Age?" He doodled on his daily calendar.

"I've read a few of Karen's religious books, Mark! Some truths never change."

"What? Like the Bible?" he asked, thinking Victoria was way too uptight.

"Yes! *The Bible.*" Victoria's temper escalated a notch.

"The Bible's changed, too. You've just forgotten a few details."

How dare him!

"I've forgotten a lot of things, but the truths of the Bible aren't included. God is absolutely Sovereign, never changes, and His grace spans eternity!" Victoria stood her ground. "Mark James, God loves you even if you don't recognize it!"

"Whatever you say." Mark's playful tactics had failed.

Victoria bit her lower lip until it hurt. If there were words to adequately describe how she felt about Mark James right now, she was positive that filth would spew out of her mouth!

"I'm sorry, Vicki," he apologized. "Apparently I've upset you. I was out of line to deride your opinion of the Bible. But society didn't change overnight."

"Like I did," Victoria admitted.

"People voluntarily made the changes," Mark continued. "The vast majority of people approve. It took twenty-five years for us to arrive where we are today."

In the sewer, Victoria concluded.

Mark's words became a blur on the edge of her thoughts as she considered all that was unholy and accepted in society. Would she never be able to openly read the Bible again or communicate her faith? Who would dispel the lies society had foolishly embraced if not Jesus Christ?

The emotional strain of loss was so pervasive Victoria could almost feel its prickly branches cutting into the very fabric of her soul. *Dear Jesus! End this terrible nightmare.*

"Vicki, did you hear what I just said?"

"Some of it." Victoria turned her attention to Mark. "I know it's not all your fault that society has changed or Jeffrey died. Life happens. But after decades in a time capsule, I've returned to a world I don't recognize. And you've changed, too."

Did he really want to know how much? The years of lying had

eaten away at his character and his association with Dick Branson hadn't helped. Talked out, Mark said, "Thank you for giving me the benefit of the doubt where Jeffrey is concerned."

Have I really? Mark was not innocent when it came to tampering with her life and controlling circumstances.

"I'm sorry if what I said about religion has hurt you, but it's important that you accept what life has handed you," Mark finalized his comments. "We can't change destiny."

Victoria hoped that Mark was wrong, having always trusted in the power of faith. Surely, Jesus had purpose in all this.

"Sweetheart, I still love you as much as I ever did, despite our differences." Mark bared his heart. "I want us back so bad I can taste it. When can I see you again?"

Although Victoria disagreed with her former lover's fatal attitude toward changing society, she didn't think arguing her point would make a penny's worth of difference to him.

"Tomorrow is the day Karen and I go to Nashville."

"To see your mother." Mark checked his calendar. "I wish I could go with you, but I have three surgeries scheduled in the morning."

Victoria offered no opinion.

"Which reminds me, I've made an appointment for you."

"What appointment?" Victoria recoiled. "For tests?" She deplored hospitals since they made her think of death more than life, despair more than hope. Did she have to go?

"A week from tomorrow, if that's all right."

"I suppose it's inevitable that I have a check-up."

"It's important to make sure you're in good health. If there's anything wrong with you, it's best that we know."

"I suppose . . ." Victoria despised the idea.

"Can you come over later for dinner?"

"No, I can't." She wouldn't place herself in a compromising position ever again.

"Can't or won't. I've been too hard on you."

"Yes, you have, but that's not the only reason."

Mark sulked a moment. "Should I ask why?"

"I've already made supper and I plan to retire early. I want to be rested and at my very best when I see my mother for the first time in twenty-five years." Or so it would seem.

"I understand," he said.

"We're leaving at five sharp."

"Ouch, it hurts even to think about getting up at that ungodly hour!" Mark chuckled, his mood lightening. "Promise to phone me when you get home tomorrow evening?"

"I will," Victoria agreed, satisfied that they were ending the conversation amicably.

"Until tomorrow . . ." Mark hung up the phone.

Victoria clutched the receiver until the phone line moaned. Every day was a unique challenge chockfull of surprises.

WEDNESDAY, APRIL 23

28

Startled by the buzzing alarm clock, Victoria leaped from the bed and raced to the shower with serious intent and prayer. Today she would face her mother with a new set of memories, an important milestone in her recovery.

Karen heard the *5 a.m.* alarm sound but decided to snuggle between her sheets an extra few minutes while the programmed coffee maker finished dripping. But if she didn't rally soon, Victoria Number III would be madly knocking on the door.

Not as enthralled with her prospective trek to Nashville as apparently her mother was, Karen stumbled into the bathroom and peered at her tawdry image in the mirror. Crow's feet and dark circles hounded her drawn, hazel eyes.

The trauma of recent events had taken its toll.

What concerned Karen most was her grandmother's reaction to her mother's weird amnesia. She would be the last one to mention the potential pitfalls of true confession and risk snuffing out her mother's enthusiasm. Let Mark's *Little Vicki* deal with the issue.

Victoria and Karen left the condo around *6:45 a.m.*, which didn't put them much off schedule. However early they arrived, they couldn't get in to see Kimberly Ann Martin until ten o'clock. Green Gables had its non-negotiable rules.

The day was unfolding nicely, the skies bluing as the sun made its entry over the horizon. Halfway to Nashville, Karen needed another cup of coffee and suggested they stop for breakfast. Pulling off the interstate, they rolled into the parking of a Cracker Barrel Old Country Store. The front porch was lined in rockers with hungry people waiting.

After Karen had placed their names on a waiting list, Victoria milled around in the curio shop looking to buy a gift for her mother. When they were seated fifteen minutes later, she immediately ordered two strong coffees with cream.

"I think I'll have the Uncle Hershel's country ham breakfast," Karen quickly decided, looking to her mother for a decision.

Not very hungry and on edge over facing her mother, Victoria was delighted to see that Cracker Barrel hadn't changed one iota since the eighties. As always, its inviting fire leaped in the gigantic stone fireplace and lovely designer quilts hung on the walls next to historical photos of unknown people.

"I'll have an orange juice and an order of biscuits," Victoria decided, thinking time had truly played a trick on her. While only a couple of months had passed since she had last seen her mother, it felt more like twenty-five years. How could she possibly explain flip-flopped memories when she didn't understand it herself?

"What's wrong?" Karen noted her mother's unrest. "Spill it, or I'll squeeze it out of you!" She didn't mince words. "This day was supposed to make you happy."

"I am happy, dear." In many ways, she was. "And I thank you for driving me to Nashville." Worry dragged down her spirits. "But I am a wee bit nervous about our visit."

"Oh?" Karen lifted her eyebrows. "In what way?"

"Although I've obviously visited my mother many times at Green Gables, I'm afraid my memory lapse will upset your grandmother and ruin everyone's day."

"I had the same thought earlier," Karen admitted. "We'll just tell Grammy the truth. She's still spry enough in her thinking to accept whatever changes have occurred."

"You think so?" Victoria felt encouraged.

"We were there on the first Wednesday in February," Karen recalled. "You talked to Grammy about marrying Mark and she was absolutely thrilled with the decision. Goodness, she thinks Mark James hung the moon." *And she would be right.*

"Oh, dear," Victoria lamented. How would her mother react when she learned that there would be no wedding? Even Karen didn't yet know of her decision.

"Something else bothering you, Mother?"

Luckily, the server arrived with their coffees in the nick of time to save Victoria from an awkward response. A congenial college student, Andrew was bent on airing his political opinions regarding a philosophical paper he was writing on Communism.

A captive audience, Victoria and Karen politely listened until their entrees arrived, choosing not to offer an opinion.

"Eat heartily and enjoy!" Andrew grinned and departed.

When Victoria had finished her biscuits, she couldn't resist snitching a third one from Karen's plate. Feeling calmer for having confided in Karen, she pondered over telling her how she felt about Mark. Didn't her daughter have a good head on her shoulders?

Well, except for a blind spot when it came to Mark.

No, thought Victoria, *the timing doesn't yet feel right.*

In quiet reflection, she half-listened to Karen's response to their astute waiter's political views. "So, Mother, what do you think of the idea of redesigning our world economy?"

Duh. Victoria drew a blank, never having been the slightest bit interested in politics. Voting in elections every two years had been the extent of her involvement.

"Mother!" Karen scoffed. "Surely you have an opinion."

"Well . . ." Victoria swallowed hard, "it seems to me the U.S. Treasury has too long been influenced by powerful men like Greenspan," she recalled a news article she'd once read.

"Who?" Karen didn't recognize the name.

"Alan Greenspan, the decision-maker for setting interest-rate standards for the U.S. Federal Reserve Bank. My goodness, his opinion could spin the stock market into Loony Tunes back when." Victoria was pleased that she had an intelligent opinion.

"Of course, Greenspan," Karen quipped. "However, I must admit I'm impressed with your answer. Really! I had no idea you cared the slightest for politics. You do seem different."

"Different? As opposed to what?" Victoria was curious.

"Well, from the way you used to think and act before your dramatic street experience." A smile curled her pink lips and spread.

"My resurrection from the past." Victoria slathered orange marmalade on her stolen biscuit. "Just my old self kicking in again, I guess! However, politics is not my forté."

"Shall I fill you in?" asked Karen.

"Might as well." Victoria sighed.

"While mass communications made the world seem smaller, religious and political opinion widened as ethnic groups polarized to strengthen their centuries-old mores and values."

"You're talking about the Arabs and Jews, aren't you?" Victoria leaned forward with interest, recalling the age-old battle. *"There is nothing new under the sun"* still applied.

"Yes. And Americans were just as guilty for defending Christianity. It took a while for the world to come to its senses and quit fighting over religious preferences," Karen went on.

"Faith is something worth fighting over," Victoria declared.

"Maybe," Karen said. "But doesn't God want peace?"

"Yes. Peace that passes all understanding. Jesus was talking about salvation, dear."

"Whatever," said Karen. "Anyhow, the problem has been resolved. A very smart business man chaired a committee that proposed an acceptable solution to religious conflict."

Victoria haughtily tossed her napkin on the table. "The creep took our Bibles away!"

"No, he didn't!" Karen nervously glanced around the room, lowering her voice. "I know you don't remember, but it's unwise to openly criticize the leadership."

"And why not? It's a free country, isn't it?" Victoria was tired of everyone's tiptoeing around the truth. "It's obvious this so-called 'man of the hour' has stolen a precious freedom from Christians. Our right to keep faith!" She didn't care who heard.

"There you go again, my melodramatic mother." Karen launched into a lengthy political discourse regarding how the restored society worked. No, it wasn't Communism. It was something God-given, the voluntary surrender of human wills.

"Humph." *God-given, my eye.*

But after listening to Karen's reasoning, Victoria soon realized that world politics had become awfully tricky. *Had the end times arrived?* She was reminded of Bible prophecy.

Only Father God could answer that question. Even the Son didn't know the exact hour of His return to Earth. Future generations were to look for certain events that signified Christ's return, the moment He would slip back through space and pick up His redeemed church. Multitudes would be caught off-guard, fresh out of holy oil and left in the dark, stunned over the disappearance of millions of people.

Wondering if she would be ready, Victoria knew that being counted among the saints came down to a personal decision: *To believe in Jesus Christ, or reject His Holy Spirit.*

Karen's description of America's role of world politics hadn't come as a total surprise to Victoria. The United States Army had always acted as the world's protector.

And now, NATO was on the brink of formulating a plan to stabilize the ailing world money markets.

Victoria feared how people would react to total government control, being policed by international armies, and influenced by a charismatic personality she instinctively distrusted: Alexander Luceres Ramnes, the world's newest pseudo-savior!

"Do we still elect a president?" Victoria had to ask.

"Of course." Karen weirdly smiled. "But all nations must answer to NATO. It's best that way, Mother. We don't have terrorist attacks and religious conflicts plaguing us anymore."

Where were brave men like Abraham Lincoln and Theodore Roosevelt? Victoria wondered. *Good men with strong Christian character who stood for justice? Had the world sunk so low that only the return of Jesus Christ could save it?*

"I suppose it's time we got on the road," Karen said, walking to the front of the restaurant to pay the bill with her Universal Credit Card. After Victoria had visited the restroom, they ventured outdoors and climbed inside Karen's Cadillac.

Once on the interstate, Karen embarked on a sore subject. "Mark said he couldn't dissuade you from reopening Dad's case."

Mark said . . . "That should please you, dear."

"That you intend to track down Dad's killers doesn't please me either," Karen clarified her position. "When you first came home from the hospital in 1989 with amnesia, I was forced to accept a mother who didn't know me. For years, I lingered between despair and hate for *all* that had happened to our family. There is no way you can understand how alone I felt."

"That's terrible, Karen. I had no idea . . ."

"I had a mistaken-identity marriage in my twenties—as you now know. And frankly, my dear, I just want the past to take a hike."

"I understand, Karen. I really do." Victoria peered through the low-glare, shatterproof plate-glass car window. Not a cloud infected the pristine sky. If only life were so blissful.

"Then you'll drop this crazy investigation?"

"Because you asked, I'll give it some consideration," Victoria replied. A red bird flitted by her window, a sign of good luck. She would receive it as a sign of God's guidance.

Hands clutched to the steering wheel, Karen realized how truly unpredictable her mother was. She would say one thing, then do another.

"Really, I will." Victoria recognized Karen's doubt.

Mother and daughter had little to say the remainder of the trip into Nashville. Karen took the 440 Exit ramp that connected into I-65 South. Twenty minutes later, they reached the Cool Springs' Mall exit. Green Gables was located across the interstate near a movie theater.

Karen pulled into a parking space and switched off the key. Victoria climbed out of the car and peered at the impressive federal structure. So this was where her father died.

They were met at the door by a guard and required to prove their identities. After signing a guest list, they were shown into a spacious solarium, bright with sunlight and filled with lush tropical plants. There, they were instructed to wait for Kimberly Ann.

Decorative cages containing exotic twittering birds of many colors hung from the overhead beams. Soft music piped through an intercom system soothed the psyche. Seated quietly before a bubbling fountain, drinking in the pleasant sights and sounds of prefabricated nature, Victoria felt as if the facility were dulling her senses to prepare her for the worst.

"How was my mother when we last visited her?" Victoria turned to Karen. "Grammy's health appears to be failing somewhat, but she was in good spirits," she answered.

Victoria looked up and saw Kimberly Ann Martin being escorted into the solarium by a nurse wearing white. Her mother's fragile face appeared troubled as she grasped the sides of the rolling wheelchair. Karen should have warned her.

Failing to steady her emotions, Victoria was overwhelmed by the intense moment. The only memory she had of her mother reached back to 1989, a week before her accident.

Age had drastically altered Kimberly Ann's physical appearance. Her once thick brown hair had thinned, barely covering her pink scalp. Cruel age lines etched her pasty-white face and dark circles rimmed her eyes. Worst of all, her mother's once-brilliant gaze had withered into a bare glimmer over time as memories slowly deserted her beautiful, rose-garden mind.

While Victoria wrestled with the initial shock, Kimberly Ann's gorgeous smile instantly put her guests at ease. "Karen, my little lamb?" A hacking cough interrupted her speech. She blew her nose with a tissue and sneezed.

"Has Mother been sick?" Victoria quizzed the attending nurse.

"A little cold. Nothing critical." The nurse seemed complacent, irritating Victoria to the core. "Has the doctor seen her?" She thought that even a little lung problem unattended might be a problem at her mother's age.

The young nurse challenged Victoria's statement by refusing to answer and briskly walking away. "I don't like her attitude. Isn't she paid to care?"

"Grammy? Karen knelt beside the wheelchair. "How are you feeling today?" She straightened Kimberly Ann's knitted shawl.

"I guess I'm fine," she loudly replied.

"She's a little hard of hearing," Karen told Victoria. "Grammy? Mother came with me today. She brought you a present." She laid the unwrapped afghan in Kimberly's lap.

"Vicki?" Kimberly Ann clapped her hands as her spirited gaze zoomed on her daughter. "I thought you'd be married by now," she loudly announced. "Where's that good-lookin' doctor of yours? Where's my Mark?" Glee exploded in her round, clouded eyes.

"Mother," Victoria said, hugging Kimberly, "you don't have to speak so loudly. We can hear you just fine." She couldn't help but be troubled by her mother's physical condition.

"It's these blamed hearing aids!" Kimberly tried to adjust the squeaky volume. "I don't see Mark? He here?" She strained her neck to survey the room. "Where's my favorite boy?"

"Mark didn't come with us this time, Mother. He's working." Victoria noted her daughter's drawn expression. Apparently, Kimberly had declined more than Karen realized.

"And Paul?" Kimberly inquired. "Where's our Paul?"

"Grammy?" Karen leaned close to Kimberly's face and patted her wrinkled hand. "Paul was killed in an accident two years ago?"

The bad news stole her grandmother's smile.

"Oh, sure I remember. Things get foggy sometimes, but no need to sign any papers yet." Kimberly's frail hand trembled on the cane lying across her lap.

Victoria sensed her mother's concern. Somebody at the hospital had probably already approached her about signing for voluntary cessation. Still alert enough to realize how her husband had died, she had to be frightened. Who wouldn't be?

"Mother, you don't ever have to sign those voluntary cessation papers," Victoria burst out. "You can live with us."

"No, she can't!" Karen exclaimed. "Don't give Grammy false hope. She can't leave Green Gables, not ever."

"That's ridiculous!" Victoria's blood pressure skyrocketed. "I'll take my mother out of this hospital anytime I please!"

Did the government dictate private affairs?

Karen grabbed Victoria's arm and pulled her to the side.

"Mother, now you listen to me good. This institution has rules. When Grammy and Big Daddy signed on, it was a lifetime commitment. Using personal assets as payment for their extended health care, they agreed never to change residences. That's the way it is, and it works wonderfully for most people."

"I don't care how much this institution has brain-washed its senior citizens!" Victoria had endured all the rules she could stomach. "It's morally and spiritually wrong to insist that these residents sign a document agreeing to assisted suicide!" *Right was right.*

Tongue-tied by fear, anger slowly settled into Karen's lovely face. "We'll discuss this matter when we get home."

"I don't want my mother to die in a place like this!" Victoria declared. "I want Kimberly Ann Martin to meet Jesus at a ripe old age. With dignity! And in my arms!"

"Grammy can't do that," Karen argued in whispers. "I know you mean well, but you can't change the legal system." She jerked her mother's arm. "Don't you dare say another word!"

"Well, I sure as . . ." Victoria fought back a whole slew of ugly words. "I certainly intend to talk to Mark about this!" She struggled with rage. "I'll hire a lawyer if I have to. Fight the system! Somehow, some way, I'll get my mother out of this predicament!"

"Oh, Mother!" Karen was at her wit's end.

"Girls, girls," Kimberly cried. "Victoria, you know better than to fight with your sister!"

Victoria and Karen did a double take. Victoria's younger sister had been dead since 1966. A hit and run on the street in front of their house. Kimberly Ann was exhibiting signs of senility.

Shortly before noon, a nurse came to reclaim Kimberly Ann, ending their visit. When Victoria asked if her mother might stay a little longer, the nurse refused. The client's stability depended on routine and the rules were non-negotiable.

After Grammy had been strolled away, there was nothing more that either Victoria or Karen could do but go home. They would need to reschedule another visit. But would it be too late to save Kimberly's life?

It wounded Victoria's heart to think she might never see her mother alive again in the flesh. And due to Kimberly's delicate physical condition, she had not shared her memory dilemma.

Another time, maybe.

THURSDAY, APRIL 24

29

Thursday morning, Victoria took a big chance in cornering Cory Lindsey outside the Olde Soda Shoppe.

When she grabbed his arm rather forcefully, the lad eyed her suspiciously, then instructed his three buddies to go on inside and order him the usual.

"Sorry." Victoria promptly released Cory.

"Hi, Miss Victoria." The lad crooked his head at her. Hands stuffed in his pants pockets, his chestnut eyes were the size of quarters.

"The other day when we talked, Cory, I forgot to ask you if Gloria Gordon had any relatives still living in Fernwood." She glanced around to see who might be watching.

"I don't think so, uh," Cory replied. "Is some'n wrong?"

"I certainly hope not," Victoria said. "I need to find her."

"I think Miss Gloria's brother used to live in Somerville," the boy recalled. "My grandpa still talks about Blazin' Burn Gordon and how good he could kick a football."

"You've been very helpful, Cory. Thank you." Victoria handed him a five-dollar bill.

"I know, keep it a secret." He looked up with a sly grin.

"Exactly." Victoria winked, thinking that Somerville was only a forty-five-minute drive from Fernwood. Since Burn was her *only* lead, this was a trip she couldn't afford to put off.

Yesterday she and Karen had traveled to Nashville to see her mother. Although they had returned home long before dark, she hadn't phoned Mark as promised. By now, he would be hot on her trail. Victoria hurried home to prepare for her Somerville trip.

"Karen, why are you still here?" she asked a little too abruptly, feeling like she'd been caught with her hand in the candy jar. "I mean . . . why aren't you at work?"

"I took an extra hour for myself," Karen replied. "Anyhow, I don't have a real estate appointment until eleven thirty. Do you need me to do something for you?"

"No, I'm fine." Victoria acted casual, peeling off her sweater. "What time shall I expect you for supper?" She saw no reason to reveal her little manhunt when she could easily make the drive over to Somerville, check out Burn Gordon, and beat Karen home.

"Late," Karen replied. "Don't wait supper on me. I'm helping with Toni Kippinger's bridal shower tonight."

"Oh," said Victoria, recalling that Toni had played on Karen's school softball team in the ninth grade. "I have a few things I need to do." She disappeared into her bedroom.

After Karen had driven away, Victoria packed an overnight bag just in case the unexpected occurred. Making sure the lights were turned off she locked up and left the condo, whistling a Disney tune from the *Seven Dwarfs.*

Involved in speculation, the drive to Somerville seemed brief. Living with misplaced memories proved tricky, Victoria was fast learning. But somewhere in the troubled hand that life had dealt, there was bound to be a winning card.

Turning up Burn Gordon could be her big fat ace!

By the time Victoria entered Somerville city limits she was passing quaint renovated neighborhoods. The town had not leaped into the future so quickly as Fernwood. Let the townspeople count their blessings they'd missed dealing with another Dick Branson.

Sighting an Exxon Station, Victoria pulled her blue Mercedes up to a fuel pump and shut down the engine. Owning no credit card, she ventured inside and approached the cashier.

"Oh, hi," she said. "Mind turning on Pump 10?" She handed over two twenties, more than enough cash.

"Sure." Dora punched a lever behind the cash register. "Got coffee in the back. It's free so help yo'rself. Want me to pump for you?"

"Yes, that would be helpful." Victoria decided a cup of hot coffee sounded wonderful.

While Dora filled the Mercedes with high-test, Victoria milled around the store staring at the variety of candies. *Don't you dare!* She didn't need to pig out on sugar. Reaching the back of the store, she filled a Styrofoam cup with coffee and added cream.

As Victoria exited the shop, she spotted a public phone booth beside the women's restroom. Possibly, Burn Gordon's number was public knowledge. It was worth a look.

"Nope!" She decided after perusing the listings. "Burn must have an unlisted number!" Victoria slammed shut the directory.

Then realizing that *Burn* was probably a nickname, she checked for listings under the first names of *Burney* and *Rayburn.*

Batting zero again, Victoria reentered the store and thanked Dora for pumping the gas. "Keep the change," she told her.

Downtown Somerville, Tennessee was laid out like most southern county seats: a county courthouse at the center surrounded by century-old mom-and-pop shops on the square.

Victoria stopped at the first enterprise that sold books and magazines. After squeezing into a parallel parking space, she scrambled out of the car and loaded adequate coinage into the parking meter. God forbid she get a parking ticket that placed her in Somerville.

Inside THE NOSY BOOKRACK Victoria struck up small talk with a saleslady operating a computer behind the sales counter. "So how long have you lived in Somerville?"

"Excuse me?" The woman glowered over half-rimmed, blue plastic reading glasses.

"I was just inquiring how long you've lived in Somerville."

"Just a sec," she said, keying data into a computer.

"I didn't mean to interrupt." Victoria browsed through the magazine racks, glancing up now and then at the blond who appeared to be around her age.

"Now! To answer your question, I've lived in Somerville most of my life." She stretched, yawned, and resumed keying in her data. "Name's Josie if you need any help."

Not wanting to appear overly inquisitive, Victoria milled around the shop another five minutes, randomly thumbing through magazines. *How To Interpret Your Karma* and *Picking Your Personal Psychic* were two article titles particularly disturbing.

I'll pass on those magazines. Victoria grew jittery.

"Can I help you find something?" Josie abandoned her computer and walked over to visit with Victoria. "I need a break anyhow."

"Thank you." Victoria managed a smile. "From the looks of your store, you have just about everything." She would despise promoting New-Age materials.

"Yeah, it's keeping records to please the IRS that's hard. Just when I think I've nailed down a computer program, technology changes on me. If you ask me, progress stinks."

"I fully agree!" Victoria found common ground. "The Internet stumps me even worse." Kathryn Billingsly's astute skills came to mind.

"Hey, you're not alone," Josie professed.

A big-boned woman with a round face, flag-blue eyes, and bleached blond hair, Josie carried her extra pounds well in her chartreuse pantsuit. And she had a fantastic smile.

"Guess it's our age," Josie remarked. "You can't teach an old dog new tricks, as the saying goes. Still, I try like the dickens to keep up with progress."

"You have a very interesting store." Victoria picked up a couple of books, biding time.

"You're not from here, are you?" Josie curiously asked.

"No. How did you know?" Victoria selected a copy of the area newspaper over her other choices.

"I know just about everybody in town," Josie spouted. "I'm a fourth-generation Donaldson. Nobody knows exactly how our family ended up here, but we all stayed."

"I'm from an old bloodline, too," Victoria remarked. "My name is Victoria Tempest. My ancestors, the Martins, moved to Fernwood prior to the Civil War. I can't think of anywhere better to have raised a family."

"Oh, Fernwood's quite a progressive little city." Josie scooted around the sales counter and plopped down at her computer screen, cursing when she realized she'd lost some data.

"Sorry," Josie apologized for her language. "You know somebody who lives here?"

"Yeah." Victoria found it easy conversing with Josie. "The brother of a friend of mine lives here. Burn Gordon. Played big-league football back when. Know of him?"

"Blazin' Burn Gordon!" Josie's eyes widened with interest. "Everybody in town knows of him! Burn was a show-stopper all right, a real pillar of this community for many years."

"Was?" Victoria's eyes blinked as fear impacted. "Is he dead?"

"Oh, no!" Josie said. "Burn moved away to Southaven a few years back. Heard he opened up a new business there. Something related to football equipment, I think."

"Mississippi?"

"Tha's right," Josie answered. "You ever been there?"

"Not that I recall." Victoria was disappointed she wouldn't be talking to Burn today about his sister's mysterious disappearance. "Well, I'll get going now. If you're ever in Fernwood, Josie, look me up."

"Stop in any time, Victoria. Doors are open nine to five."

"Oh, I'll take these." Victoria laid a *Memphis Commercial Appeal* and a *Better Homes and Gardens* magazine on the sales counter.

"That will be eight dollars and forty-five cents."

"Thanks again, Josie." Victoria paid cash, picked up her merchandise, and ventured outside. A steamy heat was settling over West Tennessee. "Oh, brother," she mumbled. The weather was shaping up to spontaneously ignite an afternoon thunderstorm. She hated the idea of driving home in the rain.

Thinking that her NOSY BOOKRACK detour hadn't been a total waste of time, Victoria counted her blessings that at least she had learned Burn's real name: Colburn Stanley Gordon.

No use stopping now! She made a snap decision and headed out of Somerville going west, her final destination Southaven, Mississippi. *Look out, crooks, here comes Sherlock!*

Somewhere down the highway, subconsciously tapping her fingers to keep beat with a Garth Brooks' country tune, Victoria concluded that proving Branson Meatpacking Company was operating on environmentally unsafe soil should take top priority.

If Jeffrey had been working on a lawsuit involving Branson's environmental negligence at the time he was murdered, then Dick Branson would have motive to break into his office to steal files. With proof of wrongdoing, she could go to Dick and demand the truth.

While in Memphis, why not contact a reputable detective agency? She stepped on the gas pedal.

As Victoria saw it, a crossroad loomed before her. Critical answers lay at the end of each avenue, all important in solving Jeffrey's murder. Regardless which road she took, there would likely be roadblocks, probably dangerous ones. One person could not explore all the avenues at once. But one good detective working in her behalf would double the effort.

Around one thirty, Victoria rolled into a McDonald's on the outskirts of Memphis and ordered a quarter-pound burger with large fries and a Coke. Discarding any guilt for the luncheon choice, she needed those fat calories to energetically pursue her investigation.

Her next stop was a public phone booth outside a K-Mart Shopping Center. Flipping through the Yellow Pages, she spied several impressive ads listed under *Detective Agencies.*

Probably firms with worldwide connections. Too well connected for her liking. No. Victoria closed the phone book. The person she wanted would be described as a small-time investigator, not unlike herself. An unconventional type who didn't mind bending the rules a bit as long as the job paid well.

Now where could she find such a person?

Victoria took the I-240 northern route around Memphis, following the West I-40 signs to Little Rock. When she spied the

Mississippi River Bridge up ahead, she exited on Danny Thomas Boulevard and headed downtown to find the county courthouse.

Passing the St. Jude's Children's Hospital on her right, she went a little farther and made a right on Third Street. Just as the McDonald's manager had said, the eighteenth-century Shelby County Courthouse stood on the corner of Third and Adams.

With no available parking spaces out front, Victoria continued down Third Street and turned left behind the courthouse, spying the SHELBY COUNTY OFFICE BUILDING on her right.

At the end of the short street running between the back of the courthouse and the county office building, Victoria paused at a stop sign. Looking to her left she spied a high-rise public parking facility a block away. *Thank you, Jesus!* She would park there.

Victoria rolled through the open gates, punched a button, and waited for the machine to spit out a metered parking ticket.

Following a circular maze to the fifth floor, she parked her Mercedes Benz between two junkers and hopped an elevator going down. Sprinting through the main lobby of the 100 NORTH MAIN BUILDING, she exited on Adams Street and glanced around.

It was evident that over the years many of the city's older structures had been demolished to make room for modern high-rise office space. *So-called progress.*

To Victoria's left, a skip and a hop from the Mississippi waterfront turned tourist trap, she caught sight of THE PYRAMID, a huge sports arena constructed back in the seventies.

Mud Island River Park, an amusement area, was just over the hill in the middle of *Ol' Man River.* And sandwiched between Main and Front streets was a super-shopping mall that swallowed the cobble-stoned streets, paving them with indoor customers.

Archaic trolley cars were on track again to transport pedestrians from one location to another, but Victoria preferred walking.

The City of Memphis had developed alongside the banks of the mighty Mississippi River to accommodate the early-American shipping industry. Steamers had chugged up from New Orleans, or down from St Louis, to collect West Tennessee's valuable cotton commodity and redistribute the bales to smaller communities along the waterways.

Victoria guessed that Beale Street would have survived the turn of the century with its many restaurants and entertainment attractions. Black musicians thrived in this area. By now, the old Peabody Hotel would have employed several new generations of strutting ducks. The Memphis Chamber of Commerce was to be applauded for doing a great job in preserving the character of the old city while embracing progress.

Change, so much change. A tear slipped down Victoria's cheek as she realized how time had marched on when she hadn't.

Take away the nosy tourists, the lofty buildings, and all the hoop-de-la. Give her the weathered stone streets and crumbling earthen buildings! The bustling rough-rousing nineteenth-century businesses, the tap dancing shoeshine boys, robust blacksmiths and carpenters! Hard-working citizens who had exhibited good work ethics with purpose.

Lost in time, drop her off anywhere!

Above Victoria, a lingering spring haze thickened with cloud coverage promising to deliver afternoon thundershowers.

With a light spring in her step, she hurried down Adams Street toward the county courthouse, plagued by the rapidly rising heat and humidity.

Hurrying across the street, she mounted the steep concrete steps of the governmental relic and passed the statue of *Justice* on her left. Blinking back tears, she could almost feel Jeffrey's presence. *Why had justice failed him?* She continued her trek to the top.

While still struggling with sad memories, Victoria stepped through the open doorway of the courthouse and was met by a guard who requested an official court pass.

Of course, she didn't have one. She learned that only people whose court cases were being tried that day were permitted inside.

What now, turn tail and race home? I don't think so!

Victoria trudged back down the steps and began walking toward the waterfront. Making a left on Main Street, she passed the front entrance of the 100 NORTH MAIN BUILDING. A fog of shoppers passed as she pushed through the revolving glass doors.

Seconds later, Victoria spied The Yellow Rose Café on the next corner. Hot and already spent from thwarted plans, she walked the short block and ventured indoors.

Met by a draft of cold air and the odor of hamburgers cooking, a sweet-smiling hostess offered her a 1950's red metal-top table by the plate-glass window. Collapsing in a plastic cushioned chair, she peered up at Marsha and said, "Please bring me a Coke."

In City Park across the street, carefree children frolicked on the gym equipment, not a bother in their young heads.

What should I do now? Victoria belabored her choices. *Look for Burn as I originally planned, or head home?*

Marsha promptly returned with an icy Coke. Meditatively sipping on it, Victoria contemplated her insecure future. Twenty minutes later, with no leap of insight, she paid her drink tab, left the restaurant, and hurried down the street to get her car.

Like a lost goose, Victoria stood shivering at the entrance of the 100 NORTH MAIN BUILDING, at her wit's end to know what came next. *Dear Lord, lead my steps!*

When she lifted her head, she noticed a modern copper-colored high-rise building across the street. On the chance she might locate a friendly face, she crossed the street to have a look.

Refreshing cold air slapped Victoria in the face as she stepped through the revolving door. The Memphis Municipal Building was a high-tech, beautifully furbished expression of space-mania.

As if being led by an unseen hand, Victoria walked across the corridor toward an office clearly marked BUSINESS LICENSES, and peered through the door's clear window glass.

Mustering courage, she entered the office and approached a clerk standing behind one of the counters. "Excuse me, sir," she inquired how to go about locating a good attorney.

Help must have been written all over her face because the older gentleman took pity on her and listened.

"Not that I really have to have one today," Victoria reasoned with the clerk, "but any good attorney must know how to find an old-fashioned, hungry private eye."

"You want somebody expensive? With enough clout to get the evidence you need?" Mule-eyes peered over his spectacles, sizing up Victoria. "You have money, I assume."

Victoria affirmatively nodded.

"What kind, Miss? Divorce? Accident?"

"I really just need a list of attorneys, if you know where I could find such an animal." She wasn't up to games.

Just the facts, Ma'am!

"Tried the Yellow Pages?" He grinned.

"Yes, but I'm looking for a smaller operation." Victoria ignored the clerk's attempt at humor. "A firm with one or two lawyers will do. My case is not all that important, just a matter I need cleared up," she was evasive. "It's personal."

Mule-eyes sighed. "Isn't everything?"

"I'm sorry, I have to go." It had been a mistake coming.

"Hey, don't give up yet, lady! I might just know a fellow that fits that description." The clerk began drawing a map on a notepad.

Victoria leaned across the counter to watch.

"Get off the interstate on Perkins Road. Right here." Mule-eyes pointed to the map. "Go south for a couple of miles and look for a shopping center on your left—Sagewood's the name, I believe—with a big movie theater at one end. No way you can miss it!"

Nodding, Victoria erected herself to escape his garlic breath.

"Down at one end, you'll find an attorney office." He glanced up. "You wanna see Devin Baldwin. He's a distant cousin of mine. I forget how many times removed, but we got the same last name."

With a wink, Mr. Baldwin handed over his sketch. Victoria took the map and thanked him.

"Just tell Devin that Larry Baldwin sen'cha."

30

Time was a big factor. Victoria grabbed Larry's road map and hurriedly departed the municipal building worried that Devin Baldwin's office might be closed by the time she arrived.

Scampering through the lobby in record time, she hopped an elevator and pushed the button for the fifth floor. *Wait for me, Devin.* She leaped into her Mercedes and spun out of the parking lot.

Following the well-marked road signs to the I-240 South ramp, Victoria nervously maneuvered her Mercedes into the four-lane expressway traffic, hugging the steering wheel for dear life, keenly aware that time had never been a friend.

Dear God, keep me safe and order my steps.

As the I-55 Southaven Exit loomed before Victoria, she resisted the urge to cancel all her other plans and track down Burn Gordon. *One task at a time*, she reminded herself.

Thirty minutes later, looking ragged and feeling distraught, Victoria traipsed up two flights of stairs and spied a young man in the process of locking up his office. "Wait! Stop!" She frantically waved, rushing toward the young man.

"What?" The attorney whirled around to see who addressed him. A startled expression coursed his handsome face as Victoria came to a crashing stop. "Are you Devin Baldwin?"

"Speaking." Alarm cringed in his expression.

"Your cousin Larry said you might be able to help me." Victoria was panting like a dog after a rabbit. "Larry Baldwin. He said you would remember him from the family picnic."

"Larry?" Devin took a moment to think. "Oh, yeah, the courthouse Larry!" He grinned as his gray matter made the right connection. "My ol' cousin sent you?"

"Mr. Baldwin, I really need your advice concerning a personal matter." Victoria was struggling to breathe after running up the steps.

"Sure." Devin glanced at his wristwatch. "Call my appointment secretary in the morning and set up a time. I promised my boy I'd take 'im to a ball game this afternoon."

"This is important!" Victoria impulsively grabbed Devin's arm. "Money is no object." She was rich, wasn't she?

A quizzical expression crossed Devin's face as he brushed Victoria's hand from his arm. "Lady, you've got my attention. I'm all ears." He set down his brief.

"I have an urgent matter that—" Victoria could tell Devin was torn between listening and leaving. "Really, mine is!" She insisted. "I'm in dire need of a private investigator."

"I thought you needed an attorney," Devin sighed. "Look Miss, everybody and his uncle thinks their problem is urgent."

"Victoria Tempest," she introduced herself with a handshake. "I apologize for my abruptness, but I'm in a rather distressful situation. A matter I'm not at liberty to discuss."

"Georgie Hendricks." Devin's steely-gray gaze hounded Victoria's big brown puppies as he shuffled his antsy feet.

"Excuse me," she reacted, batting her dark eyelashes.

"Georgie Hendricks. A reputable PI." Devin fumbled with his car keys in preparation to leave. "You lookin' to get the goods on an unfaithful husband?" he curiously asked.

"Something like that," Victoria replied, thinking going into details would delay the both of them.

"You don't want to talk about it here," Devin concluded. "That's fine, I understand. But if you ever do, our conversation will be confidential."

Victoria grew nervous at the dark clouds billowing on the western horizon in advance of an approaching storm front. She dreaded driving home. *In the rain, and in the dark.*

"Wait a sec." Devin dug a business card out of his coat pocket and jotted a number on the back. "Here." He handed it to Victoria. "You can reach Georgie at this number."

"Thank you, Devin." *Yes!* "If your detective friend can help me get the information I'm after and I need the future assistance of an attorney, I promise to call you." She owed him.

"Sure." Devin looked as if he'd heard that line before. Grabbing his briefcase, he mumbled a goodbye and vanished around the corner of the stairwell.

No longer in a hurry, Victoria retraced her steps and reclaimed her car. At the other end of the shopping center, she found a row of phone booths located outside the Sagewood Movie Theater.

Unfortunately, the parking lot was crowded with a bunch of rambunctious teenagers waiting for the next scheduled movie. And those who didn't have cellphones were standing in line to use the next available payphone.

"Oh, that's just great," Victoria complained.

Was this a bad idea or not?

While waiting for her turn to use the telephone, a din of angry clouds grumbled overhead. Reminiscent of the stormy night that had terrorized her on April 13, 1989, the specifics of Victoria's accident began to replay on her mindscape like an old horror flick.

Thirty minutes later, the phone swallowed her change.

Going nearly bananas when Georgie's tape recorder clicked on, Victoria had no option but to leave a sketchy message with the payphone number. By then, it had grown dark and cold rain slithered down in sheets.

Fortunately, with the disbursement of the last movie crowd, the youthful gangs quickly shuffled into the theater. Reclaiming her booth, freezing without a warm wrap, Victoria hovered inside the phone booth anxiously waiting for Georgie to return her call.

Georgie, I don't have forever. She began to worry that the detective might not call back. Here she sat alone, shivering in a phone booth not knowing a soul, nobody to watch over her.

Two hours passed and the latest movie-going crowd noisily filed out of the theater and took off in all directions. Tired and discouraged, she guarded her booth like it was golden, despite the fact a number of angry teens tapped on the glass door to oust her.

It was after seven and Victoria still had the long drive back to Fernwood ahead of her. Karen would surely beat her home and worry that she wasn't there. Then she would call Mark and they would both worry. They might even call the police!

Squelching a panic attack, she realized when she got home—if she did get home—she would be required to explain where she'd been and what she'd been doing.

"Oh, Georgie, please have a heart and call."

Fifteen minutes later, she grabbed the ringing phone.

"Hello!" She pounced on a salutation.

"Hey, this is Georgie. What's up?"

"Thank you for calling back." Victoria identified the voice as female. Good. A woman detective would surely understand her dilemma better than a man ever could.

"My name is Victoria Tempest. I'm calling from a payphone at the Sagewood Shopping Center on Perkins Road. Next to the big theater," she defined the exact location.

"Yeah, I know the spot."

"I'm from out of town and need your help with a matter."

"Where from out of town? Who gave you my name, lady?"

"I live in Fernwood," Victoria replied. "Larry, the one who works downtown at the municipal building in auto licensing, he told me how to find Devin Baldwin."

"Enough said," Georgie cut in. "I do work for Devin. So how can I help?" She opened the door for an explanation.

"Obviously, I need a private investigator or I wouldn't be calling," Victoria said. "It's complicated, Georgie. Do you think we could meet somewhere?"

"Tonight?" She considered the idea. "Yeah, why not?"

"You say where." Victoria didn't care.

"How 'bout O'Charley's? Oh say, in thirty minutes?"

"Yes, that's good for me, but I need directions." Victoria's evening was improving. Even a storm couldn't stop her now.

"Get back on Perkins Road and go south about a half mile. You'll see the restaurant on your right. I'll be the gal wearing a man's haircut and western blue jeans."

"I'm on my way!" Victoria was uplifted. *Thank You, Lord.*

"I've gotta silver medallion around my neck. What about you?"

"I'm wearing a green pantsuit and wagging a big battered alligator purse," Victoria identified herself. *Look for the tired and bewildered.* She said goodbye and hung up the phone.

Seeing the late hour, Victoria realized it was impossible to meet with Georgie and make the drive home to Fernwood before Karen discovered she was missing. Knowing how her concerned daughter would react, panic would likely drive her to call the cops.

No, Victoria decided, *I'll have to leave a phone message with a reasonable explanation.* She inserted enough coinage to make the long distance call.

After five rings the message center clicked on. Good, Karen wasn't home.

"Karen, this is Mother. Just calling to say that I'm spending the night with a friend." Her eyelashes fluttered. "A girl friend. See you in the morning."

That done, she raced to her car to avoid getting rain soaked.

Georgie had given excellent directions, so the drive to O'Charley's didn't take long. The restaurant wasn't all that busy if you counted the cars parked outside.

Victoria locked her car, hurried inside the restaurant, and approached the hostess at the front desk. About to give her name, her eyes fell upon a stunning silver medallion roped around a long, muscular neck. Gratefully, recognition rested in Georgie's poignant gaze.

"I'm Victoria Tempest." She walked over and shook the investigator's hand, her eyes glued to the medallion—possibly a family heirloom hand-carved by an Indian artisan.

Georgie, a bit abrupt on the edges, had a mystique about her that lived up to her husky voice. A tall, lanky woman in her thirties, she wore her blue jeans hung-slung off her hips. A series of silver studs pierced her right earlobe as she jammed hands into her pants pockets.

"Georgie Hendricks," the PI said in a raspy alto voice, her mannerisms as flamboyant as her brilliant turquoise eyes. "I already put our name in."

"Thanks for meeting me on such short notice."

"No problem." The PI half-smiled.

The wait was brief and a young hostess escorted them to a table. With a quick casing of the restaurant, Georgie gave Victoria a nudge and said, "Let's get to it."

Get to what? Victoria took a seat in the booth and accepted the menu the hostess handed her, taking a moment to study the investigator sitting across from her.

Georgie's flawless olive complexion, short raven-black hair, and high cheekbones unmistakably marked her as Native American. She had no problem with that. God loved peoples of all nationalities, primarily interested in the condition of their souls.

"So why did you want to see me?" Georgie turned cold stony eyes on Victoria, digging deep into her psyche.

"I'm not in a hurry if you're not." She didn't want to rush so important a meeting, suspecting that beneath Georgie's all-business, raging masculine demeanor lay the remnants of a troubled young woman. "Why don't we take the time to eat first."

"Eating is good, I'm hungry," Georgie agreed.

Lightning flashed nearby, followed by crashing thunder. Victoria let out a little peep as the night dragged up her old fear of storms, causing her heart to pound in her ears.

"You okay, Victoria?" Georgie lifted a pack of cigarettes from her backpack. "Mind if I smoke?" She was already peeling away the cellophane wrapper.

"Yes, I'm fine. And no, I don't mind." She did, but she was on Georgie's turf.

"Want one?" Left-handed Georgie thumped a cigarette into her right hand. "Life is a lot harder on the body than smoking."

"No, thank you," Victoria couldn't help but smile at Georgie's defense mechanism. About now, food would push back the pull of fatigue.

The PI made a ritual out of lighting her *Virginia Slim*, casually canvassing the restaurant until her unsettling gaze came to rest on her prospective client. "So why are we here, Victoria?"

"Georgie, I'm—" the waiter appeared with ice waters, interrupting Victoria's first attempt to explain why she had called. Unfolding her napkin, she placed it in her lap.

"What'll it be, Victoria?" Georgie exhaled a smoke halo.

"Anything's fine." Victoria fanned the smoke. "You order for us." She told the waiter to put their orders on her tab, the least she could do in exchange for Georgie's time.

"Two burgers and a large order of French fries. What to drink?" Twin pools of swirling turquoise targeted Victoria.

"Diet Coke," she replied.

"Double everything!" The PI plugged the cigarette between her lips, supporting her elbows on the marbleized tabletop. "So Victoria, let's just say some guy's beating up on you."

"That's not it!" Victoria jumped as lightning struck nearby.

"Maybe you've been raped and need goods on the jerk?"

"No!" Victoria raised her voice above the rumbling thunder.

"What then?" Georgie asked. "Spill it from the gut level, Victoria!" She used graphic hand gestures. "You'll feel a whole lot saner if you empty out all that garbage."

That was exactly what Victoria wanted to do. But with Georgie, she was cautiously uncertain where to begin. Once she began purging the hurt, how much of her would be left?

"Look, lady . . . if all you wanna do is buy my supper, you could take a friend out!" Georgie wasn't fluff.

"No!" Victoria knocked over her water glass.

"Easy, girl." Georgie mopped up the liquid with paper napkins.

Victoria trembled, searching for the right words. "Look, Georgie, I realize you don't know me. I could be anybody guilty of anything. But I truly am an honest person."

"I believe you, Victoria. Say what's on your mind."

"As I said earlier, I'm from out of town." She paused as the waiter removed the mess and replaced her water. "It's hard to define my—"

"I don't have time for games, Victoria. Tell me what's going on or I'm outta here." Georgie was reaching for her backpack.

The ultimatum was all the catalyst Victoria needed.

"Twenty-five years ago, my attorney-husband was murdered in his office," she bit the bullet. "Shot to death by perps, probably after his files." Grief socked Victoria in the gut. "I was talking to him on my car phone when it happened."

"I'm hearing you." Georgie hunkered over the table engulfed in a ring of smoke as she internalized the information.

Victoria suppressed a cough. "I think I know some of the people who may have been involved, but I'm not sure—I need to get soil tests run first." Her thoughts were scattered like broken glass.

"Slow down, gal! You just lost me!" Georgie put up a hand. "What's soil tests got to do with your husband's murder?" Her voice was hushed, her gaze wild with speculation.

"Like I said, it's complicated." Victoria leaned across the table to close the gap. "And a little dangerous." Probably more than she was ready to accept.

"I like danger." The PI flicked cigarette ash in the air.

"There's a meatpacking company in Fernwood doing business on a site where an old tannery used to be located. I'm thinking the EPA may have never cleared the way and—"

"I'm starting to get the picture," Georgie jumped in. "You suspect there's a connection between the processing plant and your husband's death?"

Victoria nodded, pleased with Georgie's diagnosis.

"You want to ask questions, but you think it's too dangerous." Georgie's cigarette dangled at the corner of her mouth. "So you hire me to get the lowdown." That's how it was usually done.

"Exactly!" A bolt of lightning defined the climax as the waiter set their orders on the table.

"Let's eat, talk later." Georgie clutched her burger. "I need a little down time, Victoria." She took a juicy bite. "If you want to, you can crash at my place tonight, you're more than welcome."

Georgie was a Godsend. A second bolt of lightning influenced Victoria's decision. "Thank you, I accept."

FRIDAY, APRIL 25

31

Victoria slipped out of Georgie's apartment around *5 a.m.* Friday morning. The brunt of the storm had passed through West Tennessee during the night leaving behind a trail of cold misting rain. Closing the car door, she recognized the dye had been cast in hiring Georgie. *No turning back now.*

Victoria felt a chill invading her spine as she switched on the engine, heater, and windshield wipers. What in the world was she going to tell Karen when she got home?

And Georgie had said never to phone her. Ever. Somebody could be listening. "You have to walk on eggs when a murder is involved." *People kill to cover sins.* She shivered at her investigator's outlook on life.

That she was blind-sided by her emotions was a given. Somebody took her husband's life and that was a travesty. But at least, she had an ally now. And Georgie had promised to contact her after she'd nosed around a bit and nailed down a few critical details.

"If I show up in Fernwood unannounced, ignore me like the plague," she'd said. "Trust me, I'll be there for a good reason."

Like a little lost lamb, Victoria's thoughts wandered in open pasture. No matter how poor choices had altered the present, or what the unseen future held, she was positive that her stormy past would likely haunt her until her dying days. Although a little older, and somewhat wiser, life was still a risky adventure.

Then, hadn't unknowns always frightened her?

"Grow up, Victoria!" She gripped the steering wheel and stamped hard on the accelerator. Reluctant to dwell on negatives, she much preferred designing a spectacular future: one in which the man she loved, loved her; and the daughter she trusted, also trusted her; and the many friends who supported her, she could also support. And not question *why.*

But how could she dismiss her past? Forget about a wonderful husband who had been brutally murdered? Allow those who had wrecked her life and damaged the emotions of her children to walk away unpunished? *No*, only a coward would agree to that!

Tormented by cycling thoughts, Victoria's blame boomeranged, returning to rest on her shoulders. *If only* she hadn't been terrified of storms. If *only* she hadn't phoned Jeffrey's office because she was late. If only she hadn't heard the gunshots . . .

"Maybe Jeffrey would be alive!" she said aloud.

Dear God, if only I had a reasonable explanation. If the good people of Fernwood would tell the simple truth, perhaps I could find some degree of resolve.

However, Victoria had regrets regarding her spontaneous trip to Memphis. Frustrated over not making it as far as Southaven to question Burn Gordon about his sister, Gloria, she had also failed to phone the Methodist Hospital regarding the whereabouts of her old nurse. And it was unlikely she could slip away to Memphis again without Karen and Mark knowing it.

By next week, she would be in the hospital having tests! *And who knew the outcome of that?*

Victoria anxiously drove toward home, hoping to catch Karen at the condo before she left for work. She needed to shower, change clothes, and hustle on over to the public library and meet Beverly James on the World Wide Web at ten o'clock. *Which reminds me, I still need to get an e-mail address.*

A familiar headache born out of stress buzzed at the base of Victoria's brain as she wheeled into the parking garage an hour later, pleased to see that Karen's Cadillac was still there.

However, she should have expected a confrontation and better prepared her heart. When Karen tore open the kitchen door, Victoria cringed at her fury.

"Mother! I'm gonna kill you!" she spewed. "Whatever possessed you to pull a stunt like this?" The tirade lasted a good five minutes before she wound down and gave Victoria an opportunity to explain. "Whatever you have to say, it had better be good!"

"I'm a grown woman, *dear*!" Victoria strutted though the kitchen and slung her alligator purse on the counter with attitude. "You'd think I was the child and you were the mother! I'm not a helpless imbecile!" She matched Karen's disapproving glare.

"Oh no, you're not getting off that easy. I get home late last night and find this—this sketchy phone message telling me you're spending the night with a friend!" Karen was on Victoria's heels, fuming.

Why couldn't my daughter simply trust me? Victoria felt too fatigued to argue. "Is there anything else you want to say?"

"Yes! You don't have any *friends*!" Karen stepped in Victoria's pathway. "At least none that you recall." The centers of Karen's whipped-hazel eyes danced in the whites.

She is correct. A faint smile tugged at Victoria's lips. She had no true friends. Alone in a stranger world than science fiction might imagine, who could she trust? *Except for God.*

"Really, Mother! Have you lost it entirely?"

"Because I smiled? No, dear." Victoria calmly sidestepped her daughter. She'd definitely been out of her element, immensely relieved to be safely home again.

"Wait! I don't suppose you've had any breakfast?"

"No, and I'm starving." Victoria lent Karen her wilted eyes.

"And I don't expect you're going to tell me where you've been either?" Karen ran out of steam. "You look tired."

"I am. Any coffee made?" Victoria's gaze waltzed across the kitchen and landed on the cold coffeepot as she settled into a barstool. "Did you eat already?"

"I didn't think so." Karen shook her head. "I'll make some fresh coffee before I ask you again exactly where you spent last night."

"Good! Think I'll grab a shower." Victoria leaped from the barstool. "Something to eat would be nice, too!" She grabbed her purse and started down the hall.

"Wait, Mother!" Karen called after Victoria, frustrated and mumbling curse words.

"What?" Victoria spun around. "And, sweetheart . . . thanks for not grilling me."

Karen's angry expression melted like cheese as moist tears squatted like giant toadstools in the corners of her spacious eyes.

This was the little girl Victoria remembered. "I do love you," she mouthed, overwhelmed with endearment.

"I love you, too, Mother," Karen's whisper trailed Victoria down the hallway. "But if you think we're finished talking, you're mistaken."

Luckily, Karen already had an e-mail address that Victoria could use. Surprisingly, she swallowed the cock-and-bull story about ordering make-up products sold via the Internet.

Around 9:45, Victoria rushed off to the library to greet Beverly James, vowing to one day purchase a computer of her own and apply for a secure e-mail address. But for now, it seemed far safer to communicate from a public address.

Worst scenario, Victoria lamented. Karen might intercept an e-mail letter not meant for her eyes. In which case, she'd explain her dilemma. Surely Karen would cover her back.

At the public library, Victoria hopped the escalator to the Third Level and located a free cubicle. Embarrassed over needing computer assistance again, she was grateful that Kathryn Billingsly was nowhere in sight and her assistant was kind enough to help.

Once on line, Victoria recalled the steps to connect her with the Senior Citizens Link-up. Just as before, she roamed her little *Sherlock Holmes* icon around in the chatroom.

After a few *hits*, Beverly's red-haired character showed up and led the way into *The Private Study*. "I have an e-mail address," Victoria proudly reported.

"My message will be coded," Bev's weird robotic voice responded. "Five to one, you can guess it." Her answer struck Victoria as odd, though she appreciated the act of caution.

"What's the address?" Bev asked in a disguised voice.

"Little caps: REALKAREN at JCH dot ATT dot NET."

"Got it. Will e-mail you soon." With a zip, she was gone.

All that trouble for only thirty seconds?

About to leave the library, Victoria thought of Mark. Avoiding him any longer was a virtual impossibility. The glittering ring on her left hand stung her heart. Hadn't she promised to phone him when she returned from Nashville?

Besides, she needed to work on her tolerance. She phoned Mark from the library payphone. "Mark, this is—"

"Vicki, I know who it is," he snapped. "You think I don't know your voice by now?" he raised his voice.

"Are you angry with me?" Victoria's grip on the receiver tightened. *No doubt he was.* "I've been pretty busy."

"I heard. Karen told me you were missing all Thursday evening. For God's sake, Vicki! Where have you been?"

How dare him grill me! Mark doesn't own me, never will.

"Vicki? Are you still there?" His buttery voice said he was sorry for his outburst.

"Yes. I called to see if you'd be free for lunch?"

"You're inviting me to lunch?"

"Will you accept?" The idea was spontaneous but doable.

"Of course, sweetheart. To the ends of the earth," he replied in a lilting voice. "Drop by my office and pick me up?" He was putty in Victoria's hands. *Let her take the lead.*

"Sure. What time is good?"

"Now is fine. I didn't get breakfast." Mark's breathing quickened over a smile. "And, thanks for askin', Vicki." He was starting to believe that love did conquer all ills.

"I'm ten minutes away." Victoria hoped that Mark hadn't read too much into her invitation. It was lunch. *That was all.* "Meet me downstairs in the parking lot."

At all costs, Victoria hoped to avoid bumping into Mark's business partner, Dr. Allen Page, who was Matthew's father. If Cory's buddies failed to keep her visits to the Olde Soda Shoppe a secret, Mark would find out she had been asking questions and fuss.

No, she should keep her investigation under tight wraps.

Although Victoria's detective terminology was sharpening, she was making little headway with her murder investigation. If only she could speak to Burn Gordon. Surely he would know how to contact his sister. Then she could ask Gloria herself why she had run away when the mysterious motorcyclist entered the drugstore.

Distracted by thoughts, Victoria braked hard for a red light.

It was becoming difficult to know whom to trust. Here she had gone and spilled her guts to Georgie. An investigator, sure, but a woman she knew very little about. Still, the PI seemed capable of confidentiality. And didn't liking Georgie count for something?

Victoria accelerated the car as the light switched to green. As promised, Mark was waiting outside the Doctor's Building. Looking handsome as ever, he skipped around the car, climbed into the passenger's seat, and kissed her on the cheek.

"Hi." He sheepishly grinned as he buckled up.

"Hello, Mark." She was inwardly pleased at his sweet overture.

"That's all? Hello Mark. No *I love you, baby*," he teased.

Whipping her head toward Mark, Victoria tossed a better-watch-it-bud glance, then quickly realized that Mark was only being Mark as he fondly pinched her arm.

As requested, Victoria drove around to the back of the office building and traded vehicles with him, agreeing that it was a perfect spring day for a *topless* ride in his BMW.

Mark had a sexy way of tormenting her, for sure.

Once on their way, he suggested they pick up deli lunches and take it with them to the Chickasaw State Park, the perfect place for a relaxing picnic. When Victoria inquired if he had the time, Mark reassured her that Allen could easily handle the office scene.

So here they were, two peas in a pod, free as birds.

The topless ride in Mark's convertible proved a fabulous idea. Thursday's storm front had quickly breezed through West Tennessee, unveiling pristine skies. Victoria relaxed and began to enjoy the ride as she listened to Mark describe his morning at the office. Foremost, she was grateful that he hadn't quizzed her about where she was Thursday evening. In response to his sensitivity, she trusted him slightly more, realizing that building relationships required time and patience. And Mark seemed worth her effort.

Chickasaw State Park was all that Mark had promised. Shards of sunlight turned the lake into ripples of blue glitter. Among the lush greenery hugging the shoreline, onlookers gathered to enjoy the gorgeous spring afternoon in nature's untouched playground.

"I love this place." Victoria was enjoying Mark's company. "Thanks for bringing me here. It was a great idea." She couldn't recall a time when she'd felt more at ease.

Mark was an expert at many things, but recreation was his specialty. After locating the perfect picnic spot, he carried their lunch over to the water's edge and spread the blanket over a soft grassy palate. "Coming?" His inviting eyes sparkled brighter than the sunlit water.

"This is absolutely perfect." Victoria ran down the hill, teetering on euphoria.

"You remember Chickasaw, don't you?" Mark rummaged through the paper sack for their sandwiches. "Got turkey on rye with mustard, or ham on sourdough with mayonnaise."

"The turkey," Victoria decided. "Chickasaw?" She dug into the roots of her memory. "I recall coming here often as a youngster. All those steamy summers when teenage girls from all over West Tennessee gathered here to—" She saw the frolic in Mark's eyes. "What?"

He shook his head, chuckling as he took a bite of his sandwich.

"You know." Victoria poked Mark with her bare toe. "To meet new guys." She giggled. What else did teenage girls think about?

"And for guys to meet girls." Mark munched from a package of potato chips.

"Back then, the park wasn't so developed as it is now," Victoria recalled, removing the paper from her sandwich.

"No." Mark mumbled with his mouth overloaded. Chewing hard, he swallowed. "But the picnic additions and the new lodge are a plus, don't you think?" His eyes were full of her.

"Absolutely!" Victoria lifted her skirt above her knees to receive the sun's warmth. Mark's eyes floated to her bare legs as he popped the lid to an iced-tea can and handed it to her.

Some things hadn't changed, like picnics and desire.

Victoria's gaze swallowed the rich, green foliage and colorful flowering plants dotting the distant woods beyond. Nature had outdone itself this spring and beauty was everywhere.

"I like this, Vicki." Mark's eyes scanned her face. "Just you and me alone. Nobody to answer to." He seemingly had relaxed, too, the worry lines around his eyes disappearing.

"That's a strange remark." Victoria paused in the midst of a bite of sandwich. "To *whom* do you report, Mark?" Her fiancé was full of surprises.

"Maybe that was a poor choice of words," Mark admitted, his eyes taking a giant swath of the lake. "I wish we could take a boat ride." There was wanderlust in his expression.

"We can. We could rent a canoe," Victoria excitedly exclaimed. "Let's do it as soon as we finish eating." She felt like an impulsive kid again, as if Jeffrey were just around the bend.

"Sure," Mark laughed. "Oh, Victoria! You're so good for me."

"How is that?"

"I feel young all over again when we're together."

"I wish I believed that were possible." Victoria self-consciously swallowed. Her heart belonged to Jeffrey, not Mark.

"Give yourself a break, honey. You just need some time to make adjustments to your most recent trauma." Mark gently rubbed Victoria's arm. "In time, you'll remember."

"You think I'll eventually get my *Victoria-you-can-do-anything* memories back?" It was a joke, but far from funny.

"Yes." Mark swigged his tea. "Then, we can go back to being us." He took her left hand and kissed the ring on her finger.

"Us?" *I don't think so.* "You must think I'm a very foolish woman." She would never give herself to him again.

"No. You're too smart for that, Vicki."

"But you do think I should conform to society, and that I ask too many questions." Karen had fussed at her for researching the past.

"I don't want to go there today, sweetheart." The glimmer in Mark's eyes shaded over. Whatever tactics he tried, Vicki regressed to her old feelings.

Somehow *sweetheart* reminded Victoria of Jeffrey, his pet name for her. Mark must know that, yet he dared to call her sweetheart! She winced at becoming angry over a little thing.

"Don't think too deeply," Mark cautioned Victoria, noting her mood swing. "Let's just keep this outing uncomplicated." He should have kept his mouth shut, let her lead.

"Like a date, you mean?"

"If that's possible." Mark stuffed his sandwich wrapper in the sack. "Getting worked up will only give you a headache."

Was the date over? He wondered.

"Right." Victoria rubbed her already aching temples. "I do need to lighten up a bit. How 'bout that boat ride you promised? As soon as we've finished lunch."

"Agreed." Mark sighed with relief. "Finish your lunch."

32

By four thirty, Mark and Victoria were back from their nostalgic Friday afternoon excursion at Chickasaw State Park. All and all, it hadn't been a bad afternoon. She had required little from Mark, who had expected nothing that she didn't offer. Pining away the afternoon together had made it more difficult to draw the line between friendship and love.

Victoria thanked Mark as she reclaimed her Mercedes in the hospital parking lot. On her way home she mulled over her conflicting feelings for Mark, vacillating between anger and appreciation, wondering if she'd too quickly judged him.

Realizing her paranoia over the past ten days may have been an attempt to escape her *true* feelings, Victoria was forced to ask herself if she were afraid to love Mark. *Fear* had always been a stumbling stone. Yet, the Bible said, "perfect love casts out fear."

Victoria deemed time as a precious commodity, not counting on her memories lasting. Had Karen been correct in her mental diagnosis? Was her reverse amnesia a subliminal thing? Did her former existence clash with her present convictions?

If so, what should she do? Hire a shrink? Spend time absorbed in television? Clean the condo until it was spotless? Shop? Gossip over the telephone? Play bridge?

Give me a break, Lord!

By Wednesday she would be in the hospital having tests run. At any moment life could change for her again. *Time waits for no one.* Victoria unlocked the kitchen door and slipped inside the dark condo. Karen wasn't yet home.

She began switching on lights. Although confused and trapped in tunneling thoughts, at least she was keeping a diary of her activities and evaluating her progress. And wasn't Georgie busy doing whatever investigators do?

Karen was wrong, she had a friend. There was Sarah at the police precinct. When the officer explained the procedure for requesting old accident records, she would hire a lawyer and obtain her report.

Victoria gazed at Mark's diamond shimmering on her left finger. Truth was hard on the surface, too, not easily penetrated. She jumped when the front doorbell rang. *Mark*?

She hurried to the front door and opened it. "Yes?"

"Mrs. Tempest?" A woman around Karen's age stood on the porch. "Yes? I'm Victoria Tempest," she replied.

"I'm Toni Kippinger, Karen's friend. Is she here?"

"Toni!" Victoria pulled Karen's grade school buddy through the door. "Girl, I never would have recognized you in a million years."

Victoria wanted to bite her tongue.

"That bad, huh?" Toni sighed, her eyelids drooping slightly.

"No, it's nothing like that." Victoria smiled. "Would you like to come inside?" She despised her former judgmental comment. "You look good, Toni."

"Uh, thank you." The girl clenched her fists as she brushed past. "Nice pad. Karen's done some redecorating, I see." She wore a rather boyish crewcut.

"Why don't we sit in the den, dear?"

"Sure." Toni slumped into the corner rocker.

"I have hot tea or soda," Victoria said.

"Nothing for me." Toni glanced out the sliding glass doors.

Easing over to the sofa, Victoria sat down. "I don't suppose Karen told you about what's recently happened to me, about my memory dilemma?" She peered into Toni's tan eyes.

"No." Interest rested in her curious expression. "Actually I knew that you were in an accident years back. Amnesia, wasn't it?" She leaned forward, palms resting on her knees.

"Well, a little over a week ago, I got my memories back!" Victoria announced. "It surprised the dickens out of all of us."

"No? And that's good news, huh?"

"Good and bad." Victoria wavered with her hand. "When my former memories reappeared, my more recent ones flew the coop." Her life sounded like a barnyard soap opera.

"I don't understand." Toni crossed her lanky legs.

"Simply said," Victoria continued, "I don't recall the past twenty-five years of my life. It's as if time stopped after my accident, as if those years between never existed."

"Oh, wow!" Toni's eyes lit up. "So that's why you didn't recognize me!" Relief swept across the girl's face.

"Exactly! Making the transition hasn't been easy."

"So I must look a whole lot different, huh?" she grimaced. "Rough and gruff around the edges?" Her smile dulled. "Old."

Victoria laughed. "No, Toni. Nothing like that! You look just fine to me. Great! But you're not in grade school anymore, are you? So what can I do for you today?"

"Is Karen around?" Toni glanced down the hall.

"No, but I expect her home at anytime," Victoria replied, grateful she had told Toni the truth about her condition. "Why don't I make us a snack while you wait for her?"

"Thank you, but I really can't stay," Toni begged off. "I just came by to leave off some photos of the bridesmaid outfits I've selected." She reached inside her backpack and pulled out her prize. "Would you give these to Karen?"

"Mind if I take a look?" Victoria opened the photo flap.

"Of course not." Toni grinned. "You're welcome to come to the ceremony if you'd like." The jock of a girl peered strangely at Victoria. "It's a small affair. Only a few friends."

"Who's the lucky guy?" Victoria took one look at the photos of females dressed in various styles of tuxedos. "Toni, these look like outfits guys should be wearing!"

Somewhat embarrassed, Toni dropped her gaze.

"What is it, Toni?"

"Didn't Karen tell you?"

"Tell me what?" Victoria laid the photos on the coffee table.

"It's a same-sex marriage," Karen's friend made eye contact.

"I didn't know," said Victoria, unable to accept the idea of a homosexual marriage since the Bible called the union an abomination. Worldly people embraced many inconsistencies.

***

That Dick Branson was troubled over Victoria Tempest's recent escapades was an understatement. His goon had followed her all the way to Memphis on Thursday before losing her in the hellish afternoon traffic, reporting she had disappeared.

"Now, what business did Victoria have in Memphis?" Dick scratched around in his desk drawer for a loose cigar.

From another source he learned of her recent visit to the Fernwood Police Precinct. *Busy little lady, Mark's Vicki.*

However, he was aware that the nosy witch had received a parking ticket earlier that Wednesday and had a legitimate reason for being there. But why had she hung around the precinct and talked to that female cop? Sarah *somebody*?

Dick realized that the charming woman had become an uncomfortable presence in his life. A beautiful rose, no doubt, but bearing excessive thorns.

No, Victoria Tempest was definitely up to something. He could no longer afford to sit around and second-guess her agenda. It was time to take action.

If Victoria Martin Tempest was a powder keg about to ignite, he certainly didn't intend to be caught unprepared in the wake of her explosion. *Nosirree*!

SATURDAY, APRIL 26

33

Victoria was aroused from a disturbing dream early Saturday morning. Pans banged loudly in the kitchen. Karen. *What time is it?* She rolled over and sat up in the bed.

Yawning, Victoria crawled from the crumpled satin sheets and stumbled into the bathroom like a zombie. Fifteen minutes later, having cleared her mind of threatening nightmares, she ventured into the den with a more presentable attitude.

"Good morning, Karen."

"Is it?" Her daughter scowled, briskly wiping the kitchen counter of its sinful stains.

"I heard you in here." Victoria noticed the messy pots stacked in the kitchen sink. "Baking something special?" The odor of spices nudged at her nostrils.

"Yes. A batch of brownies for a party I'm attending." Karen whipped out a box of powdered icing and poured it into a glass blender, acting as if she'd slept on a bed of nails.

Prickly and defensive, why is that?

"Oh, Karen . . ." Victoria gathered her courage.

"What is it, Mother?" Hazel eyes were pointed daggers.

"I don't mean to interfere with your cooking," she cleared her throat and climbed on a barstool, "and certainly not with your life. But there is a matter I want to discuss with you."

No time is perfect. Victoria gazed at her distraught daughter.

Karen's spatula resumed movement. "About what, *Mother*?"

Mother. The word sounded almost spiteful coming out of her daughter's mouth. Had she so miserably failed at mothering?

"I've been thinking about myself," Victoria vigilantly continued, "and wondering what I was like before I awakened in the middle of the street nearly two weeks ago."

Karen snorted as her hard-boiled, autumn eyes warily cut a path across the kitchen. Victoria guessed her timing stunk.

"I really don't think you want to hear what I have to say on that subject!" Karen stirred the chocolate batter with a vengeance. "I suggest you forget about analyzing yourself this morning and enjoy a cup of coffee," she grimaced.

"No, I won't. I really need to understand what motivates me." Victoria propped her elbows on the counter. "All I'm asking for is your opinion."

"Interesting . . ." a smirk tore at Karen's mouth.

"But would you pass me a cup of coffee first?"

"Sure." Karen rewarded her mother with a warm mug of Maxwell House and collapsed on a barstool beside her "How far back shall I go—five, ten, fifteen, twenty-five years? Does it really matter?"

Victoria was wounded over Karen's insensitivity. When had her daughter become so bitter, so cruel? Every word out of her mouth pulsed with anger. Could she be objective when it came to judging her own mother?

"I'm the cook. So put in your order, Mother!"

Victoria bit her lower lip. In lieu of Karen's caustic mood-moment, she uncomfortably shifted in her seat, questioning whether she could handle hearing her daughter's opinion.

"Actually, Karen . . ." she said, already having plowed in too deep, "I try to imagine what one day was like in the life of Victoria Tempest. Oh, say a month ago?"

"That's reasonable." Karen scooted a big bowl of icing across the bar and began spreading it on top of her warm chocolate brownies. "Let's see, where shall I begin?"

Victoria swallowed hard, seeing that her daughter relished the opportunity to reward her with forgotten facts.

"Let me see . . ." Karen's hazel eyes enlarged with thought, "on a regular week day, you usually got up about the time I left for work. Around nine thirty, I would estimate."

"That late?" Victoria reacted. "I never had breakfast with you?" She'd always thought of herself as the early bird that got the worm. *Had amnesia affected her so adversely?*

"Never. You didn't like breakfast," Karen announced.

"But I love breakfast!" Victoria protested. "Ham and eggs, an omelet. Toast with strawberry jam. My mother used to make me a big breakfast every morning and I ate like a pig."

"Not so with the new, uh, sophisticated Victoria." Karen licked her sticky chocolate fingers, glaring at her mother's disturbed expression at hearing an up-close, personal assessment.

Snotty, Karen means. "When did I start to change?"

"From the moment you came home from the hospital—that would be in early August, twenty-five years ago." Karen's pupils dilated with recall. "You were a different person."

Didn't genes matter? "It must have been awful for you and Paul." Victoria inwardly struggled with how she'd become so different. *Or did environment shape an individual?*

"Devastating!" Karen softly rasped. "You can't imagine."

Victoria grieved over the emotional baggage Karen was carrying. It was *their* fault—hers and Jeffrey's. She should have known better than to drive in a terrible storm, and Jeffrey should have somehow prevented those crazies from killing him!

Together, they should have protected their children at all cost.

"I'm so sorry, dear!" Victoria struggled with how to make it right after all these years.

"You've suffered, too. And I forgave you long ago." Karen sequestered Victoria's gaze. "Eventually I accepted that what had happened to our family wasn't my fault."

"Of course, it wasn't your fault, sweetheart."

"For years, I blamed myself for not begging you to stay home that stormy night. If you had, the accident wouldn't have happened."

But Jeffrey would still be dead. "I'm so sorry."

"Years passed and you never regained your memories. After Paul died," Karen peered at her mother, "you became seriously interested in Mark. He started coming over regularly."

"For lunch?" Victoria needed clarification. "And?"

"You wanted to be alone," Karen snapped. "Of course, I left the condo."

Karen wasn't talking about lunch. It was no secret that she'd shared an apartment with Mark in Jackson. "Did I have a job?" Victoria was ready to move on with other issues.

"No. But you clubbed Fernwood to death!" Karen chuckled.

"Whatever do you mean by that?" Victoria huffed.

Karen's lips swelled with amusement. "Well, Mother, you were a faithful member of the a ladies bridge club, last year's secretary of the Women's Civic Awareness Committee, and a yearly participant in the women's golfing event held at the Branson-Fernwood Country Club."

Golf? I played golf? Why didn't Mark tell me?

"And let's not forget about your trusteeship on the Union Federal Bank Board, or your crucial role as a financial sponsor of our fair city's Chamber of Commerce." Karen paused to appreciate her mother's expression, somewhere betwixt a grin and a frown. "Then there was your work with the handicapped at the hospital, and occasionally you subbed in your Sunday school class for Miss—"

"Stop! Enough! I get the picture!" Victoria could stand no more enlightenment.

But Karen wasn't yet finished.

"Oh, yeah! You were Miss Socialite!" Karen boasted, aware that she was stripping her mother down to a raw nerve. "And prepared to do almost anything anybody asked of you."

"No wonder Mark is upset with me!" Victoria digested Karen's incredible description of her former life. "He must think I'm some kind of maniac, running around town and demanding answers about my past like I have the world by the tail!"

"I'm afraid it's all too true." Karen's belligerent overtones weakened. "But it is the unfortunate impression you've given most of the people who once believed they knew you."

Karen's honesty was refreshing. She would give her that.

However, her next statement capsized what little faith Victoria had left in her self-worthiness.

"Frankly, Mother! You haven't acted very responsibly!"

"Wow! Now that was a low blow!" Victoria envisioned herself in a new light. "All because I was missing one night?" She grasped what this exploratory surgery was *really* all about.

"You bet," Karen's voice tightened. "One night of not knowing whether you're alive or dead is quite enough trauma." The truth suddenly burst forth. Karen had been frightened.

Victoria's face expressed wipeout.

"Forgive me if the truth hurts, Mother," Karen said. "As you may have noticed I'm in a rotten mood this morning. Although I am irritated at you, my anger has absolutely nothing to do with you or your life or how you feel about Mark."

"Then, what is it about—no, scratch that question." Victoria grasped her daughter's hand. "Thank you for being truthful. After all, I did ask for your opinion."

"That's all you have to say in your defense?"

"Yes. I know I'm a mess, but I truly want to make some sense out of the remnants of my life," Victoria admitted, despite her wounded ego dangling off a cliff.

"I know you do, Mother." Karen squeezed back tears, unable to hide her affection. "It's true I'm angry with you, and probably unfair. But you taught me that love conquers all."

Did I? Although the truth sometimes hurt, it was always cleansing.

"Actually, Mother," Karen offered a last opinion, "if I were to take a hard look inside your heart, I'd be forced to admit I prefer the newer Victoria over the other two versions."

"Really?" Victoria's spirits skyrocketed at Karen's revelation.

"Absolutely!" Karen declared. "Mind if I make one little suggestion?"

"Of course not." Karen's sunshine smile warmed Victoria as she prepared for the worst.

"Really, Mother! You must schedule an appointment with a

hairdresser," Karen's proclamation turned into a rage of giggles. "Your gray roots are despicable!"

Laughter erupted from Victoria's lips as Karen's contagious joy infected her. "Would you help me, dear? I don't know where to begin or who to call anymore."

"Sure." Karen's laughter subsided as she hopped off her barstool. "I'll even schedule a thirty-minute massage and a manicure for you. After what I just said, you deserve it."

"Do you think we could do that today?"

"I'll get on the phone and see what can be arranged," Karen bubbled with enthusiasm. "And Mother?" Tears were astir.

"What?" Victoria hugged her precious daughter.

"You never used to ask for my help with *anything*."

34

Victoria's scandalous beauty makeover was exactly the punch she needed to lift her ailing spirits. Anxious to show off her new image, she hurried home, disappointed that Karen wasn't there to see the results of her appointments. Maybe Mark would call or come by.

Standing before the floor-length mirror in Karen's bedroom, Victoria pictured Mark's reaction when he saw her. "You're a knockout, baby!" he was bound to say. *Was she?*

The massage and sauna had done wonders for Victoria's muscle tone and skin. After receiving a toasting in the ultra-light tanning machine, the hair stylist grabbed hold of her.

"You need a different look, honey," Gaylord had remarked before trimming her hair in a sassy wedge. Reluctantly, she'd agreed to trade outdated brown for a shade of pewter-auburn.

When Gaylord had performed his magic, Victoria noted how the haircut lent balance to her face and the color raised new life in her oversized bronzed eyes. Afterwards, the manicurist had replaced two handfuls of damaged fingernails with acrylics, painting them a lighter shade of Victoria's hair color. Ready to take a breather, the stylist offered her a sparkling soda.

Last came the cosmetic artist who maneuvered through a series of facial creams and defoliating techniques before applying a thin layer of natural beige to Victoria's face.

Using various brushes and tools to arch and darken Victoria's eyebrows, Crystal had outlined her eyes in dark brown, lengthened her eyelashes with mascara, and applied a rosy blush to her cheeks to produce an almost-embarrassed look.

"Done!" The salon crew had declared. "Victoria Tempest, you are beautiful."

The bill was healthy, but she hadn't minded. She'd left the salon feeling like a couple of million bucks! To top off the experience, she'd visited a designer shop and purchased a spiffy new outfit positively different from anything she'd ever worn on her usually tired body. Thrilled at her refurbished image, she danced in circles singing the familiar show tune "There's No Business Like Show Business."

The makeover had boosted her morale, a feeling not unlike being released from a time capsule. She prayed that God would reshape her into the person He wanted her to become.

When the newness of the makeover began to wear off, Victoria calmly viewed herself in the mirror again. It was true; her image had been revolutionized. In only a few short hours, her caterpillar image had been transformed into a stunning butterfly.

Meet the Y2K Victoria Tempest, world!

A little disappointed that Karen wasn't home to receive her two gifts, Victoria was certain she would appreciate the expensive mint-green cashmere sweater from Mandy's Dress Shop, and forever cherish Granny Martin's string of pearls.

A family heirloom, passed down for generations, the pearls had been presented to Victoria on her wedding day. "An early inheritance," her mother had declared. "Granny Martin wanted you to wear these pearls at your wedding ceremony. Family is all that matters, all that lasts."

"Now," Victoria removed the pearls from her jewelry box, "it's my daughter's turn to feel blessed."

Didn't Karen deserve to own her family's most treasured heirloom? Especially since she'd already missed out on so much tradition. The time to restore her faith in family was now.

Outdoors, light wilted on the western horizon, emitting shades of bloody hues as the sun receded and darkness won out. It was almost seven o'clock and Karen was still not home.

Anxious to show off her new image, Victoria kept her fingers crossed that Mark would pop in to say hello. *Probably not*, about now the would-be golf pro was likely at the country club wrapping up a Saturday afternoon game. *Would he think of her?*

The ringing phone startled Victoria.

"Mark?" she grasped the receiver.

"No, it's Sarah. Is this Victoria Tempest?"

"Yes?" Victoria was caught off guard. "Who is this?"

"You know, girlfriend. This is Sarah Boswell. We met at the police station."

"Sarah!" *That Sarah!* Victoria ignited with excitement. "Did you find out how to obtain a copy of my accident report?"

Things were looking up. *Thank you, Jesus.*

"I did some nosing around," the officer explained. "Seems you gotta hire a lawyer and file a petition in court to obtain those old reports. Probably not on computer, packed away in some ol' dusty basement," Sarah lamented.

Victoria's silence reflected her disappointment.

"Hey, girlfriend! Now don't go getting down in the mouth or nuthin' like that. I do have one idea," Sarah professed.

"I hope it's a good one," Victoria declared.

"A friend of mine says her father knew the cop who filed your accident report." Sarah paused to let her words sink in. "I just thought . . ." Sarah chose her words carefully.

"Thought what?" Victoria's heart pumped faster.

"If you knew the police officer's name was Rhe-mus Hornsby it might help."

"That's an unusual name." Victoria jotted it down. "And it does help." He might be able to tell her who called 911 and reported her accident.

"Spelled RHE hyphen MUS. Real name's Rhe Muscle-shoals Hornsby." Sarah giggled. "Named after that famous dam in Alabama, 'cause that's whur Rhe-mus got conceived."

Victoria laughed, too. "So where can I find Uncle Rhe-mus?"

"Now that's the kicker," Sarah scoffed. "Seems that Rhe-mus is quite old now, way up in his eighties." Victoria heard breathing over the phone. "He had a bad stroke a few years back and lives with his daughter, who ain't no spring chicken herself."

"And?"

"Don't think Rhe-mus talks much anymore."

"But he can still *think*?"

"Last time my friend heard, he was still making enough sense you could tell what he was talking about," Sarah reported. "Haven't heard in the last two weeks how he's doing."

"Oh, dear. Can he still write?"

"No, girlfriend! I said he had a stroke," Sarah was curt. "Rhe-mus is partially paralyzed and too blame old to do much of anything! He might not even remember you."

Victoria's disappointment sapped her former enthusiasm.

"Well, Sarah, I don't know if I can learn anything new from Rhe-mus, but I'd sure like to try." Victoria would talk to a fence post if she thought it would tell her how to get hold of her accident report. She had to face the fact that nobody was going to make it easy for her.

"I didn't say he was *dead*, child. Just disabled. His daughter's address is 1115 Balcony Avenue. They live in a new complex over on the south sector of the city."

"I'm surprised Uncle Rhe-mus hasn't moved into one of those assisted-living institutions and signed a voluntary cessation commitment." Victoria sighed.

"Now, that's a distinct possibility." Sarah mulled over the idea. "Last I heard, though, he still lived at this address." When Victoria didn't respond, Sarah added, "But I wouldn't let no grass grow 'neath my feet if I was you. Uncle Rhe-mus ain't gettin' no younger."

"I'm not!" Victoria heeded the officer's warning. "You've been a big help—would you be willing to accept a small financial gift for all your trouble?" It was the least she could do.

"Friends don't take payoffs, Victoria." Sarah smiled through the phone. "I might need a favor myself one day." Everybody needed a little help one time or another.

"Count on it, girlfriend. And thanks." Victoria was hanging up the phone when she heard the front door bell ring.

"Coming." She stepped lightly to the door and opened it. "Mark!" He carried a large bouquet of spring flowers in one hand. His shocked expression came as no surprise as he looked her over. "Come in." She yanked him through the doorway. "And breathe."

"Vicki!" Mark handed over the bouquet of daisies and baby-breaths. "These are—what in the world did you do to yourself?"

"Oh, this . . ." Victoria spun around in a circle. "Like it?"

"I gotta say it's different." Mark blinked. "You don't look like the same person you did yesterday." His gaze swallowed every curve. "That dress blows my senses."

"So you approve?" Why did it matter if he didn't?

Mark didn't answer with words. Before Victoria realized it, he was up close and personal, his moist kiss surging through her senses with anticipated passion. "How's that for an answer?"

"Very . . ." Victoria was breathless, "stimulating."

"Do you have dinner plans?"

"No, I was hoping you would ask." She led the way into the den. "Could I fix you something cold to drink?"

"What are you serving?" Mark's eyebrows lifted.

"Nothing alcoholic." Victoria eyed him sharply. "I'm not that new. I have Diet Coke, tea, or coffee. Take your pick."

"Ice tea is fine." Mark tilted his head sideways. "So Vicki . . . tell me why you changed the way you looked? I have to say I loved you just the way you were."

Mark's observation pleased Victoria.

"I did it for me, Mark. But I gather you approve." She traipsed over to the refrigerator and filled two plastic tumblers with ice.

"I must admit you do look stunning!" His voice trembled.

Stunning. Victoria inwardly smiled, lending him her eyes. Did she enjoy his company simply because she was lonely and missed Jeffrey's company so terribly? *Be careful.*

"I was just thinking how you always manage to astound me." Mark's lower lip trembled. "Just when I believe I have you figured out, there you go changing on me again!"

Victoria smiled. "So how was your golf game?"

"My score was decent." He swiped a tear from under one eye, his tenderness showing. Victoria knew no more about golf than she did about bridge, although Karen said that she had played both.

"It's getting hot outdoors." He loosened his shirt collar as his eyes wandered down the hallway. "Karen home?"

"No." Victoria handed Mark his glass of tea and sat beside him on the sofa. "Would you get mad at me if I ask you a question?" He had before, but the picnic seemed to have mellowed him.

"When you say my name like that, Vicki, how can I say no?" The liquid in Mark's tumbler sloshed in his nervous hand. "No one's ever touched me as deeply as you do."

"Goodness, Mark James, you do have a way with words!" A lump lodged in Victoria's throat. "I don't mean to tease you, just carry on a conversation. Isn't that what you want?"

"Yes, it is." He fondly grasped Victoria's left hand and squeezed it. "And more."

"I'm not ready for more," Victoria clarified her position.

"What do you want to know, Vicki?"

"My Bible. It was with me the night of my accident. Did it ever turn up?" Surely he would tell her if he knew.

"I have no idea," Mark replied, sipping on his beverage. "That's the first mention of a Bible I've heard about. Have any chips?"

Chips? "Do you think it could have burned?" she asked.

"I said I don't know anything about it!" Mark's tone bordered raw, his turbulent blue eyes narrowing with distaste. He was upset over her question. That was nothing new.

Victoria glared at Mark. *Is he lying?*

"Since your car didn't burn, however, I must admit it does seem odd your Bible wasn't found," Mark offered an opinion.

"Do you think someone might have taken it before the EMS arrived?" She wasn't about to let the subject drop.

"Stolen it? Why would anybody do that?"

"I have no idea," Victoria replied, disgusted.

"What I don't understand is why you care." Mark twisted his head her way. "You haven't read your Bible in years, Vicki."

A smothering silence stole Victoria's response. "That may be true, but now I feel differently and want it back."

"I understand. It's the memory thing."

"Regardless of how I've acted before, I want to know what happened the night of my accident. All of it, good and bad."

"Oh, Vicki!" Mark set his tumbler aside and reached out for her right hand. "Don't you realize it doesn't matter anymore?" He tenderly kissed the back of her knuckles.

"Quit patronizing me and help me with this!"

"Vicki!" Mark stood up and pulled her into an embrace. "It isn't healthy for you to always look back."

"Don't you dare tell me how to think!"

Trapped in Mark's vise, she couldn't move. "Let me go." His eyes evolved into an untamed flame-blue. "Stop it! I can see where this is heading." She pushed against his chest.

Mark released her, anger pulsating on his face. "Drop this silly notion of investigating your accident, Vicki. If you did find your Bible, you'd only have to turn it into the authorities!"

"That's absurd!" Fear boiled to the surface.

Was Mark right? A cold wind blew through her heart. Could she no longer own a Bible and freely read it?

35

Dick Branson fondly ran his forefinger over the embossed invitation he'd received from Rome earlier that morning. *Finally, my official invitation to attend NATO's June festivities.*

Short of death, nothing could keep him from attending the world's grandest shindig. Why, everybody who was somebody would be there. Ambassadors and presidents, kings and queens, wealthy women and powerful businessmen like him, plus a few unexpected guests.

One article in *Business Week* reported how the National Alliance Treaty Organization had planned to formally announce their chairperson to the reorganized Economic Common Market Council. *Hogwash, that wasn't news!*

Dick clutched his valuable invitation. The important people already knew who would claim that position. Grapevines worked well. Hadn't Alexander Luceres Ramnes been the one to convince people that a world without religious conflict was within human grasp?

Nosiree, nobody understood world politics better than Luceres. A summa cum laude graduate from Harvard University, he was an idealist with revolutionary ideas and visions of carving out a perfect world. But certainly Dick hoped, not one that discounted personal favors. *Hadn't his entire career been built on good and bad men extending him favors?*

Who could fault Luceres for bringing about religious equality? The world was due a bloody break. Abolishing the overbearing religious factions was the best thing to happen on Planet Earth since Jesus Christ. *Who cared who saved the world as long as somebody did?*

Terrorists had threatened the world, setting off bombs in cars, airplanes and buildings. It had been anybody's guess what radical Muslim or Christian sects might decide to do next. After the 9/11, 2001, bombing of the New York Twin Trade Towers, Muslim terrorists put the fear of Allah in Americans. People didn't feel safe walking the streets, and with good reason. Threats thrown about like confetti spelled war. Iraq became a battleground.

Over the decades, oil-hogging Arabs had waged wars against any ethnic group who didn't embrace their religious beliefs. *Holy Toledo!* Everybody became somebody's target—politicians, athletes, missionaries, business folk, children. Didn't matter who you were or where you lived. No one was exempt from the malicious acts committed in the name of religion.

Something had to be done. So Luceres had wisely approached NATO, requesting their permission to establish a committee to study the outrageous religious problem.

Nine months later, Luceres' ingenious ideas were birthed when the International Religious Ethics Committee submitted a sound plan to NATO. The 2011 Alliance had immediately sanctioned IREC's brilliant guidelines, issuing a mandate for nations to end the bloodshed over religious differences.

A holy truce was declared, backed up by the United Nation's World Militia and the powerful United States Armed Forces. Good ole GIs making history again! Made a man proud to be an American.

Dick kicked back in his swivel chair, thumbs tucked in his tight belt, grinning like a bear who just found honey. In a rat's nest world, NATO's boy genius might well be the next world leader.

Oh, at first some folks didn't take kindly to the religious mandate. Christians balked like babies, screaming heresy. You'd have thought the world was about to come to an end.

Televangelists hopped on the subject, lambasting IREC's recommendations as radical liberalism. Then, on Easter 2012, the fighting around the world suddenly ceased.

The news media ate it up. Reporters roamed the globe to interview religious folk, to ask them why they decided to cooperate, hoping they'd admit to coercion. *Didn't happen.*

Nosirree, Dick chuckled. People of differing faiths were sick to death of ordinary folks dying violently. They'd been praying for somebody to step up to the plate, knock a victorious home run and tell them exactly what they needed to do.

Religious leaders everywhere sat up and took notice. *Hallelujah*! For once, the news media had done a good job!

The networks reported how millions of ordinary people were demanding world peace so that men and women, husbands and wives, brothers and sisters, God's children of all races, could safely walk the planet again. Overnight, *unity* became a noble theme.

Now that has to be some kind of world record!

Shortly afterwards, representatives of all religions met to redesign their doctrines, to define a common thread of divine thought that would unify all religions: *brotherly love.*

Jesus Christ of Nazareth had declared the nobility of loving your neighbor as yourself. Buddha had liked the idea. So had Mohammed. And the Jews saw nothing wrong with it.

Luceres had envisioned peace, and don't think NATO wasn't beholden. Nations could move toward stabilizing the world's shaky Internet, stock-driven economy without the threat of ethnic cleansing and holy terrorism. The world was finally at peace.

Praise to Luceres!

He was deemed a man of humility with unbiased convictions. It had been reported that Luceres wanted the Catholic Pope to give the invocation at the final banquet to be held at the J. W. Marriott Coliseum in Rome, Italy, on June 20.

Let no one claim Luceres has no respect for religion.

Dick lit up a Havana, kicked back in his swivel rocker, and inhaled the pungent smoke.

No, sir. Time and time again the man had modestly refused the glory people tried to pin on him. Only a noble visionary could have convinced the good people of every faith to agree. A very tricky feat to unify the world in thought.

But Luceres had, and life was good.

When world peace had actually resulted, NATO had begun talk about restructuring the world's ailing economy. They weren't yet finished with the savvy politician from Italy.

And Luceres would do it for fun, having already made his millions in stock market investments. Perhaps enjoy a little glory in the process. *But that was human, wasn't it?*

Hell's bells! A paperless currency would simplify international business transactions. The New World Order was about to explode. *Earth will become a Paradise.*

In perfect health, with an IQ that topped the charts, the charismatic twenty-eight-year-old bachelor seemed eager to use his talents to save the world. Having traced his ancestry back to the Old Roman Empire, Luceres would maintain his home office in Rome where the Vatican City housed its Catholic Popes and the ancient cities of Pompeii and Campania had once stood.

Wouldn't you know a few fools had the gall to suggest that Luceres was the Antichrist! *Ridiculous!* Dick cursed. Blamed Christian sects were at the root of the trouble.

Rumor had it that Grandma Ramnes named her only grandson after Alexander the Great. A psychic of sorts, she was reported to read the stars like a pro. Astute in ancient history, Grandma was an expert on the topic of the rise and fall of Babylon.

Why, before Luceres had even learned how to walk, she prophesied his destiny for greatness. *And the boy had the faith to believe!*

Dick propped his bulky feet on his expensive desk. Nice things were for abuse, so a person could feel good about his own little kingdom.

Oh, he was aware that no one had ever considered him great. As much as Marjorie loved him, he had his human weaknesses in her eyes. Heroic men like Luceres were random acts of destiny. Most humans were too stupid to envision greatness.

When the drug cartel had looked to him to smuggle their wares, hadn't he seen his future written on the wall? *Wasn't that a little bit ingenious on his part?* The wisdom to accept what he didn't want to change. Dick chuckled, coughed, then grinned. He only hoped he'd be lucky enough to taste a little of that forbidden fruit Luceres had bitten off.

Success was a fine reward for hard work.

Staring the burning butt of his cigar in the face, Dick wondered what it would feel like to be noble for one day? Cursing, he stamped flat feet to the floor. Didn't somebody have to be bad? So the good guys would have something to do? That was his job.

Jeannie buzzed to announce a faxed memo had arrived. Stretching from the fatigue of heavy speculation, he made his way up front and jerked the memo from the machine and read it.

> *To Whom It May Concern: On April 26, 2014, a representative of the Tennessee Gas Authority will be checking for a gas-main leak on the Branson Meatpacking Company site. Please give our authorized representative clearance to complete our safety check. Thank you very much.* *The TGA*

"Jeannie!" Dick barked. "See that this memo is carried out!" He was a little concerned over the edict. "And, Jeannie. Tell whoever comes to steer clear of my buildings!"

SUNDAY, APRIL 27

36

Victoria awakened Sunday morning feeling refreshed. Life was not perfect but it was improving. In time, Mark and Karen might even be persuaded to see matters her way.

Karen claimed she had a sinus headache and didn't feel like attending church services.

Deciding to go alone, Victoria slipped in the side entrance of the sanctuary and located a seat close to the front. Glancing around, she was relieved that Mark hadn't seen her arrive.

Good. She could focus on the sermon without any distractions.

As usual, Dr. Daye's discourse was challenging. When the service ended, Victoria glanced around the auditorium. Evidently, like Karen, Mark had developed a convenient headache. *His loss.*

Victoria returned home around noon and found Karen's note stating that she had gone to the office to work with a customer.

Fine by me. She was perfectly satisfied to spend the afternoon alone, praying and recording in her diary. Maybe she'd get comfortable and soak in some sunrays first.

After changing into shorts and a halter-top, Victoria took her tuna salad out on the veranda. Spring had spun another remarkable day with temperatures approaching the mid-seventies.

Mid-afternoon, she returned to the den to read some Bible passages. Psalm 121 was a remarkable scripture. *Why not memorize it?* She began to hide God's Word in her heart.

I lift up my eyes to the hills—
where does my help come from?
My help comes from the Lord,
the Maker of Heaven and earth.

He will not let your foot slip—
he who watches over you will not slumber.

Indeed, he who watches over Israel
    will neither slumber nor sleep.

The Lord watches over you—
    the Lord is your shade at your right hand;
the sun will not harm you by day,
    nor the moon by night.

The Lord will keep you from all harm—
    he will watch over your life.
The Lord will watch over your coming and going,
    both now and forevermore.

Shortly after three o'clock, Mark phoned and asked Victoria to accompany him to their Jackson apartment one last time, claiming he was thinking of letting the unit go on May first.

After he had promised to behave himself, Victoria reluctantly agreed to drive over with him. And Mark was punctual as agreed upon, showing up at her door at 4:15 p.m.

"What a perfect afternoon!" he exclaimed as Victoria stepped into his flamboyant sunflower-yellow BMW with its sexy canvas top rolled back.

"I missed you at church this morning." She made eye contact. "Where were you?"

"Oh, I had business to tend to." Mark offered no specifics, applying a heavy foot to the accelerator. "You need to be home early?" His sapphire-blue eyes perused her.

"Nope." She hoped she wasn't giving Mark any leeway. It didn't take much to stimulate his masculinity. And, certainly, she had no intention of playing house with him.

"I suppose you're wondering why of all days I asked you to accompany me to our apartment?" Mark took a sweetheart curve, laughing as she was forced to lean his way.

"Doesn't matter as long as you do the right thing."

What a tease! Victoria got a whiff of Mark's cologne and realized that she enjoyed masculine company even if he was determined to torture her. She had missed Jeffrey terribly the last couple of days. Needing to be held again, she longed for physical intimacy. *Of course, married, and to the right person.*

"As I said over the phone, the lease on our apartment is up May first," Mark raised his voice over the noisy engine, casting an energized gaze. "I gotta tell ya, Vicki, we have good memories there." He sighed. "But the apartment isn't the same without you in it."

Victoria was pleasantly bewildered at Mark's sincerity, but offered no comment.

"You still have a few personal items there, you know. I thought you should take what you wanted before I have the Salvation Army haul everything away."

What things? She shuddered. *Intimate articles?*

Mark's nostalgic gaze locked on a flock of birds flying high overhead. "Look, Vicki!" he pointed out the front windshield. "There, to your right. Up high."

"I see them!" She shadowed her eyes from the dazzling sunlight. "The flock seems to know exactly where they're going." It was an observation, not meant to be philosophic.

"I wish I did." Mark solidly grasped the wheel as he spun onto the interstate, heading north toward Jackson. "Where are we going, Vicki? I mean *us*." His expression was sincere.

She was not insensitive to Mark's concern. He had a right to know. After all, they were still engaged. But considering her mental disability, it was a difficult question to ponder. And apparently her feelings were stronger than she first believed.

Jeffrey was never physically coming back to her. His absence had created a void she obviously hadn't been able to fill over the years. Like any other woman, she yearned for love and fulfillment.

And, according to Biblical principles, a widow was at liberty to marry again. Wasn't it obvious that Mark loved her very much? Why else would he put up with her abrasive behavior? So how should she answer him? Did she truly know her own heart?

"Vicki?" Mark's voice captured Victoria's attention.

"I'm considering your question, Mark. Really." She clasped her clammy hands in her lap, lending him her eyes. "You're a kind man, Dr. James." She peered at her very best friend.

"Kind? That's all?" Mark reacted like a wounded puppy.

Picking up speed, he accelerated the car to over eighty miles per hour. But Victoria didn't caution him. He was a very good driver and the weather was favorable.

"I can't make a commitment to marry you," Victoria decided. "At least, not yet."

"Vicki! We've already set a date." Mark's icy blue eyes brought a chill into the car. "The invitations came in last Friday." His lips sadly sagged in the corners. "Please, honey."

"What can I say, Mark? Except I'm sorry."

"Wait!" Mark struggled for an intermediary solution. "By not yet, do you mean not until Jeffrey's killers have been caught?" His foot was nailed to the accelerator.

"Huh?" However she answered would prove unsatisfactory.

"Like a fool, I suppose I assumed the wedding was still on." His shoulders jerked with emotion. "I should have seen this coming the first day Karen called me over to check you out."

His speeding started to worry her.

"Talk to me, Victoria."

"Yes. No. Of course, I want to solve Jeffrey's crime, but I'm also confused about how I feel about you." It was the truth.

"You are?" Mark swallowed. "You mean that?" The wind picked up outside and whipped at the car. "You still do have feelings for me?" He reached out for her hand.

"Of course, I have feelings for you."

"So you solve Jeffrey's murder, then what?"

Mark's mind was not on driving. "Hey! Watch where you're going!" He was over the yellow line and cars were honking.

"What's holding you back from marrying me?"

The BMW picked up more speed. Victoria held her breath as the speedometer gauge registered 90. "Please slow down, Mark!" Fear of an accident flew through her like broken glass.

"I need to know, for my own sanity." Mark eased his foot off the accelerator. "Is there any doubt how much I love you, Vicki?"

Here goes. "I have good reason to believe that you know more about Jeffrey's murder than you've admitted." Victoria wanted to be honest. *Didn't he deserve to hear the truth?*

Stung by Victoria's words, Mark's head did a forty-five.

"But I don't intend to press you for an answer." She sucked in oxygen to steady her thrumming heartbeat. "If we are ever to become one, there are two things I urgently need from you." She prayed he wouldn't get mad.

Mark's face exhibited a smorgasbord of feelings—anger, hurt, compassion, longing, love and fear—vacillating emotions that visibly displayed his confused loyalty. "So tell me."

"I need to know if you've been straight with me about Jeffrey." Passion rose in Victoria's throaty response. "And equally important, I want to know if you're *born-again*?"

Victoria's demands walloped Mark in the gut.

"Hear me out!" She feared he might interrupt. "I know I've changed, Mark. Drastically, if what others say is true. And it's nobody's fault. But I refuse to marry anyone who doesn't share my religious convictions. That's just the way it is."

Mark's sullen gaze was glued to the pavement as he swerved the car onto an exit ramp and pulled into a roadside park. Rolling to a stop, he killed the engine and glared through the windshield while contemplating a reasonable response.

Mark looked like such a little boy in trouble she wanted to tell him to forget what she had said and let him off the hook, but she didn't. His answer was too important. When his troubled gaze twisted her way, the windows of his soulful eyes emitted shame.

Here was a "double-minded" man who didn't fathom his own heart or truly know where his loyalties belonged. The Bible had aptly described such men as "lost" souls.

"Mark? Don't answer until you feel ready," Victoria uttered with supernatural patience as the Holy Spirit led her to witness.

"Just hear me out. Open your ears and heart and carefully listen." The moment was serene, electrified with human emotions.

Mark nodded, hiding tears beneath his downcast lashes.

"I must first apologize to God because I wasn't the Christian I should have been over the years." Emotions clogged Victoria's passageways. "I let the world's glitter entice me to live sinfully. I neglected to study God's Word or I would have known better."

Mark squinted at Victoria through glassy-blue eyes as her sincere words began to unmask the sin and shame buried in his hardened heart. Yes, he'd once professed to believe, but like a withering plant, he'd since chosen the world over Christ Jesus.

Dare he reconsider God's purpose in his life?

"It's true I can't recall the years following my accident . . ." Victoria couldn't stop shaking. "But if I had stayed in the Word and prayed over my choices, I—" she gulped back tears—"I never would have entered into an unholy relationship with you."

"Oh, Vicki." Mark scrubbed his leaky eyes.

"I'm so very sorry I led you on." Soaking tears wet Victoria's cheeks. "It was so unfair." She cringed when Mark let out a sad wail, like a wounded animal caught in a vise.

"No, let me finish," her voice intensified. "I'm aware it's no longer popular to believe in Jesus Christ. Or to profess that He's God's Son, the only way to obtain salvation . . .

"Or that the *Holy Bible*, like other religious books, has been reconstructed to reflect a popular belief in self-worth and brotherly love." Victoria's teeth were chattering.

"Which in itself seems good. Except the newer version leaves out the most important truth. That Jesus Christ was born to save people from their sin!

"And, although it's unpopular today, probably even dangerous for me to witness to you," Victoria spilled the contents of her heart. "You should know that I'm willing to die for my faith if it comes down to that," she declared with conviction. "Mark? Are you?"

Mark wiped his wet face with his hands, too traumatized to speak.

"If it is God's will . . ." tears pulsed with each sulking gulp, "I will find my Bible and read it from cover to cover, memorize its truths. I will uphold my Christian faith despite what others may think." It was a statement of faith she would never forsake.

Unsure of how long they sat crying together in the car, Victoria refused to interrupt the work of the Holy Spirit, diligently praying that Mark would repent and choose Jesus.

"Vicki, I don't know what to say." He blew his nose with his handkerchief. "I've never been so moved." Conviction gripped Mark until he believed his heart would implode.

"I care about you, Mark James." Victoria squeezed his hand. "Deeply, as a friend. And otherwise, probably more than I choose to—" emotion stole her voice. "But if we're not on the same wavelength, how can we be equally yoked in a marriage?"

Where did all this come from? She applauded her boldness.

After awhile, Mark withdrew his hand from Victoria's, shook his head and ignited the engine. He didn't utter one word during the remainder of the drive into Jackson.

Let him think. Victoria was satisfied that she'd presented the gospel message, pleased that she'd given Mark a window to consider a response to God. *His soul is worth the wait.*

A perfect gentleman, Mark showed Victoria into the beautiful love nest she'd personally decorated. It made her sick. She told him to give everything away, that she wanted nothing.

Any keepsake would only serve as a reminder of her former sinful life. Victoria realized that Jesus was performing a powerful work of conviction in her, both painful and cleansing.

Mark never said whether or not he was born-again. Though his lifestyle indicated otherwise, perhaps there was still a move of the Spirit on him. Unwilling to talk much about anything, he simply locked the apartment for the last time and asked if she were hungry. "No," she said before he escorted her back to the car.

The day was ending when Victoria stood on her front porch

and sadly mumbled "goodnight." Mark pecked her on the cheek, his thoughts far away and private.

Staring into his unreadable face, she could feel the invisible wall building between them. Mark had emotionally shut her out. Grieved over his inability to acknowledge God, she couldn't even thank him for a lovely time.

When the door was closed, and tears had been spent, she suspected that Mark had basically written off their relationship, although he hadn't yet asked for his ring back. She should probably be the one to give it back.

But was she ready?

Somewhere in the Bible, Victoria recalled a Scripture describing how friends and family would turn on true believers in the last days. Suddenly, she felt terribly alone. Abandoned.

Were these indeed the last days?

MONDAY, APRIL 28

37

Monday morning, when Beverly James' e-mail spit out a message on Karen's home printer, Victoria was not surprised. However, the contents of the document stumped her.

"What are you doing, Mother?" Karen glanced over her shoulder. "What's that?"

"Uh, this thing?" Victoria flipped the paper over, looking up at her daughter. "It's an e-mail from a friend. The one who sells cosmetics over the Internet." Lying came too easy.

"So what did your friend have to say?" Karen folded like a chair on the carpet. "About the makeup?"

"It's all cosmetic jargon!" Victoria nervously waved her e-mail, afraid Karen would see the deceit crouching in her eyes. "It's only a list of supplies and prices," she explained, troubled over the real message squirreled away in Bev's letter. "It wouldn't interest you."

"It might. Maybe I'll order something, too," Karen challenged her mother. "I'd like to see the list, Mother. Hand it over." Karen put forth an upturned palm with resolve.

"I don't think so." Victoria held the letter in one hand behind her back. "Besides, the formula is designed for older skin."

"Oh," Karen replied, thinking it odd that her mother was so secretive about buying cosmetics. "Well, I guess sharing is overrated." She recalled the cookie commercial. "Anyhow, I have to get dressed and head on over to the office. Gotta contract brewing."

Brewing would aptly describe Victoria's churning emotions regarding Bev's puzzling e-mail message. When Karen had driven away, she reread the one-page encoded letter four times, trying to recall Bev's exact words when they'd last spoken via the Internet.

Then it dawned on her: "Five to one, you'll get the message."

Yes! She suddenly understood how to unlock the meaning!

Locating a ballpoint pen, she began counting the words in

Beverly's letter. Every fifth word, she circled. When she'd completed the task, she decoded the message:

> *Paid off to leave town. Brand son key to solution.*
> *Expensive choice to truth. Care full. Ex- knows details.*
> *Don't call again. Beverly.*

Victoria shredded the letter and flushed it down the commode, more from anger than caution. A conspiracy did exist and Mark knew. Who else was involved in the cover-up?

Head throbbing, Victoria realized the woman she had once trusted and called her *best friend* either couldn't or wouldn't talk. But if the roles were reversed, would she act any differently?

Victoria glared at her sad image in the bathroom mirror. Shadows cloaked her tired face. Lying had undermined her Christian integrity and taken its toll on her physical health.

Bottom line, after all the trickery, she still had no proof to proceed with the investigation. Bev had not revealed anything she hadn't already known or suspected. *So what was a girl to do?*

But wait for Georgie Hendricks to do her job.

***

Dick Branson's cute red-haired secretary was buffing her fingernails Monday morning when the lanky gas lady walked up to her desk. "What can I do for you?" Jeannie asked.

Wearing an official-looking gray uniform with a TENNESSEE GAS AUTHORITY label sewn into her jacket pocket, the TGA gal said, "I'm here to check for a gas-main leak."

"Oh, yeah," said Jeannie, recalling the memo.

"You the one to give me clearance?"

"That's me!" Jeannie smiled, brushing away the excess nail fluff from her desk. "Sign right here." She pulled a black guest book from the shelf. "What's the problem?"

"Nothing we can't fix," Allison Black, a.k.a. Georgie Hendricks, replied. But of course, the signature on the registry would be a forgery. Her half-sister wouldn't mind loaning her name this once to help out a friend in trouble. And Victoria Tempest needed all the help she could get.

"Here's an official visitor's badge." Jeannie was having trouble keeping her eyes off of the silver medallion roped around the gas mamma's neck.

Georgie took note and said, "It was a gift from my great grandmother."

"Old Indian artistry," Jeannie noted. "It's beautiful." She stared into the TGA gal's turquoise eyes, feeling as if she'd stolen a disturbing peek into a universal pair of swirling black holes. "That's all I need. Good luck."

"Anything else I should know?" asked Georgie

"Oh, yeah. Don't go near any of the buildings. Boss's orders."

"No problem." Georgie was already pinning the official guest tag to her jacket pocket as she walked out the front door. Getting inside Branson had been easier than she envisioned.

Greeted by a flawless spring morning with temperatures in the high fifties, Georgie took a moment to appreciate nature as the scintillating sunlight fired up the colorful buds lacing the tree limbs in the distant hills. She only wished Allison could see it.

The sudden flutter of bird wings momentarily captured Georgie's attention. Glancing up, she saw that a lone robin camouflaged by a royal-blue sky had taken flight. Somehow she identified with the little critter, feeling her flight was skittish, too.

Georgie continued her journey along the sidewalk leading off to the left of Branson's huge complex. Snug against the drab-gray buildings where landscaped beds filled with green shrubs and blooming perennials.

Georgie whistled. Dick had gone to some expense to adorn his property. Did "pretty is as pretty does" apply? Probably not.

Stepping off the sidewalk, she trekked down a gravel pathway and crossed a grassy plain south of the complex. Heading for a hilly section, she kept a sharp watch for any clues that suggested illegal dumping. Dick's grounds seemed . . . too clean.

Like he was hiding something.

Loosely wearing her deceased half-sister's TGA uniform, Georgie went about checking the gas main leaks using a hand-sized computer program that told her what to do. Not too many years before, Allison Black had worked for the company.

Before she had OD'd on cocaine. Like Victoria, Allison had experienced her fair share of grief.

Georgie periodically glanced over her shoulder to make sure she wasn't being followed. Suspicion came natural for a private eye. Pausing to catch her breath, she pulled from her backpack a survey plat that she had obtained from the Hardeman County Courthouse earlier that day and studied it.

Branson's connecting buildings were laid out like a big capital T on the property, not so different from the mid-twentieth-century architectural designs used in constructing public high schools.

Dick's secretary had issued a warning for her to steer clear of the buildings, but nobody said she couldn't check out who and what came in and out of those gray concrete structures.

A matter of interest to Georgie was the recorded deed, which did not state the original amount Hearty Meats had paid for the twenty-five-acre plot formerly leased to a tannery.

The property was purchased in 1984 for $1.The names of the corporate owners remained anonymous since a title company closed the transaction using a power of attorney.

Why all the secrecy?

Georgie folded the land plat and returned it to her backpack, took a swig of cold water from her thermos, then continued her journey to the top of the steep embankment.

After locating the perfect overlook approximately a quarter of a mile south of the main plant, she settled her things among a clump of trees and cast her gaze on the terrain below.

It was a great spot to fish . . . for *fishy* things.

With the warm sunshine against her back to neutralize the chilly breeze astir, Georgie used her binoculars to begin her real work. She only wished the invigorating morning could be shared with

Allison. Inhaling the fresh air, she kept her eyes peeled on the landscape below.

It wasn't too long before Georgie glimpsed a tanker truck rumbling down a gravel road headed toward the south entrance of the storage plant. Upon arrival, the driver first steered the puffing diesel away from the building before cautiously backing up to a wide connecting ramp.

A double set of metal doors yawned open as four men dressed in grungy-gray dungarees hustled outside of the main building to speak to the driver. A few minutes later, the driver climbed out of his rig and the entourage circled around the back of the truck.

Georgie cursed when she lost sight of the motley crew, but they soon reappeared on the other side of the ramp, smoking cigarettes and jawing as they indulged in casual conversation.

A tall man wearing an official-looking gray-and-navy uniform hurried outside, using animated gyrations as he barked a command. Nobody seemed in a big hurry.

Probably on break, Georgie guessed. *My turn*, the PI leaned against a tree and lit up a cigarette.

She wasn't in a hurry either. A good investigator totally understood the value of patience. Over the years experience had taught her that the more important events in life occurred unexpectedly. Like capturing a bird in flight with the click of a camera, or observing a fleeting rainbow. The expert, whatever the field, must be prepared to react when that rare window of opportunity opens. It was especially true in solving a murder case.

Fifteen minutes passed before any posture of work resumed at Branson. Through her binoculars, Georgie observed the activities taking place. Like busy insects, a team of workmen scurried from the cavernous warehouse, moving the heavy crates with dollies down a ramp toward the open end of the smoking steel tanker.

So what was really inside those boxes? Packed meats? Or something more lucrative, like diamonds or drugs?

Granted, she was a professional investigator and suspicious by nature. But from the way Victoria had described Dick Branson, it was hard to imagine him as an upstanding, law-abiding citizen, innocent of all sins.

No, it was doubtful Dick earned his millions packing meats.

Having done her homework before coming to the site, Georgie knew that a Miami-based investment group had formerly purchased a dozen warehouses in Florida in 1979 and used them for packing processed meats. A year later, Hearty Meats became a corporation.

Then, in January of 1983, an attorney representing Hearty negotiated a long-term lease on the abandoned tannery property north of Fernwood, Tennessee. Construction began and the new plant opened in '84. And for a time, the packing company rocked along with marginal profits. Until early 1991 when Dick Branson purchased the operation.

By no means a rich man, where did Dick get his money?

Overnight, Branson Meatpacking Company exploded with growth, its tentacles reaching into major industrial cities such as Seattle, San Franscisco, Los Angeles, New Orleans, Miami and New York. *Who knew that meatpacking could be so lucrative?*

And it appeared that Dick preferred that his plants were located in cities near major shipping ports for easier worldwide distribution of his meats. *Or international smuggling?*

Was it coincidental that Dick Branson had arrived in Fernwood six months shy of Victoria Tempest's automobile accident and her husband's untimely demise?

Or, Georgie's criminal speculation leaped, had the start-up of Hearty Meats somehow been linked to the break-in at Jeffrey Tempest's law firm on April 13, 1989?

If that happened to be the case, and Dick Branson had a secret he wanted to keep, Victoria's renewed interest in her husband's murder was certain to push his panic button.

Georgie cursed when she looked through the binoculars and saw a hand pointed her way. Dousing her cigarette, she hastily gathered her equipment and hustled down the backside of the hill.

Circling around the rear of the property, she stumbled into a pond filled with inky sludge.

"Ug!" She mewed. Ankle deep in oily mud Georgie's frown dissolved into a grin. *The bird in flight!*

In a haste to lease the old tannery property to Hearty Meats, apparently the landlords hadn't bothered to properly dispose of any chemical residues left from tanning leather.

Trying not to muddy her half-sister's uniform, Georgie knelt to scoop a small amount of the sludge into a sterilized vial, gathering additional soil samples from around the toxic pond.

Then, just in case somebody asked, she used a TGA instrument to perform a gaseous test. The entire process didn't take more than thirty minutes.

After filling out an official-looking report form, Georgie packed up her gear and began walking back toward the main building, thinking that if anything weird resided in the quiet soils of Branson she would soon know it. Soil analysis didn't lie.

Quit wasn't a word in her vocabulary. PI Georgie Hendricks always got her man. *Or her woman.*

38

Victoria climbed into her Mercedes Benz Monday morning and drove over to the address Sarah Boswell had given her: 1115 Balcony Avenue. Rhe Muscle-Shoals Hornsby lived in a copycat condo complex similar to the one in which Beverly James had resided.

Rapping on the door, she waited for someone to answer.

Suspicious dark eyes peered around a half-cracked door. Uncle Rhe-mus' daughter wasn't young by anyone's assessment. Probably in her early seventies, she was grossly obese with condescending jade eyes.

"Yeah?" Katsy suspiciously viewed Victoria.

"Have I come at a bad time?" Victoria nervously asked. "I'm not selling anything."

"Who are you?" She hugged the door, her breath tainted with garlic.

"My name is Victoria Tempest. Sarah—" she suddenly realized that Katsy might not know Sarah Boswell from Santa Claus. "Your friend in traffic violations sent me."

"Oh, that Sarah!" Katsy's gaze ignited with recall. "So why you wanna talk to me? Am I in trouble?" She straightened her tank top and scrubbed her leaky nose with a hand.

"Goodness no!" Victoria gasped. "Sarah gave me your address because I wanted to speak to your father."

Please, lady, I need this interview.

"Rhe-mus!" Katsy hollered, halfway turned with a hand parked on a curvy hip. "You up to a visitor today?" She guarded the entry-way to the apartment like gold was stashed inside.

"I was under the impression your father had a stroke."

Let me come in, Katsy.

"He did, but he's better now." Katsy's twisted lips suggested that she had smiled. "Well, you comin' in?" The door swung open. "If Sarah sen'cha, you mus' be all right."

"Thank you, Katsy." Victoria entered the cluttered apartment strewn with clothes and dirty dishes. A collection of live spiders and cockroach corpses were trapped in corner webs.

"Sorry the place is such a mess." Katsy began picking toys off the floor. "Had my grandchildren over yesterday. You know how that is." Her black eyes slightly bulged.

Belatedly, Victoria didn't. "Don't worry about cleaning up for me," she told Katsy. "I just need to ask Rhe-mus a few questions. I won't take too much of your time."

"About whut?" Katsy flared like a startled cat. "Is my daddy in trouble? Been gambling over the Internet again? I'll kick his butt to kingdom come!" Blood was in her gaze.

"Oh, no. Nothing like that." Victoria swallowed a chuckle. "I was in an automobile accident some years ago, and I lost something. Your father reported my accident."

"My father ain't a thief!" She moved to block the hall entrance.

"No honest, it's nothing like that. I lost my Bible," Victoria moved straight to her point. "I just need to know if your father noticed it in my wrecked car?"

"Oh." Katsy calmly stepped aside. "Go on in the bedroom." She pointed down the hall. "You can ask my daddy yo'rself. Me, I gotta get myself dressed for work or I'll be late."

"I really appreciate this, Katsy." Victoria ventured into the dark passageway.

Rhe-mus looked like a bag of bones stuffed under navy blue sheets. His wiry hair was a muslin-gray, and his pinched-up face reminded Victoria of a dried prune. "Mr. Hornsby?"

"Folks call me Uncle Rhe-mus." The old man unsuccessfully tried to roll over in his bed. "Come closer, can't see you so good," his frail voice revealed his ill health.

While Uncle Rhe-mus critiqued Victoria like a true policeman, she edged around the box-spring mattress until her body shadowed his weak eyes from the window light.

"I'm Victoria Tempest," she introduced herself. "In 1989, you wrote a police report on my car accident. I nearly died that evening, left in a coma for three months."

"That wuz a long time ago." His unsettling gaze swallowed Victoria like he was tasting her. Despite his scrutiny, she was immensely grateful that an intelligent fire still burned in the centers of his drab eyes. *Uncle Rhe-mus wasn't gone yet.*

"Oh, yeah . . ." he pointed a bony finger at Victoria and coughed, "you're that Tempest lady whos' husband got kilt on the same night you tump't your car over on Highway 64."

"That's me!" Victoria was relieved he remembered. Maybe she'd learn a thing or two from the wise old cop, after all. "I'm looking for something I lost that night."

Uncle Rhe-mus coughed, wheezed, and pointed to the dresser. "Git me my medicine, would'ja?" He was obviously in great physical discomfort, gasping for breath.

Victoria hurriedly located the brown prescription bottle lying under a day-old newspaper and was about to hand it over when she realized that Uncle Rhe-mus would need her assistance.

"I'm sorry you're so sick." She unscrewed the child-resistant plastic cap and carefully measured out a teaspoon, feeding the syrupy liquid through the old man's parched lips.

The officer swallowed and collapsed on his pillow. "Ain't got nuthin' of yo'rs, child." He glared up at the dingy ceiling. "Too old and too blame tired—gotta sleep now."

His eyes shuttered and closed, a raspy snore escaping his bubbly salivating lips.

"No!" Victoria leaned close to his floppy ear and whispered, "I need to find my Bible, Uncle Rhe-mus. You're the only person I know to ask. Did you happen to see it in my car?"

The sick cop was unresponsive, hardly breathing.

"Uncle Rhe-mus!" Victoria panicked, afraid he had died.

"No," he whispered with his eyes closed. "No Bible, no whur."

"Did you see anyone else besides the two paramedics who pulled me from my wrecked car?" Victoria wasn't giving up. Rhemus could sleep later when she was gone.

Playing games or not, he was frighteningly still.

"Uncle Rhe-mus?" She studied his face for signs of life.

"No." One eye popped open. "Just me and the medics."

"Listen, I'm going to leave my phone number on the dresser if you think of anything else," Victoria said, but the old man had already drifted into the fast slumber-lane.

***

On her way home, Victoria stopped by the grocery store and picked up a few items. She was busy placing canned goods in the pantry closet when the front doorbell sounded. *Mark?*

She shoved a can of Maxwell House Decaffeinated Coffee on the shelf, peeled away her apron, and scurried to open the door. A man wearing a BellSouth uniform glared at her.

"Karen Tempest?" The stranger was short and skinny.

Victoria swallowed hard as the man glanced at his chart, then lifted weird pewter eyes. A sinister darkness eroded his near pleasant expression as he tilted his head to one side.

"No, I'm her mother." Victoria held to the door, just in case she decided to slam it.

"Phone Company," the man sourly spit out his words, forcing a smile. "Got lines down in your neighborhood. I need to check your phones." His eyes skittered past her to the den.

"Sure." Victoria backed out of the way, trying to decide if she should stalk Weird Eyes or let him do his job. "Call me if you need help. I'll be in the kitchen." *Watching you.*

"Got a phone in a bedroom somewhere?" BellSouth asked.

"Got three phones," Victoria called back. "One on the desk in the den, and one in each bedroom. Help yourself."

She hastily began pulling fresh vegetables from paper grocery sacks and throwing them in the sink to wash, leery of the stranger's presence in her home.

Sneaking a peek around the corner cabinet, Victoria spied a phone upturned in the repairman's hands. Weird Eyes gave her the creeps. Although he appeared official, he was a nameless stranger.

"Did you give me your name?" Victoria called out.

"Carl." He continued working. *Pretty trick for an older woman*, he thought to himself.

"If I can help, let me know," Victoria reluctantly offered.

"I'm fine." Carl shielded his work with his back to prevent the classy broad from seeing him unscrew the phone's metal plate, wondering why anyone would want to bug the pretty lady's phone lines. *Not his problem*, he glanced to see if she was still watching.

Nope. Let her wrestle with her groceries while he did his job. He'd get his work done faster that way. Carl prided himself in the fact he was paid well for what he did.

Always the professional, he had an instant uniform for almost any guise. Deception was his natural gift, and this job was coming off without a hitch. He'd slap a little gizmo inside each of the three phone frames and split.

Not a problem, Carl enjoyed seeing the woman squirm.

Victoria grew uncomfortable as the telephone repairman disappeared into Karen's bedroom. An even worse scenario was the prospect of trailing Carl to observe him.

What if the repairman wasn't who he claimed to be? This Carl character could be a pervert, or worse, a serial killer. *Suppose he took her attentiveness wrong and . . .*

Victoria's hands trembled as she slid the washed vegetables inside the crisper drawer. She kept her eyes on the oven clock, counting the seconds until Carl came back up front.

"Thanks." Carl reappeared five minutes later. "I'm finished."

Victoria nodded, operating on remote control to counter fear.

"Your lines all checked out A-OK," he announced, waving a fond goodbye as he slunk toward the front door. "Call me if you need anything else." *I do mean anything.*

Victoria trailed Weird Eyes to the front door.

Full of himself, Carl grinned, relieved that no hitches had complicated his assignment. Too bad he wouldn't be spending a little more time with this sultry beauty. She'd be soft to touch, and he loved smelling her perfume.

No, Carl decided. *That would be unprofessional.*

"Wait!" Victoria called out to the repairman.

Carl froze in his tracks. *Just let me go.* He'd make the lady sorry if she didn't. "What?" He stuck his head around the door.

"Did you leave a card? Just in case I have a problem?"

"Darn, left them in the truck." Relief abated Carl's fears. "I can get one if you like?" he put Victoria off. People usually didn't like to cause trouble. He waited for her decision.

"Oh, never mind," Victoria discarded apprehension. "Go on, you're busy. I'll phone BellSouth if I have a problem." She just wanted the repairman out of the condo.

"You sure?" Carl made it a point to be cordial.

"Positive."

"See ya!" Carl pranced out the door. *Yep, there were plenty of rewards for crime.*

39

Dick was perched on a barstool at the Branson-Fernwood Country Club sipping on his second vodka cocktail when he noted the time on his gold Swiss wristwatch. *5:05 p.m.*

The watch was a Daytona from Rolex that he'd purchased in Zurich. *Eighteen sweet karats!* It certainly hadn't come cheap, though it wasn't as expensive as an Audemars Piquet Grande that easily retailed at a cool sixty grand in the jewelry stores.

Life was expensive.

Dick anxiously twisted in his chair. Wiping the watch's shiny surface clean with a cloth napkin, he considered how it never missed a beat—unlike his son who was already late.

5:10. Dick shook his head in disgust.

What was keeping the kid?

By now, Victoria Tempest would have had her visitor, nasty punctual efficient Carl. He would soon know the woman's every move. She'd slip up in time. Everyone did.

Dick gulped down the devil's one-hundred-proof brew. Victoria had no idea how he was about to open up her life like a book and read it. His surveillance recorder was just waitin' under his desk to record her every phone conversation.

Just let little Miss-management try something!

He thought of how most people couldn't make it through a day without talking to somebody. Why, if he'd known Alexander Graham Bell a century ago, he'd have been the first to invest funds in his telephone invention. The man had exhibited vision, unlike most people.

Impatiently tapping his glass on the bar, Dick was counting on Victoria soon making a mistake. No second-guessing her moves ever again. He double-dared Mark James to interfere. The meddler had to be stopped before she did serious damage to his business.

It was five minutes later than the first time Dick glanced at his Rolex. Jon should know better than to stand up his daddy. Gracious, he'd left the boy a phone message over an hour ago telling him to hightail it on over to the country club.

Didn't the kid ever check his messages?

Dick was worried about his son. Jon wasn't acting normal, hadn't phoned or bothered to show up at work in almost two weeks. Sure, he'd told the kid to take a hike when Victoria was lookin' to talk to him. *But a two-week hike?*

He gulped down his drink and ordered another.

Did Jon think his daddy was made of money? Who did the boy think was gonna mind the business when his daddy was gone? Dick shook his head. It was stupid to worry about all that. In a rat's-nest world, he was filthy rich. Jon didn't need to work anyhow.

Heavily sighing, Dick glanced at his watch again. Regardless, being rich was still no excuse for Jon boozing his time away with frivolous motorcycling, beer-guzzling cronies.

The kid was older and ought to act more responsibly.

A worse idea, Jon could be shacked up in some motel with a common tramp. Dick realized in a snake's eye, he would buy youth again if it were for sale.

His son should wake up and realize that life wasn't forever, live more cautiously. In a world rampant with infectious diseases, millions had already died from AIDS and other weird viruses. Being a good papa, he'd sure hate for Jon to beat him to the grave.

However, with the advent of genetic human replacement parts, people had the potential to become gods in a decaying world. "Dick? Are you alone?" A voice from behind asked.

"Huh?" Dick spun around in his barstool and faced Mark James. "Oh hi, Mark." He resumed his lazy slouch at the bar and ordered another Absolute, a total of four.

"Nice to know you're glad to see me." Mark occupied the barstool beside Dick. "What's going on?" He opted for casual conversation before getting into the real reason why he'd come.

"Now, boy!" Dick's head cranked toward Mark. "You got my attention with that loaded question!" He took a sip of high-test before pursuing a philosophical rabbit chase.

"Would you be referrin' to my golf game or what?"

Dick was full of himself. Mark glared at the old barracuda, wondering why he let friendship put himself through the agony. His foul-mouthed companion was the most obnoxious person he knew.

"Well? Cat got your tongue?" Dick motioned for the young barmaid to refurbish his glass. "Or," Dick turned to Mark, "maybe you're lookin' at this pretty thing standin' in front of us with something more personal in mind." He hitched up his baggy pants.

"Might as well make it a double martini," Mark told Gena, glaring at Fernwood's mover-shaker. He had a more urgent agenda than playing word games. He'd come to pick Dick's brain regarding Victoria, whose meddling had become his problem, too.

Earlier that afternoon, Karen had phoned Mark at his office to discuss her mother's irrational behavior. On Thursday, she'd been missing all night. Who knew what Victoria had been doing or where she'd been? And she wasn't telling.

When Gena placed Mark's drink on the bar he said, "Put it on my tab."

The puzzling factor in the Victoria-equation was the mysterious e-mail correspondence that she received on Monday from a cosmetics saleslady. In all the years he'd known Vicki, she'd never had the slightest bit of interest in surfing the Internet.

So why suddenly now?

Oh, Vicki had been quick to explain how Kathryn Billingsley had helped her get on line at the public library, but both he and Karen knew that she had never ordered anything door-to-door and absolutely despised telephone solicitations of any description.

Always a classic hands-on shopper, it was totally unlike her to place an Internet order. *No*, Mark decided. Purchasing cosmetics wouldn't be on Vicki's prioritized list. She had one obsession on her mind: solving Jeffrey's murder!

So who was on the line with her?

Mark glanced over at Dick, rolling his cold glass between his hot hands. "What?" The tycoon belched a fiery breath. "You got somethin' to say, say it!"

Mark's sigh was so deep it was barely detectable.

"I just need to ask you a few questions, friend." He took the subtle route to unveiling the truth.

"Well, I thought our conversation would eventually touch on the subject of Victoria."

Wise guy Dick was on to Mark's agenda.

Twisting his head to one side, Dick amorously checked his mirrored reflection glowing behind the glass shelves filled with clean mugs and glasses. "Love does rare things to men."

"I think you were right, buddy." Mark downed his martini, the searing alcohol setting his taste buds afire as he tossed his scheming buddy a sideward glance.

"I'm always *right*!" Dick nursed his liquor glass to swollen lips. "I guess you realize you've been sittin' there like a knot on a log for nearly ten minutes?" His eyes were glazed.

"Yeah." Mark instructed Gena to replenish his empty glass. He was getting drunk and didn't care. It made accepting the past easier. "Guess I've been tightening down my thoughts."

Dick chuckled. "Me, too. Nothin' wrong with that, friend! It's been a crappy day. Been waitin' for the chip-off-the-old-block to show up. Looks like I've been stood up."

It was a rare moment when Dick let down his guard, unmasking his true feelings. In his own shallow way, Mark thought the selfish manipulator truly loved his son.

"Don't know what's got into that boy lately," Dick said.

"Is Jon all right?" Mark liked the softer side of his confidant. "Seems like he's had problems since Paul Tempest's death." Now that he thought about it, Jon was seldom around.

"The kid's got a sensitive streak." Dick moaned. "Anybody with half a brain could see that!" The old wasp stung again to cover his momentary melancholy.

Par for the course. Mark silently cursed, guessing that Dick must be terribly lonely at the top of the food chain. A man of his financial stature would need to glorify himself when others failed to do it for him. But he shouldn't forget Dick was a coiled snake and risk coming close enough to get struck.

"Just thought I'd ask." Mark let Dick's comment slide.

"So, back to my bein' right," Dick's syrupy words zeroed in on his favorite subject.

"You guessed correctly when you said Victoria was looking to bring Jeffrey's killers to justice," Mark revealed. Now on his third martini, he counted on the drug dulling his senses.

"Mark! News flash! I could have told you that!" Dick snapped his fingers, lending his drinking buddy his lazy eyes. "Ain't you heard there's no fool like an ol' fool?"

So Dick knew the score. Mark considered if he had indeed allowed his affection for Victoria to distort his perspective on the critical situation. Chivalry was downright scary.

Dick belched and raised his glass. "To Victoria Tempest, Fernwood's Nancy Drew!" His focus was fuzzy. "Whar's that kid o' mine?" He glanced around the crowded bar.

"You've had too much to drink, buddy. Time to go home." Mark climbed down from his barstool to haul Dick away before the fool embarrassed himself and passed out.

"Don'cha coddle me!" Dick held to the bar for dear life. "You lis'en good, you buzzard! Yo'r meddlin' bride-to-be's jus'anuther probl'm to solve in the great schem'a life!"

Mark listened as Dick headed off on a drunken tangent about there being nothing new under the sun and how he had everything under control, his cocky assurance forcing Mark to ask himself what nasty trick Dick had up his slippery sleeve for his fiancée.

"And just what does all this nonsense mean?" Mark reached the end of his endurance.

"Dad?" A voice behind Mark drew Dick's attention. Together they turned around and faced a showered, shaved, and sober Jon Branson. *Definitely, something new under the sun.*

"Well, I'll be," Dick cursed. His boy actually looked decent for a change. *Made a father proud*, he thought to himself. "Whur' ya been, Son?"

"Sorry, I'm late, Dad." Jon loosely stood before his father.

"Thirsty? Whut'd ya say I buy you a drink?" Dick's bleary eyes rested on his son. "Mark and I are through talking."

"No thanks, got an appointment." Jon buried his hands in the pockets of his faded Polo jeans holstered by a wide leather western belt that screamed all Nashville.

"Well, then," Dick cleared his throat, "how 'bout joining me for some sup'pa?" He switched gears to favor the family mode, the ol' stomach craving food again.

"No, can't stay," Jon declined, shifting his feet uncomfortably.

"Well then, how come you even bothered comin'?"

"Because you asked me to, Dad." Jon's lime eyes emitted a softer hue than Mark remembered, his demeanor forthright and honest, most unusual for a Branson.

"You haven't been at work in nearly two weeks," Dick wheezed, puffing on a fresh-lit cigar, struggling to focus his blood-shot eyes on his son. He wasn't feeling so good.

"You need to give *those* up," Jon remarked, more out of concern than disrespect.

Dick resented the reprimand. "Quit smokin'? I pro'bly oughta give up a lotta things, but I won't. Don't 'ntend to miss nothin' excitin' in this life, boy! And you shouldn't either."

Jon didn't respond, just shrugged his wide shoulders as he glared at his drunken daddy.

"I've got another job, Dad." Jon hitched his thumbs in his western belt. "Just came to tell you so." He drew in a quick breath. "I'll be leaving town by the end of the week."

"Just like that!" Dick stumbled to his feet. "Quittin' an oppor-tun'ty of a lifetime!" The alcohol took control. "And for what, Son?" He cursed. "Some job?"

With Dick on a tear, Mark stepped aside, disassociating himself from the family feud.

"Only a fool would miss running a billion-dollar operation for some insignificant job!" Dick snapped, wiping the sweat around the fat folds of his neck with a handkerchief.

Mark felt the electric sparks flying. He should go now.

But he didn't.

"I never expected you to understand, Dad." Jon uncomfortably glanced at Mark. "I'm going by Mother's house to tell her my plans. You might try going to see her once in a while yourself. Do your conscience some good. She hasn't been feeling well lately."

Mark was aware that Jon was a prodigy of Dick's first marriage. Seeming like a decent person, over the years Marilyn had accepted Dick's monthly check and never remarried.

"Some'in wrong with Marilyn?" Dick grabbed the back of the barstool to keep from tumbling off. "She knows she can call me anytime." His beady black eyes were half shut.

"Ask her, Dad." Jon's cool-lime gaze fell upon the multi-colored octagonal designs in the carpet beneath his feet. The awkward silence settling between father and son said a lot.

Mark wondered if he should interrupt and take Dick home.

But he didn't.

"Well, I should go now." Jon looked up at his dad, his eyes pulsing with emotion.

"Go then," Dick grumbled as Jon walked away, waving a hand like he didn't care.

At first, Dick appeared wounded, then the hairs on the back of his neck bristled in an attack mode. "Wait!"

For a second, Mark thought he was going to chase after Jon.

"I'm sorry, Dad." Jon spun around, palms upturned in a defense mode. "I can't be the person you want me to be anymore. Maybe someday you'll understand, but now is not the best time to explain." He kept walking, periodically glancing back to see if his father was stalking him.

Mark watched the veins in Dick's neck bulge to capacity. The pompous dictator had suffered rejection by his only son. His type would rather let a child walk away than apologize. He wondered if he should say something. But he didn't. *Wouldn't.*

Dick Branson had gotten his just desserts.

40

By late Monday afternoon Georgie Hendricks was back at her apartment in Memphis. First on her agenda was to overnight the Branson soil samples to a lab expert who worked for the Environmental Protection Agency. Clint Edwards wouldn't mind helping out a friend.

Besides, she had once helped Clint get the goods on his pretty but promiscuous spouse. Having personally tracked Trish to a low-life motel in Chicago and caught her in the unholy act, it turned out that Clint had a right to distrust his sweetie-pie.

Georgie held the overnight package in her left hand a moment longer before sliding it through the lateral slit in express mailbox. Payback was not something that she expected from Clint.

Friendships were much too important to mess up with return favors. However, this request wasn't for her; it was for Victoria Tempest, a nice lady who was in a heap of trouble.

Considering the tentacle reaches of Dick Branson, trust was important. And Clint had promised to have the lab results back to her by late Tuesday. "If there's the slightest whiff of anything illegal in the soil samples, I'll know it," he'd confidently said.

***

Victoria was disheartened that her visit with Uncle Rhe-mus had reached a dead-end. *Bless his heart*, a poor choice of words.

Here it was another Monday and she was fresh out of ideas. She hoped that Georgie would soon call to report her findings.

However, waiting proved agony. Sleepless beneath the bed covers, tossing and turning like a ship at sea, she fought back an onslaught of negative thoughts. Taxed by feminine instinct, a shadowy voice reminded her to watch her back.

Killers are lurking out there!

Victoria rolled over in the bed and considered her next move. When she spoke with her savvy detective, she would ask Georgie to track down Colburn Gordon in Mississippi.

Surely Burn knew how to contact his sister, and she badly needed Gloria's input. Victoria flipped over on her back and stared at the moonlit ceiling, thinking that every lead she had cultivated dissolved like smoke in the wind.

Even more disconcerting was the idea that someone was constantly watching her. Hadn't Beverly James' sudden promotion and Gloria Gordon's monetary windfall come on the heels of her visits? Both had fled town over the same weekend.

Probably not by choice.

No, Victoria shivered. *I definitely have an adversary.*

Despite Georgie's explicit instructions never to phone her apartment, Victoria had already decided that if her smart PI didn't soon make contact, the agreement was off.

I'm taking the bull by the horns, Georgie. So you better hurry.

Shrouded under the bed covers, depression descended on Victoria like murky fog settling in a bog. In less than forty-eight hours, she'd be at the hospital having brain scans.

Only God knew the outcome of those tests.

How could one phone call hurt? Victoria rolled over on her side, eyes wide open watching the moon shadows eerily dance across the walls.

Belaboring the lack of physical evidence, in the absence of reliable witnesses, she had no proof of any wrongdoing. *Zilch.*

There was no murder case to reopen.

Where are you, Gloria? And why did you run away?

No! Locked inside Gloria's dizzy fun-loving brain were critical details that would help solve Jeffrey's murder. Victoria crawled from the bed and switched on the lamp. Taking her diary from its secret hiding place, she opened the pages and began to write:

April 28, 2014

Dear Diary:

It's good to be able to express my thoughts, if only to a person I know as "Dear Diary." Of course, Jesus knows my thoughts and what I am going to write before my words become ink. However, it is great therapy for me to clarify my thinking.

I also believe that my Bible is safe, I just don't know where it is. The Holy Spirit has been such a great comfort over the past week. In some ways, I wish that Jesus would audibly tell me what to do, but He usually doesn't communicate like that.

It appears that in these last days, in the absence of reading the Word, God's finest efforts must be accomplished through born-again believers.

However, outside of me, there appears to be few Christians left in Fernwood. At least, they have their lights under a bushel and aren't openly proclaiming their faith. Sometimes I think I must be the last Christian saved on Earth. O, my soul, perish the thought! If it's true, Jesus has already come and I've been left behind.

Summarizing my investigation—just in case I'm no longer around and somebody finds my diary—I have a few ideas I accept as truths.

 # 1 Even though Mark James says that he loves me, he's still keeping secrets. That presents a problem in our relationship. How can I trust him with my heart?

#2 Dick Branson is somehow involved in a cover-up conspiracy to mask the facts surrounding Jeffrey's death. Mark probably knows and is afraid to tell me. Which leaves me with one resource: Georgie Hendricks.

#3 Perpetrators who broke into Jeffrey's office may not have intended to kill him, as Karen pointed out. Maybe they only meant to steal some information pertinent to a case that he was working on at the time. Knowing that my phone call alerted the perps to Jeffrey's presence and hastened his death grieves me.

#4 I still don't know why Jeffrey returned to the office that stormy night.

#5 Beverly James has warned me on more than one occasion that it is dangerous to inquire about my accident or Jeffrey's murder. The message she e-mailed me confirmed my suspicion that Mark and Dick are thick as thieves.

#6 Karen, my only daughter, whom I dearly love, does not see things my way. Afraid of her own discoveries about her father's death, she isn't willing to rock her comfortable boat. It seems unwise to expect her help with my investigation.

#7 PI Georgie Hendricks appears to be my only reliable friend to date. Willing to take risks, she assumes personal responsibility for her clients and acts like the super investigator she knows she can be. I think more to prove her worth to herself than to please her clients. (I'm sorry that girl is hurting so much. I hope to witness to Georgie one day about the love of Jesus Christ. She desperately needs Holy Spirit relief from sin and hurt that only God's grace can deliver.)

#8 God is faithful and loves me deeply! May He send His angels to guide and guard me! And Lord Jesus, please help me get my Bible back!

41

Karen had flipped over in the bed so many times she was tangled in her sheets. Why was her mother's light still on? When she'd tried her door a few minutes ago, it was locked.

Not the first time, either. What did she do late at night that required locking her door? Karen wondered. Mark had a right to be concerned. Her mother needed her head examined. *Tie her mother up, check her into the hospital, and give her back her original brain.*

Today marked the two-week anniversary of Victoria Martin Tempest's bizarre rebirth under the dawning streetlights. In the twinkling of an eye, she'd been transformed into this new entity, unlike the first or second version. *Watch out, world! The mythical creature from the black lagoon is loose*!

Crawling from the bed, Karen limped into the bathroom and studied her scraggly image in the vanity mirror. Dark circles rimmed her eyes from lack of sleep. Ghostly gray plagued the roots of her dark hair. The corners of her lips sagged unhappily.

Guilt stalked her. But what scared her most was the idea that her mother might actually locate her father's killers and see justice served. And, in the aftermath, get them both killed. *Then where was the justice?*

Scooting into bed for a second round with the sheets, Karen thought she understood why her mother thought so differently. It was her Christian upbringing, her unyielding faith that God would somehow restore her life and make all things right. *Baloney!*

Years ago, Karen had believed in God, even trusted Him a bit. Hadn't she made a public profession of faith at ten? Got baptized? "Washed clean," her pastor had put it.

Seriously, once she even believed that prayer changed things. But as time passed God stopped listening, so she'd quit talking.

Karen yawned and rolled over. The sheets were winning. It was that *holy seed* thing. Her faith hadn't taken root. Choked out by the cares of the world, she'd become a dried-up seed bearing no roots. Karen punched her pillow hard. *Maybe her mother's way was better.*

But then, in her own defense, what kid wouldn't be angry when both parents were stolen from the nest? Why she was jealous of her mother's gullible certainty in God's existence was a puzzle.

Karen kicked off the hot sheets, sat up, and scrubbed her scalp viciously. How could her mother be so positive God was *always* in control? That Jesus loved all human souls equally? He wasn't out in the world's pasture searching for lost sheep.

My mother is delusional.

"I tried to believe in you, God. I really did," Karen softly whispered. "Didn't I pray for my mother to recover after her accident? Didn't I ask you to punish my father's killers?"

But YOU never answered. Were you too busy?

Oh, Karen knew that her mother would argue that God had His own timetable for answering prayers. No answer meant wait a while. But why did God end her mother's amnesia now? Then not give her real mother back?

Years ago, Karen had been devastated over her mother's accident. On that tragic night when her father died and her mother lost her identity, life had changed for her, too. That was why she had stopped trusting in God.

Sure, she attended Sunday church services, but not for the right reasons. It was the social thing to do, an opportunity to make sound business contacts.

In all fairness to the universal order of things, Karen thought she couldn't blame God for everything. Making a few unwise choices as a young adult had eventually led to unhealthy relationships. Bottom line, she had trusted the wrong man.

Once trapped in a rotten marriage, she'd allowed herself to become a battered wife. Rather than taking a sane way out, she had committed murder, a justifiable act in her own mind, though unacceptable in the eyes of God or man.

Karen suffered bitter remorse as tears soaked her pillow. Should the truth ever surface, she would risk imprisonment. Truth could take Mark down. *Was truth worth it?*

She only hoped her mother didn't mess up life for everyone by marrying Mark out of stupid duty. Truth wasn't her mother's friend, either.

Tuesday, April 29

42

Victoria awakened early Tuesday morning and discovered the remnants of Karen's half-eaten bagel. *Alone again.* Nailed to the den wall was the chirping coo-coo clock, its hands slowly counting the seconds, minutes and hours.

Tomorrow she was due at the hospital.

Time was a tease, anyhow. When sleeping, it appeared to stand still. In a hurry, there was too little of the commodity. When bored, it passed painfully slow.

For example, Victoria thought, the last two weeks had felt more like a century—yet there had been scarce enough time to accomplish any important goals. Had she made any headway in understanding her precarious mental situation? Or resolved any great family matters? Or come any closer to nailing Jeffrey's killers?

Clearly, she'd failed to define her relationship with Mark.

Giving up the thought-chase, Victoria drew a tub of bubbly hot bath water and climbed aboard. The ceiling stared back. Submerging, she attempted to block her thoughts and feelings.

Fifteen minutes later, she briskly toweled herself dry and put on her terrycloth housecoat. Venturing into the den, she sat Indian fashion on the sofa glaring at the phone. *Ring! Would you!*

Twenty minutes passed. *Sorry Georgie.* Victoria grabbed the phone and began dialing. The detective's message center clicked on. "Georgie . . ." Victoria groaned, "why couldn't you be there? I really need to talk to you. I think I'm losing it."

Detached from reality, she let twenty-five seconds slip by. "Uh, Georgie? You got my number." What else did she need to say? "This is Victoria. Please call me as soon as you get this message."

Pressing the Off button, Victoria let the dial tone blare before hanging up the receiver. Georgie would call, she was sure of it. She would just sit by the phone and wait.

***

Dick was doing paperwork in his office when the tape recorder beneath his desk became activated. Victoria Tempest was talking to somebody. He turned up the speaker and leaned back in his chair to listen to her. Interesting. A cocky smile smeared his pleased-as-punch face as the recorder cut off.

Using his secure phone line, he dialed his contact in Memphis. "Densil, this is Dick Branson." His snooping was paying off.

"Oh, hi. What can I do for you?" the detective replied.

"You sound busy." Dick bounced the rubber end of a pencil on his desk. *Rat-a-tat-tat-tat.* He let the sound wound down. "Got a little assignment for you if you're interested."

"Shoot!" Densil knew that Dick paid well for favors.

Dick chuckled. "Nothing as drastic as that. Just need you to do a little checking up on somebody for me. Think you can you handle that?"

"Sure, who's the guy?" Densil jumped to attention.

"The phone number is . . ." Dick barked the information. "It's a Memphis exchange. Georgie's the first name. How 'bout gettin' me a last name and a street address?"

"Done," Densil replied, ready to hang up and get going.

"Wait!" Dick wheezed. "Call me back on my private line, here at my office. And don't let no grass grow under your feet."

Dick heard the line click at the other end and hung up the phone. He didn't think he would have to wait long for an answer. Densil Derringer was a low-profile detective who earned six round figures every year doing favors for people just like him.

"Bring me a fresh cup of hot coffee," Dick buzzed Jeannie.

Things were looking up, Dick thought as he inhaled the sweet vanilla aroma of his Havana. Plopping his feet on his expensive desk, hands tucked behind his head, he waited for Densil's call.

Thirty minutes later, the detective phoned with the information Dick had requested. "Name's Georgie Hendricks. Lives at 222 Simpson, the Terrywoods Apartments. The dame's a private eye!"

"Holy Mother of God!" Dick cursed like a sailor for a few minutes before he calmed down a bit and assessed the situation. *So Victoria has hired a private eye.*

"I take it this is not good news," Densil said.

"No, it isn't." Dick wiped the saliva dripping from his lower lip with a hand. "Bill me!" He slammed down the receiver, deciding on how to handle the troubling matter.

***

The brown-wrapped package arrived at Victoria's doorstep around 4:15 p.m. Tuesday afternoon. Hearing the doorbell sound, she cracked the front door and peeked outside.

Seeing that no one was there, she picked up the package on the landing and candidly placed it to one ear. *No ticks*, she grinned at her paranoia, thinking of the weird BellSouth repairman.

Hand delivered with no return address, the package was lightweight and neatly tied with a plain white string. Her name was clearly printed on the outside in black Magic Marker.

Probably a sales gimmick. Victoria tossed the package on Karen's desk in the den and resumed her nostalgic search through the archaic phonograph collection.

Locating a recording by Bing Crosby, she recalled how his crooning voice always calmed her. Maybe his music would divert her attention from worrying over why Georgie hadn't called back.

Placing the lacquered disk on the turntable, Victoria turned on the switch and instant orchestra filled the room. With a hot cup of herbal tea in one hand, she lazily slid into the comfy folds of the sofa and prepared to enjoy Bing's soothing nineteen-forties music.

The moment of serenity was rewarding until Victoria began to contemplate the uneventful Tuesday, wondering what she had expected. Cannons to go off? A meteorite to strike?

Now that her recovery from amnesia wasn't news anymore, Mark and Karen weren't keeping constant tabs on her. In fact, she hadn't received one phone call or e-mail all day.

But that was all right. Wasn't she entitled to an ordinary day?

In one of her moods, Victoria had no desire to record in her diary, clean house or cook. Why bother? She didn't know Karen's supper plans and she wasn't the least bit hungry.

Having chosen to spend the day in quiet reflection, Victoria read a selection from *The Psalms Book*, earnestly praying for Mark's salvation and her future, whatever that may be.

Karen was in her thoughts, too. Victoria longed to be reassured her daughter was *born again*. Afraid that she'd come across like a self-righteous evangelist, unless the Holy Spirit directed, she should say nothing more on the subject of faith.

Fools rush in where angels fear to tread. She had too often jumped the gun—like when she planned an intimate private dinner party with Mark, which had turned into a disaster.

God is always on time.

However, today seemed somewhat different than others, more like playing a slow chess game. And the next move wasn't hers. It was Karen's and Mark's and Georgie's.

Karen arrived home around five with a brown sack tucked under one arm. Hearing soft music flowing from the stereo, she noticed Victoria crouched in the shadows. "Mother?"

"Yes, dear." Victoria peered at her bedraggled daughter, at a loss as to how she might help. Everyone carried baggage in life. And today, Karen's load appeared ominously heavy.

"Why aren't you dressed?" Karen asked.

"Oh, these rags," Victoria quipped, attempting to lighten the moment. Karen offered no response as she disappeared around the corner of the kitchen cabinet.

"Honey, did something bad happen today?" Victoria trailed Karen into the kitchen.

With an attitude Karen plopped her sack on the breakfast bar, shaking her head no.

Sensing her daughter's despair, Victoria longed to rock her child as she'd done in years before, wanting to somehow reassure her that everything would be just fine. But no human could make that promise. Life didn't always turn out the way you intended.

"I can tell you're worried about me, Mother." Karen recognized Victoria's concern. "Please don't, I'm just fine!" She bolted, scurrying down the hall toward her bedroom.

With a heavy heart, Victoria cranked up the coffeepot and waited for Karen to return. In a few minutes, she reappeared in the doorway wearing a pair of athletic shorts and a ratty tee.

"I'm sorry I've been so moody the last few days," Karen apologized as she sat down at the bar. "Who I am or what I do, especially how I feel, is not your concern, Mother."

Victoria had no idea how to respond to so profound a rejection. "I made coffee. Can I fix you a cup?" was all that came to mind.

"No, thanks." Karen walked over to the refrigerator and pulled a twig of green grapes from the crisper drawer. Reclaiming her barstool, she munched on a handful of the fruit.

"Honey, it doesn't take a genius to see you're troubled." Victoria carried her coffee mug to the bar. "I respect your right to your privacy, but if there's something bothering you . . ." she was careful not to apply pressure.

Karen pulled a bottle of chilled wine from her paper sack and filled a crystal glass to the brim. Turning it up to her lips, she locked smug eyes on Victoria. "Here's to whatever!"

Victoria watched her daughter down the sparkly white liquid and quickly pour a second glass. Wanting to scream *stop*, Victoria didn't. Using alcohol to dull the senses was a mistake.

Giggling, Karen tossed an arrogant glance Victoria's way. "Oh, I don't suppose you approve of my drinking, *Mother*."

Victoria swallowed a mouthful of scalding coffee.

"I hate seeing you like this, but I won't judge you since I'm not walking in your shoes." She allowed latitude for grace. "Regardless of our history, I love you very much."

Karen's eyes were crystal orbs of tears as she poured herself a third glass. "Here's to honesty, Mother!" She was obviously bent on getting drunk to drown her misery.

Frightened, Victoria placed an arm around Karen's shoulder. "Honey, talk to me." A huge lump lodged in her throat. "Tell me what's wrong so I can help."

"Help?" Karen slammed her glass on the counter, her gaze swimming in destructive self-pity. "So what is it you want to know, *Mother*? My life's rather boring."

"Whatever you want to tell me," Victoria calmly replied.

"Well, let me see where to start," Karen hiccuped, then giggled. "Since Teddy's death, I've carried a lot of guilt." She wobbled into the den, hugging her wine bottle.

Victoria followed her daughter, listening carefully.

"It's not like I haven't tried to push the past out of my mind, to tell myself what happened to Teddy wasn't my fault—that it was all just a terrible chain of circumstances."

Victoria had no idea where Karen's thinking was headed. "Maybe you should sit down, sweetheart." She guided Karen to the sofa, worried that she might fall flat on her face.

Karen rocked, then sat down. "It's gotten where I despise coming home." Hurt boiled to the surface. "When I look at you, I can't help from feeling judged."

"Oh, Karen! I'm so sorry." Victoria impulsively hugged her daughter.

"Stop!" Karen's upturned palms signaled alarm. "I don't want your sympathy!"

"I'm not sympathizing, Karen." Victoria distanced herself. "Giving Teddy drugs was wrong." She desperately wanted to help Karen resolve her grief. "Please hear me out."

Karen slouched on the couch, hugging her bottle like a teddy bear.

"I've been a terrible mother," Victoria admitted, staring into Karen's sad, upturned eyes. "I've been so busy dealing with my own problems I failed to see how much you were hurting."

Karen offered no response.

"I apologize for my selfishness. God knows, I'm not your judge and jury."

Karen sucked in a sob. "Thank you for saying that, Mother." She sat the wine bottle on the table beside the sofa. "Maybe I'll have that coffee now."

"Good." Victoria marched into the kitchen and returned with Karen's steamy mug, taking a seat on the sofa beside her troubled daughter.

"I just don't know how to get past memories of my bad marriage," Karen confessed. "I need a new handle on life, a good man in my future. I want to be loved, Mother."

"Everyone does, dear." Victoria thought of Jeffrey. "I love you."

"This cloud over me is suffocating my future." Karen crawled from the sofa to the floor, now in her own world. "Know what I mean?" Her muddy-brown eyes were sappy with tears.

"Yes, I do, sweetheart." Victoria crawled to the carpet to sit beside Karen. "Your father's unresolved death makes me feel exactly the same way—like all the blame rests on my tired shoulders. I keep thinking that if I'd done anything differently, he might still be alive."

Karen nodded, then scrubbed her leaky eyelids with the back of her fists.

"You see, dear," Victoria said, "we're not so different after all. Mother and daughter: the stormy Tempest duo." Her words made Karen grin. "I haven't been the perfect mother, but in certain ways, you've failed, too. We both desperately need God's love."

Karen's glazed eyes focused beyond the pale sunlit sliders as darkness descended.

"Mother, I don't believe in God anymore." She dropped her head between her knees. "Not once has God has ever spoken to me. He can't be real!" The crux of the matter surfaced.

Victoria felt partially responsible for her daughter's impoverished attitude toward God. Certainly, she hadn't set a Christian example in the past twenty-five years. Having endured more than her fair share of fiery trials, Karen should learn how God restores relationships.

I will show her. Victoria gathered Karen into her arms. Gently rocking her little lost lamb, she couldn't recall a time when she had felt so close to her daughter. Jesus, too. If only Karen could experience the cleansing of grace, she would know how faith works.

Faith in Jesus Christ was what Karen needed most in her frazzled life. In fact, it was what all humanity needed.

43

"What's this, Mother?" Karen noticed the brown-wrapped package bound with white string lying on her desk. Popping off the floor, she picked up the item to examine it.

"It's addressed to you, Mother," she remarked. "Hmm, no return address."

"Probably some sales gimmick," Victoria replied, uninterested.

"Mother!" Karen's eyes brightened. "Maybe this is the cosmetics samples you ordered from your Internet friend." She flipped the package over to view the back.

"Oh?" Victoria hadn't thought of that. Something coming from Beverly James?

"Wait!" Karen pressed the package to one ear. "No tick-tocks, just checking." She laughed as her mood improved. "A local representative must've delivered it to our door."

Victoria wished that Karen hadn't seen the package. If Beverly James had indeed sent her something, she wasn't sure it was safe to share the surprise with Karen.

"Here." Karen shoved the mystery package into Victoria's hands. "You open it, while I make us a fresh pot of coffee." She hustled off to the kitchen.

The package almost felt hot in Victoria's hands. Perhaps Bev had finally come to her senses and decided to share information. She ripped away the wrapper with anticipation.

"What is this?" The color washed out of Victoria's cheeks.

"Can't hear you, Mother!" Karen's voice rose above the puttering coffee maker.

Who in the world? Victoria clutched the cellophane-wrapped package of Lady Havana Cigars in her right hand. The first person who came to mind was Dick Branson.

But why would he send her cigars when he knew she didn't smoke? Victoria's hands began to tremble. Something didn't feel quite right. What was happening to her? The room tilted slightly to one side as her vision dimmed. "Oh!" Victoria grasped the arm of the sofa to keep from falling.

"Mother! Did you open your package yet?" Karen's shadowy voice echoed through the corridors of Victoria's mind. "What's wrong?" She was in a dark canyon, sinking deeper.

What's wrong, what's wrong? Questions were in Victoria's thoughts she could not verbalize.

Through a misty veil of deepening darkness, the gift slipped from Victoria's heavy hand and sailed through the air in slow motion, disappearing beyond the periphery of her vision.

"Moth—, are—-ill? Do you—-me—call Mark?"

Karen's voice was a cacophony of distorted syllables in Victoria's ears. "Help" was trapped somewhere in her parched throat as she wiped salt crystals from her parched lips.

Helplessly sinking to her knees, she began crawling across the carpet like a wounded animal. Assaulted by gigantic waves of nausea, Victoria clutched her stomach and screamed bloody murder.

An instant later, the floor rushed up in her face at great speed as an inky fog descended, closing off her vision. Tumbling forward, she lost consciousness.

***

Mother, Mother, Mother! Victoria heard her name being called over and over again through a swirling black lagoon. Like a door opening, a shaft of brilliant light pierced the darkness in her mind, inviting her into the presence of its radiating peace.

But a voice, Karen's voice, pulled Victoria back. Needing her. Pleading with her, telling her to hang on. There was darkness and light, silence and confusion. Lying inside a dimly lit coffin, strange faces hovered over her. *Demons*?

No! Victoria realized that she was riding inside an ambulance. Somewhere sirens screamed. Something tightened on Victoria's right arm. *Dear God! What's happening to me?*

***

Karen downed two cups of coffee while waiting for the Emergency Medical Service to arrive. Afraid to move her mother, she covered her with an afghan.

Watching the clock, she paced the room like a caged animal debating over whether to call Mark. The second the EMS team bolted through the door, they spotted Victoria lying crumpled on the floor and began their tedious work of reviving the victim.

Karen observed the madness from the kitchen, refusing to come unglued. Three medical technicians took turns working over her mother, screaming and pushing one another aside in a frantic attempt to resuscitate their patient.

Leaning helplessly against the humming refrigerator, Karen didn't know how to help, wishing that Mark were there. He always knew what to do. The uproar pushed her to near hysteria as the medics used sensitive instruments to poke and probe her mother for vital signs.

The medicinal odors were all too familiar. *She's dying*, Karen decided. Attempting to pray, she realized that she didn't know how. But if God were real, He would know her mother's heart and help her. In that idea, Karen found some consolation.

Fifteen minutes later, when it became obvious to the paramedics that they weren't succeeding, someone barked a command to hoist Victoria onto a stretcher. Voices were loud and movement was frantic as the EMS team made preparation to leave.

"Coming along, Miss?" a young technician turned to Karen.

"What?" She zoomed in on the moment. "Yes, of course."

Outside, Karen had waited until her mother was safely inside the ambulance before rushing to get her car. *Don't leave me again, Mother!* The little girl inside whimpered.

And now, here she was tailing the ambulance, dialing Mark's cell phone number. "Thank God!" Mark answered. "It's Karen." She hurriedly described her mother's incident. Mark didn't receive the news well, insisting on a blow-by-blow account.

"It happened so fast." Karen's clammy hands were shaking so hard she could hardly hold to the steering wheel. "I was in the kitchen making coffee. Mother seemed just fine . . ."

No, she didn't see what actually happened, Mark kept interrupting. Karen didn't want him to know she was still foggy from the alcohol she'd consumed earlier. *It's not my fault.*

"Try to remember, Karen," Mark pressed. "Any small detail could be crucial. Did Victoria eat or drink anything?" His voice was urgent, demanding.

"Coffee. But I had some too and I'm fine," Karen answered, attempting to keep up with the ambulance. The phone line popped. *"What?"* Mark's voice jumped a decibel.

"Mother said something, but I couldn't hear her over the noisy coffee maker," Karen recalled. "By the time I returned to the den she was on her knees crawling across the carpet."

"There's got to be more, Karen? Try to remember!" Mark refused to accept the bare facts. "Think, baby." His grilling pushed Karen to the breaking point.

"After applying ice packs to her forehead I tried to revive her, but I couldn't. So I covered Mother with an afghan and dialed 911. Mark, I've never been so frightened."

"Calm down, sweetheart." He could feel Karen's fear. "I'll meet you at the hospital in a few minutes. Try to stay calm." He'd been way too hard on her. "EMS knows what to do."

"Do you think Mother will be all right?"

"Your mother is a trooper," Mark was reassuring. "Be careful driving and I'll see you shortly!" His cellphone was clutched to his chin as he grabbed his coat to leave his office.

"I'll see you soon," Karen responded.

Sirens screamed in front of her as the ambulance bullied its way through Fernwood's late-afternoon traffic. It had begun to mist rain, reminding Karen of how her mother had said it always stormed when something important happened in her life.

Please don't storm.

Karen couldn't shake the image of her mother lying helplessly on the floor before the EMS team had arrived. Her body had felt cold, her breathing dangerously shallow. In the ambulance, she'd be hooked up to machines that monitored her blood pressure and heart rate.

Let the experts handle it. She dismissed her worry over the outcome.

Considering the stress her mother had been under, waking up from oblivion and tearing at life with a vengeance in an attempt to track down her father's killers, disappearing for hours with no explanation . . . this could prove the last straw!

Mark should have seen this coming! Karen blamed him. He was my mother's doctor, her lover, and he should have demanded that his Little Vicki be hospitalized to have tests run!

As if to read Karen's mind, Mark offered a confession over the phone. "I should have seen this coming and made Victoria take better care of herself. If something terrible happens, I'll never forgive myself."

Karen had never heard Mark sound so devastated. She felt the same way. But all either one of them could do was wait and see.

***

Georgie Hendricks was standing on the curb across the street from Victoria's condo when a screaming ambulance arrived.

Pandemonium broke loose as the EMS team climbed out of the van and rushed inside the condo. Taking cover in some bushes, she waited a good twenty minutes before the team came back out hauling someone on a stretcher.

Is it Victoria? Georgie strained her eyes to see, but it was too dark. The lifeless form covered in a white sheet was shoved into the back of the ambulance. A woman said a few words to the EMS driver, then she ran back inside the condo. *Karen Tempest?*

The detective feared she'd come too late to deliver the news. Clint's lab results were safely tucked inside her backpack, but it appeared that Victoria was in no shape to receive the report. *Too bad*, her client would have wanted to hear what the EPA expert had to say about the Branson soil samples. As soon as the ambulance had pulled away, Georgie ran as fast as she could in the shadows of the trees, circled around the corner, and hopped into her Bronco.

Racing after the gray Cadillac trailing the ambulance, she thought of how she'd warned Victoria *never* to call her Memphis number. Her client should have paid attention.

Now somebody else had. Georgie tried to be optimistic. When Victoria's problem had been diagnosed and she improved, the news would be just as well received. Afterwards, she was going to see the FEDS. *But what if they were involved in the Branson cover-up?*

Don't go there! Georgie curbed her creative mind.

Unsure if the Fernwood police could be trusted, or anyone else in town for that matter, she wasn't about to take any chances. No sane detective would risk challenging Dick Branson without first having secured the proper backup. The opposition meant business.

But if Victoria didn't survive, then what?

It was obvious that Victoria's phone had been bugged. How else would her enemies have known? No, the timing of Victoria's illness was too critical.

If not Slick Dick, then who?

Georgie followed the ambulance all the way to the double electronic doors of ER before pulling her truck over to the curb. Lingering in the building shadows, she casually smoked and jawed with a few strangers, paying particular attention to who came and went, hoping not to alert the opposition to her presence. It wouldn't be long before someone tracked her down.

They had her phone number, didn't they?

And inside her locked truck was damaging evidence that could take down more than a few perps. When Dick Branson realized she'd taken his soil samples, the hammer would fall.

Georgie, you'd better get a good plan!

44

Mark contacted a neurosurgeon before rushing over to Hardeman County General. Fit to be tied, he found Karen in the ER waiting. The hospital staff was talking stroke.

With the head trauma Victoria had experienced in the past, Mark agreed it was a distinct possibility. He insisted, "Karen, don't worry. Doctors can perform miracles today."

But his comforting words dumped a weighty load of guilt in his plate as he considered how many people would be relieved if Victoria never woke up.

Unfortunately, it would relieve some of his stress, too.

***

Dick Branson received a phone call the minute Victoria was admitted to the hospital.

"You know what to do next," he barked instructions to his watchdog before hanging up.

In no hurry now that his plan was in motion, Dick's emotions switched from high gear to idle. The deed was done. Give Victoria a few hours and she'd be feeling worse.

Give her twenty-four hours and she'd have no worries at all.

Besides, the minuscule amount of chemical used on the cellophane wrapper of the cigars was virtually undetectable. The woman had problems already, didn't she? The fine citizens of Fernwood already knew that she had a delicate condition. Hadn't Victoria passed out on more than one occasion? Who would suspect that anyone wanted to kill that sweet, beautiful lady?

Certainly not him! Dick flexed his biceps. *What motive could he possibly have?*

If Mark James dared cause trouble, he would be *eternally* sorry.

***

Georgie's mind leaped to several options. She could spring

Victoria forcefully. Or she could create a diversion to slip into her room unnoticed and find out what had happened.

Locating a pay phone across the street from the hospital, she dialed a publicized 800 number. "Is this Channel 5 News?" Georgie asked, disguising her voice.

"Who's speaking?" a reporter responded to the hotline number.

"No name, please. Got a spicy tip!" She threw herself into the part. "Try this one on for size, sweetheart. Two weeks ago, this lady gets her memory back after twenty-five years of amnesia. Then, late this afternoon, she collapses at her residence and is hospitalized—"

"Got a name?" the reporter cut in. "Which hospital?" She was taking notes. "Victoria Tempest. Got it." She wrote faster. "Hardeman General."

Georgie kept talking until the phone line at the other end clicked and she knew Channel 5 had bitten into her story. Soon, all chaos would break loose.

***

The dimly lit hospital room was steeped in medicinal odors. Victoria moved in and out of consciousness with the knowledge that a huge shadowy figure guarded the doorway. She didn't know why, but she felt entirely safe. *God is in control.*

In a vacant hospital room across the hall, Dick's informant hunkered in the shadows, keeping an eye on the victim's room. Frustrated that he couldn't do his job, he called his boss on his cell phone. "Is it done?" Dick rasped when Jake identified himself.

"Can't get inside her room." No name was mentioned.

"I told you, don't do anything but watch her," Dick squealed, weary of incompetent employees. He heard Jake curse.

"The chemical will do the job all by itself," Dick said in a calmer voice, expelling a wheezy cough. "If anyone goes inside her room in the next hour, I want to know it. Got that?"

"Oh, I don't think you have anything to worry about," Dick's brute responded. "Some guy a whole lot bigger than me is standing guard at the victim's door."

"What the—?" Dick reacted. *It wasn't his guy.*

***

After consoling Karen a bit, Mark consulted with Vicki's neurosurgeon, Dr. Glen Andersen. Apparently the test had ruled out brain damage, although it had indicated some abnormality. Since she showed coma tendencies, Glen had placed his patient in the Third Floor Trauma unit for overnight observation. Until Victoria awakened and had further tests, he couldn't be certain if she'd experienced a mild stroke or had only fainted.

"If it's a stroke," Glen advised, "we simply need to keep our patient quiet for twenty-four hours before prescribing treatment. Meanwhile, I'm giving Victoria anti-coagulants to dissolve any blood clots."

"Sounds reasonable to me," Mark answered, more frightened than he would admit. Vicki was a survivor.

"I hear you're engaged to the patient," Glen remarked. "Pretty lady, your Victoria." He crossed stout arms over his barrel-shaped chest.

"Yes, she is." Mark's heart eclipsed as he considered the possibility that Dick Branson might have done something to precipitate Victoria's sudden illness. What was it Karen had said? Victoria had received a package before she became ill?

Cosmetics, she thought. *But what was really in that package?*

"Glen, I need to go back to Vicki's place," Mark made a snap decision. "I'll have my cell phone turned on if you need me quickly." He shook his colleague's hand. "And Glen, thanks again for coming to Victoria's rescue on such short notice. I'll be in touch."

Karen was on pins and needles when Mark located her. After detailing Dr. Andersen's diagnosis, he reassured Karen that her mother was in capable hands. Borrowing her front door key, he rushed out into the night. A storm was brewing. Not a good sign.

Mark was grateful that he'd parked his BMW close-by in a covered spot reserved only for doctors. Shielding his head from the drizzling rain with a hand, he leaped behind the wheel and zoomed out the hospital exit.

Ignoring every red light, he busted his tail to reach Victoria's place in record time. On the western horizon, an unsettling storm gathered steam. Twenty-five years before, on an evening such as this, the course of many lives had been altered.

A foreboding silence shrouded the condominium complex as Mark used Karen's key to let himself inside the unit. While his vision adjusted to the inky darkness, sounds acutely escalated—the slithering rain against the sliders, shifting rafters popping from blustery winds. Tornado warnings would be out. April did that to Tennessee.

Strobe lightning lit the den. EMS had ransacked the place, overturning furniture in a concerted effort to help Victoria. Beneath the wet soles of his shoes, coffee stains dampened the light-beige Berber carpeting. He'd call Karen's cleaning service tomorrow.

Hitting the switch to an overhead light, Mark realized the electricity had crashed. *Wonderful*, he waited for spasmodic lightning to brighten the crime scene, cursing the fact he hadn't thought to bring along a flashlight.

Seeing no package that fit Karen's description, Mark wondered if one of the orderlies might have picked it up. He'd better check with the ambulance service when he got back to the hospital.

***

Kelly Nobel, mid-twenties and ex-model for *Teen* magazine, received the Channel Five coma victim assignment.

"Here!" The anchor queen assigned her assistant, Tina, to research the data banks on any news related to Victoria Tempest while she arranged for an on-location interview.

"I need Vic and Tom," Kelly ordered, retrieving a tube of lipstick from her purse to replenish her lip color as she walked. "We'll take the Channel 5 van! This is a happening story." She batted teal-blue eyes.

Tina hopped in the van beside Kelly, relating the sketchy details of the victim's history she'd retrieved from the Internet.

"Just listen to this!" Tina burst forth in full throttle. "Nineteen eighty-nine, this gal's in an auto accident resulting in a ninety-day coma. At approximately the same time she crashes, hubby gets X'd at his law office!"

"Go on." Kelly mentally designed a scenario to dazzle her TV audience as the news team sped across town toward the hospital. Stroking her naturally blond shoulder-length hair, she realized the proper handling of the story could earn her network recognition.

"This story has potential," she verbalized her thoughts. "We can't afford to miss any of the details!" She glanced over at her assistant who was still perusing her Internet printout.

"Get this!" Tina exclaimed. "It appears the police never convicted the perps who killed Victoria's husband, Jeffrey Tempest!" She paused for effect. "And . . ." she left the door open.

"And Victoria Tempest didn't recall one single detail about that fated night when she awakened with amnesia ninety days later," Kelly said, laughing.

"*Nada*," Tina remarked. "The amnesia lasted for twenty-five years according to my information . . ." words evolved into thoughts as she wondered who reported the incident.

"And?" Kelly rolled her hand at Tina, anxious for the rest of the story.

"And two weeks ago, Victoria suddenly regains her memory and wants to know who killed her husband." Tina dramatically paused. "Then, bingo!"

"Our history-maker gets herself zapped an hour ago!"

"Exactly!" Tina winked. "Sound suspicious, huh? Like maybe it wasn't accidental?"

"Tina, you've got a morbid imagination!" A grin spread over Kelly's pretty face. "And that's what I like about you the most!"

"Exactly." Tina laughed.

45

Victoria was sleeping soundly when Mark James quietly slipped into her hospital room and stood at the end of the bed. He and Karen were taking turns visiting, and then only for a few minutes. If Vicki would only wake up, he could ask her about the mysterious package.

"Baby, I hope you can hear me," Mark whispered as lightning blinked through the hospital window. "Come back to us, Vicki, we love you. Come back to me. I love you."

"I'm so sorry I've disappointed you," Mark walked around and stood at Victoria's side, leaning over to rest his rough chin against the soft pillow's edge. "I'm ready to tell you the truth, honey. *All of it!* Just come back to me, please!" *Don't die on me now!*

Lurking across the hall, Dick's detective overheard what the doc told the pretty lady. He didn't think his boss would take kindly to Dr. Mark James' proclamation, and that maybe it was his duty to report how the stupid doctor had recently converted sides.

***

Georgie Hendricks waited in the hospital parking lot for the Channel 5 News team to arrive. *Good, it was Kelly Nobel.* She'd create a little hellish ruckus.

The news team leaped from the van and rushed inside ER as the emergency doors electronically opened. Georgie high-tailed it into the hospital following close behind.

"You can't come in here!" A heavy-duty nurse blocked Kelly's way. "Stop! I'll call Security!" She was an imposing deterrent. "Get some help, somebody!"

Paying no attention to the warning, the Channel 5 News team skirted around the nurse in a rush to reach the elevator at the end of the hall before Security arrived.

Punching a red button, they waited for the steel doors to crunch open. "Get in!" Kelly screamed, shoving her assistant aboard first, moving to the back of the elevator to make room for her camera crew. "Come on, Tom. Let's go. Now!"

Georgie smiled, deciding to wait for the next elevator.

Ascending with her news team to the third floor, Kelly remarked, "Hospital keeps trauma victims on Third. The Tempest gal's gotta be there! Follow my lead."

When hospital Security showed up and blocked all the elevators on the main floor, Georgie hit the door to the stairwell. No one was stopping her now.

"What the heck!" an orderly barked as the news team crashed the third floor. "Notify the front desk! We got trouble on our hands!" Somebody else screamed.

Not the least bit discouraged, Kelly headed for the nurse's station and pounded the counter with a fist. "I'm here to see Victoria Tempest," she said with admirable determination.

"You're not supposed to be in here, young lady!" An obese nurse looking like Dracula's mother shoved up against Kelly's flat belly.

The star reporter's cheeks blossomed into a flame red as she backed off. "Roll the cameras, Vic!" The room was instantly flooded with gleaming stage lights. "Five, four, three, two, one . . ." she counted down.

"This is Kelly Nobel reporting from the Third Floor Trauma Unit of Hardeman County General Hospital in Fernwood, Tennessee," Channel 5's star-reporter began her spiel.

"That's enough!" Nurse Dracula placed a wide hand over the camera lens. "You don't wanna law suit, little lady!" She wrestled to seize Kelly's microphone.

Scowling protests of brutality, Kelly jerked loose as Tina ran interference. Lifting the microphone to her sultry red lips, Kelly continued. "Approximately one hour ago, Victoria Martin Tempest collapsed in her home and was rushed to Hardeman County General Hospital for emergency treatment."

Kelly swung her head to the right as a second camera took over, zooming in to capture the reporter's pretty face.

"Apparently, Mrs. Tempest, former coma victim, has recently

recovered from a twenty-five year bout with amnesia according to an anonymous caller."

Kelly paused. "Channel 5 News has been advised Mrs. Tempest plans to reopen her husband's unsolved murder case . . ." the words flowed off her tongue like sweet nectar.

Simultaneously, security personnel scampered off two elevators, knocking Tina to the floor as they encountered opposition.

"Watch out, Kelly!" Tina screamed a warning.

"We're going network!" Tom excitedly screamed from behind his camera. "You're live on national, Kelly Baby. Make it good!" He focused the lens on the anchor's face.

"I'm Kelly Nobel, Channel 5 News, reporting live from Fernwood, Tennessee, at Hardeman County General Hospital where news is breaking . . ." the vivacious reporter reiterated the sketchy facts for her enlarged audience minutes before she was assaulted by the hospital authorities.

"Did you get that, Vic?" Kelly's hands fought back.

***

Dick had just walked into his living room and flipped on the television when he caught Kelly Nobel's speech. Grabbing the phone, he called his informant at the hospital.

"Jake? What the devil's going on over there at the hospital?" Dick feared he was losing control again.

"Can't hear you," Dick's private eye bellowed. "Got reporters and security personnel coming out of the walls. Gotta split now. Catch you later." The phone line fell dead.

"Wait!" Dick screamed as his watchdog rudely cut him off.

Cursing obscenities, he realized he'd need to take care of Victoria Tempest himself. Stupid incompetents didn't have a clue when it came to real guts! *This job required a pro.*

***

Georgie Hendrick's Channel 5 diversion was ingeniously successful, but she still couldn't get inside Victoria's hospital room. Some dude, big as Godzilla, blocked the doorway.

Probably FBI or CIA, Georgie reasoned as she hung in the shadows down the hall and waited, questioning if the monetary rewards outweighed the hassle. Having serious second thoughts about her involvement with Victoria's problem, she considered how meeting with her client once didn't qualify her to evaluate the woman's total involvement with crime.

However, Georgie still thought Victoria ought to know that Dick Branson was operating on unsafe soil, and technically had an illegal land lease. *But not tonight.*

46

Wearing a green orderly's uniform borrowed from the laundry room, Jon Branson rolled a gurney down the hospital corridor. He glanced around to see who might be looking and shoved open the door to Victoria Tempest's hospital room and walked in like he belonged there.

The pretty lady was ghostly pale lying on her shadowed deathbed. Too bad she'd received a lethal dose of his daddy's wonder cure for intruders. More than a few people had wanted to harm Victoria so he'd come to help. He glanced at the dripping IV.

Not so many years ago, he'd received training as a medic while serving in the National Guard so safely disconnecting Victoria from her restraining hospital equipment shouldn't prove all that difficult. But first he had to inject the antidote.

Well, here goes everything.

"Victoria, you don't know me," Jon whispered, "but I'm here to help." He had not seen the spectacular warring angel guarding her door. The vision was there to scare opposing forces.

"What?" Victoria's brown eyes fluttered a couple of minutes after Jon had dispensed the chemical antidote into her bloodstream. "Where am I?" She felt groggy.

"Don't be afraid. I've come to rescue you." Jon smiled.

"I know you." Victoria moistened parched lips with her tongue. "You're that motorcycle guy from the *Olde Soda Shoppe*, the one who spooked Gloria Gordon!"

"Take your time and don't talk too much." He disconnected tubes.

"Who are you anyhow?" Victoria weakly pointed a finger.

"My name is Jon Branson."

Branson? Fear crouched as Victoria made the family connection. "Dick Branson's son?" Panic chased the breath out of her.

"No! Don't be afraid!" Jon removed the last of Victoria's dripping IVs. "I promise I won't hurt you." His gentle lime eyes fondly targeted Victoria. "I'm here to help, Victoria. Trust me."

"Humph. Why should I trust you? Your father hates my guts."

"Well now," Jon suppressed a grin, "that's pretty strong language for a lady, but not so far from the truth. You just follow my instructions and everything will work out just fine."

"No! I'm not leaving this room until you tell me why you're helping me!" Victoria's attempt to sit up failed. "My daughter will soon be here to take care of things."

"Shuu!" Jon listened for noises in the hall. "Escaping will be much easier on both of us if you peacefully cooperate. I can assure you I have only your best interest at heart."

Victoria nervously sighed. Whether she liked it or not, she was at this courageous man's mercy. And nothing was more appealing than putting her hospital stay behind.

"Wait! Why are you helping me?" Victoria pushed up on an elbow, her vision clouded. "Please, I have to know." Strength was not returning rapidly enough for her to escape alone.

"Why? Does it matter?" Jon looked down at Victoria.

"Of course, it matters!" *The games that people played.*

"Simple. I've known good and evil. And I like good better."

Jon's voice had a sweetness about it that would calm an angel, thought Victoria. She felt a peace, despite her distrust of him.

"Trust me." Jon patted Victoria's arm.

Trust you? "Do I have a choice?"

Jon's strong hands felt soothingly cool to Victoria's hot skin as he used the bed linens to transfer her onto the gurney.

"Just take it nice and easy and you won't get hurt," he advised.

Victoria desperately wanted to believe Jon. But trust was a problem. "Fine, Jon. You tell me why should I trust you? I certainly don't trust your father." She needed answers.

"And with good reason." Jon maneuvered the gurney to get it to the door. "Now I need for you to be quiet."

"You said you liked *good* better." Victoria grasped the sides of the gliding gurney to keep from falling off. "What changed you?" The room was spinning around her.

"Quiet." Jon cracked the door and peeked into the hallway.

Beside the nurse's station, hospital staff representatives were involved in an ongoing argument with the Channel 5 News team. And Kelly Noble wasn't leaving anytime soon.

Looking in the other direction, Jon saw that the stretch of hall lying between Victoria's room and the service elevator was clear. It was time to leave. "You okay?" he said to Victoria, hearing thunder crash outdoors. Miraculously, the hospital lights blinked out.

"*Good.* Let's go!" Jon spun the gurney into the hallway.

Heading the opposite direction from where the commotion came, he arrived at the end of the corridor just as the auxiliary power kicked back on. Yawning widely, the elevator doors scrunched open.

Certain that no one had seen them leave, Jon pressed the Lower Basement button. An uneasy feeling advised him that somewhere, lurking in the shadows, were his daddy's evil eyes.

The elevator's bright spray of ceiling lights uncomfortably pierced Victoria's vision as the descending motion intensified her unbalanced equilibrium. Speculation chaotically coursed her mind, then settled down to one question: *Where is Jon taking me?*

Seconds later, the elevator doors reopened and the gurney moved again, the ride as bumpy as the county fair's rollercoaster. Soon, they arrived in the hospital parking lot.

Old Fear was lurking somewhere in the dark shadows cast by the ghostly florescent light. Beyond the hollow concrete walls, thunder rumbled and lightning sizzled.

Here Victoria was, alone with a total stranger, at Jon Branson's absolute mercy should he decide to harm her.

"Wait!" Victoria pushed up on one elbow.

The gurney halted as Jon walked around the side to face her.

"What changed you?" she rasped. "Please! I have to know."

Crossing his hairy muscular arms over his chest, Jon's cool lime gaze burned a hole through Victoria's heart as she realized, for the first time, how very different he was from his deceitful father. "Your Bible," he proclaimed, his expression reflecting integrity.

"What?" Jon's answer stunned Victoria. "My Bible?"

"Yes, the one you've been looking for—I have it." Jon tucked the loose ends of Victoria's sheets under the mattress. "I'd love to tell you all about it, but I really think we should get out of here before someone realizes that you're missing and sounds the alarm."

Victoria nodded and closed her eyes.

God is on His throne and still in control.

THE END

DON'T MISS THE NEXT BOOK
IN THE *RESURRECTION DAWN* SERIES
THE CHRISTIAN FUGITIVE
In the Continuing Saga of Victoria Martin Tempest

After fourteen challenging days following Victoria's recovery of memories at dawn on April 14, 2014, she still doesn't know who broke into her attorney husband's office and murdered him. Speculating that Mark was involved with Dick Branson in a cover-up led Victoria to hire a detective to investigate Branson Meatpacking Company for operating illegally on environmentally unsafe soil. About to report her findings, PI Georgie arrives in Fernwood and spies her client being hauled away in an ambulance.

Creating a media diversion with the Channel 5 News Team, Georgie fails to get a hearing. A warring angel has been stationed at Victoria's hospital door to protect her until help arrives, deterring Dick's hired thug from harming her further.

At the conclusion of Book 1, brave Jon Branson slipped inside Victoria's room and administered the antidote to his daddy's lethal drug. Happy to learn that Jon was the anonymous caller who reported her accident, she is ecstatic that he also has her Bible.

Meanwhile, as Book 2 opens, Karen Tempest and Dr. Mark James put their heads together and fail to understand how Victoria slipped out of the hospital without help. Worried that she is in no physical condition to be on the run, they wait impatiently for the police to do their job. Like two fools in a sob story, they turn to alcohol and each other.

Dick Branson has serious questions about Mark's loyalty. To keep a sharp eye on the detective duo, Mark and Karen, Dick invites them to attend the Rome festivities in honor of Alexander Luceres Ramnes, a rising star in the New-World Government.

Victoria soon discovers that somebody has filed false charges with the Fernwood Police and that she has been upgraded from a missing person to a murder suspect.

Romance may even be on the horizon as a new man emerges in

support of Victoria's mission to solve the crime committed against her husband.

As the story deepens and widens, Victoria gains insight to what happened the fated night her attorney-husband died. New friendships bring delight into Victoria's life as danger heightens, faith deepens, and she learns to depend on friends and trust God more.

The Author, M. Sue Alexander

ABOUT THE AUTHOR

Author-publisher, M. Sue Aexander, has been involved in writing most of her life, whether in penning an article, a children's story, or a gospel song. Reared on the grounds of Western State Hospital for the mentally ill, where her father was the resident dentist for thirty years, she has a vivacious imagination that threads through her unusual stories. A 1958 graduate of Central High School of Bolivar Tennessee, Sue earned higher educational degrees from Union University and the University of Memphis. She and her husband reside on a farm near Nashville, Tennessee and keep close contact with their three grown children and six grandchildren. Trusting in Jesus Christ, Sue believes that God often gives ordinary people extraordinary assignments and has accepted the challenge to create this heart-warming, spine-tingling novel depicting hardships as the Antichrist rises to rule.

CREAM PARLOUR
CASHIER